To Charles
with your country's
Thanks!

ICE MEN

A NOVEL OF THE KOREAN WAR

Steven Spruill

STEVEN SPRUILL

ISBN: 1-4392-2523-0
ISBN-13: 9781439225233
Library of Congress Control Number: 2009900297

Visit www.booksurge.com to order additional copies.

Advance praise for ICE MEN

"As a navy corpsman assigned to the 1st Marine Division, I lived what this novel is all about. The author has really done his research. Reading ICE MEN took me back to that first year of the Korean War. The characters are so real I fell in love with the MASH nurse. Many of us who fought to keep the people of South Korea free are still around. If you want to know what we remember, read this book."

Chief Petty Officer Lou Legarie, U.S. Navy (Ret.)

"1950, in the cold winter of Korea, a year to remember in the history of the United States, and a year that the Marines and U.S. Army will never forget. ICE MEN is one hell of a novel of that year. In it, Steven Spruill captures the sacrifice, the triumphs, and heroism of brave Americans in a gripping, heart throbbing, historically accurate account of one of our most challenging periods of war, through the eyes of a grizzled veteran Marine sergeant and two Army officers. ICE MEN is a great read."

Lieutenant General Mike Hough, U.S. Marine Corps (Ret.)

"You do not need to be a soldier or marine to feel the Korean summer heat, or, after the disastrous decision in late 1950 to proceed North of the 38th parallel, the penetrating cold along the banks of the Chosin Reservoir. In Ice Men, Steven Spruill ensures we feel the mud and the snow—and see the blood. While the weather and destiny slowly close in around us, it also pushes us insistently into the picture he has reconstructed. We find ourselves experiencing the terror, facing the challenges, witnessing the brave acts and suffering the essential mind-numbing weariness of war. Infrequently, just as it was in Korea and is in wartime, like a thin shaft of light in a gray landscape, we glimpse one of love's faces, and that fleeting look stirs in some the superhuman strength necessary to put one foot in front of the other and continue on, and on, and on. Steven Spruill captures it all.

He understands both history and our warriors. You will not forget Ice Men."

Rear Admiral Dave Oliver, U.S. Navy (Ret.)

"A terrific novel, ICE MEN has everything—action, adventure, heroism, and loads of heart, all set against an unjustly forgotten war. One of those rare novels that enriches as it entertains."

F. Paul Wilson, NY Times best-selling author of By The Sword

About the Author

Steven Spruill began writing professionally while in graduate school at The Catholic University of America. His first novel was published by Doubleday in 1977. He completed his dissertation on creativity and earned his Ph.D. in clinical psychology in 1981. Fifteen of his novels, a novella, and eight short stories have been published by Doubleday, St. Martin's Press, TOR, Berkley, and various magazines. Spruill's work has also sold in over twenty foreign countries. Several of his novels were selections of The Literary Guild and the Doubleday Book Club. Three of his medical thrillers were condensed in Good Housekeeping magazine. Both Kirkus and Publisher's Weekly have awarded starred reviews to Spruill's work. Writing under the pseudonym "Steven Harriman," Spruill recently ventured into non-fiction with "Absorbing SpongeBob: Ten Ways to Squeeze More Happiness Out of Life." In 1995, Spruill received the Catholic University of America's award for "Outstanding Achievement in the Field of Literature." ICE MEN is Spruill's sixteenth novel. He lives in Arlington with his wife Nancy, a senior executive at the Pentagon, and their two outstanding cats, Bebop and Lula.

Acknowledgments and Dedication

I am grateful to Sam Fernandez, Esq., General Counsel of the Los Angeles Dodgers, for his many insights into ICE MEN. Good lawyers, like novelists, must find the right words. Great ones like Sam find the heart of the matter. My deepest thanks, as well, to Douglas E. Winter, editor, biographer, fellow novelist and good friend for his astute edit of the manuscript. Any errors are mine.

The three main characters of ICE MEN are fictitious. However, the details of each battle are, as nearly as possible, faithful to historical documents and to the recorded memories of those who were there. The challenges portrayed in this novel, faced by the 1st Marine and 7th Infantry Divisions, and the 1st MASH, are not fiction, but fact.

With gratitude and respect, the author dedicates ICE MEN to those who fell, and to Chief Lou Legarie and all the other survivors in whom the war is with us still.

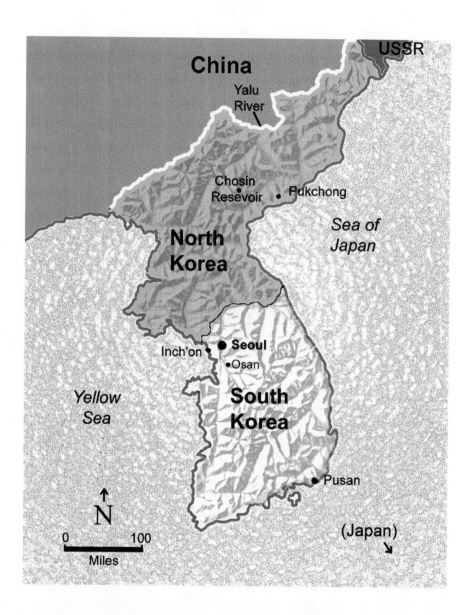

On June 25, 1950, North Korea launched a surprise attack across the 38th parallel into South Korea. Within four days, they took Seoul; in another four, they captured the port city of Inch'on, 25 miles to the west. They then attacked Task Force Smith near Osan, killing 150 and routing the Americans. President Harry Truman ordered General Douglas MacArthur to airlift more forces to Korea ASAP to reinforce the staggering U.S. Army. The enemy U.S. leaders had sorely underestimated continued to push American and South Korean troops south toward the sea. The retreating defenders blew up bridges and fought desperate delaying actions at high cost: By July 31, U.S. losses totaled 6,003 —1,884 killed, 2,695 wounded, 523 missing and 901 captured. On August 2, the 1st Provisional Marine Brigade came ashore at Pusan, the strategically-vital port at the southern tip of Korea. Unlike the army, the Marine brigade fielded many veterans of World War II, combat-tested in the Pacific. Five years earlier, Japan had been their enemy. Now it was where they sent their wounded.

"The Korean War" chapter in: *U.S. History,* St. Clair Press, New York, 1972, 1991, 2009.

1

17 August 1950, Pusan Perimeter, 1600 hours:
Watching the barrage, Harlan Hood tried to believe. "Time on Target" they called it, the big one-fifty-fives pounding Obong-ni ridge. Shells screamed overhead and slammed into the forward slope as Marine air flew sortie after sortie against the hill, wing cannons thumping. Mortars popped in a constant, ripping rattle, darkening the sky like the volley of a thousand archers. Raining down, the rounds blasted the reverse slope. Dirt geysered from the hillside, columns of black smoke rising from the flaming underbrush. There go my cover and handholds, Hood thought.

Four more fighters screamed overhead to pour fire on the towering hills that made up the ridge, a last mechanized punch before a fresh wave of Marines would go up. Hood watched men from the second battalion stream past him, double-timing it away from the front, holding bloody arms or clutching their sides, many limping along supported by buddies on either side. Sweat streaked the filth on their faces—four in the afternoon and still a hundred degrees, a vicious heat that melted your bones and sucked the strength from your muscles, forcing you to gobble salt tablets to stop the trembling. The retreating marines hustled along, clearly relieved to be putting some distance between themselves and the hill. A report a few minutes ago had the second battalion taking more than sixty percent casualties in the opening assault.

And we're next.

Hood felt a tingling ache in his fingers.

"Lookit those poor bastards," Jimmy said beside him.

"Relax, corporal. They've done all the hard work. When the heavy artillery and air get done, all we gotta do is mop up." That was the theory. The reality was that Time on Target, while way better than nothing, was rarely enough. To finish the job, you needed boots on the ground, bayonets fixed.

Abruptly, the thunder of bombardment stopped.

To Hood's right, the sergeant for Company A's third platoon yelled his men into line; Hood resisted the urge to do the same with his squad. It would only ratchet up the fear, better to wait a little. Peering up into the smoke that billowed from the ridge, Hood saw trees burning here and there. Blackened craters from the 155s pocked the hillside. In the relative hush, he could hear machine guns chattering to life, North Korean emplacements that had survived the shelling now firing into the retreating backs of the second battalion's rear guard.

Hood spat beside his boot, feeling a fleeting burn of cynicism. That was artillery for you—lots of explosions and smoke, and when it was all over the bad guys stuck their heads out like turtles and started shooting back.

A sergeant from the retreating F Company hurried closer along the winding road that bordered a lower slope of the ridge. Hood caught his arm and he stopped, Sergeant DePriest—Duane.

"What's the story, D?"

DePriest blinked at him as if trying to make his face out in the dark. He tried to speak but his voice came out a strangled croak. Hood handed over his canteen and D drank, wiping his mouth as he handed the precious water back. He looked weird, different, and Hood saw that his eyebrows and lashes had been burned off.

"Gotta watch out on your right," DePriest rasped. "We kept taking heavy fire from the right flank. Couldn't see where it was coming from but it was murder. Pinned us down behind a wall right at the bottom of the hill. It was an hour before any of us could even start up the slope. I lost three guys and two were wounded—gotta get to battalion aide, see how they're doing."

Hood released him and he hurried away.

"Shit," Jimmy said.

Hood gave him a warning frown, then looked pointedly beyond him. The rest of the squad stood around, trying to look nonchalant, but taking their cue from the two of them.

"We're gonna kick ass," Hood said, "and take this hill."

Jimmy forced a grin. "I'll be right behind you. Or, better yet, on your left."

Hood shook his head. "What D said about the right flank is probably old news. The lieutenant told me Army's got the hill on our right. By now they'll have secured it. They'll cover our flank."

"Whatever you say."

Lieutenant Morrison stalked past, a big cigar clamped in his jaw. "Line 'em up, sergeant, we're going in."

Hood marshaled his squad. They'd already done the pre-battle ritual, rubbing Corporal Bouden's prematurely bald head. They'd said their prayers if they were the praying type, which even the atheists tended to be when facing swarms of lead.

"Listen up," Hood said. "We just pounded the sons of bitches on that hill with a lot of heavy ordnance. Some of them survived it, but they're all shook up. They're half deaf and their stomachs are churning. They can't see good because of the smoke. Now's the time to get up there and show these gooks what happens when they shoot at United States Marines. As you go, look for cover above and on your right. Work your way up. Stay on the move as much as you can, but keep your asses down and do it right. We're gonna have this hill before the sun sets and make the second battalion buy us beer for a month back in Tokyo."

The men standing around him gave a little cheer. He slapped a couple of backs, at the same time turning them around to head up the road together.

A hill crowded the road on one side; from the other, rice paddies stretched away, a swampy obstacle that must be crossed to reach Obong-ni Ridge. The initial slope rose in a series of terraces farmers had built to corral enough land to grow some peas and red peppers. A low, stone wall separated these terraces from the steepening rise to the ridge far above.

The wall must be where Sergeant DePriest and his men had been pinned down. Hood scanned the rise beyond. Some scraggly pines had survived the bombardment. Good—not all the cover and handholds were gone.

Ahead, shimmering in the heat, Hood could see the forward units of the first battalion, a long line of men in forest green humping packs toward the objective. His squad was keeping good order, staying together in the swarm of men on the road. As they rounded the hill, the men flowed to either side of a North Korean tank—a Soviet- made T-34 taken out by the air bombardment or maybe a bazooka. Beyond the tank, the column parted again to let box ambulances, horns blowing, edge through to the rear. As they passed Hood he could hear moans and crying from inside. His guts twisted, but at the same time he felt the familiar, savage excitement.

Battle.

Only a few weeks ago, he'd been bored out of his skull, waiting to get out of Camp Pendleton, then waiting again in Tokyo, sitting around itching to get over here, get into the action. He hadn't survived Iwo Jima to die on this hill. Let the enemy do the dying.

The column of 1st Battalion infantry around Hood left the road now, trotting along the dikes of the rice paddies toward the terraces at the base of the hill. Leading his squad, Hood found his own narrow bridge of dirt through the swamp. Ahead, he could see men beginning to fall with a strange, balletic grace, as if they'd simply had enough of running and wished to kneel in the rice and lay over for a rest. A sense of unreality swept him, making the falling men seem less than real, as if this were a play.

He had his own role to worry about now—he would go forward and keep going; others might fall but he would not and neither would his men.

Checking over his shoulder, he saw Jimmy right behind him and the rest following in Jimmy's wake. The marine column had spread into a decent skirmish line now, fanning along the lower slope.

Hood vaulted onto the first terrace. Part of him noted that, in addition to peas and peppers, the Korean farmers had planted some cotton. It took him back to Mississippi, before the family had moved to Georgia, the hot lazy days of summer. The pack on his back felt light, his legs powerful as he jumped to the next terrace, the next, seeing someone from the squad to his right straighten and fall back. Picking up speed, he vaulted the terraces until he reached the wall DePriest had mentioned.

Scrambling to it, he motioned his squad to line up behind him along the wall. Peeking over, he saw gouts of dirt kicking up in front of him. To his right and above, in the distance. he could see a hazed-over hill paralleling Obong-ni ridge. It was covered in green, no smoke rising from it.

Good—if the hill were still in enemy hands, surely it would have been targeted by the 155s and marine air.

But if Army did have control of it, where was the damn crossfire coming from?

He motioned the squad to stay down, tight against the wall. The stone's coolness shocked his sweat-soaked shoulder. A ripe smell hit him, two dead marines stretched out ten feet his side of the wall, their mouths gaping, half-lidded eyes gazing up at the boiling sky.

Anger burned in his throat. Who had left these men behind? Marines always took out their dead.

I'll see to it on the way back down. After we take the hill.

Inching up for another look, he saw shells stitching the dirt a few feet from the wall, where they had to go, probably a fifty caliber machine gun, but he still could not tell where it was coming from.

5

"Are you sure the army took that hill over yonder?" Jimmy murmured in his ear. "I don't trust them dogfaces."

Machine gun shells hammered the top of the wall, now, and Hood ducked lower. Jimmy turned away from the fresh burst, his shoulders cringing down, hands pulling his helmet tighter as flying chips showed the barrage walking to him.

"Time to go, Jimmy."

"Sarge, we're pinned down."

"We'll wait for the fifty caliber to stop. While they're loading a new belt, we haul ass over the wall and into the pines up slope."

"A pine tree ain't gonna stop no machine gun."

"They gotta see us to shoot us."

Hood watched the wall. Abruptly, the stone chips stopped flying. "Let's go!" he yelled. Pushing away, he scrambled across the killing ground, jumped the corpse of another marine and dashed uphill. Behind him he could hear the squad pounding over the hardpan rock and dirt.

The slope steepened, forcing him to lean forward. Clawing the dirt, he found holds on rocks, scrambling on all fours into the pines. Eyes stinging, he sucked down the hot brew of smoke and air in an effort to stoke his lungs.

From the corner of his eye he saw Jimmy, not on his left but on his right, in the direction of the crossfire, always brave when the moment was on him. The corporal gave him a thumbs up, hugging a stunted pine tree. His face shone with sweat.

To his left Hood could see marines scrambling up the hill along a finger ridge. Murderous fire raked them; men fell and rolled, arms and legs flopping, down the steep slope.

"Come on," he shouted to the rest of the squad spread out beside and below him. Taking a side-winding route from one scrub pine to the next, he worked his way across and up the slope. Adrenaline chased away his fatigue; glancing down, he caught tilting glimpses of Jimmy struggling up behind him, the rest of his men now out of sight below.

A big rock above beckoned, jutting from the hillside. Churning through blackened dirt and ash, he dropped to his hands and knees to keep from pitching backward off the hill. He could hear an NK gun now, another fifty-caliber machine gun, firing from the top of the rock.

Looking to both sides, he saw men in green working up the hill around him. One grabbed his gut and leaped back, falling down, rolling until he came up against a tree stump. Hood felt his teeth clench.

That machine gun had to go.

Pulling a grenade from his belt, he started to draw the pin—

No, it would drop back down on him and explode. Gotta get higher.

The side of the rock formed a V-shaped gully with the ground. His boots slipped as he started up, and he had to stow the grenade and use both hands on the rock, grabbing for holds to pull himself up. The machine gun sounded louder now, and then it cut off, and he could hear a Korean up there yelling an order, probably for a new belt of ammo.

Just a few more feet, Hood thought, working his way up the rock.

The overhang increased, forcing him to stop. Clinging to fissures below the overhang, he tried to set the toes of his boots. Far below, he saw more marines swarming over the wall and starting up the hill. A dizzying wave of vertigo swept him. If he moved a muscle, he'd fall.

But he had to move, now, or he'd tire and then he would fall.

The machine gun above him started firing again. Hood reset his left hand, fingers hooking tight into the rock creases, freeing his right to inch down to the grenade. His toes ached, curled down hard where he'd set his boots. Finding the grenade, he plucked it free, not much of a toss, only four or five feet up and a few feet back. Biting the ring, he pulled the grenade off the pin—thousand one, thousand two—lofting it up and over in a hook shot, hearing a deafening bang as the rock punched him.

Losing his grip, he slid back down the gully until he could stop himself by digging his hands and boots into the dirt. A body in a blue-green uniform dropped past him, one arm stumped, spraying blood. Hood let himself slide down past the base of the rock, picking up speed, and then someone caught his arm—Jimmy, holding onto him with one hand, and to a root with the other.

The corporal's mouth worked, yelling words Hood couldn't hear through the ringing in his ears. He realized the grenade had deafened him. He got his feet dug in again, and Jimmy let go of him and resumed trying to crawl up.

A blank moment of furious effort, and Hood found himself on top of the rock where the machine gun had been firing, looking at what was left of the gun and one body, maybe the armor carrier who had kept the ammo coming. A bloody rock pillowed the NK's head, his neck at a sharp angle, one arm hidden under his back.

I killed him, I did this.

Hood's throat clutched with nausea; at the same time, he felt a grim triumph. Marines would live—maybe his own boys, because of the bloody mess he'd made of this man.

Hood headed up the hill, his M-1 still strapped to his back, useless on the steep grade. The pitch decreased a little and he found a path angling up and around a jutting rock.

At the same instant, an NK rounded the base of the rock and jerked his rifle up.

Grabbing behind him in near panic, Hood found his .45 and yanked it free as the NK fired. He felt his shirt tug back above his collarbone. He fired back, missing, then hitting the NK in the foot. Blood sprayed and the man went down on one knee, losing his rifle. Hood scrambled across the slope toward him, firing the .45. Blood spurted from the NK's chest and he dropped, cart-wheeling down the slope.

Rounding the rock, Hood saw another enemy soldier coming down at him. The man raised his rifle, yanking at the trigger but if the thing was firing Hood couldn't hear it and nothing was hitting him. He squeezed the suddenly unyielding trigger of his .45, feeling no kick—damn, he was out of ammo too.

The NK charged him with the bayonet; Hood slapped it aside as the man crashed into him, rocking him back, too small to bowl him over. He grappled the Korean into a clench, neutralizing the rifle and bayonet, and wrestled him down, rolling on top.

The man bit his arm; in a burst of rage, he pounded the Korean's face, feeling the shocks dimly through his knuckles. The soldier went still and he leapt off, rammed another clip into his .45, and scrambled uphill.

He was hearing again—screams all around him, marines crying out for corpsmen. He saw an NK lieutenant loading his rifle. He fired the .45 and the officer gave him a startled look, then coughed and fell. Craning his neck to see up slope, Hood realized he was more than halfway to the top.

Exhilaration flooded him. Gonna make it—!

Something smacked his thigh, like a baseball bat. Grunting, he fell flat and scrambled behind a rock. He could hear shells peppering the other side, a murderous stream of fire coming from the right flank again. He wanted to lift his head, see where the hell it was coming from, but the fire was too intense. Gritting his teeth, he checked his leg, saw blood pouring into his pants, turning the green dark.

"You're shot!" Jimmy, shouting from nearby.

"No shit!" Hood located him about ten yards over, behind his own rock.

"You gotta go down to battalion aide," Jimmy yelled.

"Forget it."

"I'll take the squad up, you get on down now, come on, sarge."

"I try to go down, they'll just shoot me. It's quicker to go up."

"Do what the corporal says!" Lieutenant Morrison, joining Jimmy behind his rock, the lieutenant chomping his cigar, incredibly still lit, throwing off puffs of white smoke.

"I'm fine," Hood yelled.

True enough. The leg felt numb, but he still had control of it. He had to get to the top. Why didn't they understand?

"You get your ass back down this hill, sergeant, and that's an order," Morrison bawled.

"Lieutenant—"

"Now!" Morrison jabbed a pointing finger back down the slope, adamant.

A bitter disappointment filled Hood. Crying out loud, it was just a through and through, only the muscle, he could tell after all this time.

He saw Jimmy start toward him and that did it; gonna get his corporal killed if he didn't follow orders.

Pissed, he turned over on his back and started sliding down the slope, giving Jimmy and Morrison a little wave to show he was all right. Digging in with his feet to slow himself, he felt distant jabs of pain from the leg, and then out of nowhere someone punched him in the side, rolling him over onto his stomach again.

He slid down and down, barely feeling the rocks against his belly, convinced now that he was dreaming all this. He went on sliding, his side on fire, burning with each breath, more pain even than that bullet on Iwo. Probing his side, he felt the entry wound, just beneath his rib, or maybe right on it. The rib blazed with pain as he touched it, and he realized it had been splintered by a bullet.

The bastards had shot him again!

He tried to shout for a corpsman. The air scorched his lungs, forcing him into a jag of coughing that wouldn't stop. Through a haze of tears he saw bullets raking the slope just above him, kicking out stones and chunks of dirt, that same murderous fire from the right flank.

The rattle of gunfire dwindled with the pain in Hood's side, the sunlight dimmed and he wished he had some water to drink, and then the world went soft and melted away.

The United Nations asked President Truman to appoint a supreme commander of allied forces in Korea. Truman named General Douglas MacArthur, who wasted little time sending the 2nd Infantry Division and two regimental combat teams to Pusan to help the 1st Provisional Marine Brigade and General Walker's 8th Army defend the Pusan perimeter. On August 29, the British 27th Infantry Brigade would join them from Hong Kong. Walker's forces, too thin to fully defend the Pusan perimeter, broke into small, mobile forces to counterattack wherever enemy troops breached the lines. Air strikes from U.S. bases in Japan and offshore aircraft carriers harried the North Korean forces and disrupted their supply lines. Moving at night to avoid air attack, the enemy pressed to within fifty miles of Pusan. U.S. losses, already costly, continued to rise. MacArthur, fearing defense alone could not continue to prevent his forces from losing their last toehold in Korea, decided to go on offense. He devised a bold and desperate plan to launch an attack behind the enemy front, to sever their overextended supply lines. The hammer of this strike was to be the newly formed X Corps, consisting of the 1st Marine Division, the 7th Infantry Division and, to treat their wounded, a new MASH unit, the 1st, then forming up in Japan.

(Ibid)

2

27 August 1950, Tokyo General Hospital, 2200 hours:
"What's cookin', blondie?" Bed 59, one of her malaria cases, whispering so he wouldn't wake the wounded on either side. The night glow of the ward gave his face an ultraviolet sheen. Bonnie wrung out the washcloth in its basin by his cot and gently blotted the sweat from his forehead. His fever had broken, but new heat was already baking through the cloth. What was cookin' was him.

Pressing two aspirin into his palm, she poured his tin cup full of water. "Drink it all, corporal."

"Yes'm." He drained the cup and patted the cot beside him. "Plenty of room for both of us, lieutenant."

She continued down the row, conscious that normally she'd have played along. A little innocent horsing around with the wounded could lift morale, but it would be no kindness to encourage the corporal's flirtations an hour and twenty-nine minutes before she walked out of his life.

Bonnie felt a gloomy touch of resignation—so much for treating this last shift like all the others. Knowing it was her last colored everything; mundane details she'd stopped noticing months ago bloomed with sentimental significance. She would miss the soothing drone of the ceiling fans; the way captured light bloomed in the IV bottles, making them look like magic

13

lanterns hung to protect the wounded. Even the smell—that pungent mix of Brilliantine and tobacco, shaving soap and sweat. Blindfolded with only your nose to guide you, you'd think you'd stepped into a frat house.

Probing her hip pocket, Bonnie felt a stab of alarm, then remembered she'd packed the notebook in her duffel bag. If she'd realized all these choice little epiphanies would hit her at the last minute, she'd have waited. Soon as she got back to quarters, she'd dig it out and write this new stuff down while it was fresh. Years from now, when she was safe back in the States, the notebook would be a doorway back to her younger self, her own words keeping alive what would otherwise fade. Fifty pages she'd filled up with neat writing in just four weeks—exotic sights and sounds of Tokyo, what life was like on a military postop ward with people from all over America, and the mystery she'd come here to study.

On that, she was getting a little more material every day, a piece here and another there, and her next billet was sure to give her more still. Her notebook would never make the best seller list. Maybe she'd be the only one ever to read it. But if her ship sank on the way to Pusan, she wasn't getting on a lifeboat without it.

Bonnie stopped at Bed 65, a kid who'd just lost his right leg below the knee. He didn't know that yet—only hours since the surgeon had sawed through above the shattered bone. A nose-prickling tang of iodine rose from his cot. Mercifully, he was still asleep because of the morphine drip hanging above his right arm.

She eased the roller valve back a fraction to loosen its pinch on the tubing. Holding her Timex next to the little bulb chamber in the drip line, she watched the second hand with one eye and counted drops with the other—a hard trick at first, now as easy as taking a pulse. Checking IVs was a never-ending duty. As a bottle emptied, the dwindling weight of the morphine would cause it to drip slower, leaving the wounded to wake up groaning.

One good thing about this being her last shift—she wouldn't have to tell this kid about his foot. Some unlucky nurse on the morning shift would have that sad duty: *You had gangrene, soldier. It would have killed you. The only way to save your life was to amputate. I'm sorry.*

Some men would curse or cry. Some would turn their heads away and not look at or speak to you again. Or they could be amazingly brave. A few would even crack a joke. Awesome.

Bonnie swallowed against a tender ache in her throat. A fraternity was exactly what these men were, hazed by bullets and shrapnel, initiated in their own blood. Maroon bathrobes were their blazers, their patch the Purple Heart. The club met every evening when they'd huddle around their crystal radios for the war news, Chesterfields and Lucky Strikes nesting between their fingers. The blue smoke carried their breath above the fans to mingle with the ward's ghosts.

Bonnie loosened the sheet around the soldier's leg, tenting it over the stump. As she turned away, an unexpected shape plucked the edge of her vision, bringing her head around. There—down the ward between the two long rows of cots, standing still as a giant mannequin. Goose-bumps skated along her arms, and then the statue flowed into life, one hand rising to remove his officer's cap and tuck it under his arm. A tall Army officer, 6-4 if he was an inch, shoulders like John Wayne, a single gold bar on his shoulder.

Just standing there, staring down at the cot in front of him.

How had he gotten in without her hearing? At night, the scrape of a boot on tile would shoot the length of the ward. Big men *could* be surprisingly quiet—how many times when she was little had Uncle Daddy inadvertently startled her, floating up behind her, his size fourteen wing-tips dispersing his weight like snowshoes?

Bonnie realized that the target of the lieutenant's gaze was Sergeant Hood, the marine who'd been airlifted in a week ago. A bullet wound in the leg, healing nicely, and another in his lower chest which hadn't done as well. An interesting guy, Hood, different from the other patients. Not just older, he had that watchful stillness, a self-contained poise. This man had been a professional warrior for most of his adult life, an area of interest to her, and she'd filled a page in her notebook speculating about him. So far, no answers, only questions.

The sergeant awoke, his head lifting sharply, as if his visitor's stare had set off an inner alarm. Rolling his legs out of bed, he sat on the edge.

The two men traded words, too far off for her to make out, the tone low but sharp.

Step in, tell them visiting hours were over? Neither was looking very friendly.

But, so far, they weren't bothering anyone else.

Give it a minute; see what happens.

The lieutenant plucked the cap from under his arm and circled it in his hands as if nervous—or mad, maybe, needing to bleed off steam. He looked about her age, twenty-two or -three. Great hair, thick and black, tapered at his neck and over the ears but full on top, grooved straight back by some attentive combing—no slap-dash army barbers for this guy. Clean, strong jaw with a Kirk Douglas dimple; dark, arching eyebrows.

Hood made quite a contrast. His marine haircut looked self-administered, buzz- cut nearly to the skin on the sides, leaving a black, shoe-brush bristle on top. Scars marred every knuckle of his outsized hands. The deep creases that framed his mouth like parentheses made it seem like he was smiling when he wasn't. Handsome was the wrong word for Hood, but he did exude a certain rugged appeal.

The tall officer said something and Hood sprang up. At five and a half feet, standing didn't buy him much, and the ramrod straight posture had to be hurting his rib. The same bullet that had splintered it had nicked a lower lobe of his right lung. The resulting infection was what had forced the 8055 MASH to evac him to Japan. After three days of the lung being drained twice a day and penicillin pumped in, Hood was insisting he was fine, ready to rejoin his platoon. A doctor would make that decision but, if it was up to her, she'd keep him awhile. He was faking recovery, she was petty sure, hiding his pain.

The voices of the two men rose. The lieutenant took a step toward the sergeant. Hood didn't back off.

The man in the next cot stirred and rolled over, squinting at them.

Time to break this up.

As she approached, both men stopped talking and turned. She said, "I'm afraid visiting hours are over."

"The lieutenant was just going," Hood said.

Appraising her, the army officer held out a hand. "Sam Foxworth."

"Lieutenant Brisbane."

Her hand was hardly small, but his enveloped it, huge and warm, holding on for an extra beat. "I'll go quietly," he said, "if you'll tell me when you get off duty."

Hood made a disgusted sound in the back of his throat.

Ignoring him, Foxworth said, "Is Lieutenant really your first name?"

"I'll walk you to the door."

She could feel Hood's gaze on her back as she ushered Foxworth out. Matching her pace, the lieutenant made no sound, his big feet confirming a talent for silence.

He said, "When you get off, maybe we could go for a drink."

"Are you a friend of Sergeant Hood's?"

"I wouldn't say that."

"Then why visit him?"

"Have a drink with me and we'll discuss whatever you want, including the sergeant."

"Goodnight, lieutenant."

At 2300 hours, as Bonnie walked off the ward for the last time ever, her sense of the moment's dramatic significance evaporated as she saw Sam Foxworth standing where she'd left him.

He grinned. "Ready for that drink?"

"You don't give up."

"Depends on the situation, Lieutenant Brisbane. May I call you Lieutenant?"

"All right, I give up. It's Bonnie."

"Bonnie Brisbane." He squinted reflectively, as if tasting wine. "Bright sound, a connotation of happiness, and of course the alliteration. Good name."

"My father wanted to call me Wilhelmina."

"Then we'll drink to your mother."

You've got that right, she thought.

But a drink?

The bon voyage party the nurses were throwing for her wasn't until tomorrow. This was her chance to get some answers about Sergeant Hood.

As for whatever Lieutenant Foxworth might want out of it, what he'd get was another handshake.

By the time they crossed the arched, wooden footbridge into Tokyo's Shinjuku sector, it was nearly midnight. A trickle of sweat eased down Bonnie's back, following a fault line ironed into the starched khaki. Where had this heat come from? Back home in Michigan, with only a few days left until September, the nights would be starting to cool down, but here there was no sign of impending fall, the air steamy and thick, moths fluttering in the yellow haloes of the street lamps. The broad avenue teemed with foot traffic despite the hour, lots of late dinners in progress, the smell of fish so strong the taste shimmered on her tongue. The men streaming past on either side were all shorter than her, look-ing enough alike to be from the same family—identically black hair, most of them dressed in a civilian uniform of white shirts and baggy gabardines. Working their way past each other they bumped shoulders as if it were nothing. The few women stood out—bright, flowered skirts twirling on the young ones, older ladies favoring kimonos. The women never bumped; they flowed through the crowd balancing invisible books on their heads.

What did Sam have in mind, bringing her here? From what she'd heard, Shinjuku was a pleasure district, everything from kabuki to call girls. Noisy place, vendors shouting, old men pushing carts of hot sweet potatoes, orange ice, paper fans—even cheap sunglasses though the sun had set long ago. Noodle stalls, tearooms, and willow houses lined the street across from the canal.

"There it is," Sam said, pointing to a thatched roof. A sign for Asahi beer flashed against a cobalt sky.

She followed him to the wicker gate at the entrance. Cement steps led down to a door below street level, black paint, no window, just a notice displaying the Army of Occupation's coveted "A," without which Japanese restaurants and beer halls were off limits to U.S. soldiers. A week of melting heat had made the paint sticky enough to hold the notice up without tape.

Passing into the haze of the bar, she pulled a deep breath, purging the fish odor with the cleansing burn of tobacco. Joint was hopping, loud with laughter, simmering from the heat of packed bodies. Damp zones bloomed on uniformed backs; Bonnie had the fleeting hope her own sweat wasn't staining through. A juke box just inside the door crooned "Mona Lisa" in Nat King Cole's voice, too low for most of the crowd to hear.

A Japanese woman at the bar noticed Sam. Her face lit and she hurried toward them between black lacquered tables of drunk G.I.s and giggling Japanese girls.

"Evenin,' Mamasan," Sam boomed. "May I present Lieutenant Bonnie Brisbane. Bonnie, this is Lulu."

The woman bowed briskly. Her poodle skirt, jet-black hair, and pancake makeup worked well enough at a distance, but this close even the soft glow of the bar's paper lanterns couldn't hide her age, more grandma-san than mama-san.

Taking Sam's arm, she yelled, "Come on—I save nice table for you."

Following Sam and Lulu toward a smoky corner of the bar, Bonnie noticed how spiffy he still looked, his shoes spit shined, the trousers sharply creased; no wet circles on Sam's back. He'd make a good recruiting poster, she thought, a handsome young Army officer, the photo of him saying, "Put on this uniform and look like me."

"What you want to drink?" Lulu asked.

"Coke on ice," Bonnie said.

Sam ordered a Bud, turning to her as Lulu hurried off. "You don't drink?"

"Sometimes." She thought of Uncle Daddy, always smelling of beer when he came around. Apparently, visiting his children for an hour had been an ordeal for which he'd required fortification.

"You're safe with me," Sam said. "I'm an officer and a gentleman."

"Is that why those two women at the bar keep waving at you?"

He turned to look. The two Japanese women, not much older than schoolgirls, wore poodle skirts like Lulu, apparently a theme in her bar. They were grinning at Sam, trying to wave him over. Clearly, he was a familiar sight to them. Bonnie saw with amusement that a flush had crept up his neck.

Before he could say anything, a girl arrived with their drinks.

Bonnie held her Coke against her forehead, savoring the cold shock of the glass on her skin. She said, "What's your connection to Sergeant Hood?"

Sam squinted, as if the smoke had stung his eyes. "Must we talk about him?"

"Who better? You?"

"Let's try you. What's a nice girl like you doing in a place like this?"

"I was just asking myself the same question."

"Not Lulu's—Tokyo, the United States Army."

"Why wouldn't I be in the Army? Because I'm a woman?"

"Because you're smart."

Maybe Sam shouldn't be Army's poster boy after all. "It happens that I *am* smart, but you couldn't know that just from looking at me."

"I know it from listening."

She went back over the few words they'd exchanged but could recall nothing particularly brainy she'd said. "If you're so down on Army, what are you doing in it?"

"The uniform. Good way to get dates." Straight face, but joking, surely. Not the sort of thing you'd say to impress a girl. You wanted to do that, you'd talk about serving your country or feeling it was your duty.

She checked the patch on his shoulder, a black hourglass on a red field. 7th Infantry—a reserve division. "You got in the Army through ROTC?" she asked.

He shrugged. "Seemed like a good idea at the time. World War II was over. Who'd have guessed we'd get ourselves into another spat in just five years? The most powerful nation in the world, hanging on by its fingernails to the ass end of Korea."

She gave a genteel cough.

"Sorry."

"No, no. That's a very. . .colorful metaphor. Let me guess— you were an English major."

"History. Figured I'd teach high school and put in my weekends in the reserve and all would be well. Next thing I know, the North Koreans jump the fence and I'm sharing a big, drafty room with a lot of other sad sacks at Camp Fuji."

"Hey, free travel, see the world."

He rolled his eyes. "It hasn't been boring, I'll give it that. Just eight weeks ago my division was a joke, down to half strength because it hadn't gotten around to replacing all the GIs it sent home after World War II. Those who'd stayed on were drawing cushy occupation duty in Japan. Then the North Koreans attack, and I get called up with a lot of other reservists. About the same time, old Sygman starts sweeping up Korean civilians and putting them in uniform."

21

For a second she drew a blank, then the name clicked: Sygman Rhee, president of South Korea.

"But guess what," Sam went on. "All the Koreans who wanted to be in the national army were already in it. So the guys Sygman's nailing in his sweeps are kids in their middle teens, old shopkeepers with gimpy legs, men too slow to duck and hide. The ROK generals don't want 'em. Some natural born sucker high up in our chain of command looks around, sees that 7th Infantry is still way under strength, and says, 'Hey, guys, we just found 8,000 more soldiers for you, isn't that great?'"

Sam made a cast-off gesture with one of the big hands. "Long story short, a third of my division suddenly doesn't speak English and has no idea which end of a gun to hold."

"Can't you train them?"

"Remains to be seen. We've been working day and night to squeeze ten weeks of basic training into two or three. Hard enough if your trainees understand what you're saying to them. Eighth Army's getting chewed up over there. Rumor has it we're less than a week from being thrown into the breach, and we're nowhere near ready."

She tried to think of something upbeat to say. "I hear the Marines are starting to turn things around. Sergeant Hood's battalion took an important ridge the day he was wounded."

"He tell you that?"

"Actually, no. Hood's not much of a talker. I got it from others on the ward."

Sam scanned the room, taking in the girls at the bar again, making it clear he didn't want to talk about the sergeant. But he'd better—that was the deal.

As she opened her mouth to remind him, he said, "MacArthur's got a huge fleet massing at Yokohama and Kobe. Word is, it's to carry us and the 1st Marine Division to Korea."

First Marines, Bonnie thought. Hood's division, which he's so hot to rejoin. "To reinforce Pusan?"

"I don't think so. The fleet includes a lot of amphibious transports—landing craft. You don't need those to dock at a friendly port, you need them to launch an amphibious assault on a hostile shore, which right now includes just about every inch of Korea's coastline except for Pusan."

She thought of D-Day newsreels she'd seen during her senior year of high school, grim footage of men slogging ashore against concrete bulwarks and razor wire. Jumping off landing craft and disappearing over their heads because the boats had pulled up short. Of a long beach littered with bodies, more bodies rolling back and forth at the surf line.

Horrifying.

"Are you scared?"

"You bet."

She blinked, surprised. A man admits he's afraid. A first. As her hand itched for the notebook, she felt her interest in him grow. "Wouldn't the Marines be the first ashore? Storming beaches is what they do. You guys will go in afterward and hold the ground the marines take."

"Normally, yes, but this time there's a joker in the deck: The task force is commanded by General Almond. He's Army, not Marines, and he'd like nothing better than to prove GIs are as good at storming a beach as any old leathernecks. . . ."

Sam stopped, blinked, and shook his head slowly, ". . .and how did we end up talking about me? I think the original question was, what are you doing in the middle of all this?"

She hesitated. Maybe if she gave a little, so would he. "The army put me through nursing school. I owe them some time."

"Why didn't you just take out a loan for school?"

She snapped her fingers. "Damn, I should have thought of that."

He hooked a hand toward himself, fishing for more.

Forget it. She wasn't about to tell a total stranger how Mom had emptied bedpans and changed soiled sheets as a licensed practical nurse, pooling her income with Grandma, who cleaned houses on the side, the two of them trading off child care to hold the family together. My mother and my other mother, she thought. Living in a rented, second story walkup, no house as collateral, what bank would have loaned such women a dime?

She said, "I really can't tell you why I joined."

"Can't or won't?" A slow grin spread across his face. "You joined up to be around men. You've got a thing for soldier boys."

"You've got a lot of nerve—"

"Don't tell me, let me guess. You have no brothers."

"What's that got to do with anything?"

"But you did have a father," he mused. "The one who wanted to call you Wilhelmina."

"Not really." *To hell with it.* "He left home when I was four and my sister was two. To be precise, Mom threw him out. He was playing around on her with two or three different women, so she told him to hit the road. She let him visit us, but he only managed that now and then and he was never a father to us." She'd meant to be matter-of-fact, but she could see in his sudden, rapt attention that her bitterness had leaked through.

"That's rough."

"It wasn't, actually. It was just how things were."

Sam signaled the bar for another round. "How'd your sister take all this? She join the army, too?"

"Nope. Found herself a husband as soon as she got out of high school, a real prize, or so she tells herself. The pompous jerk expects her to have his pipe and slippers waiting when he comes home from his job. He's a bank teller, for God's sake, but you'd think he was a vice president. Diane waits on him hand and foot, his wish is her command. She tells herself that's what a proper wife does."

"She's scared she'll lose him, like your mother lost your father."

"But Mom didn't lose him. I told you, she threw him out."

"That's *your* take, which is why you're not afraid like your sister." He studied her. "Or maybe you're afraid in the opposite way."

"What does that mean?"

"You're afraid men are all bastards like your father."

"You do presume a lot, lieutenant."

"You're right. I'm sorry." He sounded genuinely contrite, and her indignation faded. She had never talked about this with any man and, truth was, it felt liberating. He was a good listener, warm and sympathetic at all the right points, and the fact that he was a stranger and she'd probably never see him again made it easier.

"Mom went through hell trying to get Unc—her husband out of her life. So, yeah, if I'm feeling like I want to be a little bit careful before I jump into marriage, maybe you can understand it."

"Absolutely."

"Good."

"So, will you marry me?"

Bonnie nearly blew a sip of Coke out her nose.

He spread his hands. "Can't blame a guy for trying."

"What if I'd said yes?"

For a beat, nothing, and then he grinned. "You'd have made me the happiest guy in Tokyo."

"Right. I'll bet it wouldn't have taken you thirty seconds to get out that door. You'd run, not walk."

The grin stayed put, looking sprayed-on now.

She laughed and sat back. I just saw through a man, she thought. A pretty slick one. Maybe the past month has taught me more than I think.

Clearing his throat, Sam said, "So. Do you like working at Tokyo General?"

"It's been fascinating."

"Past tense? Does that mean you're leaving?"

"Tonight was my last shift. I've volunteered for MASH duty."

His eyes widened. "You're joking."

"Nope."

"Which MASH are you joining?"

"The 1st. They're just forming up."

His eyebrows shot up.

"What?"

"The 1st MASH is assigned to X Corps, which is made up of the 1st Marine Division and the 7th Infantry Division. You'll be following me around Korea. If I get shot, you'll get to help pull the bullet out and change my bandages. How's that for romance?"

"Right up there with washing out your socks."

He grinned and then, abruptly, his smile faded. "Seriously, Bonnie, MASH units set up pretty close to the front. You could be overrun. It's very dangerous—"

"Life is full of risks, Sam. Tokyo General has been a good warmup, but most of the wounded sent back here have already had their lives saved and are out of danger. I'd like to get up close enough to the front to get in on some of that glory, feel like maybe I saved someone myself." And while I'm at it, she thought, find out how men act when their lives are on the line.

I'm not looking for a man, Sam, I'm looking at men.

Speaking of which.

"Let's talk about Sergeant Hood" she said. "Earlier you told me you aren't exactly friends with him so, I repeat, why did you come to see him tonight?"

Sam frowned. "What do you care about Hood?"

"Uh-uh, lieutenant. You promised if I had a drink with you, you'd tell me whatever I want to know about you and Hood. So give."

Sam sighed. "No big deal. I was checking up on him for a mutual friend."

She waited.

Drumming his fingers on the table, he looked around the bar as if for an escape hatch. "Hood used to date a woman I know," he said. "She knew he was in the 1st Provisional Marine Brigade down in Pusan, and she read in the *Times* that the brigade was taking a lot of casualties. She made phone calls to Ft. Pendleton and found out Hood had been wounded. She asked me to look in on him."

"What was all that tension between you two?"

"What tension?"

26

"Come on, Sam."

"I never thought he was particularly good for my friend."

"He abused her?"

"Ran out on her. Deserted her for his beloved Corps."

Tossing it off, but she could hear the resentment. Had this woman been a romantic interest of Sam's? That would be odd, with the age difference between him and the sergeant.

She said, "Sergeant Hood had a visitor a couple of days ago, a civilian who used to be in the Corps with him during World War II. I overheard him call Hood 'Gunny.' Marine gunnery sergeants have a couple of rockers and the crossed rifles. Hood's a three striper buck sergeant. Do you know what that's about?"

"You'll have to ask him."

"You know, though."

Sam said nothing. Interesting. Clearly, he didn't like Hood, and yet he was passing up a chance to badmouth him. If Hood had been a gunnery sergeant, he'd been busted down, and you'd think Sam would tell the story with relish. Was this some male code of behavior?

I'm missing too much here, Bonnie thought.

"This woman Sergeant Hood 'ran out on.' She means a lot to you?"

"Can we please change the subject?"

She pushed her chair back an inch. "Time I got back to the hospital."

"She's my mother, all right?"

"Your *mother*? Sergeant Hood dated your mother?"

"Not dated, married. Till death do us part. Or, in Hood's case, the Corps."

Bonnie felt her jaw drop. All at once she could see it—the dark hair, the cheekbones. Sam's eyes were brown, not gray, and Hood was a lot shorter, but the arched brows were identical, and the big hands.

Sam's were now twisting the Budweiser long-neck around and around on the table top. His last name had thrown her off—Foxworth.

27

I've really put my foot in it.

Embarrassed, she said, "Actually, I do need to get back."

Sam leaned toward her, his eyes hot. "Go ahead and ask. You want to know if Harlan Hood is my biological father? The answer is yes. So what?"

She knew she should stop, but she couldn't, it was too fascinating in a dread, train-wreck way. My father ran out on me, she thought, and Sam's ran out on him. She felt a sense of connection to him that she'd have thought impossible five minutes ago. "Did you see him much when you were growing up?"

"I saw him enough. He'd come in wearing that spiffy marine uniform, smelling of Old Spice, and he'd pick me up and give me big hugs. He'd take me around, buy me ice cream cones, and as soon as his three day pass was up he was out of there. I'd try to hang onto his leg and Mom would have to pull me off. Then they separated and, after awhile, I got over him. Mom remarried and I got a real father. For reasons I can't fathom, Mom still cares about Hood. She wanted me to check up on him and I did. I'll tell her he's fine and that's that."

She stared at him. "It can't be that simple."

"Sure it can."

She sat back and looked at the expressive, movie-star face, now carved from stone, the sergeant's big hands and black hair and arching eyebrows expressing themselves through his son the lieutenant. Sam sitting here telling her his father didn't matter while his jaw clenched so hard she could see all the little muscles of his cheeks.

Fascinating.

And what he'd told her—the 1st MASH, the 7th Infantry and the 1st Marines heading out together to do the bloody thing that set men apart from women.

But not from this woman.

Bonnie had the sudden conviction that tonight wouldn't be her last with Sergeant Hood or Lieutenant Foxworth, not just because they'd be going to war together, but because Sam wasn't done with her—and she wasn't done with him. He'd hooked her

28

with his story of his absent father. And she'd hooked him with her blond hair and baby blues and her C cups and whatever else it was men saw when they looked at her.

Sam wants to have sex with me, she thought. I don't have to be a genius about men to know that. He doesn't want to marry me, but he'll try to get me into his bed.

And while he's doing that, I'll get inside his head.

I'm going to need more notebooks.

General MacArthur considered several locations along Korea's west coast for his proposed strike behind enemy lines. He picked Inch'on for two reasons: First, it was only 25 miles west of Seoul. A victory would position X Corps to push rapidly inland and retake Seoul, which would deal a crushing blow to enemy morale. Second, Inch'on was known to be a hazardous port because of its shallow approaches and narrow time windows of navigable tide. From the technical standpoint alone, an amphibious landing there would be extremely hard to pull off. MacArthur was betting the enemy would conclude he wouldn't dare try it—and would therefore defend the port too lightly. Two of the Joint Chiefs of Staff opposed this gamble, but Louis Johnson, Secretary of Defense, backed MacArthur, and President Harry Truman backed Johnson. The invasion was scheduled for September 15, when the tides would, very briefly, accommodate a huge fleet of landing craft.

(Ibid.)

3

3 September, Yellow Sea, USNS Private Sadao S. Munemori, 1030 hours:

"We got a problem, lieutenant."

Sam slid his finger along the edge of "Korea Today" and re-seated the paper clip he was using for a bookmark. Two long days out of Yokohama, this had to be Sergeant Hartung's two dozenth complaint, no letup even when Typhoon Kezia had sent the platoon—everyone but Hartung—lurching to the rails to puke. "We got a problem," always turned out, "You got a problem." The real question was, what was Hartung's problem? Why the petty interruptions and his constant flirtation with insubordination—like now, eyeing his superior officer's book with just enough scorn for it to register but not enough to call him on it. "What problem do we have, sergeant?"

"Couple of the KATUSAs are going at each other."

KATUSAs—Koreans Augmenting the U.S. Army—but Hartung's translation was Koreans Aggravating the U.S. Army. "Do you mean they're fighting, sergeant?"

"Correct, sir."

"And you can't stop it?"

"Oh, I could stop it, but you said no banging heads."

Sam felt a warning pang at his temples. His eyes still ached from puking all yesterday. Damn but he missed Sergeant Rawlings.

31

They'd found the perfect groove of the lieutenant not bugging his sergeant and vice versa. The platoon at Camp Fuji had practically run itself. Rawlings, the lucky stiff, was still *with* that platoon—M Company, 31st Battalion. Whereas, Sam thought, I get reassigned to a different battalion and company, in charge of a platoon of total strangers and the sourest sergeant in the U.S. Army. All because their previous lieutenant managed to run over himself with his own jeep.

"Why are the men fighting?"

"Men?" Hartung made as if to spit on the deck, then thought better of it. "I said KATUSAs, lieutenant. They ain't men and they never will be."

Sam waited him out.

"How should I know what the little bastards are fighting about? Neither one speaks any English and I don't speak gook."

"Gonna use that word, maybe you could save it for the North Koreans."

Hartung rolled his eyes as if it were his own patience being taxed. "Sir. There's bad gooks and worse gooks, and gooks who aren't so bad, but a gook is a gook."

Sam scanned the section of hold that quartered the 2nd platoon of C Company. The USNS *Private Sadao S. Munemori* was named after a Nisei—a U.S. soldier of Japanese descent. A "Jap" to Hartung, except that this particular American martyr had won the Medal of Honor in World War II for throwing himself on a grenade to save his buddies of Anglo descent. A noble name, Munemori, deserving of an aircraft carrier, not this floating sardine can of a troopship. The *Munemori* left a lot to be desired in both room and comfort, especially for lieutenants and below. Endless partitions of sleeping quarters provided the bare basics, hard steel underfoot, the aisles murky as a steam tunnel under the dim, round overhead lights. Row upon row of bunks, floor to ceiling, the mattresses so tightly spaced you had to get out of bed to roll over, so close on the next row that two men had to struggle to pass each other in the aisle. Bad enough, without the whole area smelling of vomit.

So where was this alleged fight? Nothing going on in the platoon's area except a couple of poker games. Stooping, Sam tried to see between bunks into the next aisle. Shifting tides of legs cut off his line of sight.

"They're out in the starboard alley," Hartung offered at last.

"And you left them there fighting?"

"It's mostly screaming and finger pointing but, they keep it up, someone not under orders to nursemaid 'em is gonna crack heads. That's why I came to you. Sir."

"Lead on, sergeant."

In the starboard alleyway, two Korean kids draped in outsized U.S. Army uniforms yelled at each other. A circle of KATUSAs three deep hemmed the two principals in, shouting encouragement to their man—looked like every Korean in the company was here. Where was that kid from Taegu who'd learned English working in a PX before the Korean press gangs had swept him up? There—the one with the round head and ears sticking out. "Private Kim!" Sam shouted.

The boy gave him a blank look. None of the others paid him even that much attention.

Setting his fingers to his mouth, Sam let out a piercing whistle. The crowd stopped shouting and stared at him as if he'd just landed from Mars. A memory popped into his head of when Mom was out of the apartment, Hood teaching him to rattle windows with that same whistle, practicing until old Mrs. Peasely in the next flat would start banging on the wall.

Harlan Hood coming for the weekend and thinking he was being a real father.

The two antagonists were still yelling and pointing. Stepping between them, Sam found the scrap of muscle over their collarbones and pinched down. To the casual observer it would look like a friendly hand on the shoulder, but if you got the pressure right, the only way the pinchee could avoid serious pain was to hold still. Another trick from Hood's inexhaustible bag.

One of the boys yelped and Sam eased up. "Private Kim: front and center." He gave the kid from Taegu a hard stare to show him he was busted. A small guy like most of them, looking way too young—thirteen or fourteen, though surely that couldn't be right.

Kim stepped forward.

"Do you know what these two are fighting about?"

He shook his head.

"Ask them."

"He already knows," Sergeant Hartung snarled. "Don't be lying to the lieutenant."

Kim let loose some rapid-fire Korean but neither boy would answer. One of the crowd behind Kim said something; nodding, Kim turned and translated: "Lee called Choi a coward." No indication of which was Lee and which was Choi. Clearly, Kim's aim was to get out of this with a minimum of ratting.

"Why did he call him a coward?"

With a reluctant grimace, Kim gave in. "Because Choi was crying in his bunk last night. He doesn't want to be a soldier. He wants to go home."

Don't we all? Sam felt a pang of sympathy for Choi but knew not to show it. "Private Kim, the sergeant is going to order everyone back to their bunks. You translate. I want you to stay, though." Sam cued Hartung with a nod.

"All right, you worthless scum, get your skinny asses back to your bunks right now, that's an order."

Kim said three or four words, and the crowd dispersed, a few casting fearful glances back at their two comrades still immobilized in Sam's grip.

"All right, Kim, now tell these two they are to stand still when I let go."

"No problem, Boss." Kim said a few words and Sam let go. The two stood, riveted, as if he still had hold of them.

"Which is Lee?"

"That one is Lee and that one is Choi."

"Tell Lee he is to leave Choi be. No more insults or teasing. You understand?"

"Yes, Boss."

"We say sir when we talk to a lieutenant," Hartung barked.

Sam resisted the urge to roll his eyes. Either the sergeant was unaware of his own frequent lapses in the "sir" department, or he had a flair for irony he'd kept well hidden up to now.

"Yes, sir." Kim turned to Lee and spoke a few sentences.

Sam said, "Tell him to nod if he understands. Tell him I'll take it as a promise. Make it clear to him that, if he goes back on his word when I'm not around, he is the coward, not Choi, and he will lose face with me. Plus Sergeant Hartung will give him latrine duty for a week. Make him understand this."

Kim spoke again, at some length. Lee swallowed, nodded.

"Tell him to look at me, not you," Sam said.

Kim spoke and Lee turned and gave a spastic bow.

"Okay, he can go."

"I should get back, too," Hartung said. "Make sure everything's all right."

"Hang on, sergeant. Do we not have a buddy system that's supposed to keep things like this from happening? Where are the two American guys in our platoon assigned to pair up with Lee and Choi?"

"I don't know."

"Find them. I want you and them waiting at my bunk when I get back."

"You sure you want to do that—"

"You have your orders, Sergeant Hartung."

". . . Yessir," hesitating just long enough to show his displeasure.

Watching him stalk off, Sam rubbed his temples while Kim waited and Choi stared at the deck. Now what? How did you tell a kid ripped away from his home and family and forced to serve in a foreign army not to be a crybaby? A kid who might be drowned within a week, or if he could get ashore, shot. Did you tell him to have a stiff upper lip when you, yourself, couldn't sleep at night for thinking of that water, the bullets coming at you until the sound and light went away forever?

Sam returned his hand to Choi's shoulder, gently this time. "I understand why you cry. You miss your family. But you wouldn't be able to go home right now, even if I said you could. The North Korean army is between you and your family."

Kim translated while Sam fought back a wince, the headache at full gallop now. "We are going to make the North Koreans go back where they came from—you and I and the rest of your platoon. And then your parents and your brothers and sisters will be proud of you, because you will have helped save them. In the mean time, the platoon is your family. Lee is your brother, and sometimes brothers are mean. Then the father has to step in, like I did here—"

Watch it!

"—I'm not your father, but I will do my best to see you get back to him and your mom. In return, you will make sure no one can see or hear when you cry. When we land in a day or two, I'll need you. You help me and your brothers, and I'll do all I can to see you get back home when it's over. Okay?"

Choi had started nodding, looking up more as Sam talked and Kim translated. Now, he mumbled something in a husky voice.

"He says he is sorry he shamed himself."

"There's no shame in crying, Choi. Many others are home-sick and afraid, too. You feel how you feel. It's what you do that counts with me. As long as you do what the sergeant and I tell you, you can be proud."

"He says he will try."

"Okay, he can go."

Choi headed away toward the platoon bunks, rubbing his shoulder. Way to go, Sigmund, Sam thought sourly. If I'd wanted to be a father, I'd have married Emily, or Patty, or maybe Jennifer.

"You did good, boss."

Sam gave Kim an appraising look. "You speak English very well. What did we train you for at Camp Fuji?"

"Armor bearer." With a rueful expression, Kim rubbed at his pipe-stem arms. "That ammo is heavy."

"You're off that. I'll tell Sergeant Hartung. When we go ashore, you stick close to me. You'll relay my orders to the Koreans in the platoon."

"Will do, lieutenant." He gave a big smile.

"That's all, private." Kim bounced on his way, looking lighter from just the thought of a future without all that weight on his back. God, how did I get myself put in charge of kids? Sam wondered. I'm the man who will probably get some of them killed. Did I think ahead at all?

His headache worsened, squeezing his brain like a vice cranking tight on his skull. Danger was getting closer every minute. They were in the Yellow Sea now, after rounding the southern tip of Korea where Hood had taken a bullet in the lung. Was the old man somewhere nearby right now, on one of the Marine troopships? No doubt he'd pushed for a discharge so he could join the party, as he'd think of it. What a hard-ass, Sam thought. I come to ask how he's doing, and he gets in my face about taking fire from a ridge "you dog-faces" were supposed to have under control.

And royally pissed that I joined the Army instead of the Marines. He didn't say it, but that's what's really chafing him, it's gotta' be.

Good.

Sam's smile faded. What wasn't so good was the effect Marine disrespect of Army might have on his immediate future. Hood's low opinion multiplied by the entire Marine Corps is what had given General Almond his itch to prove the 7th Infantry could storm ashore as well as any Marine. Now that the armada had steamed past Pusan, the entire coast of Korea from here north was a hostile shore. Wherever the landing took place, Almond should wise up and let the marines go in first.

Sam pictured a fearless Buck Sergeant Hood in a landing craft joking with his squad as the shore and battle loomed. The man might run from everything else, but bullets he could face.

Then he imagined Hood spread-eagled in the surf, floating back and forth with the tide, dead and gone from this world. Maybe then, at long last, his ghost would wish he'd deserted The Corps for his family, instead of the other way around.

Sam tried to picture himself climbing down the side of the *Munemori* into a landing craft. The thought, alone, made his heart pound. What had possessed those GIs on D-Day, crawling down the swaying sides of their ships into the clumsy, box-shaped boats that would speed them into a hail of bullets? Maybe they'd tried not to think about it, but how could you not? Your life on the line. Catch a bullet in the head or heart and it was no more cold beers buzzing down your throat. No sweet smell of grass on the ball diamond, sliding into home plate, dust flying up around you. No girl in the back seat letting you put your hands on her breast or thigh to find out how she compared to the others, exploring that wonderful warm softness while your blood spun. How could you say, "all right, sir, you're ordering me to jump into that water up to my neck and try to get to shore before a bullet pokes my eye out and smashes my brain, and by cracky that's just what I'm going to do."

Sam shook his head. Why didn't men refuse to get into the landing craft? Was it really worse to be called a coward than to die? If General Almond has his way, Sam thought, I'll have to order my kids to get in the boats and maybe say goodbye to their lives. I'm your lieutenant, and I say go, now you go.

What if they won't?

"Yo, Foxworth."

Turning, Sam nearly bumped into the captain. Loomis's neck seemed to have swelled another inch—must've found a way to pump iron on the troopship. With the square jaw and the straight-across angle of his cap, his head would look right at home on a totem pole. Probably a college P.E. major who'd taken ROTC *hoping* for another war.

"Got a minute?" Loomis asked.

"Sure."

"We haven't had much time to talk since you took Lieutenant Rhodes' place. I'm sure by now you know you inherited a less-than-shipshape platoon."

"They seem all right so far, sir."

Loomis raised an eyebrow. "Either you are an optimist, Foxworth, or you have your head in the sand. Between the KATUSAs and your men from the stockade—"

"The stockade!"

"Surely Sergeant Hartung told you about them."

"I believe I'd remember that. . .sir." Indignation boiled up in him.

Loomis frowned. "Sergeant Hartung should have told you when you took over the platoon. Well. Okay, it's this way: To help beef up the division, the brass arranged early release for prisoners doing time in the 8th army stockade. You've got five of them, Privates Silverman, Hufnagel, Logan, and Sherwood, and Corporal Cinquemani, who if I remember right was busted down from sergeant."

"Well, damn it, what were they in for?"

"Are you taking a tone with me, Foxworth?"

Sam blew out a breath. "No. Sorry."

"Logan and Hufnagel were in for theft, Silverman for going AWOL for a month, Sherwood for assaulting an MP, and Cinquemani for gross insubordination to a superior officer."

Sam called up mental images of the men—yeah, the five who kept to themselves, tough guys forming their own little gang within the platoon.

"Don't take it so hard, lieutenant, you don't have as many as some of the other units. Would you rather have more KATUSAs?"

"I might."

Loomis blinked. "My point is, you got plenty to do to get your men into shape, and not much time to do it."

"Yes, sir. Are we going in with the first wave?"

"You'll get that in the next briefing."

"But you know?"

"Relax, lieutenant. Whatever comes, we've trained on it."

"With respect, captain, now who's being an optimist? If Army has to—"

Loomis held up a hand; scanned up and down the long companionway as if checking for spies. "You didn't hear this from me but, as it happens, we are not going ashore with the first wave, or the second either. General Smith persuaded General MacArthur that storming beaches is the job of Marines."

"Good." Relief swept Sam, the strength of it taking him aback a little. *Am I that chicken?* "I mean, Army reserve call-ups can't hope to do it better than guys who fought their way ashore in the Pacific in the last war."

"That was Smith's argument." Loomis sounded disappointed. "Remember, everything I'm telling you is zip-lipped until the official briefing." He leaned closer and Sam caught the licorice scent of sen-sen. "Our target is Inch'on, right smack in the middle of the country. Gonna cut the supply lines of that shitload of gooks been giving our guys hell down south. God willing and with reasonable luck, the marines will take the beachhead, and the minute it is secured, we will land behind them and push inland as fast as possible to take Seoul back from the enemy. That's where the real fight's gonna be, Foxworth."

Sam thought of the map he'd just been studying in his book. Seoul, the capital of South Korea, was only a couple day's march inland from Inch'on. Since early in the war it had been in enemy hands, which meant the North Koreans had had plenty of time to dig in and harden defenses.

Loomis lowered his voice another notch: "We have reason to believe Inch'on is not as heavily defended as it might be. The NKPA is counting on the shallow water of their harbor to defend them. The approaches can be navigated only when high tide is at its peak for the month, but our timing's right and Navy knows how to work with tides. My prediction, the marines will take Inch'on before they know what hit 'em. Then we'll be right in the game."

"Taking Seoul," Sam said.

"Yeah. Like I said, that's gonna be a bitch. They got at least twenty thousand defenders there now. As soon as we hit Inch'on, it'll set off alarms with the enemy down around Pusan. They'll tear ass back north to reinforce Seoul. They get there before we do, we'll be facing fifty to a hundred thousand defenders. Street fighting, Sam, block by block, going up against tanks and artillery, with enemy shooting down at us from every window and doorway." Loomis's eyes lit as if he were plotting strategy for an upcoming football game, where, win or lose, you could soak your bruises afterward.

"What's our regiment's part in this?"

"Looks like we'll be circling in from the south to attack the city and block off enemy troops trying to get back up to reinforce. Oh, yeah, lieutenant, within a few days we'll be under fire, no question." Loomis studied him. "If you're wishing you were back with the 31st, buck it up, son. We all gotta play the hand we're dealt. I were you, I'd start with Sergeant Hartung. He was in the last war, and he could be a help, but not unless you make it happen."

"I'll get right on that, sir."

Loomis eyed him. "You're not one of those complicated guys, are you, Sam?"

"Simple as they come."

"Because I hate complicated guys. I've got enough to do without having to figure my lieutenants out. And you've got plenty to do, too, getting on top of your platoon. You don't have much time."

"Then I guess I'd better get started, sir."

Loomis squinted at him for a measuring second. "Right. Carry on, lieutenant."

Troopship USS General W.A. Mann, 1300:
Waiting for the meeting to start, Bonnie began to wish she'd skipped seconds at lunch. The conference room, buried deep in

the bowels of the ship near the steam turbines, had been warm when she'd walked in. Now it was downright hot, simmering in the combined body heat of thirty doctors and nurses crammed together, bulkhead to bulkhead, on folding chairs. By comparison, LuLu's bar back in Tokyo had been springtime in Canada.

"Front row, center?" Laura whispered behind her. "You are such a suck-up, Brisbane."

"Lemme' alone. It's my only hope of staying awake." Good, Bonnie thought—if Laura was back in needling form, the hurricane must truly be over. Still some wallow in the ship's motion, but not compared to last night, with its screaming winds and violent, corkscrewing seas, the ship plunging through waves so enormous the impacts had flung people from their bunks. Seasick nurses and doctors throwing up all around her, and somehow she'd come through without a hiccup. Typhoon Kezia had veered away hours ago, but the usually-crowded noon mess had looked like a Baptist church at Yom Kippur. Was it her fault the cooks had made too much? In the Brisbane household wasting food was only a cut below skipping class or lying to your mother.

Covering a yawn, Bonnie felt her jaw pop.

"That must be the briefer," Laura said, "over by the door. What's he waiting for?"

Turning in her seat, Bonnie watched Laura fan herself furiously with a flat, stick- handled gizmo. It looked like an outsized ping pong paddle except for the painting of Jesus—a classic camp meeting fan, looking about as natural in Laura's hand as feathers on a fox. With her long legs, shiny dark hair, and mischievous mouth, Laura Lidner was a poster girl for sin.

"Get me out of this, Brisbane, and I've got a pint of Seagram's Whiskey with your name on it."

"Don't you want to know what we're heading into? C'mon, it'll be interesting."

Laura groaned. "You're bringing my nausea back—"

"At ease, people."

The booming voice snapped Bonnie back around. Colonel Barton Lipscomb had taken up station behind the lectern. She reviewed what she'd heard about him. Far East Command Surgeon's staff, trained in psychiatry; administrator of a field hospital during World War II. He looked reasonably bright, a big man, with shrewd eyes and a commanding air. A little too big—his paunch strained his uniform. Thinning brown hair and drooping fat under his chin marked him as old, at least fifty. The armpits of his uniform were dark with sweat—gross.

"Doctors and nurses, if I may have your attention, I'll say my piece and you can get back to your cool staterooms."

Polite laughter from the nurses up front salted with uncharitable groans from the young draftee docs in the back.

"Consider the heat a part of your training," Lipscomb said. "I was down in Pusan in August for a site visit to the Double Nickel—that's the 8055th MASH—and that was really hot, over a hundred most days I was there. Just remember, fall is coming, and then winter, which in Korea is far harder to take than summer heat. But that's another story. Let me be the first to welcome you of the newly formed 1st MASH to the front."

The murmur of male voices still going on in the back of the room died away.

"That's right, the front," the colonel repeated with a relish bordering on sadistic. "As you may know, this huge armada of ships around us is also transporting the 1st Marine Division and the Army's 7th Infantry Division to Korea. The 1st MASH will be assigned to these two divisions as their forward hospital—their first resort after their battalion aid stations."

Tell me something I don't know, Bonnie thought, then realized this probably *was* news to most of those present, who had not, after all, gotten the advance scoop from Sam. Ah, Sam—ever since that night at LuLu's, she'd been seeing him in her mind. Last time a guy had imprinted that vividly was Gregory Peck, after she'd watched "Twelve O'clock High" three times in two days. Now there was a man!

And she must file Sam in the same drawer—F for fantasy. A guy that handsome must have had a lot of experience with women. The heat in his gaze, his undivided attention had been flattering but also very practiced, like a veteran quarterback running through his play book. If women were a game to Sam, she had no interest in running up his score.

No, what intrigued her was his issues with his father. Sam's had deserted him, just as hers had. If a chance came, they should get together and talk about it. Just don't bring him in on a stretcher, Bonnie prayed silently. Him or his father. I'd rather see neither one of them again than that.

"In two days," Colonel Lipscomb said, "the 1st and the 7th, backbone of General Almond's X Corps, will launch an amphibious attack on a defended harbor and city. You will be told which city and given other details in briefings tomorrow. Today, I'm here to start preparing you for what will come. How many of you doctors were doing surgical rotations before you so kindly decided to join us."

"Did he say doctors?" Laura, leaning forward behind her.

"Who cares? Put it up."

Laura gave her a reproving nudge in the back.

"Six of you," Lipscomb said. "Good. Anyone work ER?"

Bonnie again held a hand up, but Lipscomb, looking over her head, appeared not to notice. "Excellent, you have an ER resident with you. Young man, you'll have a slight head start on your colleagues."

"Except for me," Bonnie said.

Lipscomb blinked down at her, his face pinking. "You have training in emergency medicine, Lieutenant. . . ?"

"Brisbane. Yes, sir. I worked the night shift at Chicago General."

"Indeed. Then I presume you've helped treat some gunshot and knife wounds."

"Yes, sir."

"Well, as I was saying, you and the young man in back have a head start, but only a slight one. In two days, the amphibious assault will take place, and the 1st MASH will go in right behind it. As I speak, the forward destroyers and cruisers of our task force are closing in to start the bombardment of the harbor and its defenses, which includes the city itself. With luck that bombardment will leave intact a building of sufficient size for you to set up a hospital and begin operating. And operate you will. My old friend Colonel Martin, here, will be asking you non-surgical doctors to assist the surgeons in areas such as anesthesia, and if things get bad, you will end up doing some cutting yourself."

Lipscomb's big head swooped around to stare at her again. "Lieutenant Brisbane, you say you've helped patch up gunshot wounds?"

"Yes, sir."

"Have you ever seen a leg or an arm mangled by a grenade?"

"No sir."

"Have you seen men cut nearly in half by machine gun fire, but still, somehow breathing?"

"No, sir." Bonnie resisted the urge to ask, *Have you?*

"Well, you will. And when you do, there will be no time for shock or fainting."

"I don't faint, sir."

"There's always a first time. You probably think I'm browbeating you, young lady, and maybe I am, but I'm a walk in the park compared to what you're going into, and my job, with what little time I have today, is to give you some psychological preparation for what is coming so you can land on the beach and start doing your jobs. Before the week is out, you'll have sawed the arms and legs off living men to help them go on living. You'll feel a natural hesitancy, even with what you know about the speed with which gas gangrene can poison the system. But you'll do it, because you'll be the only hope they've got. I want you all to get one thing straight right at the get-go. Part of the time, God willing, you won't be doing much except treating dysentery and maybe a few cases of malaria. But when there's a battle, the floor of your building or tent will be sticky with blood, and you'll be operating for days at a time on men torn open in ways you never imagined, and by days I mean day and night. You'll have no time for fancy surgery. Take off the arm or leg, clean out the gaping chest or belly, sew the man up, and bring the next one in."

45

Lipscomb aimed a sweeping frown at the men in the back of the room. "Some of you doctors, fresh out of medical school, may think this is a good place to practice this or that new procedure you read about in a journal. It's not. Work fast, save the life if you can, then move on to the next."

Colonel Lipscomb brought the frown home to her again. The dark circles had spread out under his armpits. Pulling out his hanky, he mopped his glistening forehead. "Lieutenant Brisbane, any questions, before I go on? Any comments?"

"No sir." I embarrassed him, she thought, so now he's mad at me. Poor baby.

"You find this amusing, Lieutenant?"

She realized she must have smiled. "No, sir."

"Well you had better get whatever it is out of your system because, where you're going, there won't be much to laugh at—"

Rolling his eyes up, the colonel contemplated the ceiling. A second later, Bonnie saw the lectern sailing straight at her, shot forward by his buckling knees as Lipscomb sat down hard on the floor, his back against the wall, then flopped over on his side. Fending the lectern off, Bonnie scrambled to him, the room suddenly utterly still around her, like she'd stepped into a surreal 3D painting. Colonel Lipscomb's eyelids were open, the pupils rolled way back, like he was trying to see into the top of his own head. His mouth leered and little bubbles of spit flecked his lips. Planting two fingers under his jaw, Bonnie felt the racing pulse, strong and regular. A palm on his chest told her it was rising and falling, no problems with respiration.

"Laura, get his feet up on the chair," she said as she pulled the knot of the colonel's tie loose. His neck was so fat she couldn't get the button undone. Grabbing the points of his starched collar, she ripped apart hard, popping the button loose. Lipscomb's liberated larynx made a gargling sound; at once, his color improved.

The room flowed back to life around her, a doctor kneeling beside her—Jeffery Wittschiebe, one of the surgical residents. "How about that," he said. "The colonel's a fainter, himself. Must be the heat."

"Or the aggravation," said one of the other doctors.

Jeff's mouth squirmed, his cheeks bulging, trying to hold it in, then he burst out laughing. Others joined in.

Bonnie had a premonition of being back in her quarters with Laura, laughing until she cried. "Stop it you guys. This could be serious."

"True," Jeff said. "I am a trained physician, you know, Nurse Brisbane," imitating Lipscomb's stuffy voice.

The fallen colonel's eyelids began to flutter.

Bonnie reached for his wrist to take his pulse.

"Lieutenant," said a voice behind her, "I do think it might be best if you let Dr. Wittschiebe handle this." Glancing up, she swallowed her retort. It was Colonel Martin, head of the 1st MASH, her commanding officer. The laughter died away; Chester Martin was the adult supervision of the group, a couple of decades older than the other doctors, and the only army lifer in the bunch. He said, "I know Colonel Lipscomb pretty well. If you're here when he wakes up, it'll embarrass the hell out of him and he will not feel grateful for that. Believe me when I say you don't want to be any further on his bad side than you already are."

"Yes, sir."

In the hall, Bonnie leaned against a bulkhead. *Great start, Brisbane.*

On the other hand, she'd probably never see Lipscomb again, and what could he do, anyway? Accuse her of making him faint?

Heading back to quarters, she started composing today's entry for her notebook: *Why do men assume we are weak?*

Her mind went back to the grim scenarios of combat and bloody ORs Lipscomb had been painting. If even half of what he'd said was true, MASH duty was not for the weak.

Resolve flowed through her. I am not weak, she thought. I'm strong, and I will stay strong, no matter what comes.

On September 15, 1950, the 1st Marine Division stormed ashore at Inch'on in two waves on the morning and evening tides. The US Navy performed brilliantly, as did the Marines. Losses were far lighter than feared. MacArthur's bold gamble ended in total triumph. By September 16, the marines had pushed inland far enough to prevent North Korean artillery from shelling the unloading areas on the beaches of Inch'on. The first elements of the 7th Infantry Division came ashore September 18, as marines drove the enemy from Kimpo Airport between Inch'on and Seoul. To the south, along the Pusan perimeter, the North Korean attackers at first fiercely resisted General Walker's 8th Army offensive timed to coincide with the Inch'on landing. Within days, the enemy began fleeing north, some in panic, others to reinforce Seoul against the coming American and South Korean counterattack.   (Ibid.)

4

17 September, near Ascom City, 0100 hours:
After a couple hours of uneasy sleep, Hood climbed past Jimmy from their foxhole to make rounds. Middle of the night, and the rule in a war zone was sleep whenever you got the chance, but it wasn't working. Restless, his unconscious mind gnawing on some bone it didn't want to share just yet.

Plus the leg was bitching. Hadn't felt it in the rush of the assault on Inch'on, or the next day when the 5th regiment had moved out of the city, heading for Seoul at an easy walk. Shot in the lung less than a month ago, but that was okay. Now it was the lesser wound, the leg, that bothered him. Two bullets it had taken now, same leg both times, first from the Japs in WWII and then, last month, shot from that damn hill the Army was supposed to have taken at Obong-ni. The leg didn't like cold. First time in months it had been anything but stinking hot and, just like that, it was too cold, the chill settling to the bottom of the foxholes, some of the men pulling on field jackets to keep from shivering.

Hood worked the leg, climbing the moonlit rise toward the top of the hill the colonel had selected for the battalion. Good ground, easy to defend, with a 360 view of the countryside east of Inch'on. Back west, where they'd come from, a few lights flickered in Ascom City, a small, undefended town just inland of Inch'on. Beyond that, at the Red, Green and Blue beaches where the amphibious assault had been made, the sky above the conquered port glowed from lights the engineers had set up so the work of unloading an armada of supply ships could continue throughout the night—hundreds of thousands of C-rations, tons of water, Sherman tanks, trucks, jeeps, artillery, communications equipment, tentage, ammo, medicine—everything two divisions and their headquarters and support units needed to stay on the march.

Hood turned around to look east, where they were headed. Within a mile of the sea, the land had begun a slow but steady rise, more and more hills ahead, cutting off any nighttime glow from Seoul—a city of millions about ten miles away across the Han River.

Tomorrow, according to the topographical maps, they'd find a final notch through the hills and enter the flatter country that formed the delta of the Han River. Once they'd crossed the Han, the land would rise again, with more steep hills guarding the approaches to Seoul. The going was sure to get tough at that point, but that was a couple days off.

So what was eating him right now, enough to roust him from sleep?

On the surface, all seemed well. Inch'on, which could have been bloody murder, had gone off almost without a hitch, from the boat-work of coxswains who'd had little or no time to drill, to the cooperation of the tides, to the weak showing of the defenders, who'd seemed almost surprised, though they'd had at least a few days to see it coming. Inch'on would go down in history as a daring and incredible victory, the kind generals and the people back home loved—quick, with low casualties, everything coming off right.

But Inch'on was history, now. The push to Seoul was on, and that would not be so easy, though it was going fine so far. To the south, the 5th regiment of the 1st Marines had closed up its right flank with the 1st regiment. In a day of easy advance, not a single NK had been spotted.

Why?

That was the question, the reason his brain wouldn't let him sleep.

Hood ambled over to the foxhole Barstow and Rittenhouse had dug on the highest ground available like good veterans should. A helmet showed above the rim. Hood prodded it with the toe of his boot. Barstow's head rolled back and then his eyes popped open, and he straightened, faking like he'd been awake all the time. Below, Private Rittenhouse slept like a baby, his head resting on his drawn-up knees.

"One guy awake at all times, Hollywood," Hood murmured, "you know that."

"You say so, Sarge."

"I say so."

"Even though there isn't a gook in sight."

"Especially when there isn't a gook in sight. I'm serious—look at me when I'm talking to you, private. You want to sleep, you wake up Rittenhouse. When I come back by here, I'd better see eyeballs on one of you."

Barstow gave him an exaggerated set of owl-eyes. "Gotcha."

Hood turned away and lit up a Lucky. Now that the lung had pretty much healed, it was a pure delight, dragging the soothing smoke into his lungs. . . .

What the hell?

It came again, a wracking snore from one of the new-guy fox-holes. Hood headed for the crater Steinberg and Cockburn had dug as their home for the night. A stone from his boot trickled over the edge and the barrel of an M-1 poked out at him, making him dodge back from a Private Steinberg all too ready to blow his head off.

"Easy, boy!" A little too much alertness in this foxhole.

"Sorry, sergeant."

Hood leaned over the edge. Cockburn was sleeping curled on his side, an army blanket over his shoulders and butt, the big legs sticking out. The mashed-up nose, probably broken and re-broken on various gridirons, was producing the racket, a serious, magnified snore that a general back at headquarters could afford and Bo could not.

"Once we start mixing it up with NK," Hood said, "You wake him nights when he snores like that."

"Wake this golem? Do I look like I have a death wish?" his eyes big behind the round spectacles.

"Do it, Steinberg, or you might be dead without the wish. Enemy infiltrators love snorers to death"

Turning away, Hood looked for the lieutenant's spot, also near the top of the slope. The big rock, there. More bunker than foxhole, it had been dug out by new guys Eddie Jakes and Pete Mendenhall after a broad hint from the veteran Rittenhouse. The lieutenant always gallantly protested that he ought to dig his own hole, but the veterans knew he hated entrenching tools worse than flesh wounds. The fastest way into his heart for a new guy was to "volunteer" and most were willing enough to seize the opportunity in the hope of future considerations like three-day passes.

A flashlight glow seeped from under the rock. Looked like the lieutenant couldn't sleep, either. Unslinging his M-1, Hood sat on the edge of the hole.

Morrison glanced up from his map, nodded, and went back to staring at it.

He didn't look so good. His shoulders sagged, and he'd picked up dark rings under his eyes. Hood saw that he'd skipped shaving for a couple of days. His mouth was a tight crease, that habit he had of sucking in his lips and biting on them whenever he had serious thinking to do. His cigar, sticking out to the side, had gone dead.

Sliding into the hole, Hood scanned the map. Seoul was a big splash near the center, about ten miles from where they sat.

"Sure wish I knew how many defenders we'll be going up against," Morrison muttered.

"What are you hearing?"

"At least a division, and G-2 thinks more units are already beating feet from the south."

"Thinks?"

"When do they ever know, sergeant? Only reason they call it Intelligence is it sounds better than Eeny-meeny."

"Guess that's why we're awake."

"I'm on it, sarge. No sense both of us losing sleep."

"The NK should be harassing us," Hood said, "trying to stop us or at least slow us down so they can reinforce Seoul. They've got those Russian T-34 tanks, lots of artillery. They should be pounding us on the road and in our encampments. Instead, nothing."

"Which means?"

"They've laid a trap somewhere along the route between here and the city and are sucking us into it. Don't tell me you haven't been thinking on that, too."

Morrison grunted assent.

"Want to do something about it?"

The lieutenant gave him a wary look, the dark circles under his eyes exaggerated by the flashlight glowing up along his cheekbones. "Like what?"

"In the last war, I was with a recon platoon. I'm pretty sneaky. I could take Jimmy and run up the road a spell, see if I can find out where the NKs are hiding."

"I'm from New York, sarge. How far is a spell?"

"Far enough to get a read on the situation, but not so far we can't get back in time to warn you. You'll be moving the platoon out in the morning, so our way back to you can only get shorter."

Lacing his hands behind his head, Morrison lay back and squinted at the rock above. "Battalion will have its own recon platoon out tonight."

"They can't be everywhere and they've got a lot more to think about than our platoon. Our boys are our job, lieutenant, and when it comes to looking after them, there's nothing like a couple sets of our own eyes and ears."

"Well, I can't let you have Jimmy. Someone's got to keep an eye on the squad while you're out."

"Then I'll take Hollywood."

Morrison's gaze slid down off the rock onto him. "Barstow? Why him?"

"Because he's light on his feet and smart."

"He'll think he's in a movie."

"We are in a movie, lieutenant. You start thinking this is real, you'll get scared, and it won't be half as much fun."

"Between you and me, Hood, I'm scared right now."

"Of course you are, sir. Only natural. But, when your men are looking, you'll go on acting like you're not scared, just like you been doing. Seeing you, they'll act brave for their buddies. It is a movie, lieutenant. We couldn't do it if it weren't for acting."

Morrison studied him. "Sometimes you amaze me, Sergeant Hood. You make me wonder why you're not a major instead of a buck sergeant. Or, let's say, a gunnery sergeant."

Hood suppressed a sigh. He'd expected this back in July, when Morrison had first taken charge of the platoon at Camp Pendleton, just before the 5th regiment was tapped to form the core of the regimental combat team for Pusan. Surely a world class worrier like Morrison would check out the records of his sergeants.

"Gunnery sergeants are glorified clerks for the brass," Hood said.

"A good bit more than that."

"Not in my case."

"That why you punched out your major back in W.W. II? You were tired of being his clerk and wanted to get a squad back?"

"You got it."

Morrison grunted. "That's not what I heard. I heard your battalion was in a fire fight on Okinawa, and the captain of your company went down with a chest wound, and this major—the battalion S-2—gave you an order that would have gotten a lot of men killed. You tried to make him see that, and when he wouldn't, you cold-cocked him in his tent and gave the company the right order, saying it came from the major, and saved a lot of men."

"That how they wrote it up?"

"No, that's not how they wrote it up, damn it, as you very well know. That is what Jimmy told me. The way they wrote it up was refusing a direct order and striking a superior officer. In view of your earlier bronze star, and everything you did to deserve it, instead of a court-martial, they let you plead to brig time and busted you back. Way I hear it, they were going to take one rocker, and you insisted on both."

"Squad leader's where I belong. It's what I want."

"What about the stockade time? That had to chafe."

"The regs are there for a reason. You hit an officer, you get the book thrown at you."

Morrison gazed at him. "So. If you disagree with one of my orders, and I won't listen, you'll refrain from popping me on the jaw?"

Hood cleared his throat, getting more uncomfortable by the minute. What was this, battlefield jitters? The lieutenant had been standup so far, first at Camp Pendleton, then scrambling up the Pusan hills with the rest of them, scared, but doing it anyway, what it was all about. An Annapolis grad, which meant he was probably bright as hell, but he never flashed it. Ambitious academy lieutenants had a tendency to get too many of their men killed, but so far Morrison hadn't shown any recklessness. Hood remembered the first thing the man had said to him after being assigned to the third platoon back at Pendleton: "Sergeant, there's stuff I know and stuff I don't. I need you to back me up on what I don't know. In front of the men, we play our parts, but when it's just us you can say anything. Help me and we'll get as many of these guys out alive as we can." More polished, but words to that effect. So far, Morrison had been about as good as an officer could get.

"You'd listen," Hood said.

"But what if I didn't? What if I felt you were who's wrong?"

"Look, sir, you give me an order, I'll obey it."

"Even if you thought it would get men killed?"

Hood sighed. "With respect, Lieutenant, this is bullshit. Nobody knows what he'll do until he gets there. I try to do what's right, as best I can see it. If I'm wrong or if I gotta do wrong to stop a worse wrong from happening. . . . Well, thinking about it gives me a headache. I get in that situation again, I hope I'll do whatever's right, and that's all I can say."

Lieutenant Morrison nodded. "That's all I can ask. Take Barstow."

"Sarge!" Hollywood, lying in the tall grass beside him, gripped Hood's arm, his voice a bare whisper. "You hear that?"

Flat on his belly, Hood listened. Chirring crickets, wind whispering through the grass, and then it came to him, the faint moan of an engine up the road toward Seoul. Damn! He'd always been the first to pick up warning sounds. Had the big naval guns pounding Inch'on before the assault taken the edge off his hearing?

His and not Barstow's?

Maybe age was finally catching up with him. Hollywood was, what, twenty?

Hood parted the tall grass with his arms so he could see the road, a pale ribbon running between two moonlit hills. The engine sound welled into a rasping groan, and then he saw the truck rounding the opposite hill, slowing as it rolled through the crease. It stopped below them seventy yards down-slope and idled in the road. The truck's lights were off, the windows of the cab black, not even a dash light on inside.

"Gooks," Barstow whispered.

What was this, an advance guard of the enemy probing forward? Hood tried to estimate how far he and Barstow had come, staying on the slopes above the Inch'on/Seoul road, keeping low in the weeds as they worked their way beyond the marine front lines. Maybe a couple of miles forward of American lines? The truck continued to sit there, a canvas-backed troop transport, big enough to carry twenty men and whatever equipment they could get between their feet.

A nerve twitched in Hood's spine, that warning shiver he sometimes got when someone was looking his way. He could almost see the driver and the man in the seat beside him scanning the hills that flanked the road. Hood kept his arms out in front, holding the weeds apart, afraid to let them spring back together in case the eyes in the truck might be on them.

They can't know we're up here, so what are they doing?

The passenger door of the truck swung open and an NK soldier stepped down and stared up at the hill, hands on his hips, that cocky stance some of the Jap officers had favored back in the last war, and to tell the truth, he'd seen on some Marine brass, too.

"I'm getting a bad feeling about this," Barstow whispered.

"No shit." Hood stared back at the North Korean officer, willing himself inside the man's head. Either the gook was psychic and knew there were a couple of U.S. Marines up here in the tall grass or he was sizing up the hill for some special purpose. Like laying an ambush to catch the advancing column in the morning.

The North Korean went to the rear of the truck and lowered the tailgate. Troops dropped from under the canopy, fourteen, fifteen, sixteen of them. Then someone handed down a mortar. Two more—from the size, Russian 120 mm jobs that would pack a nasty punch. And now a recoilless rifle—two, three of them—also Russian-made, lethal enough to knock out tanks if the mortars didn't do the job. Two heavy machine guns, tripod-mounted and water-cooled, followed the recoilless rifles off the truck. They'd be for repelling any effort to rush the hilltops from the road. Two men working each gun could mow down hundreds trying to get up the slopes with nothing but tall grass for cover.

Hood thought about the Army's Sherman tanks he'd seen rumbling down a causeway before the regiment had moved out from Inch'on. They'd be essential in the assault on Seoul and they were no doubt coming up the road somewhere behind the 5th Regiment.

"Damn," Barstow whispered.

"Yeah." We have to get out of here, Hood thought. He was about to motion Barstow back when an ugly thought struck him. Raising his binoculars, he studied the dirt road bed ahead and behind the stopped truck. Now that he'd told himself what to look for, the moonlight revealed what he feared—circles of disturbed dirt, too wide and irregular to catch your eye close up, hard to see even from here, unless you were looking for them. The ground had been disturbed in those places and carefully filled back in again. The likeliest explanation was that the NK had already prepped the site, firing down on the road to register their mortars, then filling in the craters to hide the impacts of the ranging rounds. They'd probably done it before the marines came ashore at Inch'on.

The hairs on Hood's neck prickled. Somewhere in the grass around him and Barstow would be square concrete slabs a few feet on a side, bedded in the dirt and marked so the bases of the mortars just unloaded could be returned to the precise positions they'd occupied while ranging in on the road. When lined up with the marks, the mortars would be ready to rain high explosives on a column of tanks. Instant lethality, not even an initial near-miss to give the American column some warning.

"We've got to hide ourselves," Hood whispered. "They'll be sending half those guys up here, and the other half on the hill across the road. Try not to beat down the weeds too much."

"Roger."

Hood eased back and Barstow mimicked his moves, lifting his body a few inches off the ground, fluffing the weeds to cover his trail as he backed away. When they were halfway down the rear slope, Hood caught Barstow's arm, motioned him into the shelter of a couple of small bushes.

"What?" Barstow whispered. "We've got to get out of here, warn the lieutenant, so he can pass it on."

"We could do that," Hood whispered. "But our tanks have to come this way, no choice, and if we try to send men up these hills in a frontal assault once the NK platoon is here with those machine guns, a lot of our boys won't be going home."

"So what do we do?"

"We take care of it, now."

"Shit, sarge."

Hood heard him dry swallow. "We can do it, private, if we're quiet. They won't settle too close together for fear of being seen from the road in daylight, so there probably won't be more than two in any one place—four fire teams is what I'd do, if I were them. We just watch where they settle, come up behind and use the knives. We won't make our move until the truck's gone. We'll have grenades ready, in case one of them makes enough noise to warn the others. They'll be watching the road, we'll get them two at a time, cut their throats, one deep stroke like they trained you at boot camp."

Barstow swallowed audibly.

"The worst that can happen is someone yells, and then we empty our M-1s and take off like rabbits. I'll take the lead, you stick behind me."

"I don't know if I can do this, sarge."

"Well, private, you'd better decide, because I'd hate to go against two guys and find out I'm the lone ranger."

Hollywood sat there staring at his doubled knees, swallowing over and over.

Come on, Hood thought, but said nothing. What he was proposing would be considered reckless at best. At worst, it might get both of them killed. No matter what your rank, there was a limit to what you could order a man to do. Or at least there ought to be.

"I. . .all right. Lead on, Kemosabe."

"Good." Hood watched the crest above them. Within minutes, men appeared over the rise, silhouetted against the moonlight. The count stopped at eight, moving into position in twos at points along the summit, each pair keeping its distance from the next—good tactics to avoid being wiped out in a single counterattack.

Not so good if a couple of United States Marines were already up here at your backs and you didn't know it.

The truck started again and moved off, the low growl of the engine dwindling back the way it had come until there was nothing but the wind and the crickets. Hood eased his bayonet from its sheath and gripped the blade's backside in his teeth, crawling toward the position nearest to them on the right flank of the hill. Listening for Barstow behind him, all he could hear was the whisper of his own body through the weeds. As he neared the position, he heard the two North Korean soldiers talking softly in the grass, gazing down at the road with rapt attention, as if the column of American troops and the Sherman tanks would appear at any moment. Egging each other on about the slaughter they were going to unleash? Clearly, they felt safe for now, knowing they'd hear so many troops coming well before the column could spot or hear them.

Ten yards. Slow, nice and easy, now.

Glancing back, he was relieved to see Barstow, right behind him. Hood nodded him toward the NK on the left. Five yards; three, glad for the covering chirr of crickets and the wind moving the grass all around. Hood showed Barstow his fist, popping fingers—one, two, three—and he lunged and caught his man around the chest, pinning his arms as he whipped the bayonet across in front, a bubbling sound, and a sigh of air, and he let the man flop forward in the grass.

Glancing left, he saw Barstow holding his man by the chin, blood spurting onto the ground. With a shudder, Barstow eased the body into the grass.

Low voices further up the rise bantered back and forth.

This time Barstow got out in front, probably desperate to get this over with, forgetting that haste could get him killed. Alarmed, Hood closed the gap, wincing at the rustle it caused, but the two NKs kept murmuring to each other. Barstow went right at the further NK, as Hood closed with his man, another deep stroke and the dead men twitched in the grass beside the recoilless rifle.

Up on the crown of the hill, Hood could see the next pair, the mortar man and his assistant, sitting still, in an attitude of listening. Hood motioned Barstow flat in the weeds. One of the men at the crest called out softly, his voice inquiring. Getting no answer, the man descended toward them, while his partner waited above. Bad—one yell, and the eight NK across the road would be on guard.

Barstow lay right in the man's path. Hood motioned him to stay flat, let the man past before he struck. Circling away to miss the descending NK, Hood veered toward the crest of the hill, zeroing in on the man who'd stayed put up there. The NK had adopted a wary crouch.

Lunging, Hood hooked his throat from the side, a deep stroke, then dropped back into the weeds as the NK crumpled, his air gushing out below his severed vocal cords.

Another faint burp of air from down slope; a second later, Barstow rose, circling his fist, then sank again.

Hood waited for Hollywood to come to him. He could hear the last two NK about twenty yards down and to his left talking in low voices. Hood told himself they were discussing the hell they were going to send the Americans to in the morning. He conjured in his mind members of the squad who were no longer around: Gullotte bleeding out on Obong-ni ridge outside Pusan. Simon Corkindale, lying in the 8055 MASH minus a hand. What might Simon do to himself once his brave Captain Hook jokes lost their meager ability to soothe him?

North Koreans in the same uniforms as these killers had done that. To feel any sympathy now would be a betrayal.

Barstow arrived, his eyes pale slits in the moonlight. Hood led the way along the crest to the last NK position, inching along—almost there, don't blow it now. Barstow had calmed himself enough to stay back, letting him keep the lead. Through the tall grass he could see both NKs sitting with their mortar, heads bobbing as they talked, not expecting any danger until morning. Closing with his man, Hood saw Barstow loom from the grass, his bayonet flashing again.

A grim satisfaction filled Hood. Eight down, eight to go.

Barstow lay in the grass, shaking, staring at the moon. He'd got blood on him—the smell filled Hood's head, that rich, vinegary scent of a steak before you threw it on the grill.

"You ready to get the other hill?" Hood whispered.

Barstow rolled his head. "You are a maniac, sarge, a fucking maniac."

"Take it easy, kid. No hurry. We sit a minute, then we cross the road further down and come up from behind them, just like we did here."

"We don't even know where they are."

"They'll be talking."

"I have to rest first."

"It's better we keep on."

"What if one of them manages to scream?"

"We start shooting. With this side down, the odds are a lot better for us now. We just have to make sure they all die over there, quietly if we can, guns and grenades if we have to.

Barstow said nothing, staring at him, his eyes wide in the moonlight.

"Look, son, we're not supposed to be here. They think they're safe. That's why we got the guys over here and it's why we'll get them over there, too, long as we're careful. We'll get 'em, Sam, and we'll save a couple hundred good marines from having to rush those fifty caliber machine guns in the daylight."

"Who's Sam?"

"What?"

"You just called me Sam."

Hood stared at him, taken aback. "I did not. Did I?"

Barstow took a breath, eased it out. "All right, sarge. All right."

When it was done and the other eight were dead, and the mortars and recoilless rifles had been broken down and scattered away in the bushes, Barstow sat on his rump in the tall grass, shaking so hard you could see it in the dark. Sitting beside him, Hood waited for his own legs to stop trembling so they could hike back to their platoon.

"I can't believe we did that." Barstow's voice had a slight warble, like you hear in old people.

"You did fine."

Barstow shook his head, kept shaking it, until finally he was able to stop by clamping his hands to his cheeks. "Who's Sam?"

"My son."

"I remind you of him?"

Like I wish he was, Hood thought. Not something he could say. "Yeah, you do."

"I didn't even remind my own dad of his son. He wanted me to be a Bible teacher. That's what he did—teach in a Seventh-day Adventist elementary school. Died of a heart attack two years ago."

"You're a good marine, Barstow. You proved that tonight. I'm sure your father would be proud of you."

Hollywood grunted. "I doubt it. Seventh-day Adventists won't bear arms. They don't join the marines like I did, and if they get drafted in the army, the only thing they'll do is be a medic."

"That's good. Medics are good. When you need 'em, there's nothing better than a corpsman."

"Ever read the Bible, sarge—the Old Testament?"

"Some."

"Dad read the Bible to us every evening. Some of that Old Testament stuff is pretty hard to follow, but this one passage used to make me laugh. It was a story about an army of heathens that was looking to defeat the Israelites. So God's angel of death went out at night before the big battle was to be fought and killed them. Slaughtered the whole enemy army that one night while they slept."

"Yeah?"

"Yeah. And at the end of the story—like a punch line—the Bible says: 'And they woke up in the morning, and they were all dead corpses.'"

"That *is* pretty funny," Hood said.

Barstow stared out over the waving grass. "Not any more."

After the U.S. Marines took Inch'on, General Almond was eager to move X Corps' other combat division ashore as quickly as possible to fill in behind the American and South Korean (ROK) marines so they could advance on Seoul. The 7th Infantry Division and 1st MASH hurried off their troop ships early in the week that followed the amphibious assault. They entered a shaken and unstable city where fires from the naval and air bombardment still smoldered. Security in the city was now in the hands of South Korean marines determined to punish any remaining communist occupiers for their harsh excesses committed while the North held the city. Sniper fire persisted in the streets. It was a week of uncertainty, fear, and constant flux as MacArthur's forces redeployed in and around Inch'on to defend their gains and attack Seoul. Rushed into this mix, the newly established 1st MASH set up its inaugural hospital in the outskirts of Inch'on and began treating wounded.

(Ibid.)

5

17 September, USS General W.A. Mann, 1000 hours:
"They want us to *what?*" Laura Lidner asked, peeking over the side of the ship at the landing craft far below.

"Climb down," Bonnie said.

"Sweetie, we're in the middle of the ocean."

"That's Inch'on right over there on the other side of the ship."

"I don't think so. It's a bank of clouds."

"Get with it, Lidner. Our enlisted people are already ashore setting up the hospital."

"Has anybody heard from them since they left?"

"Knock it off. It's our turn. We're going ashore."

"How about leading by example, Brisbane?"

Throwing her leg over the rail, Bonnie was struck by how unlike her leg it looked—green fatigue pants, an army boot several sizes too large. It looked like a man's leg—which, in a certain way, pleased her. If you want to understand a man, walk a mile in his shoes. A metaphor, yeah, but hey, maybe it would work literally.

A jittery eagerness filled her. Inch'on casualties had been far lighter than feared but there were still dozens of wounded in battalion aid stations waiting for the more thorough attention a MASH could give. She was about to see men who, only hours ago, had been shot or torn by shrapnel on a battlefield. She would save them if she could, help them heal and, while she was at it, learn what made them tick.

Starting her descent along the steep flank of the ship, she looked down, just as they'd warned her not to. Her stomach swooped. Waves thrashed along the side of the ship far below, making the waiting midge of a boat gyrate in the swells. The water was as gray as the ship, foaming where it hit the side. She could smell the salt in it, so amazing, different from the fresh waters of Lake Michigan.

Okay, keep going.

As she forced herself down, the corkscrewing craft looked less like a toy boat and more like something that could actually get her to shore. Two jeeps and crates of MASH supplies filled the center of the landing craft. A doctor waiting in the stern helped her in. Laura practically stepped on her head—after all that whining, she had scrambled down like a monkey. Four more nurses followed Laura, then Jeff Wittschiebe, the ER resident whose name, she had learned, was pronounced "Witch-a-bee."

The boat's pilot declared them full and cast off. Bonnie checked the ties on her life vest, then watched Inch'on's waterfront grow more distinct, Blue Beach losing its cloud-like haze and taking on detail as the landing craft bounced over the waves. To the left, the shore sprouted a causeway that connected it with a little island, and beyond that she could see the seawall, with gaping holes in it, where the main assault had fought its way ashore.

The shore was jammed with more boxy-looking boats like their own, with flat gates for fronts that could be let down so tanks or jeeps on them could roll ashore. The pilot steered between several LSTs already beached, throttling back at the last second as the prow ran up on the sand.

Hopping into a tidal pool left by receding waves, Bonnie waded ashore. Men in green swarmed the landing craft, unloading the supplies and driving the MASH jeeps onto the muddy sand. The air reeked of oil and exhaust fumes, the ground trembling from the tanks and bulldozers growling across the beach.

It sounded like a factory, metal banging metal, chains screeching on derricks, engines revving. Ramshackle buildings leaned this way and that, holed and windowless from the bombardment. Striding onto dry land, Bonnie smiled as men called to her, whistling and clapping, marines on every side stopping to gape at all these dames coming out of nowhere.

She kept going straight ahead, having no idea where until an MP pointed to two waiting trucks. Climbing into the back of one, she sat on a side bench while doctors and other nurses crowded in. Jeff settled beside her, his face looking very handsome with the acne scars lost in shadow.

The truck lurched and bumped over the beach, then, from the smoother feel of it, found a road. She smelled the salt of the sea again, laced with a mildewy tang from the truck's canvas canopy. "You ready for this?" Jeff asked.

"Are you?"

"You bet." His voice was bright with confidence. She knew from her days in the Chicago ER that emergency medicine doctors were a breed apart. Why would anyone want to treat people mangled in car accidents, or shot or knifed, or who had their heads bashed in on motorcycles? The answer, which most medical people felt uncomfortable talking about, was that you liked it—the excitement, the drama.

Jeff said, "I asked Colonel Martin to let you assist me in surgery."

"Me? Laura's the surgical nurse."

"She'll be assisting Dr. Lugenbeal. Of course, we'll all switch around if necessary as we get good at one thing or another. But to start, you're with me."

"Fine. I was afraid the colonel would put me in triage."

"You might wish he had."

"I can take anything you can, doctor."

"I just meant you can sit down while doing triage. We're liable to have some very long days and nights."

"Women can stand better than men. Lower center of gravity."

"Maybe."

"I'll bet you twenty bucks that if we get into a marathon you'll have to sit before I will."

"Uh, twenty bucks?"

Others in the truck started razzing him, calling him chicken.

"Okay," he said, "You're on."

Bonnie held a hand out to him and Jeff shook it, hanging on an extra second. Had he just given her knuckles a little rub with his thumb? Hmmm.

The truck jolted to a stop and an MP dropped the tailgate. "You're home, folks."

Piling out, Bonnie got her first look at the abandoned schoolhouse that would house the 1st MASH—a long brick building, one story, with a tall chimney in the middle. The entrance looked much like a typical ambulance portico, except instead of a drive-through, steps ran the length of the entry. She imagined Korean children skipping up the stairs and into the school, the boys pulling the girls' pigtails.

The fantasy crumbled as Sergeant VanDorn, big as a grizzly bear and grim-faced, emerged from the shadows and hurried down the steps to meet Colonel Martin, who was alighting from the other truck.

Bonnie eavesdropped as the sergeant brought Martin up to date. Supply had improvised some operating tables out of desks and benches. The place had no running water at the moment, so the surgeons and surgical nurses, at least for now, would have to scrub in using water ferried in five-gallon buckets. There were gloves, scalpels, masks, surgical needles, iodine and sutures from the medical company supplies, and plenty of ampoules of morphine. VanDorn had also scrounged a small supply of whole blood from battalion aid stations. They'd managed to get tanks of nitrous oxide, oxygen, and ether ashore, and they had plenty of saline. They'd hooked up a generator, so the building had enough juice for dim lighting.

"What about penicillin?" Bonnie asked.

Martin and VanDorn gave her a startled look, like they hadn't realized she was there listening. "Yes, sergeant," the colonel said, "what about it?"

"Maybe I can get some from the 121st Evac."

A distant beeping quickly grew louder, a box ambulance speeding toward them, sounding its horn, doctors and nurses scattering out of the way. It screeched to a stop at the entry to the school house. The driver, a marine corporal with a medical company patch, hopped out and looked around. "Who's in charge?"

"Over here, son," Martin said.

The corporal ran over, saluted, and said, "Is this here the 1st MASH?"

"It's going to be," Martin said.

"I've got a marine who won't wait. Sniper got him—one of the stragglers still hanging on in Inch'on. Shot him in the belly. He's lost a lot of blood."

"I'll take him," Jeff said behind her. "Nurse Brisbane can assist."

Martin nodded. "I'll get you an anesthetist. Sergeant Van Dorn, how quickly can you get that penicillin?"

"Half an hour."

"Get going. Wait—where have you set up the surgery?"

"Through there, second door to your right."

"Come on," Jeff said.

Bonnie followed him into the school house. It was dim and smelled of dust and mold. The floor tiles, cracked and filthy, made her heart sink. How could they do surgery in these conditions? Jeff disappeared into the room designated as OR. A second later, an orderly raced out, almost bowling her over.

"Where's the patient, Lieutenant Brisbane?"

"Outside."

"You'll have to scrub in the pail," he said, pointing to the corner.

"Got it," she said, "Go!"

She hurried into what had once been a classroom. A blackboard covered most of one wall. She could smell the chalk dust in its tray. Major Janey Folsom, head nurse of the MASH—and the only one with Army field experience—hurried in, Laura right behind her. Bonnie stripped off her fatigue jacket, found a pail of water and soap in a corner of the room and began scrubbing. Excitement bubbled in her chest. No way could they achieve truly antiseptic conditions, they'd just have to do the best they could and hope the sergeant got back fast with some penicillin.

Pulling her hands from the pail, she looked around for a rinse. The orderly ran back in and pointed at the ceiling where they'd suspended another pail with holes punched in it. He poured a bucket into it and she rinsed under the makeshift stream.

"Did you get these buckets clean?" Janey Folsom asked him.

"Clean as we could, major. They're new issue, and we gave them an alcohol wash."

Bonnie finished rinsing under the holed bucket as Jeff scrubbed behind her. She could hear the wounded man moaning as they brought him in and laid him on the table. A belly wound the corporal had said. We'll have to clean him out, she thought, and empty the stomach while we're repairing, or he could vomit and aspirate.

The orderly produced a towel and rubbed her hands down, then held out gloves, which she tugged on. The wounded marine's shirt had been removed and his bare arm dangled from one side.

"Prep him for me will you, Bonnie?" Jeff said, "I'm still scrubbing."

"Don't be too long, doctor," Major Folsom warned.

As the orderly tied her mask on, Bonnie said, "Get us some iodine and gauze and rush ten units of whole blood in here stat. No time for a full type and cross match, just be sure it's O negative."

Another orderly had run in; he ducked back out, reappearing with two bottles of whole blood. A rack had already been positioned by the surgery table, which was a wooden teacher's desk, draped with sheets. Dark blood welled out of a hole above and to the left of the marine's navel. Taking a wad of gauze from the orderly, Bonnie soaked it with iodine and cleaned the blood away. More blood was slow to well up, a bad sign, indicating that blood loss had already been extreme. In the wan glow from the single bulb overhead, the marine's skin looked pale, but it was hard to tell how much blood he'd lost in such poor light.

"Do we have a pressure?" she asked.

Major Folsom slapped a cuff on the wounded man's arm and pumped. He had not groaned again, unconscious now, but they couldn't operate without anesthesia in case he spasmed. The first orderly rolled tanks of oxygen and ether to the table.

"80 over 40," Janey snapped. "Way too low, we should stabilize him with blood, first."

Jeff appeared at the table. "You're right. Needles—we've got to get some lines going in this guy."

"Here!" Laura said, stepping in beside Bonnie. Handing one needle to Jeff, she started in on the marine's other arm, setting the needle, getting a unit of blood flowing into him, but too slowly.

"We need a third line," Jeff said. "We've got to force whole blood into him as fast as we can. Major, can you handle anesthesia?"

"I can, but what if he's had morphine? They always give them morphine at Battalion Aid, and if he's had more than one hit, he could die from the gas, with his breathing down and his blood pressure so low."

"I know it, but I can't cut him with his stomach muscles jumping. Do we have any atropine? And get some norepinephrine in here. Where's a scalpel, I need a scalpel."

"Bonnie," Laura said, "can you set this line? I'll do instruments."

Bonnie took over trying to seat a second line. At once, she realized the needle was too narrow, a twenty gauge, when they needed the blood to flow in as fast as possible. "We need bigger needles, stat!"

The orderly scrambled off.

Bonnie felt for a pulse at the Marine's neck, couldn't find one. His chest had gone still. She looked across at Major Folsom, who shook her head.

"He's dead, Dr. Wittschiebe," Bonnie said.

Jeff froze, staring down at the corpse. Bonnie had a powerful sense of unreality. This could not be happening. Our first patient, and he died before we could do a thing.

"We had no chance," Janey Folsom said in a brisk voice. "If our equipment had been here, if we'd been set up. . . ."

"Damn," Jeff said.

The backs of Bonnie's eyes prickled. Be strong, she thought. Be strong now, like you promised. Her throat burned but, with an effort, she kept her face calm, imitating the business-like expression on Folsom's face, holding the deadpan look in place even as the tears broke loose and rolled down her cheeks.

17 September, Inch'on/Seoul Highway, 2012:
"Those books and manuals y'er always reading say anything about this?"

Sam had no trouble placing the voice—Sergeant Hartung, slipping up on him from the rear of the platoon. Too dark to make out his expression, but his voice carried enough scorn on its own. Which he'd deny, Sam thought, if I called him on it.

"A book told me those are rice paddies beside the road."

"Think rice paddies'll save you if we get into a fire fight?"

"Is that what you believe is going to happen?"

Hartung peered up the road at the shuffling tail end of Company C, strung out ahead of his own platoon in the near dark of a quarter moon. "You tell me, lieutenant. You're the one reads the books."

Sam struggled to keep his temper. He was tired, hot from the march, his toes blistering from boots that no longer fit his swelling feet, and he was sick of Hartung's carping attitude which had infected half the platoon.

Most of all, he was pissed at himself for not knowing what to do about it. From the moment Captain Loomis had challenged him on the ship, he'd wracked his brain for a plan to get the platoon into shape. The main problem was Hartung. It was a sergeant's duty to help his lieutenant but Hartung's genius was for the opposite. Right behind the ranking non-com were the five ex-cons from the stockade, holding themselves apart from the rest of the platoon, and finally, worries about the KATUSAs. How would untrained civilians who spoke little English, many of whom had ducked their own army's draft, perform when the platoon did come under fire? "Lieutenant?"

Kim's voice, right behind him. "What is it?"

"Lee says the ammo carriers need a rest."

"They can rest when the column rests," Sergeant Hartung snapped.

"Lieutenant?"

"Follow your sergeant's orders, private."

"Yes, sir." Kim flashed him an OK sign. The kid was the one bright spot, a hard worker with an excellent attitude. Couldn't turn around without stepping on him but that was better than having to look for him every time the other KATUSAs needed an order translated.

"The men are tired," Hartung observed, wasting no time planting the new barb he'd been handed. He knew full well battalions marched and rested on the orders of lieutenant colonels, not lieutenants.

"Colonel Faith wants to link up with the 1st Marines tonight," Sam said. "There's nothing but North Koreans on our right flank. If the marines are going to march on Seoul, they'll need us to fight off any counterattack from the south."

"That what the colonel told you?"

Heat flared under Sam's collar. He fought an impulse to pull Hartung aside and get in his face beside the road while the battalion trudged past, give them some entertainment. With an effort, he kept his voice low. "Sergeant Hartung, my old man took one in the body at Pusan because the Army wasn't following its orders to protect a Marine flank. Other men in his unit died because of that. So if our battalion orders are to protect the marine flank, that's exactly what this platoon is going to do."

"Your father is a jarhead?" sounding both surprised and skeptical.

"That's right."

"He read a lot of books, too?"

Sam thought of Julian Foxworth. Julian did read a lot of books and he could bring tears to your eyes playing the cello. So the correct answer was yes, his old man read books. Probably shouldn't have mentioned Hood, but he had to reach Hartung somehow, and what the hell—maybe he could finally get some use out of a father whose only real loyalty was to The Corps.

"I suppose he's brass, too, your old man."

"A sergeant."

Hartung's head came around. "You're shitting me."

Sam said nothing.

"Your old man's a sergeant wounded at Pusan. Will wonders never cease? What's it like when you and he get together? You make him call you sir?"

"You're a sergeant. Do I make you call me sir?"

"No, but you want to."

Sam swallowed an incredulous laugh. "I don't give a rat's ass about being called sir for it's own sake. You can believe that or not. If you were any kind of soldier, I wouldn't have to give a second thought to whether you respect my rank."

"Permission to speak frankly?"

Sam shook his head in the dark. What did Hartung think he'd been doing? "Go ahead, sergeant."

"You never fought a day and you're calling me a bad soldier? I was taking my own bullet in the leg in the Battle of the Bulge when you were in knee pants, you young pup."

"If you say so. All I know about you is what you show me—a career soldier spitting on his duty. You know everything I'm about to say, Hartung, but I'm gonna say it anyway, because you seem to have forgotten: You and I are responsible for the three dozen men following behind us. One of us has to be in charge and the gold bar says it's me. When you fail to respect that emblem of rank in front of the men—whatever your personal opinion of who's wearing it—you undermine the discipline the Army must maintain to win battles. That could come back to hurt you as much as me. If you show the men you don't have to respect my rank, why should they respect yours? From what I've seen, that's exactly what's happening to you with the five men from the stockade."

Hartung spat on the road. "Those pogues. They're not gonna respect nobody. You said it yourself, they're from the stockade. Had my way, they'd be right back there."

"But you don't have your way, sergeant. You have the Army's way. You took a bullet for it, so it had to mean something to you once. But somehow you've lost that along the way. You've gone downhill, you surely have, and if you try to put that on me, you're just lying to yourself."

"I suppose this platoon being a mess is my fault, too."

"I'm in charge. If I let you fail in your duty then I'm failing in mine and I'll answer for it. You're good at staying just this side of the line, but I probably should have brought you up on insubordination charges by now, whether I could make them stick or not, or found some other way to get your ass out of this platoon. One reason I haven't is because I believe, with your knowledge and experience, you could be a fine sergeant again if I could just figure a way to get you there. The other reason is I'm new at this. You're only my second sergeant, and the first made things easy for me, so I have no experience dealing with insubordination. My gut tells me if I ordered you to start snapping off salutes and calling me 'sir' it would make things worse. You'll take yourself in hand or you won't. I've left it too long because I've been stumped, frankly, and now we're in a combat zone—which means your game of how far you can push me in front of the men has to end."

Sam glanced at Hartung, looking for a reaction, anything to show he'd even been listening. The scant moonlight revealed a ghost face as the sergeant looked up to scan the crest of a hill by the road. The helmet draped his eyes and mouth in shadow again. "Sergeant?"

"Were you saying something, lieutenant?"

"Oh, for Christ's sake—"

Hartung held up a hand, gazing at the hilltop again.

Sam halted with him, the platoon flowing forward around them. "What is it?"

"Thought I saw metal winking up there on the hill."

"Where?" Looking where Hartung was staring, Sam saw nothing.

"Probably just one of our recon patrols, up there making sure we don't get ambushed. Let's go, or we'll fall behind the—"

Lights flashed suddenly all along the hill's crest, followed in a split second by the crackle of gunfire, and Sam heard men crying out up and down the column. "Get off the road," he shouted. "Take cover!"

Remembering Kim, he looked around, and there the kid was, still right behind. "Follow me."

Sam scrambled off the road, waving the rest of the platoon with him, diving down the slope of the roadbed. He grappled with his M-1, the strap stuck on his pack. Kim gave it a yank and the rifle slid free. The gunfire from the top of the hill continued, joined now by the ominous, ripping thump of heavy machine guns. Sam gripped his rifle, his head pressed into the dirt, hearing the return fire start up on either side of him. His platoon—had they all gotten off the road? Popping his head up, he glimpsed a body twenty feet from him, the legs sprawled apart, the man's helmet off. Without thinking, he scrambled up, grabbed the GI by the feet, and hauled him to the edge of the road as dirt spattered his pant legs, and then he was back down the roadbed, the body tumbling after him. Rolling the soldier onto his back, he pressed an ear against his chest. He heard rasping and then someone bumped him aside—Hartung.

"Sucking chest wound," the sergeant said.

"Medic!" Sam yelled. Pulling a C-ration from his pack, he ripped open a carton, tossed away the crackers, and flattened the waxed cardboard over the wound on the right side of the man's chest. At once, his breathing eased. A medic skidded along the embankment to them. Turning, Sam saw Hartung up the road-bed again, his body flat against the bank, firing his M-1 at the hilltop. His own hands were empty.

Where had he put his gun?

"Here, boss!"

Kim handed him the rifle, and he flattened himself at the rim of the bank, squeezing off eight shots at the hilltop, dry firing until the spanging told him he needed a new magazine. It took forever to load, his hands awkward. He heard Hartung scream-ing orders to concentrate fire on the machine gun. Then, sud-denly, the sergeant was yelling in the opposite direction: "Shit! Come back here, you little bastards!"

Following his gaze, Sam saw some of the platoon's KATUSA armor bearers running away through the rice paddies, dropping the platoon's ammo packs into the marsh as they fled. He yelled at them to stop but they either ignored him or couldn't hear over the din of battle. Kim saw what was happening and jumped like he'd been stabbed. Slithering down the embankment, he screamed in Korean but the KATUSAs kept going, jettisoning more ammo to increase their speed.

Sam's helmet pinged. Turning back to the fight, he saw dirt spouting along the road as a 50 caliber mounted machine gun from the hill raked it. He looked around for a more protected position but there wasn't one. They were pinned down on low ground, at night, when no air strikes could be called in from the carriers or Kimpo.

What about artillery?

Where's the weapons platoon? he wondered. We've got ma-chine guns, some bazookas, we can't do squat with rifles and carbines.

The ground shuddered as a brilliant flash lit the roadbed—damn, the NKs were raining down mortar rounds now, white phosphorous, too damn close. If they found the range, his platoon could go up in flames.

We must be directly across from them, he thought—the main enemy concentration. Got to get the platoon moving, ahead or back the way we came.

Looking for Hartung, he saw him returning fire again over the edge of the roadbed. Before he could yell at him to get the men moving, another mortar round thumped down, the flaming edge of the blast lashing Hartung's back.

Leaping from the bank, the sergeant ran along the roadbed, screaming and clawing at his shirt. Sam sprinted after him, and then a soldier in Hartung's path caught him and flung him to the ground, rolling him—Corporal Cinquemani, leader of the stockade gang. He put the fire out in seconds, but Hartung went on squirming and yelling in pain and Sam remembered what the training manual had said about white phosphorous—how it kept on burning inside the skin even after the initial flames had been put out.

The book had said water or mud would follow such flames and smother them.

Rice paddies!

Grabbing Hartung around the middle, Sam lifted him, surprised at how light he seemed. Dashing into the rice field, he flung the sergeant down, submerging the phosphorous wounds, a hand under Hartung's neck to keep his head above water.

The sergeant's yells throttled down to moans.

"Boss, what can I do?" Kim, beside him in the water.

"Get back to the bank and take cover, we're exposed here."

"Seriously, boss," the kid said, not moving.

The boom-boom of heavy artillery came from down the road. Shells screamed into the NK positions, the crest off the hill blossoming into flame. Sam's heart leapt. The 32nd's artillery had gotten into the fight—about time!

More shells whistled against the ridge, setting the entire hilltop ablaze. North Koreans streamed in panic down toward the road, some of them in flames. Massed fire poured from the roadbed, cutting the NKs down, but still they came, desperate to escape the inferno.

Hartung stopped groaning and started cursing.

"I need light," Sam said to Kim, thinking of the phosphorous particles in Hartung's back. Deprived of oxygen, they weren't flaming now, but as soon as his skin was exposed, the air would start the fragments burning again, maybe eating deep enough to kill him before they could get him to an aid station. "There's a flashlight in my pack, back at the roadbed."

"A flashlight," Hartung snarled, "are you nuts? The gooks will see us and drop another round on us."

"We're blasting them now, sergeant; listen—that's our artillery. Go, Kim."

Kim darted away and returned in seconds with the light. Sam removed his helmet. "Fill this with mud. Scoop it from the bottom of the paddies, fill mine and yours, just keep it coming."

"Okay, boss."

Sam dragged Hartung to the edge of the paddy. Kim followed with a couple of helmets full of mud, trading them for the light. Hartung's shirt had burned off him and his back looked like he'd fallen on a bed of nails, the skin blotched under the beam of the light. Sam used a scrap of shirt still tucked into Hartung's web belt to brush his back off while the sergeant yelled and swore.

"Lieutenant!"

Glancing up, Sam saw Cinquemani.

"The gooks are on the run, sir, we're cutting them down. I sent a runner to call in an evac for the sergeant, here. Ambulance is on the way."

"Good. See if you can find a medic, we need some morphine, here."

"Right," Kim said. "Lieutenant, I watched where they dropped the ammo."

"Good. We'll go after it as soon as I'm done here."

"They were scared, boss. Nothing like this ever happened to them. They didn't mean to run. They'll do better next time."

"Fucking gooks!" Hartung growled. "They're long gone and good riddance."

"They'll come back," Kim said stubbornly. "Next time, they won't run."

"Bullshit. Fucking gooks, all of you."

"He's in pain," Sam said to Kim. "It can make you crazy."

No more phosphorous was visible in Hartung's wounds, so Sam started spreading mud all over, packing it on as thick as he could, hoping this area of the paddy hadn't been fertilized lately, because Korean farmers weren't above using their own waste, but that's what penicillin was for, and the point right now was to keep the fire out inside Hartung and keep him alive long enough to worry about infection.

"The ambulance is here," Kim said.

"Can you walk, sergeant?"

No answer. Hartung had passed out.

"Tell them we need a stretcher," Sam said to Kim.

Bonnie was chowing down on perch deep fried in batter with a pitcher of beer on the table. The place looked familiar with its red plaid tablecloths and deer heads on the wall—yeah, the Lamplighter, that roadhouse restaurant outside Muskegon where the family went for special occasions, when Grandma made some extra money cleaning house. Odd thing, the place was full of guys in old-fashioned blue uniforms, yellow neckerchiefs and cowboy hats, looking like General Custer's men. Maybe they came from that old fort blockhouse up the road from the state park—

One of the soldiers grabbed her foot under the table and was shaking it and wouldn't stop, even when she tried to kick his hand away—

"Come on, Brisbane, roll out."

She awakened in a cold rush, then tried to drift back under, but the foot-pulling started again and she flinched with shock, blinking up at the glowing ghoul face above her—Major Folsom, lighting up her own battleaxe face with a flashlight.

"We've got wounded, lieutenant, and you are next up."

"Yes, ma'am."

Crawling from her sleeping bag, Bonnie pulled on her fatigues and buttoned up as she stumbled after Folsom. Her eyes felt gummy and she was thirsty enough to chug the pitcher of beer from her dream. The classroom the nurses had taken over for their quarters had filled up with cots, and Bonnie felt envy at the snores rising all around her.

What time was it?

Late at night, early in the morning, who could tell? It had been dark when she'd fallen into bed, exhausted. All day they'd treated mostly Korean patients who had kept coming hour after hour, walking in from Inch'on, or riding ox carts, whatever they could find. A lot of burn cases and some gunshots. The great majority of the bullet wounds were Koreans—communist sympathizers who'd lorded it over their neighbors now being paid back by those citizens or shot by hard-boiled South Korean marines who'd come in behind the Americans to "clean up" their city.

In addition the MASH had admitted dozens of Korean kids with dysentery or malnutrition, many of them orphans from the battle or the shelling that preceded it. The children responded quickly once they got some food and penicillin in them. Now that more supplies had been unloaded, the hospital had much of what it needed, and they'd saved a lot of people, which felt good after losing that Marine first thing. From what Folsom had just said, the next wave of patients was not Korean civilians but wounded soldiers, which meant the battle had been joined further inland along the lines of advance.

"Where's the action, major?"

"Up the road toward Seoul. Some of our Army boys got ambushed. They counterattacked with artillery. We're getting wounded from both sides."

Bonnie squinted as she followed Folsom into the relative brightness of the medical ward. An enlisted man handed her a tin cup of coffee and she drained it to the sludge, feeling it kick through her veins to her heart.

Folsom took her to a big man lying belly down on a stretcher, his back horribly burned. "Start with him. White phosphorous. You know the drill?"

"Saline dressings, right?"

"Right. Someone had the sense to slap mud on him. Keep him wet until I can find you some cupric oxide."

"Has he had morphine?"

"I don't know. He's passed out."

Bonnie hurried to the man, a big guy, mid thirties, with dark hair and a bald spot on the back of his head. As she bent over him, she smelled a ripe, organic odor she recognized as fertilizer. Must be mixed with the mud, full of bacteria, so better get him started on penicillin right away. But Folsom was right, the mud was good. If it had been put on soon enough, it might have saved enough skin that grafting wouldn't be necessary.

"I need saline," she said to an orderly at the next cot. "Lots of it."

He was back in a minute with a tray of bottles. Gently, she cleaned off the stinking mud with the saline and assessed the skin, pleased to find good patches surviving all through the burn. They'd gotten his shirt off quick, and they must have had him wet within seconds.

"You're a lucky guy," she murmured.

"Damn straight," the man said.

She jumped. "You're awake?"

An eyelid peeled back for a glimpse of her, then slid shut again.

"Are you in pain?" she asked.

"Gave me some morphine," the man said. "I forgot how good that can feel. Mmmm." A smile touched his lips. "The lieutenant. Can't believe it. His old man's a sergeant, but all he did was read books. How could I know?"

She bent closer to decipher his mumbling. "You say your lieutenant's father is a sergeant?"

"Goddamned leatherneck."

Bonnie blinked, taken aback. Could it be? It was certainly possible, with the 7th Infantry on the march only a few miles away. She felt her heartbeat accelerating. "Your lieutenant's name wouldn't by any chance be Sam Foxworth, would it?"

The eye cracked open again. "How'd'you know?"

She grinned. "Sam."

"Son of a b—gun saved me. Knew just what to do. I was screaming, half out of my head, no good to anyone. Hurt like a bastard, but he knew what to do. Saw him reading the manual, wanted to kick his ass, but damn if it didn't save me. So now I gotta go around feelin' like an idiot."

Bonnie worked on his back, trying to make sense of the mishmash of words. Sam Foxworth, the reluctant warrior. And this was Sam's sergeant.

"S'cuse my French," the man mumbled.

"Is. . .the lieutenant all right?"

"The lieutenant is all right, yeah, you got it." The man shifted on the cot, screwing himself around on his elbows so he could look at her with both eyes. "You know him?"

"A little," she said.

"Can you get him a message for me—send it back with the next ambulance?"

"I'll try."

"Tell him I heard him."

"You. . .heard him?"

"He'll know what it means."

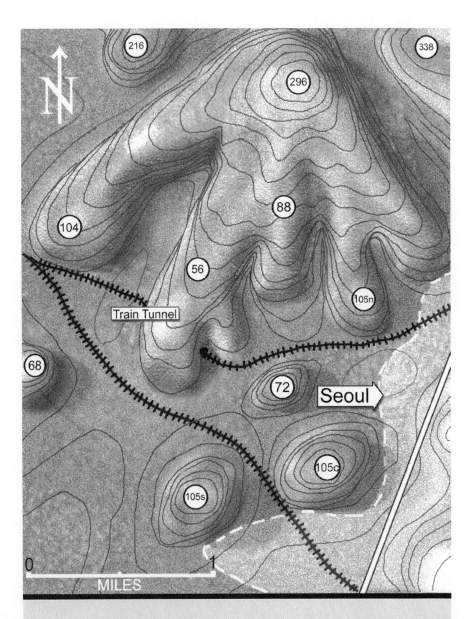

Final approach to Seoul
September 22 - 24

On September 22, President Truman pinned a fifth star on Omar Bradley, Chairman of the Joint Chiefs of Staff, making the beloved and unassuming World War II hero the ninth "General of the Army" in American history. Bradley, who was more worried about the communist threat in Europe than in the far east, would be Truman's chief advisor throughout the Korean War. His relations with fellow West Pointer Douglas MacArthur were cool. He believed General MacArthur to be a megalomaniac who cared too much for fame and glory.

As Truman honored Bradley, General MacArthur was giving his commander of X Corps, Army Major General Ed Almond, his marching orders. The most pressing aspect of these orders was the timeline. MacArthur wanted Seoul retaken as quickly as possible. General Almond publicly promised to recapture the capital city by September 25, three months to the day after it fell to the North. But the battle to do so would be far more difficult and costly in human lives than the quick victory at Inch'on.   Ibid.

6

22 September—Hill 105-S, 0500:

Hood waited for Morrison to finish his interrupted sentence. The Corsair swooped so close over the railroad shed that its roar rattled a mess kit on the window sill. The shed smelled of Morrison's beloved cigars and a musty undercurrent of rat droppings. Sledge hammers, pickaxes and boxes of rusting spikes had been pushed into one corner of the dirt floor to make room for the lieutenant's sleeping bag. Not quite dawn, and marine air was already probing across the Han River from their newly seized home, Kimpo Airfield. More "Time on Target," heading out to pound the hills, soften them up for what would be one hell of a battle. The moment was almost here, awaiting only the regimental order to move out.

". . .a medal in it for you," Morrison finished, as the thunder of the Corsair dwindled away.

"It wasn't exactly combat, sir. Hollywood and I got the drop on them."

Morrison's mouth curled sardonically around his cigar. "Sergeant, the brass don't care how you did it, just that you did it. Sixteen enemy, only two of you—if you hadn't 'gotten the drop' we'd be dropping the medals on your grave markers. I know medals are old hat for you but don't spoil it for Barstow."

"No, sir." Maybe a medal will pull him out of his funk, Hood thought. Himself, he'd like to get off the subject. The memory was still too fresh after almost a week—the feel of throat cartilage giving way, transferred from blade to handle to his palm, where it had imprinted itself in the nerve memory.

Morrison grinned at some inner vista. "I'd like to have been a fly on the wall in the NK command post when our tanks entered their ambush point. The Commie brass no doubt had their binoculars out, waiting to see us blow up, and then nothing happens, we roll right through. They must have shit bricks. Don't know if you've heard, but they set up a similar ambush for Army and caused a lot of havoc."

Hood's pulse picked up. "Where?"

"They caught the 32nd regiment on their way south of Seoul to cover our left flank. Army was able to beat the attack off by calling artillery in on the hills, but they took some losses."

The 32nd regiment, Hood thought. That's Sam's outfit. A deep unease filled him; in his mind's eye he saw Sam lying on the road, bleeding his life into the ground. His heart twisted. How could I tell his mother? How could I live with it myself?

With an effort, he pushed the dread back. The odds favored Sam being unhurt, or at least alive. He would check the MASH when he could. Right now, he must keep his head in his own coming battle or other people's sons who depended on him might die.

"Army's scrape points up how significant your and Barstow's accomplishment was. With those mortars registered in, we could have lost a lot of men, not to mention a platoon of tanks we gotta have to take Seoul back. Instead, we demo'd the six tanks the NK ran down the road to lure us into the trap, plus we killed two hundred of their infantry left exposed when the tanks blew up. So you take that medal, y'hear?"

A knock on the shed door was almost drowned out by another Corsair.

"Come," Morrison shouted.

Tech Sergeant Weiler, Morrison's ranking non-com, and Corporal Dunleavy from the third platoon ducked inside. Hood greeted them with a nod. Fellow vets of the Pacific war, both men tall and skinny. Dunleavy had a bland, Midwestern face, sandy hair. Weiler was darker, some Kraut in his bloodline, waves of black hair perpetually matted by his helmet.

Turning up the wick of the kerosene lantern on his work table, Morrison bent over the map he'd spread there. "We're here, just south of the railroad track. Our battalion has been given the immediate objective of Hill 105 South—this one right here on our side of the tracks. The rail line passes between it and the next hill—105-C. We'll be going in at 0700. According to G2, the two hills, 105-S and -C, were a training area for the Japs back in the last war, when they controlled Korea. Which means both hills are covered with field fortifications, including cement reinforced caves, bunkers and other barriers."

"Great," Sergeant Weiler muttered.

"Yeah. With Government House in Seoul only two miles away, you can be sure the NKs are looking to stop us right here. Trains have been rushing their 25th brigade to the hills from not long after we came ashore at Inch'on. I won't lie, this is a veteran outfit we're facing. I fought alongside the Commies in China. We're talking two infantry and four heavy machine gun battalions, a 76 millimeter artillery battalion, and a 120 millimeter mortar battalion—probably around 2500 men in all."

"Then we got 'em outnumbered one to three," Dunleavy said. "They don't have a chance.

Morrison awarded the joke a show of teeth around his cigar.

Hood wasn't in a mood to smile. Mortars were bad enough but that many machine guns, placed right, could hold a couple of divisions at bay.

"As soon as it's light enough for spotters out there," Morrison said, "artillery from our 11th will start pounding 105-S. The NK have undercut their foxholes into the slopes so that will give them some protection against air bursts. We have to assume they've got lots of ammo and supplies in those caves, and with that many machine guns they'll have set up interlocking fields of fire on us."

"So how do we get up there?" Sergeant Weiler asked.

"Same way we always do. Find the ravines, anything that'll give us a scrap of cover, and work our way up. Improvise. Our company will attack the hill from the front. B Company will give us supporting fire, and C will try and slip around behind the hill, come up from the back side. The Corsairs will be helping out with air strikes where conditions permit. I don't have to tell you, it'll still be a bitch. We had at least this much air prep and bombardment at Obong-ni, and Sergeant Hood caught a couple of bullets anyway. But at the very least our bombs will shake up the enemy—"

A loud thump to the west gave way to the whistle of an artillery round, and finally an explosion to the southeast against the hill— the Marine 155s starting to range in. Weiler and Dunleavy hurried to the shack's single, grimy window, and Dunleavy whooped. More thumps followed by impact explosions gave way to a steady roar as the big howitzers found their readings. Judging from the din, the artillery was firing from close behind the regimental line, maybe as little as five hundred yards instead of the usual fifteen hundred. In brief lapses between the thunder of howitzers, Hood heard the distinctive pop of mortars joining in.

He stared at the map, feeling his mind go blank for a second—not fear, exactly, but a close cousin. He blew out a long, measured breath. Hell, he felt this every time before he went up. Yeah, he'd gotten a few holes punched in him at Obong-ni, but he was here, wasn't he? Ready to go up again, and this time, God willing, reach the top. What had Morrison said? 0700—one hour.

"It would be nice," Morrison said, "if we could pound those hills for a day or two straight before going in. But think about this: Every hour that passes, more NKs will be arriving to reinforce Seoul. You think dug-in bunkers are bad, try getting shot at from every building as you go down the street. We need to get to the city itself as fast as we can."

Hood grunted and the other two said nothing still staring out the window. Morrison joined them there, peering out with the relish of a schoolboy watching fireworks on the 4th of July. The windowpanes rattled constantly and Hood felt tremors through the dirt floor. He pored over the terrain map, though he knew a map ten times as detailed could not show him a way up the hill. It came down to being there, discovering the contour of each foot of slope, finding that depression just deep enough to save you, or the rock just high enough, and getting from it to the next, jerking your head up here and there for half a second, risking a bullet to figure out the enemy lines of fire.

"That's all," Morrison said, "time to brief your squads."

Dunleavy and Weiler turned from the window. The lieutenant wished them luck as they went out. Hood pulled his knuckles from the table and started for the door.

"Sergeant."

He turned back.

"You're the best man I've got. Help me get this done." His eyes gave off a faint sheen of fear.

Hood shook off a fleeting, dark premonition; gave Morrison a thumbs up. "We'll make it, sir."

Back at the foxhole, Jimmy had a fire going, two tin mugs of water heating over a couple of candle's worth of flames. He'd swiped some of the railroad spikes from the lieutenant's shack and laid them across rocks to make a grill. Knowing Jimmy, he would carry the spikes in his pack from here on out, two extra pounds multiplied over however many miles they'd be walking and climbing, because the engineer in him had found something that worked and couldn't bear to leave it behind.

Hood felt a wave of affection, that sappy feeling he'd get before he was about to take his boys into fire again. No sweat, as long as he didn't blurt it out and embarrass them both. Bad idea to let yourself feel too much for any one of your men, but with Jimmy you couldn't help it. Only twenty-five and bald as a frog. High school dropout, but there wasn't much he didn't know about anything mechanical. Steady as a rock under fire and a big worrier the rest of the time. Damn well should be a sergeant with his own squad by now.

"You'll never get that to boil," Hood said.

"You'd rather have your coffee cold, just say so."

Hood scanned the low rise where the squad had bedded down for the night. If anyone had tried to sleep in, that was over, with the artillery now booming.

Where were his veterans?

He spotted Rittenhouse and Barstow, stooped over near the railway embankment, rolling up their bags. Couldn't see Bertleson anywhere. Probably off with the second or third platoon, trading his breakfast biscuits for packs of C-ration gum, which he chewed like a maniac all through any battle. Hood glanced south to where the railroad tracks rose across a saddle between the two hills in the lieutenant's briefing. "A" Company would be attacking the one on the right, about three hundred yards away. Not light enough yet to see any North Koreans— might be too far to see them even in full daylight—but they were there, waiting.

"Told you," Jimmy crowed.

Sure enough, both mugs were boiling. Hood handed him his powdered coffee ration and Jimmy went to work spooning and stirring, pouring a huge slug of sugar into his own mug. Hood pulled on a glove and plucked his mug from the fire, feeling the heat through the leather. "Got a cigarette, Jimmy?"

"What happened to yours?"

"Saving 'em for after we kick some NK ass today. Come on, you don't smoke."

"Yeah, but I trade 'em for Hershey bars. You know that, sarge."

"Well here you go then, you miserable little scrounge."

"Who you calling little? If I'm little, you're a midget."

Hood dug the chocolate from his dinner ration and handed it over, and Jimmy gave him the four cigarettes in the breakfast ration and one of his matches. Lighting the cigarette, Hood pulled the smoke into his lungs, savoring the bite on his tongue, the glow of well-being. Exhaling, he blew smoke rings and resisted the urge to glance at the hills again. "Get the squad together, corporal."

As Jimmy assembled the men, Hood drained his coffee, checking out the four replacements over the rim of his cup: Mendenhall, the pudgy and dark-haired one who looked like a choirboy; Eddie Jakes, Mendenhall's pimple-faced buddy who thought he was a card shark but had more tells than a kid sneaking cookies; Bo Cockburn, big and homely, his nose flattened from playing football, and Larry Steinberg, a Jewish kid from Brooklyn with round glasses and barely enough chin to hold his helmet strap.

Hood resisted an urge to shake his head. What wouldn't he give to have back the veterans these kids had replaced? The squad was still three men short, dating back to the first week in Pusan, and now nearly half the remaining nine were green as the hills. Hood waved the four over to him. "Remember what I said about going up hills?"

They gaped at him as if he'd spoken in tongues.

"You stay spread out from each other and crawl with your butts down."

They nodded, eyes big and serious.

"Don't let yourself stray too far around the hillside to the east. You do, and the NK on the other hill of the saddle will be able to see you and you can bet they'll be giving supporting fire to the NKs on our hill. I'd rather you took an extra hour to get up that hill than have to try and think up good things to say about you in condolence letters to your moms."

The four swallowed nearly in unison, adams apples bulging.

"Any questions?" Hood asked.

Bo frowned thoughtfully, then shook his head.

"Then I believe it is time for the Sacred Ritual of Luck."

Hood turned to Jimmy, who had settled cross-legged on the ground, acting blasé, as was his duty as a veteran. He tried to crank himself up from his crossed ankles without using his hands. Instead he fell back on his pack and had to be helped up by Bertleson and Rittenhouse, the three of them cutting loose with that raw laugh men blow out when they're scared. Jimmy flipped off his chin strap and pulled his helmet off. Bertleson and Rittenhouse rubbed his bald head. Catching on, the new guys did the same. As he stretched out his own hand, Hood thought, *Dear God, keep Jimmy and the lieutenant safe, and the rest of the squad, especially these new guys. Let me bring them all through alive. If it's Your will I die, please make it quick.*

"Whoa, Nellie!" Bo said.

Following his gaze, Hood saw a slim woman in marine fatigues and helmet, a typewriter tucked under one arm, talking to the captain of B Company. That reporter—what was her name?—had insisted on staying with the troops. A good looking woman.

"I didn't know they let girls be marines," Bo said.

Steinberg shook his head. "That's Marguerite Higgins, stupid."

"Who you calling stupid?" Bo said with genuine menace.

"Her. That's her name—Marguerite Higgins Stupid."

"Oh," Bo said.

Hood shot Jimmy a look. There was no replacing a wit like Simon Corkindale, now lying one-armed in the MASH back at Pusan, but Steinberg was showing some promise.

Hood felt a tug on his arm, Bob Barstow pulling him aside.

"I've got a bad feeling about this, sarge."

"That's fine. I'd worry if you had a good feeling."

"I'm serious. At least one of us is going to be dead in the next few hours, and I think it's going to be me. What you and I did to those NKs on that hill. . . ."

"Was our duty. It's over and done with, and it's got nothing to do with today. Forget about it."

"Have you forgotten?"

"Hell, yes," Hood lied.

"It's like we murdered them. They never had a chance."

"Sure they did. If they hadn't been running their mouths, if they'd watched the whole hill instead of the road in front of them, we'd be drawing flies up there now instead of them.

They knew it was a war zone and they were out to kill our buddies, and we stopped them from doing that the only way we could. Don't be a dimwit, Barstow. They outnumbered us eight to one."

"I can't get over feeling God's going to punish me—"

"Only because you're not thinking straight, son. That Bible story your old man read to you—did God punish the angel for killing that whole army during the night?"

Barstow said nothing.

"No," Hood said. "God *sent* the angel. It was God's will. The men we killed were in the North Korean army, which is looking to take over the whole country by force and make everyone do what they say. You think God wants these godless commies shoving their will down the throats of everyone in this country?"

Barstow gave his head a tentative shake.

"Look, everyone gets feelings like yours before they go into battle—you were at Pusan, you know that. It's noise your nerves throw up, like static on the radio. You've got to ignore it and concentrate on the ball-game, which right now, today, is taking that hill."

Barstow nodded without conviction.

"Sarge," Jimmy called.

Hood saw that the platoon was forming up.

"Come on, Hollywood."

First platoon had the left flank of the line, and Hood took the very end so no one could wander past him around the curve of the hill. Morrison came down the line, reminding everyone not to bunch up. Pink radiance slid over the top of Hill 105-S, capping it as the sun rose, but the slope they were going up was still in shadow, the way they wanted for an assault.

Hood felt his pulse beating between his palm and the stock of the M-1.

"Let's go," Morrison said from the middle of the platoon, and the skirmish line moved forward in a hurried walk along with the rest of the company, over two hundred men heading in a long, ragged row toward the hill. Hood kept his eyes on the slope, stomach churning, watching for the first spark of enemy fire. Shells from the 105s and 155s continued to pound the hill, blowing out plumes of smoke and debris that rained down the incline.

Two hundred yards, a hundred, the ground taking a definite upward pitch now, and Hood waved his squad forward at a trot, eager to close with the base of the hill where there would be some contour cover, but the hillside sparkled with rifle fire, then the fatter bursts from machine guns, and Hood ran faster, just get there, get up against the hill, where it would be safer. He heard a cry on his right and saw Mendenhall go down and roll, grabbing his ankle, and Jakes started to turn around, and Hood yelled at him to keep going, the corpsman would take care of Mendenhall.

The ground around them erupted from the hard rain of bullets and he ran full tilt, and the others followed him, yelling like crazy men, scrambling to where the slope steepened. Behind them, the artillery stopped firing, the sudden contrast making it seem almost a hush until the machine gun and rifle fire above reasserted their own level of racket. Hearing the faint pop of enemy mortars from the reverse slope, Hood yelled for everyone to get down, find cover. A gout of flame leaped from the hillside not twenty yards from him. Spotting a crevasse worn down by rainfall, he dived into it, buying himself half a foot of shelter.

The gully meandered up to a point about twenty yards above him. Bullets kicked clods from the bank. A shell ticked his heel and another rang off his helmet as he buried his face in the ground.

The level of enemy fire swelled, bullets swarming down the hill. Hood could see Jakes next to him, and beyond, Barstow and Jimmy, then Steinberg and Cockburn. Lower down, Jack Rittenhouse lay on his side behind a fallen tree, and further still, Freddy Bertleson, chomping furiously on his gum, was sighting up the hill, squeezing off rounds with practiced precision.

Rolling onto his back, Hood tried to see down between his feet to where Mendenhall had fallen. No one there now—good, the kid must have been able to crawl or hobble away from the firestorm.

Another shell clipped Hood's helmet and he rolled onto his stomach, flattening himself in the culvert. Damn, that was close.

Dirt, kicked up by the hail of bullets, rained on his back. He could hear ricochets off the rocks all around him. Squirming ahead, he thrust with his legs and knees, crawling like a snake until he reached a bend in the shallow trough. A patch of tall grass to his left jerked with bullets, but he seemed hidden here.

And pinned down.

Lieutenant had said 2500 NKs, and they must all be shooting at once, because if anyone lifted their head, they'd be breathing lead.

Hood listened for the sounds of B Company. They must be laying down covering fire but he couldn't hear it from the din on the hill.

Something stung his rump and for a minute he thought he'd been shot, but no, it must have been a pebble, careening against him.

Tipping his head, he glimpsed a slice of Hill 105-C, which meant the gooks over there could see him, the very thing he'd warned the squad against. Couldn't stay here, so he scrambled across in front of Jakes, then dropped behind a ridge of rock. His eye returned to what he'd glimpsed above, a darker crease in the shadowed hillside—a cave, maybe? Probably too far down the hillside to be occupied by the enemy.

If he was wrong, they'd shoot him dead from inside as he approached.

Lying right here, he was alive.

Fuck it, he thought, and lunged up, boots slipping then digging in as a bullet plowed into his pack and another rang off the blade of his bayonet, nearly tearing the M-1 from his hands, and then he was rolling into the crease, someone else right behind him—Lieutenant Morrison. Hood crawled deeper into the crease, the jagged rock floor tearing at his knees and elbows.

When he was sure the lieutenant had room to get out of the field of fire behind him, he stopped.

A sharp ammonia smell filled his head, making him cough.

"That's from all that smoking," Morrison said.

"You should talk."

"I wasn't shot in the lung a month ago," the lieutenant pointed out. "And cigars are different."

The rock all around them muffled the gunfire outside. Hood felt a heady pleasure at being out of the line of fire. They had a chance to survive now—just stay right here, yeah, until everyone decided this was crazy and went home.

"Sergeant, what do you think we've got here?"

"It's no bunker, too small. A natural cave, I'd say."

"Think it goes deeper?"

"One way to find out."

Hood crawled deeper, cutting off the gray light from outside, feeling his way. The stone ceiling pressed down on his pack, and he felt a spasm of claustrophobia. Breathing deeply, he forced his rigid shoulders to relax. I got in here, I can get out.

"Sergeant?"

"Hang on."

He ran an arm deeper into the crease, feeling the floor angle down. Pushing with his legs, he squirmed into a roomier area big enough for him to sit up. Moving deeper into the hill, he was able to rise into a crouch, then stand. He looked back at the cave mouth, a crease of gray light, notched by the helmet-shaped silhouette of Morrison's head.

"This would make a great clubhouse," he said.

The lieutenant scrambled to join him; Hood could just make him out in the dim light as he stood and looked around.

"Think it might go somewhere interesting?" Morrison asked.

"I doubt it. Like you said, the Japs used this area for training for years, and the NK had plenty of time to recon the hill before we got here from Inch'on. If this hid a way to the top, they'd have either left a squad here or sealed it with explosives. . . ."

"You're probably right—"

"Shhh!" Hood said. Listening, he heard it again, a faint "bonk," almost musical, reverberating through the cave. Twenty seconds later, it came again, a concussive thump with a flute-like overtone, like someone blowing into a coke bottle. "I think we've got a mortar emplacement somewhere above us, sir. I can hear it firing, but the way sound is in here, I can't tell if it's near or far."

Someone rolled into the cave and let out a sound between a grunt and a sob. Morrison whipped out his .45. Reaching over, Hood eased it to the side. "Steinberg?"

"Yuh-yes."

Morrison holstered his pistol.

"What's the matter, son?" Hood asked.

"I got shot in the *tokhes.*"

"Your balls?"

"His ass," Morrison said.

A laugh burst from Hood before he could stop it.

"Oh, right, suddenly I'm the boy with two butt cracks—in the sign of the cross, yet—and my own sergeant thinks it's funny."

"Are you all right, soldier?" Morrison asked.

"It only creased me but it hurts like a *Dybbuk,* if anyone cares."

"Private Steinberg, I want you to call down to the platoon, tell them to hold position. Then you will guard the entrance to this crease. The sergeant and I are going in deeper."

"Yes, sir," his voice firming up.

Morrison pulled his flashlight from his pack and switched it on, playing the beam over a jagged chimney of rock above. Brown splotches clung to the walls, and in a second Hood realized what they were. "Bats," he said. "That explains the smell. It's their piss."

"Terrific," Morrison said. "I wonder if they're rabid."

"The North Koreans will probably kill us before we could die of rabies."

"Good point."

The *bonk* came again, reverberating down the chimney. Hood tore his gaze from the bats and looked at Morrison's face, garishly lit from below by the flashlight. "Are you thinking what I'm thinking, sir?"

"Not unless you're thinking you should have kissed Marianne Shoren that night in the snow back in college."

Hood laughed. "I didn't go to college, sir. I was thinking that the NK explored this little crevasse and decided it led nowhere because there wasn't a mortar firing when they checked it out."

"And we're getting the sound because there's a crack in the rock where they've set the mortar."

"Right. Either it's been there all along or the mortar concussions are creating it. The rock is taking quite a recoil kick every time they fire. They keep it up, they're liable to crack open a good-sized hole up there. Give us a way up this hill from inside."

"After you, sergeant."

Hood shrugged out of the pack and laid his rifle beside it, keeping only his .45. and the grenade belt across his chest. He backed into one wall and found hand and footholds on the other, working his way up in an awkward crawl. Each time he shifted higher, sharp edges of rock pressed painfully into his back. The stink of ammonia grew stronger, stinging his lungs. Bats everywhere, barely room to place his hands—and then they were flying all around him, swooping with a chorus of chittering noises.

Morrison let out a string of curses, and the flashlight beam wavered, fell away.

Hood waited in the dark, feeling his heart pound, and then light bathed the chimney again.

"Okay." Morrison said. "Okay. Nasty things. I hate them."

"Anything that eats mosquitoes can't be all bad," Hood pointed out. "You coming, sir?"

"How much further?"

Hood took a look up the chimney. "It's about thirty feet to the top. I can see a sliver of sunlight now, coming through up there."

"Okay, I'm right behind you."

Hood worked his way up, his back raw. Finally the chimney widened and he felt the lip of a ledge and pulled himself into a space under the ceiling of the chimney. The concussions were loud now, the *bonk* sounding every twenty seconds or so—an efficient crew. If they didn't slow down their rate of fire, they'd melt their tube.

Hood offered a hand, groped until he found Morrison's wrist, and pulled him up. As the lieutenant settled on the final ledge, panting, Hood peered at the faint veil of light filtering down through the crack in the rock. A gritty crackle accompanied each thump of the mortar, now. Bits of dirt and stone rained down.

"How many do you think are up there?" Morrison asked.

"Their mortar teams are usually two or three guys, just like ours."

A good-sized pebble stung Hood's outstretched hand, and the light level rose abruptly. "I think it's about to give way."

"Grenades or .45s, sergeant?"

"Grenades first, then we go up shooting."

"That Steinberg's a card, isn't he?" Morrison said. "Think he's really shot in the ass?"

"Probably. He's the sort of man that happens to."

"A *shlimazel,*" Morrison said.

"Are you Jewish, sir?"

"My mother is, so, yeah, I guess I am."

The mortar thumped, and more debris rained down. "One more ought to do it," Hood said. "Get ready." He plucked a grenade from his belt, found the pin and held it.

Thonk.

An earsplitting crack, and a big chunk of rock hurtled past, another, and light poured down alongside a booted leg. Morrison grabbed the leg and yanked and Hood glimpsed the North Korean hurtling down past them, the man too surprised even to shout. Hood pulled the pin and leaned from the shelf, bracing a hand on the far wall. A hole the size of a tire gaped above him, still raining debris from its edges. A Korean head appeared, silhouetted against the sky, jerking back as Morrison fired with the .45. The gunshot deafened Hood in the confined space; he pitched the grenade through the hole and shoved himself back into the protective slot, pulling Morrison with him.

Seconds later, an explosion sent more rock plummeting down, and he heard men above screaming over the ringing in his ears.

"Now," he yelled, chinning himself through the hole, scrambling to his feet and blinking in the sudden glare. He gave Morrison a hand up. Two dead NK lay with the shattered mortar, the third no doubt lying, broken, at the bottom of the chute.

The emplacement had been chipped out of the rock with small explosive charges which had probably started the crack in the rock on which they'd set up. To the west, a machine gun fired from the mouth of a bunker cut into the hill. Pulling another grenade, Hood started for the bunker, then heard the lieutenant yell.

Spinning around, he dived as a squad of NKs came at them around the curve of the hill, firing their rifles.

The lieutenant went down and Hood lobbed the grenade over him.

The lead NK fell on the grenade as it went off, his body humping from the ground, then settling, and Hood knew he had only seconds. Pulling the .45 from his belt, he fired off the clip, seeing the next two fall and the others duck back around the curve.

Morrison lay too still, his .45 beside his hand. Hood scooped it up and ran at the enemy squad, cursing, firing, and two more went down. The others ran from him, but beyond them, he saw more coming.

Too many.

He dropped back into the hole, pulling the lieutenant after him, his feet spread wide to catch either side of the chimney. Morrison was a dead weight on his shoulders.

Hood slithered and lurched down the chimney. A hand on his leg told him he was almost down. He stepped on the body of the North Korean, barely feeling it as Steinberg helped pull the lieutenant through beneath the low overhang.

Hood felt a blast of grit on his ankles as he slid through the crease back into the mouth of the cave. Looking back, he saw no light, and realized an enemy soldier above had dropped a grenade and it had gone off too high, apparently sealing the chimney. There would be no pursuit.

Turning to the lieutenant, Hood felt for a pulse in his neck.

Furious, groping for a pulse, feeling all around the throat, it must be there, but it wasn't.

Lieutenant Morrison was dead.

Hood stared out the slitted cave mouth at the light of day, bright now with the risen sun. His throat burned, like someone had poured hot sand down it.

Beside him, Private Steinberg had the sense to say nothing.

On September 22, the North Korean attack finally began to falter and fail along the Pusan perimeter. The US Air Force dropped leaflets informing enemy soldiers that In-ch'on had fallen and Seoul was under attack, and ordering them to surrender. Two hundred of them did so, and American troops took them into custody. B-29 bombers dropped flares over rail lines in the south, lighting up North Korean supply trains which were then destroyed by B-26 bombers. As the 32nd Regiment of the 7th Infantry Division moved to try and prevent enemy troops fleeing north from reinforcing Seoul, North Korean forces already in the area were advancing up the same road toward them. They would clash seven miles northeast of Anyang-ni. The winner would take command of the strategic hills south of Seoul. The war might be over in the south, but not in Korea's midsection. . . .
Ibid.

7

22 September, Road north of Anyang-ni, 1000 hours:
"What's your point, lieutenant?" the major asked.

Sam hesitated. Wasn't it obvious?

Maybe the major was only *acting* dense. Why, in the first place, had a senior officer from intelligence walked down the line of march to discuss tactics with a lowly 2nd lieutenant he'd never met?

He's testing me, Sam thought, *but why me?*

Never mind. He had his ducks in a row. Just last night he'd hashed over the issue with Lieutenant Lamberton, his counterpart commanding the second platoon, and with a couple of noncoms who had wandered up and joined the conversation. Major Anson would find that he'd given this plenty of thought.

Sam knelt beside the road, emptying his mind of the stink of rice paddies behind him and the thump-thump of his company tramping past and away. With his bayonet, he drew a circle in the dirt to indicate the town of Yongdung-po and a bigger circle next to it for Seoul. Next he drew in the Han River that meandered between the town and the city. Finally, a slash for the "highway" they were on now, running north toward Yongdung-po. West of Yongdung-po, he drew a "1" to indicate the 1st marine regiment which would be attacking that town right about now.

"My point," he said, "is that we're too far south."

Anson eyed the lines in the dirt with bemused skepticism. Major Tom Anson, Colonel Faith's natty G-2 intelligence officer. Stiff mustache; slitted eyes, as if bees had stung the lids. Lack of sleep, more likely. Intelligence officers were wrong more than anyone liked, and they took plenty of grief for that, but Sam had yet to meet a stupid one.

Anson said, "Are we not heading north toward Yongdung-po?"

"We're *pointed* in that direction, but we're in no hurry. We haven't even reached Hill 290, which is seven miles southeast of Yongdung-po. That's too much separation if we're going to defend the marine right flank."

"We've sent our 2nd Battalion closer."

"To Toksan-ni, which is still too far south of Yongdung-po—nearly three miles. Our 3rd battalion is even further away than we are, way down past Anyang-ni. Our regiment is in good position to oppose NKPA units coming up this road from the south, but we could do that just as well from nearer Yongdung-po. Why leave a three-mile gap between our northernmost battalion and the right flank of the marines?"

Major Anson thumbed his mustache, making the wax gleam in the sun. "Who told you our 2nd Battalion is stopping at Toksan-ni?"

"I overheard it," Sam lied, "I can't remember where."

Anson gazed at him as if his thoughts might start scrolling across his forehead.

Waiting him out, Sam kept his face impassive.

A corner of Anson's mouth quirked in a fleeting smile. "It seems you have a nose for intelligence, Foxworth. Ever thought of requesting a transfer to G-2?"

Sam almost laughed. When he'd been called up, an intelligence billet was exactly what he'd asked for, and he'd been denied on the grounds he had no training in the field. Apparently being curious all his life didn't count. Sam thought of his senior photo in high school. Under "favorite pastime" the wags on the yearbook staff had put, "asking too many nosey questions."

Was Anson making idle chat or a real offer?

Sam felt a stir in the pit of his stomach. To hand over the platoon to someone else, get out from under the burden of being responsible for thirty-plus lives—he hadn't imagined it might be possible. The men were starting to round into shape, but who knew when that would take a turn for the worse? The platoon's improved morale might last only as long as Sergeant Hartung stayed confined to the 1st MASH. And the halo effect of him rescuing Hartung and the guy with the sucking chest wound would wear off, too. Sooner or later, his men would realize he was no hero, and then all the earlier problems would come back.

But if Anson was serious. . . .

Play it cool.

"I'm happy working under Captain Loomis, sir."

"Are you?" Anson sounded mildly amused. "You've got his 1st Platoon, right, the one with five 'early releases?'" Showing that he knew things, too. "Five army criminals and eight Koreans who never held a gun before, and you like working for Captain Loomis?"

"I like challenges, sir." Sam winced inwardly. A poor choice of words, "challenge" being exactly what he was doing to the major, even if Anson *had* asked for it.

"Lieutenant, is one of your jailbirds also an eavesdropper?"

"Not that I know of, sir."

All of a sudden, Sam realized why Anson had sought him out. Someone who'd heard him discussing this in his bull session with Lamberton and the others had passed it on to Anson. The major didn't want a discussion on tactics, he wanted to know how a lowly platoon leader had found out so much of the thinking in higher councils. Apart from the need to keep tactical plans secret from the enemy, information was power, not to be passed around freely to mere second lieutenants.

Relief settled over Sam. Now that he knew the game, he could play it. If Major Anson kept digging and discovered how he'd found out what he knew, he'd almost certainly lose his source.

Time to go on offense, take Anson's mind off the leak.

"Major, it isn't just the three miles of separation bothering me. That area is hilly, full of cover. A division of North Koreans could be dug in there between us and the marines, in perfect position to hit them without us even hearing the gunfire and mortars."

"If there were a division of NK in that area, don't you think I'd be aware of it, lieutenant? It's my job, after all, not yours. For all you know, I've had recon patrols all over those hills. You do understand that, as a 2nd lieutenant, it is your responsibility to have your platoon ready to fight, not to advise senior officers on strategy and tactics."

"With respect, sir, you're the one who brought this up. It puts a black mark on our regiment if the NK attack the marines from a flank we're supposed to be controlling. Did X Corps task the marines to maintain contact between flanks, or did they give that mission to us?"

Anson looked both vexed and amused. "Are you *grilling* me, Foxworth?"

"Wouldn't it be us, sir, so the marines can concentrate on taking the town?"

"What are you, twenty-two?"

"That's right, sir."

"A college-boy reservist, am I right?"

"I'm done with college, I'm no boy, and this isn't the reserves any more, sir."

Anson nodded, and nodded some more. "You've been shot at a few times, and you think that gives you the wisdom to know what's right for the regiment? Talk to me again when you've killed an enemy soldier. Bring me the gun or the helmet of someone you stopped from killing one of ours."

Sam felt a flush warming his face. "Sir, whether I've shot an enemy soldier or not, isn't my duty to give a superior officer my opinion if asked?"

"Your duty, and mine, is to our regiment of the United States Army. You haven't pointed out any threat whatsoever to that regiment. And yet you are questioning how an order is being carried out by superiors above your rank—mine, too, for that matter."

"Are you saying us staying too far back *is* deliberate?"

Anson looked uncomfortable. "'Too far' are your words, not mine. We have been given not just one mission but two—guarding the 1st regiment's right flank and cutting off the Anyang-ni corridor from the south—"

"Which we're doing—with overkill. Why settle for that, when a simple move north will allow us to do both?"

Major Anson reddened. "Are you trying to provoke me?"

What's wrong with me? Sam thought. I should be getting on Anson's good side, so he'll want me transferred to him. "I'm just asking questions, sir. Do you know for a fact that no sizable NK force is in those hills on the 1st's right flank?"

"I don't answer to you," Anson snapped. "This discussion is over."

"I apologize, sir. I mean no disrespect."

Anson continued to glare at him. "In the army, lieutenant, it is not what you mean but what you do that counts."

"And sometimes what you don't do?" *Put a cork in it!*

"Less often, Foxworth. Far less often, what you don't do. Maybe that's what you could learn from this."

Either Anson had his equanimity back or he was a good faker. Strolling back up the bank to the road, he rejoined the column. Sam rose and brushed off his knees, feeling deflated at the missed opportunity, a chance to impress an intelligence officer into taking him on, and instead he'd antagonized the man.

"Yo, lieutenant." Cinquemani, veering down from the road toward him.

Returning his salute, Sam felt a little better. Here, at least, was one bright spot. Julius Cinquemani, five-foot-four, curly black hair, as tanned as if he'd just left his father's vineyards in Italy. Short he might be, but he had shoulders like a davenport, and a good head on top of them, even if he was an ex-con.

109

"The platoon's up the road a piece, sir. Thought I'd better come check if you turned an ankle."

What I turned, Sam thought, was an opportunity—into a disaster.

Cinquemani glanced at the dirt map. "You discussing tactics with the major?"

"His idea, corporal, not mine."

"Permission to speak frankly, sir?"

"Go ahead."

"When brass asks your opinion, it's best to give 'em theirs. That major looked pretty red in the face when I passed him. I can't count how many times I've wanted to set straight someone who outranks me, but no good has ever come of it, no matter how right I was. I've learned that the hard way, sir."

"I'll have that engraved on my canteen." Sam scanned the road. It was so packed with troops they'd make better time catching up with C Company if they stayed on the margin between the road and the rice paddies.

Sam started walking and Cinquemani hurried on his short legs to keep up.

"Corporal, you're a World War II vet, right?"

"That's right, sir. I fought in Europe."

"Ever fight with marines?"

"You mean fight with 'em, or against 'em, like in bar fights and such?"

"I meant in a joint campaign."

"No. I've thrown some punches when they got in my face. Jarheads got an 'attitude' about Army. I don't know what their beef is. Probably something from way back—they got memories like elephants."

Sam remembered Hood's needling back at Tokyo Hospital, his obvious contempt for "dogfaces."

"Marines think we can't fight for shit," Cinquemani went on. "That we bug out when the going gets tough. Most of it's just talk, leathernecks thinking they're better than everybody else. Far as that goes, there might have been times when some army unit or the other hasn't done everything the Marines were expecting."

"Like Pusan?"

"I've heard rumors about that, yeah, but I was thinking more back in World War II, some of the stories. My own view, why care what jarheads think? I was 101st Airborne in WWII. We were the toughest sons of bitches you ever saw, and I'll fight anyone says otherwise."

Okay, Sam thought. There's some bad blood between the two branches, but would Army deliberately duck orders to protect the Marine flank in Pusan, and now here? Surely not. Maybe Anson did run recon and knows there's no North Koreans northeast of us—

"Heard anything about Sergeant Hartung?" Cinquemani asked.

"I tried to get through to the MASH a couple of days ago, but the phones were out. Don't tell me you're worried about him. You wouldn't give him the time of day before he was wounded."

"True. But you hate to see a man on fire, even if he's been a total pain in the ass. And if you put the fire out, like you and I did, it gives you part interest in the guy."

"Yeah." Sam felt a twinge of guilt. He'd probably given less thought than he should have to Hartung. Pain in the ass was right and, with him gone, things were shaping up.

But he is one of my men. If we ever get a lull, I ought to borrow Loomis's jeep and go check on him.

His teeth clamped with an obscure anger—at himself, he realized. What was wrong with him? A true leader would be firmly committed to his platoon by this time. Instead, here he was, hoping for another assignment, a way out. Instead of making sure he was dependable, he worried that his men would depend on him too much. What was he doing here in this uniform? He could have arranged his life never to have to ask himself questions like this. But no, he had to take ROTC. And now he was in the Army for real, where every flaw he had would be tested and exposed—

A distant loud "whump" shook the earth under his boots. North of the column—an artillery or mortar explosion, and now the distant rattle of gunfire followed by more explosions.

Sam felt a grim vindication. I was right—there *are* NK between us and the marines—

My platoon!

Sam bounded up the bank onto the road, hearing Cinq scrambling after him. "A" Company milled in confusion, officers and sergeants yelling orders. The firing sounded at least a mile north, maybe two, where "B" Company led the regimental column. Today's order of march had "C" Company in the middle of the column behind "B," with "A," here, bringing up the rear.

Sam shoved his way through milling men unslinging their weapons. Ahead, he saw Kim working his way back to meet him. It took them a couple of minutes to catch up with the platoon. Cinquemani's buddies from the stockade had their weapons out, looking up the road, and the KATUSAs were opening up ammo packs, staying with the column this time, thank God.

"What's happening?" Sam asked Kim.

"Haven't heard yet, boss."

"Where's the captain?" Stretching up on tiptoes, Sam looked around. There—on the radio, a hand over his other ear to shut out the din around him.

He pushed through the crowd to his C.O.'s shoulder.

"Yes, sir," Loomis was saying. "Will do." Handing the headset back to his radioman, he shouted, "Where the hell is Foxworth?"

"Here, sir."

Loomis turned, his square face furrowed with stress. "B Company is under attack by a large force. They're retreating along the road back toward us. We need to set up a counterattack. But where?" He gestured at the swampy ground on both sides of the road. "Goddamn these goddamned rice paddies!"

"Can we make it to those hills?"

Loomis looked ahead to where he was pointing, beyond a bend, on the right side of the road. "Get your men up there, quick. Where the hell is Lamberton."

The 2nd platoon lieutenant was also right at Loomis's side, the captain so hopped up he wasn't seeing straight.

Cinquemani already had Hartung's squad moving, skirting the milling mass on the road. Sam relayed the order to the other two squads and got them moving.

"Grenade belt, boss."

Sam took the belt from Kim and ran after Cinquemani. Finding a break in the crowd ahead of him, he snaked through, staying on the roadbed to get out front of his platoon. The slope of the meager hill he'd spotted rose from the rice paddies on the right side of the road. Plunging down the bank, he ran up the opposite grade, his feet tangling, thick weeds dragging at his ankles. Scraggly trees dotted the margins of the hill, with a few more on top, and some boulders that might provide cover. Reaching the top, Sam looked ahead up the road. A cloud of dust obscured the rattle and pop of gunfire, loud and clear, now.

"Here you go, boss."

Snatching his binoculars from Kim, he focused in. Blurred shapes in the dust became American soldiers, running this way in all-out panic. Unnerved, Sam dropped the glasses and tried to think. Most of his platoon was on the hill now. Waving them up around the crest, he yelled orders to find a rock or tree to hide behind. "Stay down! Don't fire until I say."

Finding cover behind a big boulder with a flat top, Sam fixed the glasses on the road again. Kim joined him, crouching in the weeds beside the rock. The kid had his carbine out. His eyes shone with eagerness. Sam's mouth was so dry he couldn't swallow. He reached for his canteen, then decided there wasn't time.

The GIs were nearly to the hill, now, running headlong in full retreat. With a shock Sam recognized Colonel Faith bringing up the rear, turning every few steps to shoot back up the road, yelling at the men around him to do the same. Sam's heart lurched with admiration. What bravery! Faith could have hopped in his jeep and been at the head of the retreat.

Inspired, Sam felt his fear lifting. Unslinging his M-1, he brought it around to bear. The forward tilt of the rock table allowed him to sight down on the road.

"B" Company streamed past, running around the skirt of the low hill toward the rest of the column, which had scattered off the road to find their firing positions.

And suddenly, just like that, Sam realized he was looking down at North Koreans, only forty yards behind the fleeing Americans and closing.

Why weren't his men shooting?

"Fire!" he yelled.

The hill erupted all around him with the banging of M-1s and the tinnier pops of the carbines. NKs in the lead spun and toppled, as though a scythe had ripped through them, and others stumbled over them, bogging down the pursuit. Sam looked for a target as the NKs regrouped. A couple of dozen bravely charged up the hill toward his platoon. One headed straight for Sam's rock—he could see the brown face clearly, the small chin, the determined grimace. Taking aim, he squeezed the trigger. Blood gushed from the man's neck, the shock of the bullet standing him upright, then toppling him backward.

Sam stared at the soles of the man's boots, frozen, hearing his platoon firing all around him. Other enemy soldiers at the periphery of his vision spun and fell.

The NK counterattack faltered, the surviving NKs turning to run back down the hill. Sam got one in his sights, a clear shot between the shoulder blades, but the trigger wouldn't pull.

Yells of triumph all around him, the men emptying their magazines, reloading, and firing again, mowing the enemy down as they tried to escape back up the road.

"You got one, lieutenant," Kim yelled, exultant.

Sam managed a nod.

Company B, rallied by the colonel, had turned and were now chasing the North Koreans back up the road.

Rising, Sam felt stiff, as though he'd slept on a bad bed. He couldn't take his eyes off the man he'd shot. As if in a dream, his legs carried him down to the fallen soldier. Kneeling by the body, he saw that the man was an older veteran, a sergeant.

A Korean Harlan Hood.

His helmet had fallen off, the chin strap severed by the same bullet that had penetrated his throat. The corpse's black hair was salted with white. He looked to be in his mid forties. His jaw gaped and his eyes stared over Sam's shoulder with a look of dulling expectation.

Still in the dream, Sam watched his own hands search the man's pockets, pulling out money and a photograph, bound with a rubber band.

The photo was of a woman and child.

Sickness ate at Sam's gut. Major Anson had said to bring him a trophy, something off a dead enemy, and then they could talk. Maybe he should bring Anson this picture. And then he could listen to Anson tell him that the man had been trying to kill him, this man with a wife and kid, and Anson would be right, and he would hate him for it, just like he hated himself right now.

"Nice shooting, lieutenant."

Cinquemani, so he forced himself to wave in acknowledgment, and in that instant he knew with a bitter certainty that he'd get over killing this man. That he would throw away the picture and try never to think of it again.

And that, in doing it, he'd be throwing away a part of himself.

At the outset of the Korean War, surgery in the field was conducted much as during World War II, which had ended only five years earlier. In the case of injured arteries, the approved procedure was to tie off the bleeding stump of the damaged blood vessel (ligation) and wait to see whether enough vascularization would occur to revive the tissue formerly fed by the torn artery. In about half of all cases, new circulation was insufficient, resulting in the amputation of the dying limb. As the war began, teaching hospitals were starting to explore daring new techniques in arterial repair—principally, grafting a vein from a donor or from elsewhere in the recipient's body to restore the flow of blood through the damaged artery. To save the limb, the surgery must be done within ten hours of wounding. MASH stood for Mobile Army Surgical Hospital. MASH units deployed close to the front and moved with the units they treated. Many of the wounded in need of arterial repair did reach surgery within the ten-hour window. Even so, doctors were forbidden by the Army Surgeon General's Office to perform any "experimental" procedures such as arterial repair to try and save the arm or leg.   (Ibid.)

8

1st MASH, Inch'on, 2023:

It's only pain, Bonnie told herself. After seven hours in surgery, her spine throbbed and her shoulder blades ached. She stepped away from the table so orderlies could remove the pneumothorax. As they carried the GI away to postop, she flexed her knees and bent forward, sneaking a glance at Jeff. Bloody-gloved hands on his hips, he had bent over so far backward she could see the stubbly base of his chin under his surgical mask. He hadn't sat down the whole seven hours either—no chance, really. Their standing bet concerned exactly that—who could stay on their feet longest if the going got tough.

It was tough now. Her calves pulsed. If she could get her weight off just for a few minutes—

The orderlies hustled in with another litter. Sally Reynolds, in her sixth straight hour as instrument nurse, held a new sterile glove up for her, and she wriggled her fingers into it, then the other. Major Folsom accompanied the patient, holding a unit of blood aloft, hanging it on the rack as the orderlies settled the litter onto the table. The North Korean soldier's face was slack, his arms sticking out to each side, supported and immobilized by splints to hold the IV lines secure. It made him look like he'd been nailed to a cross.

"A bullet tore up his right biceps," Folsom said, "severe damage and blood loss, as you can see. I expect you'll have to amputate."

"How long ago did they bring him in?" Jeff asked.

"Couple of hours. He's lucky we're bothering with him. His unit ambushed our 32nd regiment boys on the road north of Anyang-ni."

Sam, Bonnie thought with a pang. Wounded had been coming in all day, some of them Army, but no one had mentioned which outfit. The last time she'd thought of Sam was a couple days ago as she fell asleep, exhausted, a few seconds of semi-lucid drift before she'd slipped under. He hadn't come by the MASH as she'd expected. No doubt he'd been busy.

Or maybe he'd already forgotten her. A little lesson in humility if she hadn't been too tired to care. Too tired even to collect her thoughts about what she was seeing and experiencing, which was mainly men bleeding and being sewn up by other men. Strong stuff, but she hadn't had time to write a line in her notebooks in four days.

"How many units of blood has this man had, major?" Jeff asked.

"Here at the MASH, three, before that, I don't know. He's B positive." With a final, cold glance at the North Korean, Folsom headed back out to pre-op.

Bonnie wondered how deeply ran the major's dislike of treating enemy wounded alongside American and ROK soldiers. She'd never talked against it directly, but that icy look wasn't the first she'd given a North Korean patient.

On the other hand, when was Folsom ever warm to anyone?

Jeff used a forceps to probe the NK's upper arm, which looked like it had been run through a meat grinder. Bonnie fingered the wrist of the mangled arm. No pulse that she could find, and the skin chilled her glove—both signs that scant blood was getting past the wound into the lower arm.

Folsom was right, it would probably have to come off.

Jeff looked up at her, his gray eyes wide above the mask. "Remember what we discussed?"

She felt a sudden surge of energy.

"Hot dog!" Hank Basham exclaimed from the head of the table. Jeff's best buddy among the doctors, and a pretty fair anesthesiologist, considering the doctors draft had yanked him from a residency in pediatrics.

"Are you with us, Nurse Reynolds?" Jeff asked.

Sally leaned over to look at the wound as he blotted it, and Bonnie did the same, seeing it clearly now, the big artery that ran through the biceps muscle. A two-inch section of it was so tattered that blood poured from it like a sieve.

Sally nodded. "I'm with you."

No one coming right out and saying it because Army surgical teams did not do arterial repair. That was the policy and the main reason was gaseous gangrene, which killed fast once it got going. Amputation was the one sure way to prevent the lethal spread of gangrene—the patient gave up an arm or leg to be sure of keeping his life.

But Jeff had filled them in on a study by a Dr. Michael DeBakey, reviewing over two thousand arterial wounds DeBakey had seen as an Army doctor in World War II. That, and a select few other studies, had suggested a method for repairing arteries.

But on an enemy soldier?

If a "gook" died of gangrene, Major Folsom might look the other way but, NK or not, this was a man, not a guinea pig. A human being.

With a shot at keeping his arm, if they had the guts to try.

"I'll replace the damaged artery with a section of his saphenous vein," Jeff said. "There should be enough other veins in the leg to recirculate adequately. Before I do it, I need a gentle way to interrupt blood flow just above the damage while we work. I can't use a suture because it might cinch the artery too tight and destroy the tissue, in which case blood flow might not resume even if the repair, itself, goes well."

"Rubber tubing," Bonnie said. "Sally's got some for Penrose drains on the tray."

"Perfect. Cut me a five inch length, Sally. Then, keep a sharp eye as I slice out the piece of vein for grafting. You'll be responsible for making sure I reverse it before I patch it into the artery. If I get it the wrong way, the valves in the vein will fight blood flow instead of helping it along. Bonnie, I'll need you to retract on the leg so I can get the vein, and also on the arm. Give me plenty of work space. Double-O silk's too damn thick for sewing the ends together. Have they shipped us anything finer, yet?"

"No," Sally said.

"All right, we'll just have to make it work."

Sally laid the haft of a scalpel in Jeff's palm. Bending over the leg, he positioned the blade parallel to the tibia bone, where the saphenous vein ran down toward the instep of the foot. A nervous sweat poured into Bonnie's cap. This would be hard enough in a well-lit, modern operating room. In here, the lights might be adequate for cleaning out wounds or sewing up fascia, but they were too dim for the close work of stitching a vein to an artery. The clamps had not been designed for such fine work—too big to set securely in such a small field, and the suturing thread was too thick, like Jeff had said.

Other than that, Bonnie thought, it's a snap.

Jeff drew the scalpel down the inside of the thigh. Blood welled up, and Bonnie blotted it away with gauze as Jeff exposed the vein. He worked the underside with the blade of the scalpel, freeing up eight inches, then cutting it loose and tying off both severed ends. Collateral circulation should take over the job of the missing vein—or so the theory went.

Sally held out a tray for the graft, reversing it so it would lie the right way when she handed it back.

"Clamps," Jeff said.

Bonnie moved in with the clamps Sally handed her, pinning shredded muscle tissue away from the leaking artery.

"How we doing on blood?" Jeff asked.

We'll need another unit soon," Sally said. "I'll get it ready."

Bonnie tried again to clamp a tattered piece of muscle away from the area Jeff needed to work. It slipped loose. There—got it!

"Good," Jeff said. "Now keep it there for me."

Sally handed Jeff the tubing, and he doubled it back into a scissor hold around the artery above the shredded part, binding the two legs of tubing together with a couple of turns of silk—snug, but not too tight. He sliced the damaged section of artery out.

"Sally, the vein."

"It goes this way," she said, handing him the tray.

"He just twitched—get him deeper, Hank."

The hiss from the ether tank swelled. Sally handed Jeff a suture and he bent over the field, his shoulders hunched and still. ER doctors were used to hurry-up surgery, and Jeff must be stitching as fast as he could, but a minute dragged by, then another, as he struggled to pull the coarse silk through without damaging the joined rims of vein and artery.

"Got it!" he whispered.

Attaching the other end of the vein to the downstream stump of artery went faster. Jeff pulled the ligature of Penrose tubing free to reopen the upstream end of the artery. The anastomosis held, no blood leaking out.

"Brilliant!" Bonnie exclaimed.

Jeff looked at her, his eyes shining between the mask and cap, holding her gaze and not breaking eye contact after a second, like he usually did. Her heart, thumping at her throat, reminded her she ought to be checking for a pulse.

"A good, strong beat," she said, "and the skin already feels warmer."

Jeff let out an explosive sigh. "Let's clean up the wound and close. You were terrific." He looked away at last, at Sally and Hank. "All of you, very good. Thank you."

Heading for the medical ward to look in on her patients, Bonnie slowed to give herself time to think. The musty hall smelled of

121

old wax and white paste. Other hints of the former inhabitants still lingered—a construction paper cat taped to the wall, an open locker with a child's stocking cap in the bottom. Hopefully, the war would end soon and kids would again fill this hall with laughter.

Had she read Jeff wrong? That long look he gave her after she called him brilliant. Simple pleasure at the compliment or more? He would hint he was attracted to her, then undercut it. One day she was Bonnie, the next Lieutenant Brisbane. He'd sit beside her in the mess then let her walk out alone, ignoring her announcement that she was going for an evening stroll.

She had come to Korea to study men, not find one, but there was something to learn in how they approached a woman. Sam Foxworth had pounced on her the minute they'd met and Jeff drifted in and out like wavelets lapping a shore, the two men opposites, a palindrome—wolf and flow.

Maybe Jeff was shy because of his face. He shouldn't be. Really, after you got used to the acne scars, he had a handsome face. And risking his career to save an enemy soldier's arm, now that was attractive.

I can't believe we did it, Bonnie thought, then reminded herself that they hadn't—not yet. The anastomosis could start leaking and even if it didn't, if the circulation was inadequate, the soldier could still die of gangrene. Either way, if Folsom realized what they'd done, they'd all be in dutch.

Tomorrow's worry. Check her patients, then hit the rack.

Stepping into the post-op/medical ward, once the school's gym, Bonnie made her way between the close rows of cots, stopping to read the chart of a patient with dysentery, then rounding the corner into the next row to check on Sergeant Hartung—

And there, kneeling by Hartung's cot, was the big bad wolf, himself.

Bonnie stopped in her tracks. Sam, in the flesh, as if summoned by her earlier thought of him. He and his sergeant were talking softly, but loud enough for her to hear. She shouldn't eavesdrop—well, only for a minute.

". . .sleeping on your stomach?" Sam asked.

"You bet I'm sick of it," Hartung said.

"They say only a few more days of dressings, the way the uninjured skin is healing in. Those stockade pogues giving you any grief?"

"Not since I made Corporal Cinquemani acting platoon sergeant."

"You're shitting me—sir."

"Give him a break, sergeant. He's the one that tackled you and kept you from becoming Hartung the human torch. He also got you the ambulance while I was packing mud on you."

"Well, that's a surprise," Hartung muttered.

"He's been doing all right. Even calls me sir."

Hartung made a face. "Gah—he's spoiling you, for sure, sir. Tell him not to get too used to sergeant duty because I'm coming back, soon as I can. You been resupplied with ammo yet?"

"Kim found most of it. We're doing all right there. The KATUSAs were all back the next morning."

"Probably wanted their breakfasts."

"They were embarrassed that they ran. First time they'd ever been fired on."

"For you, too, but you managed to keep your head and shoot back—"

Bonnie realized Hartung had spotted her over Sam's shoulder. She resumed her stride, all innocence.

"Here's your friend now," Hartung said, twisting his head to smile up at her. Sam rose and held out his hand. She suppressed a smile as she shook with him—his first instant of awareness of her, and he'd managed to touch her. He might have forgotten completely about her between Lulu's and this moment, but he was ready to pick right up where he'd left off.

And she had to admit it was a nice boost for her ego.

"I was hoping you'd get free before I had to leave," Sam said.

"Lots of surgeries today. Some from your regiment."

His smile faded. "I can believe it."

"Has it been bad?"

123

"Bad enough," Sergeant Hartung said. "From what the lieutenant's been telling me, the 32nd's been busy. Yesterday, box mines wrecked three of our tanks, and then we had to fight off an attack. Seven dead, thirty wounded—"

Sam cleared his throat, shooting a cautioning look at his sergeant. "On the brighter side," he said, "our second battalion captured a big load of medical supplies from the North Koreans. That's why I'm here—my C.O. was at the regimental command post this afternoon when the colonel ordered the supplies sent back to your MASH. Captain Loomis knew I had a sergeant here, so he volunteered a squad of my men to ride shotgun. They're chowing down in your mess right now."

"Shame on you," Hartung said, "using a sick man for your alibi. He came to see you, Nurse Brisbane."

Sam gazed at her, saying nothing to correct his sergeant.

She said, "I'm sure he's concerned about you, Sergeant Hartung."

"Naw. He doesn't even like me."

"That's true," Sam said, and both men laughed.

Bonnie bent over Hartung and lifted the patches of damp gauze dressing here and there on his back. "You're healing fast."

"Just my luck," he groused, pretty convincing had she not just overheard him chafing to get back to his unit.

Sam gazed at her. "Is there someplace around here I can buy you a drink?"

"I shouldn't be hearing this," Hartung said merrily.

"And even if you don't drink," Sam added, "we'd at least be able to ditch this guy."

She started to tell him she was too tired, then realized that, all of a sudden, she wasn't. "Okay," she said.

Down the hall, she told Sam to wait. Tiptoeing into Pumpkin Land, as Laura Lidner had dubbed the nurses quarter, she commandeered a half-empty fifth of Johnny Walker from under Laura's cot. She led Sam up the hillside behind the hospital, the bottle clinking against the buckle of her web belt under her fatigue jacket, the first time she'd ever taken a walk with a guy where she was dressed the same as him. Crickets chirred; tendrils of mist drifted and swirled over the damp grass. She could just see Sam's face in moonlight filtered by overcast—that Kirk Douglas chin and the straight nose and sculpted mouth, all the beautiful dark hair.

Had he really come back here to see her?

He'd let Hartung give her that impression, but it was also possible he'd simply brought the captured medical supplies as ordered and looked in on his sergeant while he was at it. He could have forgotten she existed and only remembered when Hartung mentioned her. *Oh, yeah, the nurse from Tokyo.*

Sam chose her favorite spot to stop, a crumbling section of stone wall left over from some ancient building on a hill now overgrown with grass and trees. Settling across from her, he took a pull on the bottle and handed it back. "You know your way around in the dark pretty well," he observed.

"I come out here when I get a chance. Gets me away from the smell of medicine and blood and all that."

"But at night? There might still be some NKs around in Inch'on."

"I doubt it. The ROK marines had a scorched earth policy when it came to ridding the city of Communists. It's as safe here as you'll get in a war zone."

She took a sip; found him watching her.

"I thought your drink was Coke, or is that only on the first date?"

"That wasn't a date, Sam." Taking another short pull at the bottle, she savored the smoky heat of the scotch, first drink she'd had since her farewell party in Tokyo, and she probably shouldn't, in case there were more wounded, but just a sip or two wouldn't hurt.

"You look different," Sam said.

"No kidding. I haven't had a bath in three days. Too busy operating, plus no bathtubs anyway, just a tent shower—a bucket with holes in it. Try rinsing your hair in that. And while we're on the subject, you don't look so hot yourself. Back in recovery I noticed your eyes are bloodshot."

"That's because you're a sight for sore eyes."

That was smoother than the scotch, she thought.

"Still glad you volunteered?" he asked.

In her mind, she saw the blanched face of the GI who'd died on the table this morning, too mangled by the mine, bleeding out despite three lines of whole blood. No time to think about it, more patients waiting, like the eighteen-year-old whose arm they'd taken off just yesterday, the bones pulverized, the arteries too shredded even to think of repair. "I knew what I was getting into," she said. "How about you?"

"All things considered, I'd rather be on spring break in Fort Lauderdale."

She smiled. "At least you're getting some preparation for your teaching—a chance to help make some history yourself."

"Yeah, but what kind?"

"Did you study Korea in college?"

"We spent a day or two on it in one of my courses."

"Jeff was telling me that China used to rule Korea."

"Jeff?"

"Dr. Wittschiebe, one of our surgeons."

Eyeing her, Sam said, "Genghis Khan conquered this country in the 13th Century. China dominated it for the next six hundred years, but the Koreans still managed to stay themselves."

"What does that mean?"

"The Hermit Kingdom. They wouldn't trade overseas and they wanted nothing to do with foreigners. In 1866, an American merchant schooner ran aground near Pyongyang. The good citizens of that town took the crew off and massacred them all."

A chill went through her. "That's really hating strangers."

"Later they decided we Americans might have a use. They were tired of being China's lunch, and worried because the Japanese and Russians were both waving their forks over them. So, in 1882, they signed a treaty of peace and friendship with us.

Turned out to be useless. The Japanese whipped the Chinese and the Russians and gobbled up Korea themselves in 1905, while we looked the other way. Japan was savage enough to make Koreans miss the good old days simmering in China's wok. Instead, they spent the next forty years as sushi, until we finally had no choice but to cook Japan's goose."

"You aren't by any chance hungry, are you?"

"I'd kill for a Nathan's Coney Island hot dog with mustard and onions."

Bonnie clenched her teeth to keep from yawning. Starting to feel tired again. Truth was, she wasn't interested in Sam the historian at the moment, she was interested in the Sam whose father had left him when he was young, like hers. From what she'd observed of Sam in Tokyo, Harlan Hood's desertion still stung. Why? She wasn't angry about her own father—at least, not near as angry as Sam seemed to be. Strange. Her father betrayed her mother with other women. From what Sam had said, Harlan's other love wasn't a woman, but the Marine Corps, defending his country.

"So-o-o-o," Sam said, "this Jeff studied history along with medicine?"

"Try and put Jeff out of your mind," she said.

"I am."

She wanted more scotch but knew it wasn't a good idea, so she handed the bottle to him. His hand lingered on hers as he took it. He didn't drink, just gazed at her in the dark. She could sense it coming, feel her heartbeat picking up despite her weariness. As he started to lean toward her, she said, "After the war, why didn't we just give Korea back to the Koreans?"

He settled back again, making it look like he'd just been shifting positions. "You sure you want to hear more about Korea?"

"It's fascinating." She batted her eyelashes, hoping he could see it in the moonlight.

"Ha-ha-h'all right, Nurse Brisbane. The thinking then was that Korea was too unstable to fend for itself."

"Whose bright idea was it that dividing Korea between us and the Russians, of all people, would make the country more stable?"

"It seems like a lame idea now, but that's hindsight. At the time, near the end of World War II, Russia was our ally. It was a UN decision, which we went along with, and why not? It was only supposed to be a temporary fix—Uncles Sam and Ivan would teach Korea how to ride its bike, then let go of the seat together as soon as the nation could pedal itself and stay upright. My own sense is that we went along with it partly because we hadn't yet really fathomed what a total maniac Joe Stalin is. We knew he had a hammer and sickle up his sleeve, but how could anyone foresee how ruthless he'd be in the next five years, slicing up Eastern Europe like so much pie? Stalin wanted Korea too, so he groomed his Commie pal, Kim Il Sung to rule the country. To be fair, at the same time, we were grooming our own horse in the south. Whatever else he may be—a lot of it not very nice—Dr. Syngman Rhee is a staunch anti-communist. Both Koreas want their missing half back, but on their own terms. Unfortunately, Stalin was a lot more serious about arming and preparing the NK People's Army than we were with the ROK. And Kim Il Sung got his Ph.D. in combat, fighting the Japanese in Manchuria and North China."

"The dictator of North Korea was on our side?"

"Stalin's side, which at that time was our side." Sam edged closer. "Enough on Korea. I'm putting you to sleep."

"I am wide awake."

"If you clamp your jaw one more time, you'll crack a molar."

"No, really, Sam. We're here thousands of miles from home, I'd like to know something about it—and you sure know a lot for just a couple of days in one college course."

"I did some reading on my own before I came over."

"I'm impressed."

"Tell that to Sergeant Hartung. He thinks reading is useless."

"Not any more." She told him about the sergeant's epiphany when the ambulance first brought him in. "He saw you reading the manual, and later you knew proper first aid for white phosphorus burns. I think he's a convert to reading."

"At least to me reading."

Laughing, she realized how good it felt—and how strange, like she'd forgotten how. There'd been little to laugh about lately.

Sam said, "Is this Jeff better looking than me?"

"Much."

"Liar. Wanna make out?"

Her heart raced, but she stifled the rush. "Where did that come from?"

"You're a beautiful woman. I'd be a fool not to want to touch you."

"To find out how I compare?

He gave her a look of reproach.

"Come on, Sam. Women do throw themselves at you, right? Ever been engaged?"

He shook his head.

"What's the longest you ever dated a woman?"

"I don't know."

"Sure you do. A couple of months, am I right?"

"Maybe I never found the right one, until now."

"Sam, you don't even know me."

"I'd like to. Couldn't we just take it a step at a time?"

"Depends on what you think is the next step."

"Come on, Bonnie. If you decide I'm just some guy on the make, as you seem to think, you can tell me to get lost."

"But that's not what you think will happen. You think we'll make out, and I'll like it so much we'll make love, and later you'll decide I'm not the one for you, and you'll move on to the next woman."

"Whoa, we're getting way ahead of ourselves, here."

"How many girlfriends have you had?"

"How would you like it if I pried into your romantic history?"

"I've dated maybe ten guys, and I've had three boyfriends that really counted—one in high school and two in college."

He opened his mouth; closed it.

"The guy in high school broke up with me, and the other two I had to break it off with when I realized I had no idea whether they really loved me. It hurt like hell to be dumped, but what surprised me was how painfully hard it was to do it to someone else. You know?"

"Yes."

Did he really mean it? Pain at breaking up was hardly the way of the wolf. He was too smooth not to have dated plenty. Surely, among all those high school girls and college women, at least one would have been right for him.

Bonnie realized she was gazing at his mouth. A hot flush came over her and she swallowed, embarrassed. She really would like to kiss him, just kiss him, but a desperate caution held her back like an arm across her chest. Uncle Daddy had been handsome and tall like Sam, and he'd broken Mom's heart. That is not going to happen to me, Bonnie thought. If I repeat Mom's mistake, I'll be the world's worst idiot.

"So," he said, "on making out—is that a yes?"

She laughed. "You know what I really want right now? I want to sleep."

Rising, he handed her the bottle of scotch.

Oh, God, I've offended him. "But it's really nice to see you again."

He reached down and pulled her up. "It's nice to see you, too. I should be getting back to my men."

He kissed her gently on the lips, his big, warm hand cradling the base of her neck. His tenderness stirred sparks in her, and she almost pulled him closer. With an act of will, she stepped away.

He walked her back to Pumpkin Land.

She shook his hand goodbye.

As she drifted into sleep, she felt warm in places she hadn't even thought of in weeks.

Warm and at the same time, frustrated.

An annoying question circled down with her into sleep: Had she, in her zeal not to be the world's worst idiot, just been the world's worst idiot?

While the 7th Division attempted to secure the area just south of Seoul, the heaviest fighting commenced on the western edge of the city. Beginning on September 22, the 5th regiment of General Oliver Smith's 1st Marine Division fought one hard battle after another, trying to break through a tough perimeter defense mounted by North Korean forces just west of Seoul. Two other regiments of the 1st division joined the 5th Marines during this period, but breaking through into the city continued to go slower than General MacArthur or General Almond, head of X Corps, liked. On September 23, Almond warned General Smith he was unhappy with how long it was taking the marines to enter Seoul. He gave Smith 24 hours to show significant progress; otherwise, he would bring the 7th Infantry Division's 32nd Regiment into the attack from the south. . . .

(Ibid.)

9

23 September, Hill 68, 0700:

"Can one of you fill me in on what's been going on?"

No one spoke up, and Hood wasn't about to go first. One of us? he thought. You're the new lieutenant, pick one.

The constant thump of artillery sent tremors through the sandbags overhead, dropping veils of dust between the girders. The bunker's dirt floor, dug out to only five feet below the beams, stank of mildew. The smell aggravated Hood, like pretty much everything else had aggravated him the past twenty-four hours. Another good man gone—as close to a friend as an officer could be. You had only two choices: sink so low you could barely lift your head, or stay mad. Mad, you could fight, and right now fight was all he wanted to do.

The silence dragged on; Corporal Dunleavy coughed and glanced at Weiler, who was, after all, the senior non-com. Weiler rubbed his helmet-matted hair, probably trying to figure out what to say to such a dumb-ass question. Surely the new lieutenant had been briefed on the tactical situation before taking over the platoon. If he wanted a readiness report—how was the platoon's morale—he should ask for that. "What's going on" was too vague.

"Well, lieutenant," Weiler said, "Yesterday, the ROK marines were supposed to take Hill 56 in the center of the regimental

133

line. When they couldn't do it, they retreated to Hill 104, which meant our platoon had to reposition here to guard both the ROK's right flank and the remainder of A company's left flank on 105-S."

Weiler sounded accusatory on the ROK setback, as if the new lieutenant were, himself, Korean. More likely Lui was Chinese, based on his light skin and his height, which looked about six feet. Name didn't sound Korean either—Fu Kong Lui.

The new lieutenant gave a laconic nod, cueing Weiler to continue.

"Ah-h-h-hm, as of now, the enemy still holds Hill 56. After four hours of heavy bombardment yesterday, Company B was able to take Hill 105-S. Companies B and C are holding it now. In all, our battalion lost thirty-one wounded yesterday and twelve killed, including our lieutenant."

Hood simmered with frustration over what Weiler wasn't saying—that Battalion had ordered "A" Company, including Lieutenant Morrison's platoon, to stay put on the lower slopes of Hill 105-S while giving "B" Company the green light to race up through them. "B" proceeded to take the hill in under half an hour because the extended bombardment, which should have been ordered in the first place, had turned the tide, leaving the NK defenders too shook to shoot straight.

They should have let us take the damn hill, Hood thought. We were there first and we had something to avenge.

He rolled his shoulders, trying to break the stiffness. Lieutenant Burch of "B" Company was no doubt strutting around up there on the summit while Company "A," who'd left their life blood on 105-S, had to slink back and guard this worthless hill in the rear. We need to be putting gooks on Morrison's tab, Hood thought. Not sitting here.

Goaded by Lui's little unvoiced prompts, Weiler covered how Lieutenant Morrison had been killed taking out a mortar emplacement with Sergeant Hood, how the platoon was short yet another man because Private Mendenhall had been evac'd back to the MASH with a leg wound. How Private Steinberg's ass had been stitched up in battalion aid and the kid allowed to remain with the squad, though disinclined to sit.

When it was clear Weiler had said all he could manage, Lui thanked him and said, "From what I hear, Lieutenant Morrison was a good man—"

"You heard right, sir," Hood said.

The dark-eyed gaze turned to him. "Something else you want to say?"

"No, sir."

"I assume your admiration for Morrison is shared by the rest of the platoon."

Dunleavy and Weiler said that it was.

"I can't replace Lieutenant Morrison," Lui said, "and it would be stupid and wrong for me to try. This will work better if you put the concept of 'replacement' from your minds. The platoon must have a lieutenant, and because Morrison is gone, they've sent me. If anyone's wondering, I joined the marines in 1944, while the war in the Pacific was still on. As the war ended I was a platoon sergeant in the 1st Division's 7th Regiment. We were sent to occupy north China, the country of my parents' birth, from '45 to '47, and I was retained in the reserves when the regiment was deactivated in March of '47. The 7th was reactivated this August at Camp Pendleton, too late to get in on the Inch'on assault. We—they—crossed the Han River yesterday, moving up to support the left flank of the division. Because my company had an extra sergeant, I was given a battlefield promotion to lieutenant in order to take command of your platoon.

"So, on the bad side, this gold bar on my shoulder is brand new. On the good side, I do have experience. Once we break through this last line of hills, Seoul will be a hard nut to crack. All I can do is my best. If you do the same it'll work out. Any questions?"

Hood felt a grudging interest. So Lui was a "mustang," promoted from enlisted to officer—not all that common. It could be good, because he likely understood the role and importance of his sergeants and corporals. If he'd done some real fighting those last few years of the war rather than support or administrative work, that would be good, too. He hadn't been clear on that point—either from modesty or hoping to pass himself off as more than he was. From what Hood had heard of the reactivated 7th regiment, it was mostly green. Whatever he'd done during the war, Lui would have seen no combat in the subsequent occupation of China.

Being a mustang might be bad if he couldn't get past it, still trying to make all the smaller decisions that should be left to his squad leaders. That would undermine respect for the non-coms and for himself, too. Lieutenants were better off not being overly friendly with the men. That didn't mean be a cold fish. Lui had yet to give a hint what he felt about anything.

"If there are no questions," he said, "our mission for now is to stay on Hill 68. We are to go on protecting the two flanks and provide fire support for the 1st Korean Marines, who are going to take another shot at Hill 56. Thank you, you're dismissed—except you, Sergeant Hood."

Hood shrugged at the looks Weiler and Dunleavy shot him as they slipped, crouching, from the bunker. When they were out of earshot, Lui said, "I had an awkward conversation with Lieutenant Burch this morning."

Hood felt his back stiffen. Burch and his damn jeep.

Waiting for Lui to go on, he realized the lieutenant's little silences might be a conscious tactic. Say as little as possible, wait for it to work on your men, goading them to blurt out more than they might otherwise. Damned if he'd play that game. He waited some more and Lui said, "Burch tells me you disobeyed a direct order and stole his jeep yesterday."

"I didn't hear any order from him, sir, and, with respect, I did not steal his jeep, I borrowed it."

"With his permission?"

"We were taking hits all around from 120 mm mortars. The lieutenant had holed up in a shack. Shacks and Jeeps are two of the enemy's favorite mortar targets, and they were ranging in. It was urgent that someone get to battalion as fast as possible to persuade them to lay an artillery barrage on Hill 105-S. I figured if I went inside the shack to ask permission, and the NK mortars found the range, we'd all be blown up, including the Jeep, and no one would get the request for artillery support to battalion. So I hopped in the jeep and took off."

"That's not how he tells it," Lui said.

Hood said nothing, waiting him out again.

"He wants to bring charges against you."

"And what do you want, sir?"

"He can bring charges whether I agree or not."

Hood played Lui's game, bouncing the silence back at him. Better to keep quiet, anyway, with the anger cranking hot in his chest. Still furious over Morrison's death, and now Lieutenant Burch was acting like a prick.

Why?

Clearly it had been right to call in artillery. Burch should be glad—his company was looking good because of it, having taken the hill after the four additional hours of bombardment. But the man was making trouble anyway. Did he think the marines could afford to lose a veteran sergeant over something so petty as a jeep commandeered for a critical mission in the heat of battle? If Lui went along with that, he was selling out his men to curry favor with a guy only one grade above him, which would be bullshit.

"Sergeant Hood, I won't tolerate any insubordination in my platoon. Or any evasion of orders either. Is that clear?"

"Yes, sir."

"You're dismissed."

"Sir, are you going to go along with Burch or not?"

"I haven't decided. I need to see more of you to know whether Burch is right about you."

"If you want to see more, then I have a suggestion, sir."

Wariness flickered across Lui's face, then the deadpan expression returned. "Go on."

"Battalion has given us easy duty for the day. Protecting flanks and providing fire support are mostly jobs for the weapons

137

platoon—our 60 mm mortars and the recoilless rifles. You don't need three rifle squads joining in, popping away at long range with nothing but carbines and M-1s. Might as well shoot 'em with bee-bee guns. Two squads plus the company weapons platoon are plenty for the mission."

"What's your point, sergeant?"

"I'd like to take my squad and reconnoiter around Hill 56."

"Why on earth should I let you do that?"

"Because I'm good at finding back doors. Yesterday, I found a way up Hill 105-S, from the inside."

"From what Sergeant Weiler said, that's how your lieutenant got killed."

Hood fought down a flash of rage. Factually, Lui was right.

"Sir, we're here to fight, and you can't fight worth a damn if you're too afraid of losing men. You know that, if you fought in the Pacific."

Letting it hang there, see if Lui would clear up the ambiguity.

The lieutenant said nothing.

"If the NKs hadn't closed that chimney with a grenade, I could have led our platoon through it and created enough havoc so the company might have taken the hill without the delay of bombardment. I was recon in the last war. Maybe I could find another way up Hill 56, make things easier for those Korean marines over there and our second battalion if they have to join in."

"What makes you think you could find something the ROK didn't?"

"It's worth a try."

"You're snowing me, sergeant. You don't want to find another way up the hill, you want to probe that train tunnel that goes through it."

Hood hesitated, caught out. Impressive—the man had done some homework of his own. "Has anyone tried it, sir?"

"I assume so. And I assume they had to fall back. The NK know this terrain, and they'd surely have men in that tunnel. If I were them, I'd leave the tunnel dark and mount a fifty-caliber machine gun on a low wall of sandbags. Silhouetted against the light, your whole squad could be mowed down in seconds from the far end."

"Not if we crawl in."

"You don't think they have a Klieg light set up in there? They hear you coming, it's lights on for them, then lights out for you."

"We won't know if we don't try, sir."

"And risk losing a squad? I don't think so, sergeant."

Frustrated, Hood made himself wait a beat, choose his words. "Sir, I'm not going to lose my squad. If I were the reckless type, I'd have gotten them all killed yesterday trying to rush that hill after our lieutenant was killed. Instead, I came back to request artillery. If that train tunnel is too well defended, we'll lay off it and tell you, so you can pass it on to regimental HQ. If it can be had, we'll take that tunnel and hold it, and second battalion can send a company through to attack Hill 56 from behind."

"Are you always this gung ho, sergeant?"

"Sir, my men would have cut off a hand for Lieutenant Morrison. His death hit them hard. They are frustrated having to retreat while B Company went up past them. They're good marines and they are as motivated as they have ever been."

"To go kill themselves some gooks?"

"That's right, sir."

Lui's eyes narrowed.

You said it, not me. "Lieutenant, taking the initiative and seizing that tunnel would be a good way to start your career as an officer and put yourself on the fast track."

Lui studied him, his face unreadable. "Permission granted."

Crouched with his squad against the railroad embankment, Hood worried about the fire they'd take going over the top. Getting here had been okay, only a few mortar rounds, until that one machine gun on Hill 56 had spotted them and opened up. The gunner was probably zeroed in, waiting for them to pop their heads up.

So we wait, too. When the ROK charges, he'll have all he can handle.

Any minute now.

Hood took a breath. *Patience.* He was clear of the new lieutenant, now, in the field and too far out to be called back. He'd get his chance for some payback for Morrison.

Why had Lui given him the green light? Career ambition?

Or maybe he's hoping I'll come back in a body bag, Hood thought—that look in his eyes when I said "gook," like I meant him. Come on, lieutenant. You're that hung up on your race, stay out of The Corps. Chinese, Puerto Rican, Negro, Indian, Irishman, we shed those skins when we joined the marines. The Corps is our race, our skin-color is Marine green. Any other way, we're not The Corps, we're a bunch of clans fighting each other instead of the gooks.

A mortar round whistled close.

"Incoming!" Hood flattened himself against the bank. The blast shoved it into him. Dirt peppered his shoulders, and he felt the little mood-lift that always came with a near miss. Jakes, Cockburn and Steinberg squirmed along the bank toward him, spooked, doing the new-guy thing of clumping too close together. They should watch the veterans—Rittenhouse, and the three B's staying spread out, Jimmy anchoring the far end of the line.

Hood motioned Jakes to the other side of him, told Cockburn and Steinberg to spread out.

"Sergeant!" Cockburn yelled, though he was two yards away.

Hood made a show of clearing his ear with a pinkie. "What is it, private?"

"How far's the tunnel from here?"

"A few hundred yards east, other side of this bank."

"East is that way, right?" Cockburn pointed into the embankment.

"You're embarrassing yourself," Steinberg said.

"Shut your pie hole. I'm talking to sarge."

"Vasco de Gama he's not, folks. Just follow me, Bo."

"Fuck you, dickweed."

Hood said, "Okay, Private Cockburn, pay attention; I'm gonna explain it to you. Out yonder the rail line splits," pointing northwest, to his left. "The bank we're hiding behind supports one fork, which keeps on going southeast. What we want is to get across to the other fork. After it splits off toward the east, it tunnels into Hill 56 over where all the firing's coming from. You'll see it soon as we clear this bank. When I give the signal, we go up and over and haul ass to that tunnel."

"So we'll be running that way, right?" Cockburn pointed to where the rail line forked.

Hood resisted an urge to grab him by the nose and shake him. He sighed. "Just follow Steinberg."

Down the line, Barstow was staring into the sheltering bank that supported the tracks as though a movie were being shown there, no expression, his head clearly somewhere else.

Back on that hill cutting throats?

Frustration filled Hood. He'd tried everything he knew to snap the man out of it. How long before Hollywood got himself or someone else killed?

Can't worry about that now.

So far, Barstow had been okay once the shooting started.

"Everyone, listen up," Hood barked. "We're about to move out. Those are rice paddies between us and the tunnel. The farmers leave strips of unplowed ground so they can walk through the paddies on dry land when they seed and fertilize. When I give the order, we'll go up and over, then run through the paddies toward that tunnel. If we take fire, get down in the muck and let the hump of dry ground give you cover. The ROK marines are attacking the hill right now, so with luck the enemy won't notice us."

Hood made sure every eye was on him, seven pale faces drinking in his words, even Hollywood at least faking attention. Easing his head over the bank, he saw that the ROK marines were charging the hill.

"Let's go!"

Scrambling up the bank and across the tracks, Hood slid down the other side on his back, then ran until the grass started to splash under his feet. In the rice paddy now, he veered onto a dike of dry land, sprinting toward the hill. He caught glimpses of the unfolding battle—the Korean marines swarming up the slope on the far side of the train tunnel, distant ant men falling under heavy fire from the summit—and then his eye was wrenched home by little geysers of water stitching across the paddy toward him. *Shit!*

"Get down!"

Diving into the muck beside the dike, he grimaced as the foul-smelling muck soaked his uniform. Shells kicked dirt from the dike just above his shoulder. Checking behind, he saw Cockburn still charging forward like a tackle rushing the quarterback. Before Hood could yell, Steinberg dived and caught Bo's ankle from behind, bringing him down. He rolled against the protective dike, somehow managing to drag Cockburn with him. Bullets kicked up spouts of water where they'd been.

"I saw the tunnel," Cockburn said, his voice croaking with excitement. "It's over there."

Hood fought off an insane urge to laugh. "Stay down," he yelled, "until I say." He saw Rittenhouse and Bertleson behind him, waiting against the same dike, Bertleson chomping his gum. The others had all found cover, as well. The machine gun was no longer firing their way, but Hood made himself wait. The tunnel wasn't going anywhere.

"This smells like shit," Cockburn said. "I ain't never eating rice again."

"You never ate it before," Steinberg said.

"How would you know? My grammaw makes rice pudding all the time, with custard and raisins."

Hood felt a heaviness around his heart. Children, he was taking children into battle.

Like your sergeant took you, when you were their age. They want to be men or they wouldn't be here. Don't let them down.

"Okay, go!"

Clambering onto the dike, Hood ran forward again, sucking air, trying for more speed. He felt a stitch in his side, the place he'd been shot, and then he was out of the paddy onto the skirt of the hill. As it steepened, he veered across the slope to the railroad tunnel, crowned by an arch of mortared stones that stuck out from the hill.

Hood checked the line behind him: Cockburn crowded his shoulder, followed by Steinberg and the rest of them spread out all the way back to Bertleson.

"Freddy, Jimmy—on me."

The two crawled along the hillside to him.

"Yeah, Sarge?" Jimmy said.

"I'm gonna climb down the far side of the arch. Bertleson, you take this side. We'll crawl inside the tunnel, keeping tight against the wall. With daylight behind us, we'll make silhouettes, so stay down on your belly. If the tunnel's lit when we go in, we'll have to shoot out the bulbs, first thing. I'll do my best, but I'll be counting on you to get most of them, Bertleson. If the tunnel is dark, you can bet they've got a klieg light ready and waiting at their end. Be ready to shoot it out the second they turn it on, before they can shoot us."

"Piece of cake," Bertleson said with a grin. He liked any plan with shooting in it. The rest clearly hadn't sunk in yet.

"We'll be crawling in the dark," Hood said, "so keep a hand out front to feel for mines."

Bertleson frowned. "Wait a cotton-pickin' minute. We're gonna go *through* the tunnel?"

"How else can we get to the other end? Come on, man, this is your chance. There aren't ten guys in the whole division that could shoot out the lights. It'll make you king of the snipers."

Bertleson opened his mouth then shut it, his eyes going distant with reflection.

Hood turned to Jimmy. "Corporal, as soon as you hear firing, lead the rest of the squad in. Concentrate your fire down the center of the tunnel so you'll miss Bertleson and me at the sides."

Jimmy nodded.

Working himself over the stone arch, Hood dropped to the far side of the tracks and flattened himself on the gravel just outside the tunnel mouth. When Bertleson had done the same on his side, Hood gave him the nod and crawled inside.

Into total darkness.

Eyes straining, he stared at the distant half-circle of light. He could see no one at the other end, but that meant nothing. If they were smart, they were doing what the new lieutenant had said, lying behind a low wall of sandbags, a machine gun crew for sure and a couple of snipers, far enough in to be cloaked in darkness—

What's that?

Hood stared, eyes watering, at a dark circle jutting from the curve of one wall. A vertical line shimmered below the circle, firming up as his eyes adjusted to the dark. A pole mount. His skin rippled cold; there was your Klieg, yeah, waiting to bathe the tunnel in light. He listened for a generator, could hear nothing over the din of gunfire and artillery behind him.

Try taking the light out now?

No. Bertleson might could hit it from here, but what if it wasn't a Klieg, just a stop signal or other piece of railroad equipment? They'd have given themselves away for nothing.

Hood slithered the rest of the way into the tunnel, the gravel stinging his knees and elbows. He glimpsed Bertleson on the other side, the dark swallowing the man like a hungry snake, his legs disappearing, then his feet. Inching ahead, Hood kept a hand out front, feeling for trip wires and patting the dirt and gravel. The din of battle receded behind him, and he could hear Bertleson now, gravel crunching across the tracks as he inched forward.

Cold stung Hood's back—a drip of condensation from the ceiling. His hand, groping ahead, touched something—

Tripwire!

Sweat turned clammy on Hood's face. He probed with his fingers: the wire was tight, ankle height, had to be a booby trap. Following the wire to his left, he found the spike that secured it.

The other end would be looped through the pin of a grenade mounted on its own spike. The wire was too thick to cut with a bayonet, and sawing on it would take up enough slack to pull the pin. If he tried to go over the tripwire, his silhouette would make him a sitting duck.

Gripping the anchoring spike, Hood tried to uproot it.

It held firm.

Both hands, now, forcing the spike a millimeter sideways toward the grenade as he lifted. Grinding his teeth, he felt the spike give slightly, a fraction more of tilt, then it moved upward, careful, careful.

It popped free.

Hood took all tension off the wire, depositing the spike beside its mate with the grenade.

He lay, his cheek on the gravel, feeling his heart pound.

A crunch to his right sent a shock through him—Bertleson, still crawling forward.

"Jack," he hissed. "Stop! There's a booby trap."

Blinding light poured from the far end of the tunnel. A machine gun started thumping; in the next instant, Bertleson's M-1 banged and the klieg light flashed and sank into darkness, fizzing and spitting.

"Good shot!" Hood cried. "Stay where you are—there's a booby trap."

"I saw it."

The machine gun continued to fire, shells sparking off the rails. A sudden, hot fury pumped through Hood. Unslinging his M-1, he fired, elbows down, at the muzzle flashes, hearing Bertleson pumping off rounds from the other side of the tracks. More guns joined in from behind, the squad inside now, laying down their own fire.

The machine gun fell silent and Hood jumped up and ran toward it.

The tunnel mouth swarmed with silhouettes, shadow men scrambling to man the machine gun again, toppling as Bertleson picked them off.

Close enough for a grenade, Hood put his arm into it—too much. Sailing past the machine gun out the mouth of the tunnel, the grenade exploded in a ball of flame.

Men passed Hood from behind, Steinberg and Bo, heaving more grenades. An explosion lit the sandbag barrier; Hood's helmet rattled with grit, his face stinging like a pin cushion. Vaulting the bags, he ran from the tunnel and stopped short as he saw NK reinforcements rushing up the tracks toward him, a platoon or more. He fired his M-1 at them, and then guns popped all around him as his squad joined in. Two of the NK fell in a tangle; the others broke and ran as if a whole company was coming at them from the dark of the tunnel.

There should be, Hood thought, anger pumping through him. Why didn't the brass think of this? He kept on firing and one of the fleeing NK went down before the rest ran out of sight behind a finger ridge.

"Cease fire!" Jimmy yelled.

Hood counted heads, his heart sinking. Where was Rittenhouse? And Jakes? He heard cursing from the tunnel behind him—Rittenhouse swearing a blue streak.

"Are you hit?" Hood shouted.

"My arm. And Jakes is down."

Jimmy started back into the tunnel.

Hood grabbed his arm, thinking of the NK that had run away, now maybe sucking up nerve for a counterattack.

"How bad is Jakes?" Hood yelled.

"I'm getting my flashlight," Rittenhouse called back. "Not much blood, and his pulse is strong. I think he's just knocked out."

"What about you? Can you walk?"

"Hell, yes—nothing wrong with my legs. My arm hurts like a son of a bitch, but I don't think they got an artery. Should I stay with Jakes or get on up there?"

"We'll take care of Jakes. You high-tail it back to our lines. Tell the first officer you see that we've taken the tunnel and we need more marines in here as fast as they can."

Hood heard him clatter off.

"I'll check on Jakes," Jimmy said.

"Make it fast. They come at us again, we'll need all the fire-power we have left." Hood led the remaining five back into the tunnel mouth, setting up behind the sandbags. The machine gun looked to be in working order despite being knocked over by the explosion. Hood set it up in the center, aiming at the finger ridge that petered out near the tracks. That's where the NK had run, and that's where they'd reappear if they come back.

"Steinberg."

"Yes, sergeant?"

"You know how to feed shells to one of these things?"

"No, but how hard could it be?"

I like this kid.

Steinberg hefted the belt of shells and glared out the mouth of the tunnel, looking every inch a hardened veteran. Jimmy returned, reporting that Jakes was conscious now, but groggy. "I think a piece of masonry fell out of the ceiling and clipped his helmet. I told him to stay put. If we have to retreat, we'll pick him up on our way."

A tight band loosened on Hood's chest. No dead, and only two wounded.

Jimmy gave him a savage grin. "We killed us some gooks, sarge."

"We did."

"Maybe we even got the one who killed Lieutenant Morrison."

"Maybe."

"And we're gonna deliver Hill 56 to the United States Marines."

Hood nodded, putting some energy into it to hide the sense of futility settling over him. No use bringing Jimmy down, too. If they could hold the tunnel, the hill would fall as Marines charged up the reverse slope and caught the enemy from behind.

Morrison would have been proud if he had lived to see it.

But he hadn't.

He was gone from this world and killing a hundred gooks, a thousand, wouldn't bring him back.

On September 23, North Korean forces continued to hold General Oliver Smith's marines back on the western approaches to Seoul. General Almond met with General David Barr, who commanded the 7th Infantry Division, and ordered him to prepare to move from defensive positions south of Seoul to attack across the Han River into the Southeast portion of the city. X Corps' 1st Marine Division would carry the GIs across the broad river by means of its 1st Amphibious Tractor Battalion and its 56th Amphibious Tank and Tractor Battalion. The 7th Division's 32nd regiment, commanded by Lt. Colonel Faith, would lead the Army advance. While these plans were being laid, the 5th Marines continued to take casualties. The more severely wounded were rushed to the 1st MASH. How many men would leave without an arm or leg was up to doctors who had to decide whether or not to follow regulations—a decision less simple than it might seem.   (Ibid.)

10

1st MASH, 1610 hours:

From the door of the children's ward, Bonnie watched the performance with a critical eye. At a distance the puppets didn't look bad, considering they'd started life as old socks donated by the doctors. Talk about crawling from the primordial ooze. She and Laura Lidner had sewn on buttons for eyes and stitched in cardboard mouths and, presto—Kukla and Ollie. Sally Reynolds rotated with Laura and her, two at a time, to work the puppets. They'd collaborated on the script—lots of slapstick accompanied by bleats and other wordless cries, because most of the kids didn't know English. In the show going on now, Sally's right hand was Kukla while Laura's was Ollie, A.K.A. Oliver J. Dragon, but looking more like a rooster with the rubber glove stitched to his cranium flopping back and forth.

Bonnie watched with nervous interest as Kukla hit Ollie over the head with a straw. The kids—victims of the real-life violence of war—were laughing their heads off, just as Laura had predicted. Bonnie could see none of the fear or revulsion she had feared. Some of the kids caught in the long bombardment had faces so stiffened with burns they couldn't laugh or even grin. They were clapping as hard as anyone.

What would happen to them when the MASH moved on?

"M" did stand for "Mobile," which meant keeping as close as possible to the front. Right now that was the last hills before Seoul, where the prelude to the battle for the city raged hour after hour. Box ambulances rushed wounded marines in from the battalion aid stations. Today they'd lost four men in surgery, two of whom might have been saved if the MASH had been closer to the front. They'd have to head forward soon, but leaving here would be tough. The school building had provided plenty of room and a familiar place for Inch'on's kids. Who would take in the children orphaned by the same artillery shells that had burned them?

The MASH near the front lines would be a tent compound with far less roofed-over space, all of it taken by medical staff and wounded soldiers. Even if there were room for the children, it would be wrong to endanger them by hauling them closer to the front.

A little boy on the front row caught Bonnie's eye, his hair burned off, his face a slick red weal, one eye closed by the scarring, but there he was, clapping with the others, and then Bonnie was in the hall, her back to the wall, tears coursing down her cheeks. She tried to stop but couldn't—just bawling her eyes out, yeah.

Sheesh—embarrassing.

Lucky for her the hall near her was empty, no one close enough to see. After a moment she got hold of herself. Whipping her hanky out of her medical coat, she wiped her face and pulled some deep breaths. At the drinking fountain she splashed cold water on her eyelids to chase the redness.

All right, worry about the kids later. She had just time for rounds in post op before she'd need to check back with surgery—

"Lieutenant Brisbane."

Major Folsom, bearing down with that forward-leaning stride, wearing the hard look that didn't go away even when she slept, according to Laura Lidner, who swore she had verified it by flashlight.

"Yes, major?"

"My office."

Bonnie's heart sank. Steeling herself, she headed down the hall, conscious of the major's boots clumping on the tile behind her. This could only be about one thing, and she wasn't ready.

Folsom's office had probably once belonged to a teacher—a cubbyhole barely bigger than a closet in which Folsom kept her administrative papers in a banged-up file. The desk was old and chipped, taking up most of the space, leaving room only for a folding camp chair in front. A lone, fly-specked bulb lit the room in a stingy half-light. Folsom motioned her to the camp chair and sat in the wooden swivel chair behind the desk.

"That enemy soldier you and Sally assisted on four days ago."

"Which one?"

"Don't act dumb, Brisbane, you're terrible at it."

"What's the problem—is he crashing?"

Folsom stared at her. "On the contrary, he's doing well—too well. I saw the wound when they brought him in. That artery was shredded, a clear case for amputation. And yet the arm is still intact and healing well."

"You say that as if it's a bad thing."

"An arm that should have been amputated, instead showing good circulation, a strong pulse—explain that to me, Lieutenant Brisbane."

Bonnie hesitated. Jeff's career and hers might be on the line, and her two choices were truth or stonewall. "Major, there have been so many surgeries I'm not sure I can recall the details of that one."

With a cold, knowing smile, Folsom settled back in her chair.

"Uh, maybe there was enough collateral circulation in the undamaged blood vessels to save the arm."

"Lieutenant, I was in charge of triage that night—you do recall that, don't you?"

"If you say so."

"I do say so, and I'm also here to tell you that I tried repeatedly to find a pulse in the North Korean's arm and could not. The chances for any collateral circulation to develop in time to save the arm were poor to none. Now, either that artery healed itself, which is impossible, or Dr. Wittschiebe performed an arterial repair, which I feel certain you would remember, since Army regulations forbid it."

"I'm sorry, ma'am, but I've scrubbed in on more surgeries in the past week than you'd see in a month in most major hospitals. You get done with one and they slide the next one onto the table, and after awhile everything blurs together. You say arterial repair is against regulations and I guess I've probably heard that at one time or another, but not enough to make it stand out in my mind, so there's really nothing to make me recall the case."

"You're lying."

Bonnie felt herself flushing. *Right. I would lie any time to save a man's arm, and you're who we have to get past, and this is the one lie that might do it. If I try to persuade you that Jeff didn't stitch a shredded artery back together, you'll shoot that down for sure.* "I don't appreciate having my integrity questioned, major."

Folsom's eyes narrowed. "Is that your answer, to talk back to your superior officer?"

Bonnie knew she'd better rein herself in, try to be conciliatory, but that crack about lying—it might be true but it was also *wrong*.

"Lieutenant Brisbane, did you or did you not assist Dr. Wittschiebe in performing an arterial repair?"

"I'm telling you I don't remember, major."

And why, Bonnie thought, do you even care?

Is it because we tried to save an arm, or that it was the arm of an enemy soldier? Feeling the question shoot to her mouth, she stifled it. She *was* back-sassing Folsom, she always seemed to when people pushed her, but she must stay focused on the goal now, which was to *soothe* the woman. "Major, I'm sure you'd agree that our role as nurses is to assist in surgery, not lead out. Why not let the doctors worry about this issue and how best to work with the regulations?"

Folsom stiffened. "We may be nurses, Brisbane, but we are not second class citizens who go around meekly doing whatever doctors tell us to do."

"I agree. A major is a major, whether a man or a woman—"

"And rules are rules," Folsom cut in. "Military discipline is essential in creating and maintaining a fighting force that can go out and defeat the enemy."

"But don't you think those same rules might in some cases conflict with the purpose of medical care, which is almost the opposite of military goals? As MASH nurses and doctors we're not here to attack and defeat but to repair and heal."

"Nurse Brisbane, the Hippocratic Oath includes the caution to do no harm. These men are not guinea pigs, and that fact is particularly problematic in the case of enemy wounded, as you would realize if you thought about it. What do you imagine the Reds would do if they learned we were 'experimenting' on their soldiers? They'd use it for propaganda you can be sure. They'd paint us as no better than the Nazis."

Bonnie stared at her, astonished. "How could anyone twist trying to save a man's arm into a Nazi experiment?"

"The communists are masters at twisting. All they'd need do is accuse U.S. Army doctors of experimenting on their wounded, and instead of denying it outright, we'd be in the position of having to explain, and at that point you've already lost the propaganda war. . ."

Folsom drew a deep breath, collecting herself. "But I didn't call you in here to debate this with you, lieutenant. Army regs forbid arterial repair. If you had forgotten that, or knew but thought it wasn't important, you will have no such excuse in the future. I see no conflict between army rules and our duty as medical professionals, and the fact is, you are in the army now, and in the army, we follow orders."

Bonnie had a sudden sense of the brittle walls Janey Folsom had set up around herself—regulations, rules, following orders no matter what. Her attitude toward the nurses was strictly as superior officer, never as confidante or friend, even though most of her staff had made at least one overture to her.

How lonely she must be.

Bonnie's heart softened. "Major, I respect your rank, and I know commanding the nurses under such extreme conditions isn't easy—"

"Extreme?" Folsom snorted. "You haven't seen anything yet. This is a walk in the park compared to what I put up with in the last war. In a month, you'll be longing for this nice, warm schoolhouse. Our boys are fighting their way into Seoul, a city teeming with millions of civilians and up to 70,000 North Korean troops. The army and marines will be in the fight of their lives. Everything up to this point has been a warm-up. If the perimeter defense of the communists is any indication, once we enter the city, wounded will flood us around the clock, with no forty-five minute breaks and no time for fancy surgery. If, when that is all over, God willing, our boys take the city, the North Koreans will have only one direction to run—north. The army and marines will follow, and we'll be right behind them. Do you know what's waiting up north, Nurse Brisbane? Mountains. The Taebek range, towering peaks, more than a mile high. We're less than eight weeks from cold weather—winters here are hard and long, especially in the mountains. So don't talk to me about extreme conditions until you've experienced them."

"I'm from Michigan, major. The winters are harsh there, too, strong winds, drifting snow, sometimes three or four feet of it. We go out and play in it."

Folsom shook her head; something in her expression sent a qualm through Bonnie. "Major, I know duty is important, and I respect you for your devotion to it. But there's more for us here than duty. Your nurses would like a warmer relationship with you. You can be in command of us, and also confide in us, let us in a little bit, and we can help each other that way."

For just a moment, Bonnie thought she saw hints of a thaw, and then the major said, "Lieutenant, there is nothing I wish to 'confide,' as you put it. You are only trying to soften me up because you are in a jam."

I'm not in a jam, Bonnie thought, unless you put me there, and why would you? You've accused me of trying to send a man back home with his arm. You've called me a liar, which is attacking my character, but what kind of character would I have if I wouldn't risk punishment to heal a patient?

Folsom stood. "Lieutenant, regulations aren't just silly rules, they're there for a reason. It's my responsibility as a senior officer to enforce them. If I see further evidence that you or any other nurse is assisting in arterial repairs, I will report you and the doctors involved to Colonel Martin for disciplinary action. Have I made myself clear?"

"Yes, ma'am." Bonnie wanted to protest, to argue more, but that would only make Folsom more adamant—and more watchful in the future. "You are dismissed," Folsom said.

Heading for surgery, Bonnie felt like yelling with frustration. The graft on that NK had gone well; Jeff had proven he could manage the procedure, and he would only get better with practice. They'd done two more arterial repairs already today, given two American soldiers a chance to hold their children in their arms when they went home from this war, but now she would have to warn Jeff to stop. If Folsom made this stick, she ought to be forced to look every day at the stumped shoulders of Marines and G.I.s she had stopped the surgical team from helping. . . .

Against her will, Bonnie imagined what Folsom would say back: If you keep experimenting, Nurse Brisbane, and Dr. Wittschiebe gets even one arm or leg wrong, and the patient develops gas gangrene because of the delay, and dies. . . .

24 September, Hill 290, 0430 hours:
The chill forced Sam awake, his mind echoing with some argument he'd been having in his sleep. An ache in his jaw told him he'd been grinding his teeth. He climbed out of the foxhole, pulled on his fatigue jacket and checked on Yongdung-po, a dull

red smear spread along the black horizon. Marine artillery had pounded the town so hard that, forty-eight hours later, the night sky still glowed from fires smoldering in the debris. The Marine 1st Regiment had taken the town and was poised to cross the Han River and attack Seoul from the south while Hood's 5th regiment struggled forward from the west.

Army seemed to be holding up its end. The 7th Infantry's 31st regiment had come ashore and captured Suwon. As for his own 32nd regiment, not only had his battalion turned the enemy around on the road, it had pushed on north to take this strategic hill, with its panoramic view for miles around.

Now if he could just put some emotional mileage between himself and the photo.

Sam stared at the horizon, the red glow advertising hundreds of new widows and orphans like the two in the photo. You could know it and still sleep—as long as you didn't see their faces. He should not have taken the photo from the man he'd killed. It had cursed him, sending the man's child to accuse him in the dream, you killed my daddy, I loved him, my mommy and I cry all the time. . . .

Sam's head jerked in an involuntary effort to shake off the image. Ridiculous. If that NK had killed me, would he be losing sleep? Pictures of my own, that's what I need—a photo of Cousin Annie and her kids. If the other guy shoots first, let him think Annie's my wife and the kids are mine, let him agonize over someone missing me.

Sam forced his gaze past the smoldering aura of Yongdung-po to the white glow of Seoul at night. He'd be leading his platoon against the capital city soon. Tall buildings, thousands of windows, snipers back in the dark, and he and his men exposed in the streets—

"Up bright and early I see."

Sam turned and acknowledged the captain with a salute. Pretty early for Loomis—usually, he stayed in his bunker until first light. He looked like he'd just been rousted from the sack, his helmet forgotten, the flattop bristling in odd directions atop the square head. He took a hand off the dispatch bag he held and returned the salute. A combination padlock secured the bag's thick flap.

"Feel like taking a ride, lieutenant?"

"Sure."

"This needs to go to Major Goss, G-2 of the marine 5th."

Sam's enthusiasm evaporated. The 5th regiment—Harlan Hood's. "What is it?"

"Spook stuff. Too sensitive for a normal courier. The 7th has gotten new orders from General Barr and we have to coordinate our intelligence estimates with the Marines. Anson wants it transferred by an officer."

"How about Lamberton?"

Loomis leaned closer, as if to read his expression in the moonlight. "What's the deal, Foxworth? A second ago, you were hot to trot. Hartung's back and fit for duty. He can take care of the platoon while you're away. Take you only a couple hours to get there, deliver, and hustle back. Major Anson specifically asked for you. Said he'd given you a heads up."

He started to deny it, then realized Anson might believe he'd agreed in principle to a mission like this. *He asked if I'd be interested in intelligence work, and I didn't exactly say no. So now he's giving me a little job to see if I'm discreet and dependable.*

Sam felt his pulse picking up. Forget Harlan Hood. The chances of running into him were slim. With a regiment of 2500 men spread over dozens of hills, he ought to be able to avoid the man. And this was an opportunity.

The relief he felt at the prospect of ditching his platoon made him feel a little shabby, but mightn't it be better for all concerned, given his ambivalence about command?

Sam took the bag.

Loomis said, "Use Cinquemani to drive you. You are to give this to Major Goss and to Major Goss only. If someone else promises to deliver it, you don't take them up on it, you just hang onto it until you get to Goss, understood?"

Sam nodded.

"Try and make it back no later than 1000 hours."

"Yes, sir."

Bouncing up and down beside Cinquemani, Sam tried to read the map with his flashlight. The road was full of potholes, the jeep's shock absorbers long gone, and Cinq was making no concessions in speed. Giving up, Sam put the map away. He saw that they were approaching the eastern outskirts of Yongdung-po, near the town's airstrip. To the west, pocked buildings alternated with smoking rubble. Three other roads angled in to join the one they were on; at the intersection ahead, the marines had set up a barrier and checkpoint.

A sergeant waved them down and made a production of looking at his shoulder patch. "You lost?"

Sam felt his temper slipping. "You'll salute me, sergeant, and you'll call me sir."

The man waited a beat, then flicked a hand to his brow. "Yes, sir. Beg your pardon, sir. I guess I just didn't expect any Army coming up this road after the way y'all disappeared on us the past three days."

Shit! Sam thought.

"Correct me if I'm wrong, sir, but wasn't your regiment supposed to cover our flank while we attacked Yongdung-po? We took fire from the south the whole time we were trying to take the town. Two of my buddies are lying in the MASH because Army bugged out. All due respect, sir, a lot of us marines are wondering if y'all got lost or if you just prefer not to get too close to the enemy."

Cinq started to lunge from behind the wheel. Sam grabbed his arm, holding him in place. Three days ago he'd gone crosswise with Anson over his fear of this very thing. The man had a right to be pissed.

"Sergeant, I don't have time for this. I've got important documents to deliver to Major Goss."

"You can leave them here. Sir."

"No, I cannot. Now I suggest you stop holding us up."

"Yeah?"

Sam kept hold of Cinq's arm. "How do we get to the 5th?"

The sergeant sighed like he'd just been asked which way was up. "Follow this road until it curves back west. There'll be a big rise there, Hill 131. Get out there and hoof around that hill and you'll find the ferry crossing. The next amtrac will take you across. It's a short walk. Sir."

"Thank you, sergeant." Sam let go of Cinq's arm; the corporal gave the marine sergeant a smile that resembled a junkyard dog baring its teeth.

As he drove on, Sam rubbed his forehead, frustrated and depressed. *We did it again. My old man took a bullet because Army screwed up—that he deserves to suffer doesn't excuse our failure. Army let the Marines down, and now we've damn well done it again.*

"This might be it, sir," Cinq said.

The road took a wide curve ahead, the headlights picking out the hill the sergeant had described. Cinq drove the Jeep off the shoulder, stopping under some trees at the base of the hill. Shutting off the engine and lights, he started to get out. "Better wait here, corporal. In their present mood, we don't want to tempt the jarheads with an empty Army jeep."

"You got a point, sir."

"I'll be back as soon as I can."

Sam slipped his M-1 strap and the document bag over his shoulder. Skirting the hill to the east, he followed the sound of rushing water to the river bank. An amphibious tractor idled at what must be the crossing point. As he approached, a sentry, barely more than a kid, climbed down off the Amtrac's cab and shined a light in his face.

Sam told him why he was there.

"I can't take you across, sir. We have strict orders on that—no single passengers except high command or accompanying a load of supplies."

"Private, I've got some critically important intel dispatches here."

"Another load of ammo is due any time now. Best I can do, sir."

Not giving him attitude but not being helpful, either. Sam turned away to keep himself from yelling at the man. Pacing the riverbank, he cursed Korea under his breath. Bonnie had said something about them making history here. If he survived, what he'd take home would not be history but a yellow coating of road dust in his mouth and stomach; the garlic and cabbage stench of the kimchee Koreans seemed to cook constantly in their huts; the everlasting stink of rice paddies fertilized with human shit. The daily pressures of trying to move his platoon to the next objective without getting any of their heads shot off; the weird, knobby hills poking up everywhere; the tedium of having to dig foxholes over and over whenever they moved on.

Hartung, Kim, or Hood, experiencing many of the same things, would weight them differently. Those who made it out of this war would carry their own unique stories, like the proverbial blind men who had felt different parts of an elephant. History books would focus on the big picture, the general impression, an averaging of truth that could never be as accurate as the millions of smaller realities that would remain untold. As the survivors grew old and died, the memories would wink out, one by one, until no one was left who knew what it had been like on the ground.

Personally, he couldn't wait to start forgetting his part in it.

Even Bonnie?

Wheeling around, Sam paced back toward the amtrac. Yeah, tall, blond Bonnie, refusing to make out with him, instead giving him the third degree on his history with women. So what if he'd had a lot of them? Just because he hadn't found the right one didn't mean he couldn't settle down someday, make a commitment. He could do that when the time was right. Until then, better to get out before you hurt or get hurt.

Ah, but that kiss, the smoky taste of scotch on her lips—

"Yo, lieutenant!" The amtrac sentry, signaling him.

The load had arrived, did he still want the ride?

By the time they'd crossed the river, dawn had broken; it took Sam another half hour to find the regimental command post, a spacious log bunker, complete with file cabinets and an eight foot ceiling, set into the reverse slope of a hill.

Major Goss wasn't there.

Seemed a squad of marines had routed a couple of platoons of NK holding a railway tunnel and the major had gone down to gather some first-hand intelligence about the other side of the hill.

Following instructions to cross the railroad tracks and then some rice paddies to get to the tunnel, Sam studied the terrain with an eye to the future moves of his platoon. The hills were enormous, covered with scrub, still smoking in places from what must have been an intense bombardment. As he had the thought, artillery started up so close the ground shook. Shells screamed overhead and slammed into hills to the east, now crowned in daylight. He prayed the shells would kill a lot of enemy, because climbing those steep slopes into machine gun fire was not the best way to bring his men through the war alive.

At the mouth of the tunnel, a marine sentry barely old enough to shave stopped him. "What's Army doing here, sir?"

He seemed merely curious, eyes ringed in dirt making him look like a raccoon.

"I have documents for Major Goss. What unit are you?"

"'F' Company, sir. Second Battalion."

Sam relaxed a little. Harlan Hood was "A" Company, 1st Battalion.

"'D' Company's around here, too," the sentry went on, "and there's still a squad from "A" Company, 1st Battalion. They're who took the tunnel."

Sam groaned inwardly. Should have known—hell, deep inside he *had* known. A single squad of marines routing an NK company, that was Harlan Hood.

"Something funny, sir?"

"Where is Major Goss."

The sentry shrugged. "Through there, sir."

161

Sam stepped past him into the tunnel. Enough daylight spilled in so he could see the rails. At the other end a knot of silhouettes milled around. What if one of them was Hood? Sam felt his stomach shrink. Just say he had to find Goss and get back to his platoon. Hood would be as happy to see him go as he was to clear out. No problem.

Inside the tunnel, the clamor of the big guns dwindled and the temperature dropped. By the time he stepped from the other end, he felt a damp chill against his skin. A marine manned a tripod-mounted machine gun pointing up the tracks toward enemy territory. His tense attention to the field of fire stirred the hairs on Sam's neck. This place was still hot, a combat zone.

A worried-looking corporal came up and saluted, a man of around twenty-five, no hair on the sides of his head under the helmet. "Help you, sir?" Looking at him like he was a gorilla escaped from a zoo.

"I've got some papers for Major Goss."

"And you would be. . . ?"

"Lieutenant Sam Foxworth, Corporal. . . ?"

"Bouden." The man's eyes widened. "You're sarge's son." He did not smile. It sounded almost like an accusation.

"Can you take me to Major Goss?"

Bouden stared at him a bit longer, then turned without a word. Sam realized he was supposed to follow. Irritated, he tried to catch up but Bouden seemed determined to stay ahead of him, almost running. What was wrong with the man? For him to know who I am, Sam thought, he must know Hood pretty well. Not one of his fans, apparently.

Down the tracks nearly fifty yards, Bouden stopped abruptly and turned. "Sir, best you wait here. Major Goss wanted a look at that hill, and your father had already been up there earlier, so Goss took him as a guide. Enemy's up there, for sure. Could be dangerous."

Sam felt himself bristling. "And you think I'm not up to it?"

"I just don't want to get sarge's son killed, sir."

"You sure about that, corporal?"

Bouden returned his stare, and Sam wondered what was going on inside his shaved skull. "You kind of look like him," Bouden said. "Your chin. And you've got the same eyebrows."

"So I'm told."

"I guess your Ma must be tall, huh?"

A sense of unreality swept Sam, like he was mired in a dream. What should he do? Okay, Major Goss was a cowboy who wanted to go out and smell the blood. So he should just retrace his steps, wait at the command post for Goss to return.

Except that might take all day and Loomis wanted him back inside the hour.

And this corporal was telling him he wasn't up to doing what Hood had done.

Sam's palms throbbed, a pulse of pure, animal fear. He studied the finger ridge that rose from the tracks, a wooded slope that disappeared half-way up in a pall of smoke from the bombardment.

This was insane. Go back to the command post; wait for Goss there.

Instead, he said, "Let's go, corporal."

"Yes, sir," Bouden said, as in "it's your funeral." Turning, he sprinted up the hill.

Sam pounded after him, the butt of the M-1 strapped to his shoulder kicking his rump with each step. The slope steepened, slowing him as he hunched into the hill, looking for places to plant his boots. He unslung the rifle, trudging uphill, now, through thickening trees. Bouden stayed on his shoulder as they climbed higher into the smoke, and then Sam realized it wasn't just smoke but a heavy fog, tainted with the smell of burning. The scrubby pines looked silver in the mist, swimming to them from a few feet in front. The bombardment continued to hammer away higher up the ridge, covering any lesser noise from above. If other men were on the move up there, no way could they hope to hear it.

And then the bombardment stopped.

Bouden went still and Sam halted too and listened. All he could pick up was a faint dripping sound, the mist condensing on the pines and pattering into the carpet of needles. The fog brightened into a dazzling mist under the invisible morning sun. Sam heard the soft crunch of footsteps, the clink of metal. He pointed that way and cupped his ear at Bouden, who nodded. They started up again, creeping now, no way to know how far ahead the others were, fifty yards or ten feet—not to mention whether they were "F" or "D" Company, or a North Korean patrol.

Sam fought an urge to call out for Major Goss. If those were NK above, they'd shoot down, and if they were marines, he might be alerting NK further up.

Bouden drifted a few feet from him, a gray ghost with a rifle. The corporal had fixed his bayonet; Sam eased his own blade from its scabbard, trying to make no noise as he attached it to the muzzle. By the time he finished, Bouden had vanished ahead of him.

Fear drove Sam ahead; a dark shape loomed in his path, and he had to pull the bayonet back to keep from stabbing Bouden in the ass. The corporal waved him forward and another shadow emerged from the mist, a marine with his finger to his lips. The ground leveled into a ridge line. Sam followed Bouden and the other marine past a smoking hut, set ablaze by the bombardment. The marine in the lead hunkered down, and Bouden with him, so Sam sank to his haunches.

He became aware of the cool mist pressing his face—a breeze blowing down the slope. If it stiffened, it would blow away the fog and they'd be exposed. Gray shapes emerged further out in front, a platoon of men rippling in the fog, and Sam advanced again with Bouden and the other marine.

All at once, the fog cleared, and there was Hood, no more than twenty yards ahead. To his right, a dark crease shimmered into focus—a trench, and Sam felt a shock as he realized it was full of enemy soldiers, Korean faces, gaping in surprise. Jerking his M-1 up in shock, Sam emptied his magazine, seeing men fall, then sprinting uphill to Hood, who stood with calm poise, his feet apart, firing into the trench, shooting North Koreans dead at point blank range in front of him. Two NK riflemen down the trench drew a bead on Hood. Frantic, Sam jammed another magazine in; before he could fire, Bouden opened up beside him, cutting down the two NK.

Marines were spinning and falling along the trench line. One of those still on his feet threw a grenade into the trench just as dark orbs arced up in return from the NK position.

"Get down," Bouden yelled.

Sam dived into the pine needles, feeling a thump of compressed air across his back. Ears ringing, he jumped up, saw Hood still standing there, firing into the trench. Dashing to him, he grabbed him and pulled him down, helmet to helmet, as a grenade sailed overhead and went off beyond in a grove of trees.

Hood stared at him, nose to nose. His eyes widened. "Sam?"

"I'm looking for Major Goss."

"He went back down." Hood said.

A laugh tore from Sam's throat.

Corporal Bouden rolled into him, sat up, and fired his M-1. Another NK sprawled back. Hood whooped and rolled onto his stomach, squeezing off rounds as more North Koreans scrambled from the trench and charged with bayonets. The white lid of fog lifted on the slope below them—the way out, except that, somehow, more NK had circled in behind them and were swarming up the hill.

Sam felt the mist on his face, tasted the crisp, smoky air. Life swelled inside him, everything clear and vivid—

And about to end.

He would go out on this cosmic joke, this God-sized, ironic gag: *My old man. Couldn't live with him, but I'm gonna die with him.*

In the meeting on September 24 in which X Corps C.O. General Almond gave his revised orders to Generals Barr and Smith (commanders of the army and marine divisions, respectively) a clash of egos took place. General Smith confronted General Almond about giving orders directly to his regimental commanders. Almond denied he had done so, but Smith backed his charge up and Almond then took the position that it was all just a big misunderstanding. Oliver Smith, chafing under the command of an Army general he felt had insulted his marines by implying they weren't fighting hard enough, had to swallow his resentment. Meanwhile, Smith's 5th regiment was still engaged in battle on the final hills before Seoul. The day would be decided when thirty-three Americans—all that remained on their feet of "D" Company, 5th Marines—charged up Hill 105 North against what had started out as three battalions of tough North Korean troops. . . .   (Ibid.)

11

Lying on his belly in the wet grass, Hood emptied his M-1 at the charging North Koreans. Knowing Sam was beside him filled him with fear and frustration. Damn kid, what was he doing mixing into a Marine battle when he could be safe on some cushy Army hill behind the lines?

A North Korean charged at him, thrusting his bayonet. Hood fired, then cursed as his M-1 spanged on empty. Flushing cold, he fumbled for the .45 at his belt, and then Sam fired and the enemy pitched back, one leg kicking high.

Shoving another magazine home, Hood trained his rifle on the trench line. "Good shooting."

Sam didn't answer, staring with wide eyes at the gook he'd just killed.

I've got to get him out of here, Hood thought. He's half in shock.

Somewhere in the fog, a man groaned, no telling if it was a marine or an NK. Jimmy yelled a warning and Hood saw a couple dozen NK downhill from them, where "F" Company was supposed to be, moving up beneath the glowing bank of mist.

"Gotta take the trench," Hood yelled. "Now!"

Worming for it on his belly, he kept slipping on the fog-soaked grass. He scrambled up on all fours to launch himself the last few feet. As he fell into the trench, his helmet spun from a shell impact. Springing up, he found himself three feet from a North Korean trying to start a belt of cartridges into a .30 caliber machine gun, fumbling at the breech—almost had it—the gook tossing him a bizarre smile. Hood shot him with the .45. Blood sprayed from between the NK's eyes as he pitched back, revealing the gunner on the other side of the mount. Metal blurred toward him at knee level. Dodging the thrusting bayonet, he felt it take a slice out of his side, no pain, his vision turning red with fury as he pressed the .45 into the gunner's forehead, inches from his own, feeling the gun buck, hearing nothing as the enemy's blood spattered his chin. He grabbed the belt the first man had dropped and snapped it into the breech. As he turned the machine gun to aim down the slope, he saw Sam crawling toward the trench at last, hell for leather, now, his jaw set with effort. Rolling into the trench, Sam landed on the dead gunner with a grunt of revulsion.

Beyond Sam, three NK rounded a bend in the trench and ran toward them. Hood handed Sam his .45, heard it banging away as he gripped the handles of the machine gun and turned the other way, firing over the edge of the trench, down the slope at the charging enemy skirmish line. The NKs crumpled under the hail of fire. Holding the trigger down, he swung the gun back and forth. As more enemy soldiers fell, the ones in the rear turned and ran, disappearing into the mist.

"Cowards," he snarled.

"Jesus!" Sam said.

Hood saw that he was staring at the mass of bodies, still twitching and jerking. One man's ammo belt blew up; he thrashed around, his tunic in flames. "Where's Jimmy?"

Sam continued to stare.

Grabbing his arm, Hood shook him and asked again.

"There's some, ah, some trees out there in the fog. I saw some marines go down trying to get there for cover, but I think Jimmy made it."

Hood felt a quick relief. "See if you can find more ammo for this thing."

Instead, Sam started firing the .45 again, and Hood saw more NKs in the trench rushing them. After two shots, the trigger froze against Sam's finger as he thrust the gun forward in a panic, trying to fire on empty. Hood swung the machine gun around. The grips pounded his hands and the sharp stink of cordite filled his head as the squad tangled with each other in a clumsy dance before settling into the bottom of the trench. "Damn!" Sam said. "That was close."

Hood stared at him with wonder. "You called me Daddy."

Sam frowned. "What?"

"Right then, a second ago. Just like when you were little."

"Bullshit."

"Corporal Bouden!" Hood yelled. "Get your lazy ass over here."

A gray figure emerged from the fog, taking on shape and color, as Jimmy sprinted to them and dived into the trench.

"It stinks in here," Sam muttered.

"The dead, shitting their pants," Hood said.

"I can't see a damn thing," Jimmy complained. "Who ordered this pea soup?"

"Did you find me ammo?" Hood asked Sam.

"I was a little busy, there."

"I'll go." Jimmy disappeared into the fog down the trench.

A damp chill had settled into the ditch, the cool, saturated air sinking into any hole it could find. Jimmy emerged from the mist with another belt of cartridges for the machine gun. Hood checked downhill; ghost shadows were forming in the fog. He brought the machine gun to bear, but Sam grabbed his arm before he could fire.

"They might be ours. 'F' Company's down there somewhere."

"You're right." Hood felt a sudden hope. If this was "F" Company, they'd have cleared the base of the hill and he could get Sam out that way.

The blurred forms darkened, sharpened, and then one of them barked a command, not in English.

Hood fired off the rest of the belt, and the shadows faded back into the mist.

Jimmy slotted the new belt into the breech.

"I'm hit," cried a weak voice out on the slope.

Jimmy started to climb from the trench.

"Hold on," Hood said. "See if a corpsman comes. He'll be more help, and we can give covering fire from here."

Seconds later, a corpsman hurried down the hill and knelt by the fallen marine, helping him to his feet, providing a human crutch as the man hobbled up the slope.

"D Company must be just above us," Jimmy said. "Should we go there, sarge?"

"Let me think."

"I'm in command here," Sam said, then stared up the hill, looking uncertain.

Hood mentally reviewed the map he'd memorized in Lieutenant Morrison's command shack. Their immediate objective that day had been Hill 105-S, but the map had also shown this final complex of hills just to the north and west of Seoul—the North Korean Main Line of Resistance. From above, the complex of hills looked like an octopus. The body of the beast was Hill 296, up the ridge-line to the north. Other ridge lines draped south from Hill 296—forming rounded tentacles of hill, with oval valleys between. This rise they were on now was Hill 56. East of here, across one of the oval valleys would be Hill 88, another big tentacle of 296. To the east of that was an even bigger tentacle—Hill 105 North, whose reverse slope looked down on Seoul, itself. That's where the marines needed to end up in order to attack the city, but North Koreans were all over these last few hills, thousands of them, manning heavy machine guns and mortars. Ahead, up there beyond Hill 56, was where they had to get, all the way to 105 North—the big tentacle overlooking the city. And they had to do it now—before the fog cleared, exposing them to NK fire.

"I'm gettin' a bad feeling," Jimmy said, peering down the slope. "The enemy is definitely down there, and they have to be up ahead, too."

"We gotta worry about the ones down there, first," Hood said. He watched the fog, no more shadows—where were they?

"Think they're trying to flank us?" Sam asked.

"That's what I'd do in their boots," Hood said. "They've come under machine gun fire twice and they aren't idiots."

"If they are circling behind our trench," Sam said, "maybe we could make a break for it now, get back down the way we came."

"And if we're wrong, we run right into them and we're either dead or POWs. No, we gotta head up the hill, connect with "D" Company, not let ourselves get isolated."

"Then we'd better spike this machine gun," Sam said.

"Right. Give me a grenade, corporal."

"I've got one." Sam fumbled at his belt.

Hood lugged the machine gun and mount to the bottom of the trench, put the grenade beneath and looked up. "Clear out, boys."

"I'll do it," Sam said. "I've got the longest legs."

"Yeah," Jimmy said, "and dogfaces are better at running."

"Very funny," Sam said.

Hood climbed out of the trench with Jimmy. Sam gripped the grenade and pin. "On three," he said. Pulling hard, he yelled, "Three!" and leapt out of the trench.

"What happened to one and two," Jimmy yelled over his shoulder, and then Sam passed him and Hood, sprinting up the slope. The grenade blasted behind and then Hood made the shelter of the uphill trees.

Someone in the copse yelled, "Marines!"

Hood pulled up as he saw five fellow leathernecks, a welcome sight, squatting on their haunches in a small clearing. One, a lieutenant, asked where they'd come from.

"Company 'A,' sir." Hood pointed to himself and Jimmy.

Sam said, "7th Infantry, 32nd Regiment. I was just—it's a long story."

Hood said, "there's at least a platoon of NK coming up from below, may try to flank you, Lieutenant. . . ?"

"Smith. We'll watch for it. Glad you're here. We need every gun we can get. These trees go on up the slope a ways, then thin out. There's a knob up there with at least six or seven NK heavy machine guns, got us bottled up in here. We've got to get past that knob. Lieutenant McNaughton's about to lead his platoon against it. You can go forward and join him or stay here in reserve."

Hood turned to Sam. "You stay here. Jimmy and I are going."

"I don't take orders from you, sergeant."

Hood felt a surge of frustration. He'd never laid a hand on Sam in anger but right now he wanted to shake him.

Smith looked puzzled—no doubt wondering what had thrown two marine noncoms and an army lieutenant together in the first place.

"Guess we'll all go up, sir," Hood said.

Smith nodded. "Good luck."

When they were out of earshot of the "D" Company marines, Hood let Jimmy get ahead a little. "Son, I know you outrank me, but what's coming I've done plenty of times and you haven't, so if you're determined to be in it, please be smart and let me lead."

Sam started to say something, took a breath. "If I think it makes sense," he said stiffly.

"That's all I ask."

Up ahead, Jimmy was easy to track, snapping twigs with his boondockers. They caught up with him as the trees thinned. The marine platoon had hunkered down just inside the tree line. Beyond, Hood spotted the knob Lieutenant Smith had mentioned. It stuck up from the rising slope like a fist. Scraggly trees clung to the sides, and he could see darker splotches, probably machine-gun emplacements, dug into the sides of the knob. Dense fog floated above the summit, hiding it from marine artillery spotters. The ground between the tree line and the knob offered little cover, only shallow gullies, a tree or two, and scattered rocks.

Someone yelled, "Go—let's go!" and the platoon moved forward in a skirmish line. Jimmy went out with the platoon. Grabbing Sam's arm, Hood held him back a few beats.

Machine guns on the hill opened up, seeking their targets; men starting to fall.

"Okay, stick with me."

Hood darted from the shelter of the trees, hurrying past Jimmy to a small boulder. He hunkered down behind the rock and Sam pressed close up against him. Dull "thoks" rattled like a sprinkler on a tin roof, a machine gun peppering the rock.

"You're shot!" Sam cried.

Hood saw his shirt was dark with caked blood. That bayonet thrust back at the trench—the blade must have caught half an inch of his side. Still so charged up he wasn't feeling it.

"It's nothing. Don't worry about it."

Sam shook his head. Mortars started popping from the tree line—the marines who'd held back in reserve ranging in on the knob with their 60s. Not much chance of hitting anything, but it would provide a distraction.

"Time to move." Hood sprinted toward a gully about fifty yards from the knob, hearing shouts and screams as he ran. Diving into the gully, he rolled tight to the side nearest the knob, Sam doing the same at his feet. Head down again, he heard enemy mortars on the knob popping, now, the impacts marching through the platoon of marines. Smoke billowed from the mortar impacts, boiling up into the lid of fog. Men screamed for corpsmen.

A mortar round fell close and Hood felt Sam's helmet flinch against his boot.

"The knob, get ready—now!" He lunged up and ran.

Sam zigged and zagged a few lengths off his shoulder, eating up the ground with his long legs—twenty yards, ten and they were there, flat against the flank of the knob, lungs heaving for air in the smoke. Overhead, rock bulges cut off any direct fire from the bunkers higher on the knob. Behind them, Hood watched the broken marine skirmish line retreat back across the killing ground to the trees.

Good. McNaughton couldn't hope to take this knob with just a platoon.

What wasn't so good was that he and Sam were now stranded.

Where was Jimmy? Planting his back against the hill, Hood scanned the field. Smoke drifted above the long grass, no Marines on their feet. Jimmy had either made it back or was keeping his head down.

Or lying dead in the grass.

Hood swallowed a sudden surge of nausea. Not Jimmy. He couldn't lose Jimmy.

"Now what?" Sam said.

"We wait. They'll be back."

"They shouldn't. Not until artillery has pounded this hill."

"That can't happen in this fog. The spotters need to see."

The cries of the wounded continued; two corpsmen ran forward from the trees. Machine gun fire cut them down.

"Bastards!" Furious, Hood listened to the cries for help. Was Jimmy among them? The remaining marines charged from the trees again. Heartsick, Hood watched them come, and fall in the weeds. Wait, he urged silently. Let the fog clear.

Again the marines fell back, leaving more dead and wounded.

"For God's sake," Sam cried, "this is a slaughter. Why is Smith attacking?"

"We've got to take these hills."

"Not right this minute we don't." Sam's face had gone pale. "These men are being fed into a meat grinder, and the order sure as hell is coming from higher up than a lieutenant."

"Sam, those hundred thousand North Koreans we were fighting down in Pusan are now hauling ass back north toward Seoul to keep us from cutting them off. If they get to the city before we do and reinforce it, a lot more of us will die in the streets of Seoul than you just saw go down in that field."

Sam stared at him. "You of all people, defending the big brass?"

"I don't give a rat's ass about the big brass. Our job—yours and mine—is to lead our men."

"Why did you leave us?"

"What?"

"You heard me."

174

Hood stared at him. "This is hardly the time—"

"The hell it isn't. We'll never make it back to the trees and you know it. We'll be dead in a few minutes. You tell me, now. Why did you run out on us?" his voice raw.

Hood felt a desperate urge to run. *Don't do this, son.*

He remembered the weight of baby Sam in his arms, that furry cry of wonder that made you want to hold onto him forever. The gawking amazement in his son's eyes, as if little Sam were looking up into the face of God instead of a jarhead marine with scars on his knuckles. The man that baby had become could have no idea how hard Iris had worked to pretend everything was all right those years in the hot, spartan duplexes assigned to married non-coms. Fans going all summer to bring it down to 85, a place of blowing dust and teething babies and endless, numbing routine.

Sam took his helmet off and rubbed his forehead, his fingers leaving tracks of dirt. "Mom would tell me you were coming, and I'd make up my mind to ignore you, let you know we didn't need you. Then you'd arrive, looking like a king and wanting to take me places, and Mom would seem all happy to see you. You'd give me those big bear hugs and I'd melt. When you took off again, I'd be mad at you for leaving and at myself for getting sucked in all over again. Then Mom started going around with Julian, and I really got mad at you for not telling him to go away. I wanted you to put our family back together. But you didn't want that. You loved the Marine Corps more than you loved us. You had a choice between us and this," waving his arm at the field of fallen marines, "and you chose this."

"That was not the choice."

"Then what was?"

"You wouldn't understand."

"Try me, goddamnit."

A mortar round from the tree line fell a little short, showering them with rock from the slope. Flashes lit the tree line, smoke rolling up as the NK mortars rained death on the few remaining marines.

But what was that?

A thin cheer, going up from the edge of the woods. Looking up, Hood felt his heart lift at the patches of blue showing through the fog and clouds. As he watched, the holes in the clouds widened. A distant scream swelled in volume, the vengeful howl of a 155 shell. Smashing into the knob above them, it made the rock against Hood's shoulder tremble. Stones cascaded down from above. Hood slapped Sam's helmet and pulled him up as more shells slammed into the knob above them.

The artillery became a continuous thunder, pounding the hill, and then a different sound rolled from the west, the drone of fighters from marine air, and Hood cheered as a foursome of Corsairs topped Hill 56 and roared in on the knob. Black shapes tumbled from the planes; he had just time to think, *Oh, Shit,* before the napalm hit, and a heat wave swallowed them.

"Run!" he yelled. Pulling Sam away from the knob, he sprinted for the tree-line, feeling his shirt sear his back, watching the ground so he wouldn't trip, because if he went down now, he'd be cooked. Smoke rolled around them, stinging Hood's eyes, and then he was into the trees, and Jimmy caught him before he could bang his head on a branch—*Jimmy, thank God!*—and Sam and Jimmy were slapping his leggings, which were smoking as the laces smoldered.

The knob was in flames, now, patches of grass burning away in the field between. Another wave of marine air swooped low over Hill 56, strafing the knob and dropping bombs that drew more cheers. Corpsmen ran into the field and began dragging back the wounded.

Lieutenant McNaughton limped over and clapped Hood on the back. "Good going, Marine. We thought you two were goners."

"Just taking a breather," Hood said.

Sam gave a harsh laugh.

Lieutenant Smith counted heads. "How many we got standing, including reserves?" he asked McNaughton in an excited voice. The two of them began to count, ending up with a tally of thirty-three.

That can't be right, Hood thought. Thirty-three out of a company of 250?

"Let's go get 'em," Smith yelled, and the marines broke from the tree-line, sprinting toward the knob. Men climbed up the sides, firing into bunkers, meeting only token resistance from the surviving North Koreans. Hood pressed on past the knob with Smith, Sam, and Jimmy out to either side of him, heading up the rise toward the big, central body of the octopus, Hill 105 North. Artillery was pounding up that way, too, and the Corsairs were strafing and bombing now that they could see the ground, swooping low overhead and wagging their wings on the way back out.

Hood was conscious of firing his M-1 into bunkers, throwing grenades then shooting men as they staggered out. The ground burned all around, smoke going up to blue heaven; the ground leveled out as they reached the crest of 105. Three Korean officers jumped from a bunker—damn, enemy were pouring out of the ground everywhere—at least a company of them, but they weren't charging, they were running away.

Dropping to one knee, Hood fired into their backs as they fled down Hill 105 toward Seoul, shooting them as they ran and watching them fall, glad to be doing it, because the ones they didn't get would be firing on marines in the city tomorrow.

Pausing to jam another clip in, Hood caught sight of Sam and Jimmy, shoulder to shoulder, shooting the fleeing enemy. Around them stood maybe two dozen marines, all that was left, firing away like hunters at a turkey shoot. Sam was snarling as he pulled the trigger, his teeth bared. Hood saw him again as a baby, back in the warmth of the apartment, flowers in the window boxes, Iris frying potatoes in the iron skillet, one eye on Sam's playpen, the radio going on a warm summer night.

Watching Sam kill and grin and kill some more, Hood was glad his mother couldn't see him now.

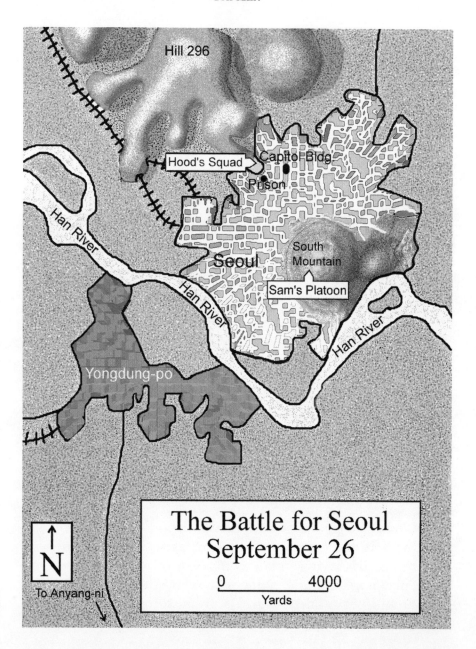

Hill 296

Hood's Squad

Capito Bldg
Prison

South
Mountain

Seoul

Sam's Platoon

Han River

Han River

Han River

Yongdung-po

The Battle for Seoul
September 26

0   4000
Yards

N

To Anyang-ni

On September 25, while the 32nd Infantry regiment attacked South Mountain in the outskirts of Seoul, the marines fought their way into the city from the west. The North Korean 18th Division gave ground grudgingly, launching fierce counterattacks wherever the marines appeared. The fight went on for two days, with the enemy firing from windows and rooftops and manning barricades made of bags filled with rice or sand. Blocking nearly every intersection, these barriers were cruelly effective, forcing the Marines to pay with their blood for each street taken. As the battle raged, ambulances rushed hundreds of wounded back to Inch'on and the 1st MASH. (Ibid.)

12

25 September, 1st MASH, 0810:

Bonnie took a seat beside Colonel Martin's desk and gazed around, curious despite the nerve twanging in her stomach. So this was the colonel's hidey hole, tidier than she'd expect for a guy, every piece of potential clutter squared away. A baseball mitt held down the papers in his out-box against periodic sweeps of breeze from the pedestal fan rumbling by the door. Between his out- and in-boxes, lined up in a row, were a golf trophy, a scorpion-in-amber paperweight, and a pair of those little scotty dogs, one black and one white, placed just far enough apart to keep their magnet bases from snapping them together.

On the wall behind Martin's desk, a framed cross-stitch proclaimed, "Home is Where the Heart Is."

Clearly, Chester Martin's heart was back home in Washington, D.C. Photos from there covered the side of his file cabinet—the U.S. Capitol Building, the Washington Monument, the Lincoln Memorial. A more personal one showed Colonel Martin posing with two fellow officers beside the gate sign of Walter Reed Army Hospital, the shadow of the photographer lapping to their feet.

The largest photo was an 8x10 of the colonel and a short, robustly plump brunette standing close together on the front stoop of a modest brick colonial. Bonnie smiled at the contrast. Out of uniform, Chester Martin was every inch the absent-minded professor—tall and skinny, those round spectacles, thinning hair, the vague smile. His wife, her hands clasped in front, looked like an opera soprano about to launch an aria.

Snapshots of two grade-school-age girls plastered the rest of the cabinet. One grinned straight into the camera in a lot of the photos, her short, tomboy hair tousled. The other girl had been captured in shy, sidelong glances, a braided pigtail showing over her shoulder.

Bonnie's chest warmed. One introvert and one extravert, she thought, just like Diane and me.

What was not like Diane and her was the father behind the camera. Both girls loved their daddy, you could see it even in the pained smiles of the shy one. Colonel Martin was an Army lifer, but the scuttlebut in the MASH was that he'd managed to stay near his family during peacetime, serving at Walter Reed as an ear, nose, and throat doc. "That's Shirley with the pigtails," the colonel said proudly, "and Vivian. Shirley's sixth grade and Viv, eighth."

"I'll bet you miss them."

"I sure do."

"There's nothing you can do, though. You have to go where the army tells you."

"Yes." His head tilted, as if he found the remark curious. He wouldn't if he knew her past. Uncle Daddy was never in the Army, Bonnie thought. He managed his own furniture store ten blocks from home. There was nothing stopping him from staying with Mom and us, being true to us.

"You have family back home?" Martin asked.

Bonnie nodded, picturing Mom and Grandma snug and secure in the bungalow she and Diane had bought for them on Roosevelt Street. Mom still worked as an L.P.N. but Grandma had totally retired, done with housekeeping work except in her own house. The Brisbane women, yeah—three of the four of them still carrying the "maiden" name Grandma had reclaimed after a marriage that had apparently been even shorter and more disastrous than Mom's.

They didn't need men in their lives, Bonnie thought, and neither did sis or I. We were all right.

Or, if we weren't, I didn't know it.

She imagined Chester Martin as her father. He was the right age, at least twenty-five years older than her. Decent and kind from all she could tell. Curious that he didn't pitch in more on the MASH wards. An E.N.T. doc might be a menace in surgery, but surely he could help out in post op and the medical wards. She could understand the doctors griping about their CO's reclusiveness after being on their feet for twenty straight hours.

On the other hand, this was Chester's second war, and maybe he was doing the best he could.

The colonel picked up a paper from his desk. Gazing at it, he cleared his throat, and it occurred to Bonnie that he was nervous, too. "Lieutenant, I wanted to go over your latest supply request with you."

"Is there a problem?"

"Well, let's see. More gauze—can't get enough of that, can we? And, oh, here we are, some four-oh silk?" He arched an eyebrow.

Her stomach felt hollow. "For sutures."

"Don't we normally use two-oh?"

"Yes, sir. But it would be good to have something finer for ragged tears or when the edge we're suturing is thin."

Martin's head tipped in a slow, skeptical nod. "Trouble is, the four-oh is hard enough to come by that we might take some heat from the supply officer."

She shrugged. Stay cool, don't overexplain.

"Remember Colonel Lipscomb?" Martin said.

The little muscles in her neck tightened.

"He gave us a lecture on the ship," Martin prompted. "Passed out from the heat."

"Sure. Colonel Lipscomb."

"From the Far East Command Surgeon's staff," giving each word a slight emphasis. "I've just gotten notice that Lipscomb will be paying us a site visit in the next day or two. I've done a quick sampling of charts to make sure we're okay. In several of the charts, I came across a certain vagueness about just what surgical procedure was used."

"Unhuh." Bonnie's mouth was dry. *Lipscomb. Damn!*

"Lieutenant, I need to know whether Colonel Lipscomb is going to discover something we'd rather he didn't."

Bonnie hesitated. Why wouldn't Martin just come right out and ask—*Are we doing arterial repairs?*

Maybe he didn't want to know; maybe he just wanted to be able to say he'd asked.

"Sir, Colonel Lipscomb shouldn't be surprised if our charts fall short of the standard of, say, a teaching hospital. As you know, we've gotten really swamped a couple of times when the battles are raging out there. We do our best with the charts, as time allows, but our first concern is keeping the wounded alive."

"Well said, lieutenant. Unfortunately, I'm afraid generalities, however well put, won't satisfy the colonel. Lipscomb is a 'by the book' sort, and he can be relentless if he thinks he's onto something." Plucking a baseball from the mitt, Chester Martin rolled it around in his hands, setting the seams different ways. He said, "I wouldn't be surprised if Lipscomb looked over our requisition records and spot-checked them against procedures and chart notes. If he were to see this request for four-oh silk. . . ."

Bonnie suppressed a groan. God, she hated indirectness. What did he want her to say? Martin restored the ball to the glove. "Lieutenant, I do want the 1st MASH to give the best care we can to the wounded in the time available under the press of battle, when they keep pouring in. I'm also charged with upholding army regulations. It's my belief that the two goals shouldn't come into conflict. I want to be clear about that."

Shouldn't conflict? she thought. Or *don't*? There's a world of difference.

She hardened her resolve. If he was leaving it to her to interpret what he meant, then her interpretation was that he was not ordering an end to arterial repairs. If, to cover his own ass,

Martin later felt he had to say he'd told her to stop, fine. If we're caught, we're on our own. "You've been perfectly clear, sir."

"Good."

Her heart sank as he tore the requisition in two and dropped it on his desk. He said, "Sutures that fine aren't available in our supply channels, anyway. You'd have to go to Tokyo to find four-oh silk. Speaking of which, next lull we get, maybe I can arrange a weekend pass for you—a little R and R. We've got planes going back and forth from Kimpo to Tokyo around the clock. I think we could manage it soon. And of course, what you choose to do while on leave is up to you."

Bonnie's spirits lifted. *What a sly old dog you are, Chester.*

"I'll look forward to that, sir."

Stepping from Martin's office, she thought about Lipscomb's visit. Of all the MASH units in Korea, why had he decided to check out the 1st? It could be a random choice, a casual decision, but somehow she didn't think so. Back on the ship, he'd embarrassed himself. She hadn't meant to be any part of that, and maybe another man would have laughed it off, or at least seen how he'd brought it on himself, but it was too much to hope that was true of Lipscomb. In his mind, she had caused him humiliation, and you didn't have to know a whole lot about men to know he was coming to the 1st MASH in the hopes of getting back at her.

If he found out she'd helped with arterial repairs, he'd have what he needed.

Outside Seoul, 1100 hours:

Hood lay on his belly on a ledge on the last hill before Seoul. The capital city was far bigger than he'd imagined, huge, almost as big as Tokyo. He'd heard the population was two million, but seeing was believing. Two million civilians, and tens of thousands of enemy soldiers looking to kill them some U.S. Marines.

"Good shot," murmured Lieutenant Lui to no one in particular. Flattened on the rock beside Hood, he gazed at the city through his field glasses. The shot he'd just praised could have hit almost anywhere—black smoke streamed up all over Seoul as Corsairs swooped and rose, new explosions bursting orange in their wakes. At this distance, you saw each smoke cloud blossom before the sound of the explosion could reach you, a constant popping and booming out of synch with the flames and carnage, as Marine Air from Kimpo and the carriers offshore strafed and bombed the city. The brassy, orange flames sent up a rising wall of heat that made the sky above Seoul shimmer.

God, it was spectacular.

Forget that and do your job.

Shifting his attention from the swarming aerial bombardment, Hood studied the city as if it were a three-D terrain map. It was far better, of course. Unlike with maps, what he was seeing now would be right where he expected when he took the squad down.

Three bigger buildings drew his eye. There in the main downtown area east of the hills was Government House—a big, western-style building with fancy stonework and columns that might have housed the mayor and city council of any good-sized American city. The air attack appeared to be avoiding it. Rumor had it that MacArthur wanted to retake the city on the three-month anniversary of its fall. Government House would be the natural spot for his ceremony, but not if he'd bombed it flat.

To the north, another long roof made a striking contrast to Government House, very old, oriental-style, with those horn-like cornices curving out from the corners and at regular intervals along the roof's edge. A royal palace, fixed in time like a butterfly in amber as the city it had ruled changed around it. Acres of green surrounded the ancient building, probably the imperial gardens.

A broad boulevard ran between Government House and the palace, with side streets cross-hatching outward on all sides. From what he could see, the old and the new mixed together all through the sprawling city—tall, modern office buildings rising next door to wooden shops and stalls like you saw in Tokyo.

Further north, and closer to the base of the hill, Hood saw a complex of squat stone buildings as long as barracks which could only be Sodaemun Prison. Guard towers stuck up from the west wall.

Were South sympathizers being executed in there at this moment as their would-be liberators stood at the city gates?

Time we got down there, Hood thought.

He wondered how the lieutenant would do in the fight ahead. The battle for Seoul ought to clear up whether he was a veteran of combat or not. He'd done all right this morning, keeping up with the platoon as it helped root out the enemy's final rear guard action on Hill 256. Resistance down the eastern slope had been surprisingly fierce. Enemy survivors of the D Company turkey shoot yesterday must have been joined by other troops during the night. Even two tank platoons rolling down the ridges hadn't turned the tide. Then that one tank fitted out for flame had gone to work licking up the enemy like an anteater with its long tongue of fire. It had broken the enemy will, gooks spilling from their trenches, scrambling to surrender, over three hundred of them marched away with their hands high, the war over for them.

But not for us, Hood thought. The winners get to keep on fighting.

Sam's bitter accusation in the heat of battle came back to him, that he had chosen between his family and this—the gut exhilaration of battle, the bond that came from entrusting your lives to the men in your unit, the hammering of your heart as facing death drove home how precious life was. All those things he did love. But the choice Sam considered so obvious was far less simple than he thought. It had not been between two loves—his woman and The Corps.

It had been between loving Iris and *telling* himself he was loving her.

He will never understand, Hood thought. A playboy like him.

Lui said, "Are the replacements ready for this, sergeant?"

"As ready as talk can make them. Maybe, with all the bombing, the NK will run before we get there."

"You don't believe that."

"No sir."

Lui edged back from the lip of the ledge and slung his field glasses. "All right, Sergeant Hood. You've got five minutes to brief your squad while I send a runner to the company command post."

"Yes sir."

Slipping back into the cover of scrub and trees on the slope, Hood found the squad where he'd left them. The seven men closed in around him, their faces expectant. "Smoke 'em if you've got 'em," he said. Steinberg rolled his eyes as Bo lit a big cigar. Bertleson added another stick of gum to the wad in his mouth. Barstow shook out a Lucky and sat there with the unlit cigarette in his mouth, staring off into space. *Damn, it Barlow. . . .*

Hood lit his own Lucky. Okay, Hollywood was still having trouble. So far, he'd been all right once the shooting started, but what waited below would dwarf anything they'd faced to this point—

That smell, so familiar—Cockburn's cigar? It's the same as Morrison smoked, Hood realized. "Where'd you get that, son?"

"Uh, Lieutenant Morrison gave it to me. Said cigars bring luck. So I been saving it."

Steinberg started to say something, then closed his mouth. No one needed reminding how much luck the cigars had brought Morrison.

"Okay, listen up," Hood said. "We're about to go down this hill into the city. Street fighting is different from what we've been doing, better in some ways, because there's lots of cover for us. Trouble is, the enemy has had his pick of the best of that cover while we've been closing in. He's familiar with the city and we're not, and by now he has set up in a lot of good places to shoot us from. Which means we gotta think like him, decide where we'd go to set up ambushes. Then we gotta hit those places with everything we've got."

He looked at the two new guys, replacements for the wounded Jakes and Rittenhouse. Milo Stempleford and Joe Clemons. Milo was a stoop-shouldered, skinny kid, a sad sack whose slumped posture would make him look old if it weren't for the mountain of curly auburn hair now hidden by his helmet. Joe Clemons was a rare one—a Negro in a combat infantry unit. A veteran marine, having served as a steward aboard various ships in the last war. But a new guy when it came to combat, getting his shot at killing the enemy, thanks to Harry S. Truman's brand new integration policy. Joe was almost as big as Bo, with huge hands and broad shoulders. The mild good humor in his face worried Hood. Carving roasts in a navy mess was a far cry from shiska-bobing the enemy on a fixed bayonet. Clemons had done all right helping mop up the slope today, but that victory belonged mainly to the tanks. Down below it would be man on man in the streets and alleys of a strange city.

"You guys get any training in street fighting?" he asked the replacements.

"Boot camp, sergeant," Clemons said, "but that was awhile back."

"It's a simple concept. We got eight men left in the squad, counting me, so we'll divide into two fire teams. Corporal Bouden, you'll take Privates Stempleford, Bertleson and Barstow. I'll take Clemons, Steinberg and Cockburn. Way it works, you put half your fire team—two marines—on each side of the street, starting at the corner. First you all fire down the street until it looks clear. Then half of your fire team starts in on the corner building across the street from it. Shoot the shit out of it, then cease fire so the the other half of your fire team, the two guys next to that building, can run along in front of it throwing grenades into the windows you smashed with your gunfire. Those two then go in to clear the building, while the team across continues to cover the entrances. When that building is clear, the team inside starts the next cycle, shooting the next building in line across the street, then cease fire and cover that building while the two guys over there throw their grenades, then go inside and clear. The two teams will alternate that way, working down the street."

"What about prisoners, sarge?" Steinberg asked.

Hood felt a stab of annoyance. Leave it to Steinberg to ask the one intelligent question that had no good answer. "I don't believe you'll have that problem, private."

"But if we do?"

"Use your judgment. The enemy may only pretend to surrender until you drop your guard, so make sure you don't. If you do take a prisoner, your first step is be damn sure he's disarmed. Then you have the problem of what to do with him. By taking a prisoner, you put yourself in the position of having to escort him back behind the lines, which means your fellow marines will have to get along without your help, as surely as if you'd been killed. Losing your support may mean one of them dies. Remember that. I suggest you think hard about it when you're deciding whether to take a prisoner or not."

"But if an enemy drops his gun and puts his hands up, it wouldn't be right to just shoot him," Steinberg said.

"I'm not ordering you to shoot him, private. Let's just say I'm advising you not to encourage surrender. If you get into a situation where you, personally, feel you have no choice but to take a prisoner, disable him and go on."

"You mean like shoot him in the leg?" Cockburn asked.

"No, Bo," Steinberg said. "You tie his hands and feet."

"That's enough on prisoners," Hood snapped. "Don't go into any room without a member of your fire team at your back covering. Be thorough but don't dawdle. That's a big city waiting down there. Any other questions?"

Men around the circle began stubbing out their smokes.

Jimmy took off his helmet. Everyone except the two new men gathered around him and rubbed his bald head, and then Milo and Joe, seeing what was happening, stepped into the circle to do it, too.

"Okay," Hood said, "watch each others' backs like good marines and you should come out of this in one piece." Giving them all a final, prayerful look, he felt in his gut that some of them would be dead before the day was out.

Seoul, 1600 hours:

Blind eyes straining, Hood hugged the dusty floor of the church and counted his blessings. Company "A," first platoon, had made it into the city without him losing a man from his squad. Steinberg and Cockburn should be safe for the moment, with good window perches in the parsonage across the street, covering the entrance to the church. The team next street over was Jimmy's worry, and there wasn't a better corporal in the United States Marines.

Now if I just had eyes like a cat, Hood thought.

Joe Clemons, where are you?

Someone had boarded up the stained glass windows from the outside, hoping to spare them from the bullets and bombs. Outside in the street, it was still day, the air smoky from the flames. In here it was dark as a moonless night, the only illumination a faint glow from stray shafts of light leaking through cracks in the boards. Hood knew he should shoot out a window or two from the inside, but he couldn't. This was God's house, and you didn't want Him sore at you right now.

"Sarge, ovuh heah!" The Mississippi drawl coming through even in his whisper.

Raising his head between pews, Hood peered toward Clemons' voice. Faint light etched the rims of the pews, laying out glimmering lines ahead of him, ten of them—ten rows to the front of the sanctuary.

"Sarge?"

"Quiet!" Hood hissed. The last thing Clemons needed was to give an NK sniper hiding in the dark a chance to home on his voice. Ducking again, Hood crawled to the nearer aisle, then toward the front. As he rounded the front pew, he was finally able to make out Clemons' big form kneeling at the other end. Crawling toward him, he stumbled over something soft—with a small arm, a thin neck. A kid, not moving.

Hood felt for a pulse. None, though the skin was still warm. Looking ahead he was just able to make out a row of bodies, some small, some enough bigger to be adults. Sickened, he crawled along the line, his fingers tangling in thick hair—a woman, her forehead still warm, the blood wet, not crusted. These poor people had been shot, no, executed, only a minute or two ago—

Which meant the killer was probably still here. Or killers.

Hood crawled faster, glad, now, for the darkness. If he saw the dead faces, he'd never forget them. One hand, groping in the dark, landed on a wrinkled, dead throat. Cringing away, he gave the corpses a wider berth, scuttling to Clemons.

"Sarge! Why would someone do this?"

"Quiet."

Hood pulled him in between the second and third pews, steering him beneath one with a couple of shoves, then crawling under the next pew himself. Revenge, that was why. The North Korean occupiers of Seoul knew the liberators of the city were coming as soon as the bombing ended. The minute the marines had started moving into the city, the commies would have had execution squads set to kill people who weren't with them during the occupation.

But in a church?

Communists don't care about church. If they're still here, they'll kill us, too.

With an effort, Hood pulled himself together. He must be cold as ice, now, for his own sake as well as Clemons.'

If they're still here, *I'll* do some killing.

A shot came from up high and whined off the tiled aisle in ricochet. Hood felt his teeth bare in the dark. Replaying the sound in his mind, he tried to pin down where the shot had come from. Hard to tell with the echoes, but definitely from somewhere to the rear and. . .above?

A balcony.

Another shot, the bullet thumping into wood near his head. Hood heard slithering sounds near him, Joe moving, and then Joe's M-1 boomed six times, the muzzle flashes illuminating his contorted face, wood splintering above, in the direction of the sniper—a balcony, yes.

"Keep moving, Joe," Hood yelled, then scrambled away, sliding under two rows of pews, hearing the sniper fire again, this time from the back right of the church. Shoot and move—this gook knew the rules, too.

Or he had a partner.

Hood heard Joe moving again, then nothing. To let Clemons know he was okay, he tapped out shave-and-a-hair-cut on the underside of the pew, then pushed under three more pews toward the rear of the sanctuary. A shot splintered the pew where he'd tapped out his message seconds ago.

Lying still, he sucked a lungful of dust and strangled a cough.

Time to move again. Lying on his back, holding the M-1 to his chest to keep it from knocking into anything, Hood used his heels to push himself along the floor. The darkness seemed denser now. He'd made it under the balcony. Rising to a crouch, he felt his way along the pew to the aisle. The altar flickered in muzzle flashes as Joe's M-1 boomed three more times, impacting the wooden face of the balcony. Hood used the distraction to grope his way to the rear of the church. Wood yielded to his touch—a swinging door into the foyer.

At once, visibility improved. A small window of ordinary glass near the stairs to the balcony had not been covered with protective boards. Hurrying past, he glimpsed flickering orange light from fires burning in the street.

He slipped quietly up the steps, stopping in a narrow hall behind the balcony. Light fell from the hatch of a bell tower at the center of the hall, bleeding through the opaque glass of a clock face up inside. The gears of the clock whirred and clacked as Hood looked around. To his left, three steps rose into the darkness of the balcony. The hairs on his neck prickled and he realized he was smelling the man—the fishy garlic odor of *kimchee.*

In the faint light from the clock tower, Hood could just make out wooden steps—squeakers, for sure. If Clemons would fire again, it would cover the sound he'd make going up. He could wait, but not long.

He felt the rage boiling up in him, tried to control it, because this was not a charge up a hill, this was hunting a man in the dark, as he hunted you. Not a man, an animal, a beast in a gray-green uniform who could shoot down helpless civilians—from his own clan, women and little children, old men.

Not a soldier, he thought. A demon.

Clemons' M-1 banged below, and Hood took the three steps on the balls of his feet, M-1 to his shoulder, looking right, then left, just as the sniper over there fired back at Clemons, the side of his face showing in the faint light of the muzzle blast.

Putting a bullet into the sniper's head, Hood dropped to his knees and dived left as a gun on the other side of the balcony opened up on him—boom, boom. Plaster showered down, and he heard Clemons below, blasting away. The second sniper screamed, and Hood sprang up, firing at the sound.

It cut off; Hood's ears rang in the sudden silence. A second later, the body of the second sniper, crashed down on the pews below.

"Sergeant! You all right?"

Wincing at Clemons' incaution, Hood waited for more gunfire, but none came. All right. All right.

"I'm okay, Clemons. I think we got them both—good shooting. Now move somewhere else, quietly, and wait for me below. I'll only be a minute."

"What are you doing, sarge?"

"Wait."

Hood felt his way to where the first sniper had fallen. The man lay on the floor, one arm flung up against a pew. Probing his head, Hood felt a satisfying wetness. He could find no pulse in the throat. Slinging his M-1, he grabbed the NK's arm and dragged him out under the bell tower. Not enough light there, so he dragged him down the steps to a landing, propping him against the wall where the glow from the small window fell. Smoke shadows writhed across the beast's face. The left side of its head was red with blood, its eyes closed, not open as death sometimes did you. The face was neither young nor old, probably mid thirties.

There was nothing in it to explain how this being in human form could have killed babies and women. A shudder of revulsion went through Hood. You didn't slaughter innocent people and call yourself a soldier. Each one of those people lying on the floor had held a different world inside them, old men with the wisdom of years, a million memories now lost, the children just on their way to wonders they'd never see—

The NK's eyes opened.

Hood jumped back, fumbling his rifle off his shoulder.

It *was* a demon!

"No shoot," the NK gasped, raising trembling hands above his head. "You no shoot, I surrender—I your prisoner, please, please." Crying, his tears making streaks through the blood.

From a dispassionate distance, Hood watched a man in a marine uniform with three stripes on the sleeve fire an M-1 rifle at the weeping demon, hitting him in the head and then the chest, the bangs distant and disconnected from him. The demon folded at the waist, his head smacking the step. He shuddered and went still.

Footsteps burst through from the sanctuary into the foyer and Clemons came upon him standing there over the body, still pointing his gun at the corpse.

"He tried to surrender," Hood said.

Clemons gave him a long look. "You did right, Sergeant Hood. We don't need his kind using up the good air of this earth. You got to guarantee he won't ever do it again, a man like that."

Cold crackled across Hood's skin, as though a scrim of ice were breaking off him.

"You okay, sergeant?"

He dropped his rifle, sick to his stomach. Soldiers didn't shoot an enemy who was trying to surrender. Steinberg, a brand new marine, a kid—even he knew that.

"He didn't have a weapon," Hood said. "It's back up there in the balcony. He begged me for his life."

Clemons started for him, holding a hand out, then stopped at something in his sergeant's face. "Take it easy, Mr. Hood. I'm sure the folks he killed here in God's temple begged too, and his heart was hard then. You think the devil won't beg for his life in the end, when he's facing that eternal lake of fire? You think he won't plead with God not to throw him in?"

"I'm not God," Hood said.

He couldn't seem to get his breathing right, like he'd been shot in the chest again, the lung refusing to pull air. Clemons took his arm, scooped up the M-1 and walked him away from the corpse, back into the dark church, down the center aisle.

The squad needs you. Gotta move on to the next street.

Clemons sat him in the front pew in the darkness. An instant later, the private's M-1 banged. Hood flinched; stained glass shattered and a long bar of smoky light flooded the sanctuary.

"Take a look," Clemons said. "This is what the man you're feeling sorry for did."

For just a second, Hood saw the row of bodies spread before the altar, saw their faces, a mother trying to shelter her child, an old man and woman with their arms around each other.

He pinched his eyes shut, *too late.*

Early in the morning of September 26, the 32nd Regiment of the 7th Infantry Division dug in atop Nam-San, a mountainous park in the southern district of Seoul. The GIs could see the flames of the marine battle nine hundred feet below in the city, and hear the din of mortars and small arms fire. They expected an attack all during the night, and at 0430, Colonel Mount's 2nd battalion staved off a determined assault that overran Fox company. A counterattack was able to regain those positions, and the enemy assault was broken. Later, Lt. Colonel Faith's 1st battalion would also come under attack. An intense firefight ensued as dawn broke. The battalion was able to hold its position. . . .

(Ibid.)

13

26 September, South Mountain, Seoul, 0330: Sam's head jerked up from the table. He tried to focus through the bleary glow of the Coleman lantern. The carbon-wax scent of kerosene filled his head; he did not know where he was. . . .

Okay, Korea. . . South Mountain. . .

. . .and this would be the gardener's shed.

On the cot, Sergeant Hartung snored softly, his face to the wall, combat boots hanging off the end of the makeshift wooden frame. By now it must be Hartung's watch, but for dozing off during his own, he owed the sergeant some leeway.

The tapping came again, what had wakened him, soft, diffident.

Sam pushed up from the table, the heel of one hand slipping as it shoved the map of Seoul away. His knees ached, bent tight in one position for too long; a vicious crick gnawed at his neck. "Who is it?"

"Kim, boss."

Sam rubbed his neck. What could the kid want? Shuffling to the door, he opened it. Kim gazed past him into the shack like it was FAO Schwartz at Christmas. Motioning him inside, Sam shut the door against the night chill.

"Swell digs," Kim observed.

Sam looked at the rakes and shovels, the moldy-smelling tarps, the bushel baskets and trowels, the rickety table and homemade wooden chair he'd managed to fall asleep on. Had Hartung been teaching the kid sarcasm? "Beats digging another foxhole. What's up?"

Kim hesitated. "I think maybe I heard a tank, boss."

Sam forced his mind around it. South Mountain, called Nam-San, was hardly the best terrain for tanks. The "Mountain" was Seoul's hilly version of Central Park, an array of shrines, arbors and monuments surrounded by woods. The steep slopes and thick tree cover would limit any tanks to the roads that meandered up to the summit.

Still, there were points along those roads where a tank could find good lines of fire. So if Kim was right, the question was whose tanks? None that he'd seen had crossed the Han with the regiment yesterday, the amtracs big enough only for troops and artillery. The 7th Division did have a heavy tank company somewhere, and just because he hadn't seen it didn't mean it hadn't been bridged, barged or forded across the river by now.

Probably ours, Sam decided. If he even heard them. "How sure are you?"

"Not real sure. Just heard that squeak and clank in my foxhole. I crawled out to listen and didn't hear it again." His eyes had gone distant with fear. A nightmare, Sam thought, and now he wants to crawl in with Daddy.

Bad idea. *I'm not your father, kid, and I already like you too much for someone I have to order into battle.*

Sam thought of Hood's corporal. His first take—that Bouden was giving him the cold shoulder because he disliked Hood— could not have been more wrong, he now realized. Jimmy Bouden had been through hell with the old man, in Pusan and here, and maybe the last war, too. He thinks Hood's his daddy— which makes me his rival for the old man's affection.

Sam's face prickled hot with resentment. Who said command was being anyone's dad? Screw that.

"It's late, Kim. If you hear it again. . . ."

The kid edged past him to the table, and traced a forefinger along the map. "That must be the big shrine, not far from here, up on the highest hill," pointing to a small rectangle on the map.

Sam hesitated, curious. "You've been here before?"

"Sure. My Dad brought me two years ago. He said it was time for me to see the capital. We stayed in a hotel and ate in restaurants. We came up here one day and walked all around. It was cool." Kim's voice, low in deference to Hartung, brimmed with repressed enthusiasm.

This might be useful, if the kid actually knew his way around. . . .

"What does your father do for a living?"

"He was a cop in Taejon." Kim's eyes turned shiny.

Was, Sam thought. Whoa—time to bail.

"The so-called People's Army attacked in July," Kim said. "The U.S. 34th Infantry tried to stop them, but the NKPA had tanks and Yak airplanes shooting and bombing. Lots of dust from the explosions, until the rain came in the evening. During the night, the NK surrounded Taejon, where we lived. The next day, more attacks. An artillery round hit the house. My father and mother were both inside and my little brother. I was in our vegetable garden in back. The explosion knocked me over. When I woke up, I saw the house burning and our next door neighbors in the street, crying. I tried to get inside, but it was too hot, and the neighbors, they stopped me." He swallowed. A single tear finally spilled, running down his cheek. He ignored it.

Sam resisted an impulse to put a hand on Kim's shoulder. Then saw it go there anyway. The kid hung his head, wiping furiously at his eyes, obviously ashamed to let Boss see him cry.

Sam thought of his own childhood, so safe and secure compared to this kid's. There had been pain, sure, and fear, moving from the walkup in Queens to the brownstone in Manhattan after Mom had married Julian. The tall house of dark stone had been forbidding at first, but then its inner calm and beauty had soothed him, the grand paintings on the walls, so full of light and color, the sweet sound of Julian's cello wafting up the stair-case in the evenings. Mom would take him to Rumplemeyers for breakfast, and to her matinees on Broadway, the fear and resent-ment leaving him day by day as he'd realized Julian was gentle and good, that he cared for Mom and him and would never leave them. Carnegie Hall had become a part of his world, the New York Philharmonic concerts. Seeing the passion on Julian's kind, round face as he helped produced the grand music, he'd real-ized that Julian's tuxedo was a uniform as worthy of respect and admiration as Harlan Hood's. In the library of the big house, Mom would take out Julian's books, holding them to her chest and smiling.

We were safe, Sam thought. I never went to sleep wondering if, in the morning, an artillery shell might hit my house and kill everyone I loved. My father left, and that hurt like hell, but he wasn't killed before my eyes, and I got a new, better father.

The kid squared his shoulders, and Sam pulled his hand back.

Kim said, "Some of the U.S. soldiers from the 34th took me with them when they escaped. That's how I got down to Taegu. They let me work in the PX until I got to be in your army." His voice, under control again, sounded proud; Sam wondered what had made Kim different from the other KATUSAs in the pla-toon, most of whom were still reluctant soldiers at best. The men from the 34th must have made a pretty good impression on the kid, even as they ran for their lives in that first powerful push of the invading North Korean army.

"I'm sorry about your father."

"Me too, boss." His eyes went distant. "If my whole fam-ily hadn't been killed, I'd have stayed in Taejon, and who knows what would have happened to me when the NKPA took over."

Sam wondered what it must be like for his KATUSAs to fight in their own country. When he had killed his first human being, Kim was at his side, firing at the charging North Koreans right along with him. I saw foreign-looking men, Sam thought, with slanted eyes who were coming to kill me. Kim saw his own kind in a different uniform.

"Do you have any relatives in North Korea?"

"My mother's brother—my uncle and his wife and kids, my cousins. I haven't seen them for a long time. My uncle moved up there when I was little to help build a damn for power in the mountains."

"Is he in the North Korean army now?"

Kim shrugged. "I don't know, boss. I hope not. I hate the North Koreans. They killed my mother and father, my little brother. I'm glad the USA is here and I can fight against the NKPA with you. If you didn't come, they'd have the whole country, and I'd have to do what they say—the same men who killed my family."

Sam nodded. Enough. Kim looked all right again, the tears gone. Time for a graceful exit. Sam steered him toward the door. "Well, thanks for telling me about the tank. Keep your ears open and let me know if you hear more sounds—"

"Major Anson knows I speak English."

Sam felt a chill of foreboding. The major, mixing into his business again. Carrying Anson's dispatch had nearly gotten him killed before he'd found Goss back at the regimental command post. And now the major was onto Kim.

"Boss, I'm worried."

"Take a load off, private." Sam pointed to an empty crate, and Kim settled on it with the happy look of a kid who has been allowed to stay up another half hour. "Tell me what happened."

"I was over there before dark today," Kim said, "while some GIs from intelligence were setting up that tent the major uses as his office. I figured maybe I might hear something good for you. Behind me, someone says, 'out of the way, private,' and I moved before I could think about it. It was the major. He seemed pleased that I understood English, like he'd been waiting to catch me."

Sam shook his head, impressed. Anson must have realized I had a spy, he thought, from the moment he drew me into that argument about covering the marine flank, and I knew more than he thought I should.

But why suspect Kim?

Most officers ignore KATUSAs as long as they aren't causing problems. That's what made Kim so perfect. He'd just happen to walk by when company captains got on their radios, or get himself put on cleaning duty outside briefing tents where men like the major discussed plans.

Clearly, Anson wasn't "most officers."

Sam rubbed his forehead, trying to think. It was probably inevitable that someone would get onto Kim sooner or later. Good translators were in short supply and, though G-2 had the market cornered already, why let even one get away—especially if, by taking him, you made it harder for a certain lieutenant to pry into matters above his pay grade?

"The next time he has prisoners to question," Kim said, "he wants me in on it."

Sam felt a twinge of envy. What about me? "Don't look so unhappy, private. Going over to intelligence might be a great opportunity for you."

"I want to stay with you."

"No you don't."

"Yes I do."

Sam felt torn; Kim was a valuable member of the platoon. He might be finished as a spy, but he was still an effective liaison to the rest of the KATUSAs, most of whom didn't speak English. "Let me explain something to you, Kim. This is a combat infantry platoon."

"I know that, boss."

"What I'm saying, the best you can hope for here is that the enemy will miss when they shoot at you. With Major Anson, you wouldn't be on the front lines. You'd have a lot better chance of surviving this war." What am I doing, Sam thought. Shut up, already.

"You need me, boss."

"I could get along without you."

Kim's eyes glossed over again; Sam felt like a rat bastard, and at the same time resented the feeling. *I never encouraged him to feel this way about me. After the way Hood sucked me in, I know better than anyone how cruel that would be.* "I just mean that some of our KATUSAs are starting to pick up enough English to get the commands. I've appreciated your help, but your skills are overkill here. You could help the major quite a bit."

"I don't want to help him. I want to help you."

Hartung stopped snoring and rolled away from the wall, lifting up on his elbows to protect his back. He blinked at Kim. "What are you two gabbing about in the middle of the night?"

Sam patted Kim's shoulder. "The sergeant needs his sleep, and you need to get back to the foxhole and listen for those tanks, all right?"

"What about Major Anson? Will you help me stay with you?"

"Let's not worry about that until it happens, all right?"

Kim held his eye for a beat, then smiled. "You'll keep me, boss, I know you will." Before Sam could answer, he was gone.

"What was that about?" Hartung asked.

"Nothing. The kid's so dumb he'd rather fight on the front line than stay behind in a nice warm tent."

"Kind of like us, huh?"

"Speak for yourself, Hartung."

At the table, Sam looked at the map where Kim and his father had visited the shrine. Your dad had no choice but to leave you, Sam thought. Mine had a choice; he traded me and my mother for the United States Marine Corps. I can't be your father, kid, even if I wanted. Damn it, it isn't up to me. Anson's a major and I'm a lieutenant. If he wants you, he gets you, and there's nothing I can do about it.

As the battle for Seoul continued on September 27, field intelligence was contradictory and confusing. Some reports had the North Korean defenders fleeing *en masse* from the northern reaches of the city. At the same time, fierce fighting continued at the barricades. Generals MacArthur and Almond, eager for the city to be retaken on the three-month anniversary of its fall to North Korea, saw what they wanted to see and sent communiques accordingly. Marine and, to a lesser extent, Army units battling in the city saw what they did not want to see—the enemy fighting back hard. In war, perhaps more than anything else, the devil truly is in the details. As the conflict continued, faulty intelligence would have enormous costs in loss of life and, indeed, on the outcome of the war. . . .   (Ibid.)

14

27 September, Kwang Who Moon Circle, Seoul, 1045:
Hood hunched down behind the Pershing tank with the six of
his boys still on their feet. Smoking one of Jimmy's Chesterfields
to mask the tank's exhaust, he pondered the significance of the
Pershing's presence. It belonged to the heavy tank company of
Sam's regiment. For it to be here instead of farther east in the
army zone could only mean it wasn't needed by the 32nd, which
was good, because the less combat Sam saw, the better.

He showed real guts, Hood thought, on the hill with me. But
the men he killed will haunt him, even though it was entirely
honorable. In a pitched battle, it's kill or be killed. He's no
soldier, not in his heart. He's too sensitive, like his mother. Just
let him keep his head down, survive, and get back to his life.

And stop asking me questions which he can't understand the
answer.

You chose the Marine Corps over us.

Hood closed his eyes. Was that really what he thought? Why
hadn't Iris told him? Maybe she couldn't bear to think about it,
or maybe she could never find the right words, or was scared if
she tried to explain, Sam might hate her too, which would leave
him with no one to help him.

She didn't do anything wrong, Hood thought. Except to love
me. If our falling in love was wrong, it was a team effort, and Iris

and I deserve all the pain, not Sam. It wasn't fair he had to go through it, but what am I supposed to do, wish he'd never been born? When we made Sam, we didn't know, we didn't get it yet.

Hood felt a stinging pain in his palm; Jimmy gave him a look and he realized he'd just slapped a Pershing tank, never a good idea.

Gotta get his head back in the game.

He swung out for a quick look at the barrier. Smoke from blazing office buildings on either side of the street shrouded the far intersection. Sweat stung his eyes—another hot day even without the fires from the bombs and artillery that had turned Seoul into a blast furnace. Through patches in the smoke, the barrier looked like all the ones before it. While the army and marines had spread out from Inch'on, the NK had been busy little beavers, damming the streets with an endless obstacle course of gunny sacks filled with dirt or rice, stacked to chest level at every intersection. It was working; the barriers had slowed the marine advance toward the city's heart to a bloody crawl. Four ambulances trying to get to the wounded had been blown up in the few hundred yards the squad had advanced this morning, seven medical corpsmen dead, poor, green Milo Stempleford riding a box ambulance back with a shoulder wound—not even a full day with the squad.

Through the swirling smoke, Hood could see the NK machine gun that was making life miserable in this latest attempt to advance—a flashing muzzle spraying the length of the street with fifty caliber shells. He could hear them ringing off the armor of the Pershing.

"For God's sake, Sarge!" Yanking on his arm, Jimmy pulled him back behind the tank.

"I'm gonna get that machine gunner," Hood muttered.

"No you're not. You're going to wait for air support to strafe them."

Hood settled his back against the rump of the Pershing. Jimmy was right, he'd be crazy, even in this smoke, to try and sneak up there.

But if some other opening didn't come soon, he was going to do it anyway.

Taking a drag that burned the Chesterfield down a quarter inch, he eased the smoke out and watched it ascend in white curls that darkened as they swirled into the pall above. Joe Clemons leaned out from beyond Jimmy and scrutinized the corporal's face, which was black as coal with sweat-streaked soot.

"By cracky, I thought I was the only negro in this outfit."

"Very funny," Jimmy said.

"Hey," Steinberg complained from the other side of Clemons. "I'm the funny man in this squad. Isn't that right, Cockburn?"

"You wish."

Beyond Bo, Barstow and Bertleson kept quiet, normal for Bertleson but not for Barstow—at least the Hollywood version. Sadly, Hollywood wasn't around any more. Barstow never mimicked Harry Truman or Douglas MacArthur any more, none of the old talk about becoming an actor when this was over.

Clemons said, "Guess I'll have to content myself with being the only handsome negro."

Jimmy waved a clawed hand. "You're about to take over as squad bald man."

"You got to get my helmet off first, corporal." Clemons pointed to the strap, tight against his big jaw. Hood was amazed and a little put off by the man's good humor so soon after the horror in the church.

Of course, Clemons wasn't the one who'd shot a surrendering enemy.

The big negro shook out a newspaper and started reading.

"What you got there, Clemons?"

"The latest *Stars and Stripes*. One of the tankers gave it to me after we wiped out that last barrier. Pretty interesting reading." He held up the front page, dated September 26—yesterday—and Hood blinked in surprise at the headline: "SEOUL LIBERATED."

"I'll be damned," he said.

Clemons read from the article in an amused drawl: "Three months to the day after the North Koreans launched their surprise attack south of the 38th Parallel, the combat troops of X Corps recaptured the capital city of Seoul. The liberation was accomplished by a coordinated attack of X Corps troops. By 1400 hours, 25 September, the military defenses of Seoul were broken. The enemy is fleeing the city to the northeast."

"Then who in hell is shooting at us?" Jimmy asked.

"I wonder if this means we can go home," Clemons mused. "Since we beat them two days ago. Just sashay on back down this street and catch the next boat to Biloxi."

"What it means," Hood said, "is that we have to get moving past these damn barricades or make our generals into liars."

"I think they already done that for themselves," Jimmy said.

"Put a lid on that, corporal. Where's that damned air support?"

"Now, sarge," Jimmy said, "it came all the other times, it'll come this time, too."

Scaling the rear of the tank, Hood grabbed the phone on the back of the turret. After a minute, someone inside picked up. "Can't we get moving?" Hood asked.

"You got a lunch date or something?"

"The longer my squad is out here, the more chance someone's going to pick us off. We gotta move in on the barrier."

"Can't. In case you haven't noticed, they've got a tube down there, some kind of anti-tank weapon, firing rockets at us. Can't shoot for shit, but if we get any closer, even a gook couldn't miss and they'll blow us to hell. On top of that, we're running short of ammo with more barricades ahead and no resupply in sight. I've got to conserve until your Corsairs soften it up."

"The hell with you, I'm going." Hood slammed the phone into its cradle and slid off the back of the Pershing.

Clemons blocked his way.

"Move, private."

"Sergeant," the big man said in a low voice, "You did God's work in that church, and He's telling me not to let you go kill yourself now."

"What?" For a second, it didn't sink in, and then Hood realized what Clemons was thinking. That he'd taken on a death wish because of the church.

"I'm fine."

"Maybe so, sergeant, but God is also telling me there's no cover down that street, and six poor dead marines, may they rest in peace, lying out there already, and if you go, you going to be number seven, and I'm to stop you."

Hood shook his head. "Son, in the United States Marines, you can talk to God all you want, but if God talks to you, you get a psychiatric discharge. Now get out of my way."

"I'll go," Barstow said. He had that distant, already-dead look in his eyes.

Hood shoved him back. "I say who goes and who stays. Sit your ass down, Barstow."

Jimmy took hold of Hood's shirt. "Sarge, listen—"

"Damn it, corporal—"

"No, I mean *listen*."

Hood heard the welling roar of plane engines from behind them reaching a thunderous pitch as the Corsair flew low down the street, its wings spitting fire. Gouts of dirt flew from the barricade, and then an explosion flared as a rocket from the Corsair scored a hit on the bags—unfortunately well to the right of the machine gun. Smoke and flames shot up, dirt flying everywhere, but it smoldered down quickly as the bags burned off.

When the smoke cleared there was a gap in the barricade, and that was all—two gook bodies being dragged from the gap, the machine gun on the other end still firing.

Then a gook rose with a tube on his shoulder and fired a rocket that screamed overhead.

Sooner or later, even at this range, one of them was going to hit the tank.

"Sarge," Jimmy said. "Why don't you and me go inside that apartment house over there, get up to the roof, and shoot down on the bastard? He's reloading every couple of minutes. Takes him about ten seconds during which there's no firing. We can blow the door with a grenade, then haul ass inside during his next reload."

"I like it," Hood said. "Clemons, if we can get that rocket tube too, the tank can move in. That happens, you and Barstow clear away the mines they're sure to have spread in front of the barrier. You other two follow them and give cover. Just stick behind the tank as it moves in and shoot any NK who rears up to pitch a grenade over those bags."

"He's coming up on a reload," Jimmy advised.

Hood plucked a grenade from his belt, pulled the pin and lofted it underhand onto the front stoop. Two beats, and the grenade went off, and the door canted back inside, hanging by one hinge.

"Nice throw," Jimmy said.

The steady clatter of the machine gun stopped for the reload.

"Go!" Hood took off for the apartment building, hopping the curb and hauling on the rail to speed himself up the steps and into the smoking foyer, his M-1 out front as Jimmy crowded in behind him.

Back in the street, he could hear fifty-caliber shells clanging off the tank again.

So far, so good.

Hood took a couple of deep breaths, half-winded from the short dash.

"Sssst!" Jimmy said, pointing.

Down the hall, a door eased open. Jimmy sighted in on it; Hood heard a high, brittle voice chattering in excitement. He pushed Jimmy's M-1 aside as an old woman scurried into the hall and bowed over her clasped hands. "Think she's glad to see us?" Jimmy asked. The woman pointed at the ceiling and shook her head, holding an imaginary burp gun in her two tiny fists, shaking as she mimed firing off a burst. She pointed up again.

Hood flashed the old woman an "okay" and waved her back into her apartment. "She's happy to see us, and there's an enemy soldier somewhere up those stairs."

"Yeah, I got that."

Slipping through the foyer, Hood angled into the steep staircase to his right. Low watt bulbs, too far apart, gave him a murky view of a red carpet runner, frayed at the edges, and an empty landing at the top.

"Cover me, Jimmy." No sense trying to be quiet on old wooden steps with all the booming outside and the crackle of small arms fire. He ran up the steps, slowing as he neared the landing, turning onto a second floor hall, his finger heavy on the trigger of the M-1, but the hall was empty.

He motioned Jimmy up behind him. "With this stacked stairway," he whispered, "we'll have to clear each hall to get up to the next floor. You cover me while I get down to the other end, then move up when I signal."

"That ain't how it works, sarge. This next floor's mine."

"I'm not going to argue—"

"Good." Pushing past him, Jimmy hurried down the hall, tipping his muzzle toward each door as he passed, then waved him up from the far end. The carpet runner with its Persian design reminded Hood of the one in Iris's flat in New York. No smell of nutmeg here, though, only the stink of cabbage and garlic mixed with a faint bite of smoke from the street.

He covered Jimmy up the next flight, then switched off with him at the top. All the doors on this floor were shut, too. The NK the old woman had warned them about could be anywhere, but it made sense he'd want a street view. If he had the right angle and a burp gun, he could hose down the pavement. He might also be here to stop attackers from gaining a strategic position on the roof. If he'd seen them come in, he'd be at the hall door of a front apartment, listening. If he was smart, he would let the fire team pass him, then step out and blast them from behind as they went up the steps—first the cover man, then the advance man, bang, bang.

Which means I'm looking the wrong way, Hood thought.

He turned away from Jimmy, who was almost up to the landing, and focused on the door right behind him. If I'm the NK, he thought, I have the door open just past the latch—so slight no one sees it unless he's looking. That way, I don't make a sound coming out.

Jimmy was waving him up.

Hood hesitated. From when the NK must have spotted them coming in, he'd have had plenty of time to scoot down the hall to a back apartment, where no one would expect him. It would give him the easier shot, straight down a hall instead of up a staircase.

Hood reached the next level. Instead of hurrying down the hall, he turned to the apartment at the head of the stairs.

Its door was a quarter of an inch from shut!

Hood felt a savage excitement. Motioning Jimmy past him, he kept his M-1 trained on the black crease. Six clumps of Jimmy's boondockers and it widened and there was the North Korean, the burp gun coming up in his hands, his face starting to look surprised as Hood shot him high in the chest. Pulling down a fraction, he hit the heart with his second shot, driving the man back and down.

Kicking the door, Hood pushed through, ready to fire again, but the NK gunner bucked and went still. Beyond him, Hood saw an old woman sitting bolt upright in a chair. A second later, the ropes registered, and the gag in her mouth.

"Damn," Jimmy said, behind him.

"Watch the door," Hood said.

He used the bayonet to cut the old woman loose. She grasped his hand, her head bobbing in thanks. Around her, he got quick impressions of dolls lined up in the alley window, flowers in a vase, paintings of more flowers on the wall.

Dragging the NK gunner into the hall by his collar, Hood took the burp gun from his dead hands. It was one of the earlier Soviet models, where you had to select for full auto—the little lever forward in the trigger guard. This one had the 71-round drum, not the smaller, detachable box which was only good for 35 rounds. The Russians had made a good gun, here. Plenty of stopping power in the 7.62x25mm caliber shells. Simple blow-back action, a high rate of fire from the open bolt position, just enough room for your other hand forward of the drum.

Leaning down, Hood closed the former owner's eyes. A soldier, this one. Easier for him if he'd killed the old woman, but he hadn't.

Hood touched a finger to his helmet in salute.

"He might not be the only one, corporal. Two floors to go. I'll take the next landing."

Once there, he checked the door, making sure it was tightly shut before starting up the next flight. On the top floor, all the doors were firmly closed. Hood scanned the ceiling for a hatch, found it at the rear end of the hall. Slinging his M-1 on his shoulder, he kept the burp gun in one hand and climbed the fold-down ladder until his head was in the well, giving the roof hatch a half-inch push to make sure it would open. If an NK sniper had gone ahead of them to the rooftop, he might have heard the shots two floors down. With luck, the fight in the street had covered it.

Hood drove the hatch open with his helmet, legs pumping him the up the ladder as the hatch banged onto the roof—

Damn—two of them crouched behind the low brick rim of the roof, getting ready to fire down.

My boys!

Ice shot through Hood's veins. He yelled. As the two NK turned, he squeezed the trigger, spraying a burst that took them both down to thrash in the gravel. He ran to the bodies, hearing Jimmy behind him.

Both men were dead, riddled.

Moving in a crouch to the low parapet, Hood popped his head over to scan the street. "The Pershing's hit," he told Jimmy.

"Our guys?"

"Fine—they're still down behind the tank, but the track's been knocked off on this side, damn gooks finally got lucky with that tube." He waited to see if the Pershing would fire on the barrier. It didn't, probably out of ammo.

"The machine gun's still popping," Hood said, "keeping our guys pinned. We get that .50 cal, they can rush the barrier."

"Can you see their gunner?" Jimmy asked.

"Helmet and shoulders."

"Anything left in your magazine?"

"Too far, a burp gun isn't accurate from here. You get down to the corner there and sight in with your M-1. When you're set, I'll pop up and spray this thing at him to get his attention. You take him down from over there."

"Got it."

Jimmy scuttled across the gravel and tarpaper roof to the corner closest to the barricade and set up. Hood rose and squeezed the trigger, churning bullets down toward the NK machine gunner, emptying the magazine with that long brrrrrrp that gave the gun its name, seeing no effect, and then Jimmy's M-1 barked and the gunner reared back, flung his arms up, and dropped behind the barrier.

Exhilaration pumped through Hood. He yelled down at the tank. "Joe, Joe!"

Clemons looked up at him. "The machine gun's down, get going, we'll cover you. Watch for mines."

Clemons, Barstow, Steinberg and Bo took off toward the barrier. Hood saw another NK move in to take over the machine gun. Firing his M-1 the same instant as Jimmy, he saw the man spin and fall back. Barstow took the lead, keeping low, his eyes on the street, pointing out paths through the mines as Steinberg passed him and tossed a grenade over the barrier. Seconds later, Bo and Clemons threw theirs. The explosions toppled large portions of the barrier forward, and Hood fired at a stunned

NK, now exposed and trying to crawl away as Steinberg heaved another grenade right over the machine gun, blowing the gun and its tripod forward into the street.

The squad climbed through the holes in the barrier, and Hood could hear the popping of their M-1s and a few shouts, and then Bo and Steinberg started clearing bags out of the center of the barrier. Barstow was picking his way forward to join them when Bo hurled a sandbag his way—

"DON'T!" Hood shouted—

—as an explosion blew Barstow sideways.

The sandbag had exploded a mine.

Hollywood lay still on his side in the rubble, his right leg ripped open, crimson blood spurting in arcs from his thigh.

Hood sprinted back to the roof ladder and dropped down into the building, hearing Jimmy scramble behind him. He bolted down the first flight of steps, the air seeming to resist. Grabbing the newel post to pull himself around, he took the hall and hit the next flight, boondockers clumping—dear God, four more flights, a hall between each, did anyone on the street know what to do? A tourniquet was the only chance, high up the leg, right away, a major artery could empty you in a minute. Third floor, and Barstow shouldn't be dying, because Seoul had fallen two days ago if only you could believe the papers. Back home, Iris would be saving the New York Times that pronounced the big battle over, keeping it on the little table by the davenport, headline up, waiting to hear that Sam had made it through all right, never dreaming he might still be in the thick of it. What would Lieutenant Lui write home to Barstow's mother—that her son had died two days after they'd declared victory? Second floor, and a door opened in the hall as he passed, forcing him to slow and turn, groping for the .45 at his belt until he saw it was just a kid, pulled back by his mother as the door slammed again.

Down the last flight and out into the street, Hood sprinted past the tank with the mangled tread. Seeing the commander's head sticking from the turret, he yelled at the man to radio for an ambulance. Ahead, Steinberg and Clemons knelt over Barstow.

Hood dashed over fallen bricks and chunks of concrete, slowing enough to avoid breaking an ankle, watching for mines, kneeling, finally, at Barstow's side.

Clemons had clamped Hollywood's upper thigh with his hand, slowing the hemorrhage some, but not enough.

"Give me your web belt, private."

Steinberg whipped it off, and Hood snatched it, fingers fumbling the tongue back through the brass buckle. He worked the loop up Barstow's leg. Clemons let go and the artery spurted again, spraying in Hood's face as he got the loop to the top and cinched it, working to set the buckle, his bloody fingers slipping on the pinch pin.

The severed artery pumped more blood, and then the flow choked off as Hood pulled the belt tight. As the bleeding subsided, he could see the stub of artery poking from the torn muscle, the skin flayed back, that pantleg gone.

Barstow's face was pale as ivory, his face slack, jaw hanging open.

Hood pulled his helmet off and pressed his ear to Barstow's chest. For a moment, nothing, and then he detected the heartbeat, weak and fast.

"We've got to get blood into him."

"Bertleson ran back to get a medic," Clemons said.

Looking up, Hood saw Bo standing back, staring at Barstow with horror, his face pale. "I'm sorry. . ." he said brokenly.

"Private Cockburn, I need you to watch the street ahead, warn us if you see any NK coming. You too, Steinberg. Find cover behind what's left of the barrier."

"I didn't mean to," Bo said.

Steinberg took the big man by the arm and led him away.

Clemons and Jimmy stared back down the street, toward the Pershing. "I don't think an ambulance can get past that tank," Clemons said. "And they have to fix that tread before it can move."

"We'll carry him back," Jimmy said, bending to take Barstow's good arm.

"Hold it—we don't want to hurt him worse." Hood did a quick check of Barstow's wounds. The blast had stripped the shoulder on the same side down to the muscle, red and raw as hamburger, and his head was cocked at an odd angle. Gently, Hood probed the back of Barstow's neck, feeling the bone, his heart sinking as he felt a loose chunk under the skin. Damn it to hell, the blast might have fractured his neck, too. They couldn't risk picking him up.

"Jimmy, you and Joe go back to that apartment we just left and bring that steel door back. It's hanging by a hinge, break it loose. We'll use it to carry Barstow."

Hood leaned close to Hollywood's ear. "Hang on, son. You're gonna be all right, I promise you."

Boots crunched through the rubble, Bertleson, stumbling to a stop, panting, hands on knees.

"Did you find a corpsman?"

"He's com. . .coming as soon as he gets done with another wounded fellah he's got back there. . .a block and a half."

"You told him to bring blood?"

Bertleson nodded, stooped over, trying to catch his breath.

Hood checked his watch. Four minutes since he'd cinched the tourniquet. It hadn't just stopped the hemorrhage, it would have cut most of any remaining blood flow to the leg. If he kept it tight, the leg would die.

But wasn't it a goner, anyway, with the major artery severed?

He'd seen plenty of legs and arms torn up less than this in the last war, and not a man he knew of had kept the limb. Loosen the tourniquet and blood loss might kill Barstow. Better to keep it tight, forget the leg and save his life.

"Stay with him," Hood said. "I'll make sure that tanker called an ambulance." Climbing the front of the tank, he rapped on the hatch. When it didn't open, he scrambled around to the rear and snatched up the phone.

"Yeah?"

"Did you get that ambulance?"

"How? We don't net on marine channels."

Shit, that's right! "Well, who's calling in the artillery? Don't you have a marine forward spotter directing artillery and tank fire?"

"Yeah, but only because Army gave him one of our radios. We're linked up on our net, not yours."

"Well, damn it, he's got his own radio, too, or he couldn't turn around and call in marine artillery. Get him on the horn, give him our cross street, and tell him to relay it to battalion aid on his marine channel."

"Christ, sergeant, I can't do that. He's bringing in salvos all around him, he's too damn busy to relay messages for one wounded marine."

"You do what I say you fucking dogface, or I swear to God I'll put a grenade under your turret right now and let God sort y'all out."

A second of shocked silence, then: "All right, all right, keep your shirt on."

"Don't just pretend to do it, either, because if that ambulance doesn't get here chop chop, you're gonna die, you got my word on it."

"I'm calling, I'm calling—Jesus."

Peering back up the street, Hood saw Bertleson through a haze of smoke, hunched over Barstow. An artillery round landed beyond the barrier with a flash of orange flame; Bertleson shielded Barstow's body as grit rained down. Hood thought of running back, but then the tankers could see him through their view slit. After his threat, they might just be scared or riled enough to cut him down with their forward machine gun. Better to let them worry about him up here with his grenades.

Jimmy and Joe ran past with the door, and it occurred to him that the tanker was right—getting a forward controller to try and save one wounded marine when so many were in danger was not a good tradeoff. What if some other marine, still on his feet at this moment, died waiting for an artillery strike that could have taken out his killer while the controller tried to get help for Barstow, who might not make it no matter what?

We fought together at Pusan, Hood thought. I took Barstow up a hill to cut men's throats, and after that, he wasn't the same. Before, he'd never have let anyone, green or otherwise, toss a goddamned sandbag into a mine field he was standing in.

The tank phone was still pressed to his ear. "Were you able to get through?"

"Yeah, we told him. Ambulance doesn't come, it's on him, so keep them damned grenades on your belt, pops, okay?" Hood heard him mutter, "fucking maniac," as the connection broke.

Jimmy and the others had gotten Barstow onto the door and were heading toward him. Slipping down off the tank, Hood found a grip on one side of the door and helped them get it back around the corner. A corpsman ran up to them, two bottles of blood slung side by side in his canteen canvas. They lowered Barstow to the sidewalk and he went to work, tying off the marine's good arm with rubber tubing.

It took him nearly a minute to find a vein that hadn't collapsed. At last he got a line started.

An ambulance screeched to a halt in the street.

Hood's hopes rose a little. Barstow's color was edging back.

Two men from the ambulance brought a litter. The corpsman held the bottle of blood aloft and Hood cradled Barstow's head to keep it stable while the others eased him onto the litter.

Hood was climbing into the ambulance behind Barstow, when a hand caught his arm from behind. Turning, he choked off the snarl pushing up his throat. It was Lieutenant Lui.

"Where do you think you're going, sergeant?" Lui's face was bloody where a bullet had taken a hunk out of his cheek, his right arm splinted from elbow to wrist, that hand clutching a .45. Whether or not he'd fought before, the new lieutenant was a fighter now. "This man's in a lot better hands than yours, now, isn't he?" Lui said.

"I want to make sure he's treated right away, sir."

"You've already seen to that. The rest of your men need you—now and here."

Behind Lui, Hood saw men from Corporal Dunleavy's squad mixing in with his own men.

"Take the rest of your squad to the next street over," Lui said. "No one's assaulting that barrier and we've got to clear it."

Hood looked back at Barstow on the stretcher, a corpsman switching in a new bottle of blood. He wanted to be with Barstow after they took his leg, tell him it was all right, he could still live, but Lui was right. Jimmy, and Bertleson and Clemons, and Bo and Steinberg, they needed him, too, and if one of them died on the next street over because he wasn't there to take care of him, how would he live with that?

Dropping down from the ambulance, he turned back to the corpsman: "Whatever you do, don't loosen that tourniquet."

"No sweat, sergeant. We know what we're doing."

General Douglas MacArthur had a widespread reputation for brilliance, but he was not above mistakes in judgment. One that would cost him in the Korean war was his belief that the Chinese were poor soldiers. MacArthur had intelligence reports to the contrary from the Korean Liaison Office, which had placed sixteen Korean agents in the north to keep track of troop movements above the 38th parallel. KLO officers in Seoul challenged the loyalty of these agents and thus took the weight from their reports. But even CIA warnings about possible Chinese intervention had insufficient influence on MacArthur's thinking. Before the war, "CIA Memorandum 301" warned that the Chinese army might interfere in any conflict near their border. On July 8, ten days after North Korea struck across the 38th parallel, the CIA issued "Memorandum 302," which opined that the Soviet Union had instigated the invasion of South Korea and that Stalin could unleash Chinese forces to tip the war's balance if North Korea faltered. That was happening now. Even so, General MacArthur, confident from his daring victories at Inch'on and Seoul, was not disposed to worry about what the Chinese might do. . . .   (Ibid.)

15

1st MASH, 1300:

"Well, well, we meet again."

Bonnie winced as Colonel Lipscomb boomed his patented greeting to the OR team at Table 2, behind her—same exact words he'd used at Table 1. She let her lip curl behind her mask: The Mighty Lipscomb, infamous throughout the 1st MASH for passing out during his own lecture. A psychiatrist-turned-bureaucrat who probably knew less about surgery than the average medic or corpsman. All yesterday, he had pored over charts, pestering the nurses about making their entries more complete, giving postop patients the third degree to see if they had any beefs. He'd gotten no satisfaction there, all the wounded swearing by their doctors and nurses.

"Okay, he's under," Hank said.

Bonnie made herself focus on the task at hand, though it felt as if she'd done it a thousand times in the past week—scrubbing another freshly shaved belly with hexachlorophene, then rinsing with saline. The battle for Seoul was keeping the MASH busy today, a steady stream of wounded pouring into surgery. This casualty was a marine from the 1st Regiment who'd taken a bayonet in the upper left abdomen, a neat slice right between the ribs.

Jeff made a big cut near the wound, and Bonnie went to work to enlarge the opening with retractors, separating first the skin, then using the stainless steel spreader to crank the muscles apart.

"That's fine," Jeff said. "I can see it. Guy's lucky—the blade went straight into the spleen and missed everything else. We'll take it out, and that will be that." He went to work isolating the spleen and tying off the blood vessels to the damaged organ to free it for removal.

Bonnie, keeping the pressure on the spreader, was acutely aware of Lipscomb behind her. In all his snooping, had he noticed the pattern in just which charts were vague? It could explain why he'd decided to scrub in—he hoped to catch them doing an arterial repair. Before he'd arrived, they'd covered their six graft cases with bandages, wrapping the four arms and two legs in a lot of unnecessary gauze so Lipscomb couldn't get a clear idea of the damage. Circulation was good in all cases, so there was nothing to tip him off that all six limbs had been clear candidates for amputation under the WWII rules still in effect.

Relax, Bonnie thought. This splenectomy will take at least fifteen minutes, and by then Lipscomb will be back in the mess hall with his coffee and donuts.

She dampened some gauze with saline and packed it in where Jeff was working to soak up the blood that spilled as he cut tied-off blood vessels away from the spleen. Behind her at Table 2, Lipscomb was chatting up young Dr. Hendricks, belaboring a tortured analogy about the "complementarity" of their two areas of training—psychiatry and neurology. "You treat the brain, and I treat the mind that lives in that brain."

Hendricks mumbled something innocuous, probably wishing he was operating on Lipscomb's brain, instead of picking shrapnel out of an unlucky marine's derrière, which was the limit of what doctors without surgical training got to do in here.

Will Lipscomb visit our table, Bonnie wondered, or avoid me? *If he wanted to avoid you, he wouldn't be here.*

Jeff cut the last blood vessels free and removed the spleen. Sally handed her a bottle of sterile saline. As she irrigated the surgical area, she felt Lipscomb at her back, his gross belly just touching her.

"We meet again."

She said nothing, gritting her teeth beneath the mask as she squirted more saline, then removed the gauze sponges she'd put in earlier.

"Dr. Lipscomb," Jeff said, acknowledging him with a curt nod. From the corner of her eye, she saw Hank Basham, pediatrician-cum-anesthetist, nod from his vantage point at the head of the table. Poor Hank, so nice he'd find something friendly to say to the devil himself, rather than risk hurting his feelings.

"What's this?" Lipscomb asked, pointing to the beaker at the foot of the table.

"A spleen," Jeff said. "Would you like a souvenir?"

"No thank you." Lipscomb's strained laugh made his belly shake against her. She stepped away, crowding the table, and he did not pursue.

"So, Nurse Brisbane, isn't it?"

"Pardon me if I don't turn around, colonel."

"Quite all right. I can see you're busy. How have you liked working in a MASH?"

"It's been. . .interesting, sir."

"I should think so, yes, indeed. Not much like ER after all, is it?"

"Nothing could compare with this," she agreed, resisting the bait, praying for him to move on. Lipscomb stayed put behind her as Jeff finished closing the muscle fascia and then the skin, suturing with practiced ease. In another minute, the orderlies would take this litter off the table and put down another. With luck, it would be another bullet or bayonet to the chest or abdomen, nothing controversial.

"Tell me the truth, Nurse Brisbane, you felt queasy the first time they brought in a battle casualty. Probably more than the first time."

"No, sir."

Jeff was working slower now, stalling as he finished. "She won a bet with me," he said, "over who could stand up longest at an OR table. I folded after eight hours. Cost me twenty bucks."

"Well," Lipscomb said, "just remember this, my dear. It's the brittle ones who break in the end."

"Yes, sir, I'll remember that." *Just go, please.*

Jeff gave the orderlies a reluctant signal, and they hurried to the table, removing the marine. In seconds, they were back with another marine. His left side was soaked in blood. A handsome fellow, with thick, dark hair. Checking his dog-tag for blood type, Bonnie noticed the last name: Barstow. He had a serious leg wound that had blown the femoral artery. A crude web belt tourniquet, caked in blood, had been cinched tight around the upper left thigh.

The only chance for this leg would be the forbidden surgery, a graft.

Laura Lidner, on triage today, had come in with the litter. "He got caught in a mine explosion," she said. "Besides what you see, he has a bone chip in his neck. That wound may not be serious—the corpsman says he was moving his arms. He's had six units of O negative."

"How long has the tourniquet been on?" The tension in Jeff's voice made Bonnie's gut throb. *We're going to do it. God help us!*

Laura cleared her throat.

"Nurse Lidner?"

"Uh, the corpsman brought him straight back. The tourniquet has been on around an hour, he thinks."

"Did they loosen the tourniquet at all?" Jeff asked.

"One time. The hemorrhage was pretty severe, and they had to give him two more units."

"Doctor," Colonel Lipscomb said in a flat, warning voice.

Jeff ignored him. "Sally, cut me a four-inch length of Penrose drain, stat."

Sally handed him the tubing, already cut, showing she was onboard, too. He looped it around the shredded femoral above the damage and cinched it tight with a suture. "Let's get that tourniquet off now. Nurse Brisbane, can you get that buckle to slide?"

She rinsed it with saline and worked the pin with her fingers, prying hard until it broke through the caked blood and the tourniquet relaxed all at once. As she removed the belt, blood welled up from smaller vessels torn by the mine blast, but the penrose ligature on the femoral held.

Jeff said, "We'll take a section of saphenous from the uninjured leg."

"No," Lipscomb said. "This is a clear-cut case for amputation. Otherwise, he'll die from gas gangrene."

Jeff looked up at him, his eyes hard above the mask. "I can save this leg, colonel."

"You don't know that, young man—"

"I've saved two others, and four arms."

Oh, man, Bonnie thought. . . .

And that was exactly what Jeff was, a man. She had not written in her notebook for weeks, but this was going in, first chance she got. She had come to Korea to study men, and she had surely found a prime example of ideal manhood in Jeff.

"Are the rest of you with him?" Lipscomb asked.

Hank coughed, and Sally seemed frozen at the instrument tray. They nodded together. Bonnie felt Lipscomb move to her side. "I'm with him," she said.

"So the three of you have willingly assisted in these illegal operations," his voice in her ear was calm, layered with relish at the revenge he could now take.

"That's right, colonel," Bonnie said. "And every surgery Dr. Wittschiebe has done has worked. Six men are going home with their arm or leg intact, instead of stumps."

"Nurse Brisbane, do you realize you could be court-martialed?"

Bonnie felt someone move up on her other side—Major Folsom, Dear Lord, just when it seemed it couldn't get any worse. Behind Folsom, a bug-eyed Laura Lidner looked like someone witnessing a horrible automobile accident.

"Nurse Brisbane, I asked you a question," Lipscomb said in a louder voice.

"What question?" Major Folsom asked.

"This surgical team has been doing arterial repairs, major. Are you aware of that?"

"Colonel, with respect, if you think any of my nurses may have acted improperly, I expect you will take that up with me."

Surprised, Bonnie resisted the urge to stare at Folsom, see if it was really her behind the surgical mask. Instead, she looked at Lipscomb, whose face was turning red.

Jeff said, "This patient requires my full attention and concentration, Colonel Lipscomb. Would you be so kind as to step back and remain quiet, or leave if you prefer."

"Who do you think you are?" Lipscomb sputtered.

"The surgeon in charge of this operating room," Jeff said. "You can court martial me later if you think it will help the wounded who come into this MASH, but as long as I'm at this table with a patient's life in my hands, I call the shots, and I am respectfully asking you to leave."

"The doctor is right, colonel," Major Folsom said. "Rank does not supersede a surgeon's authority in an operating room. That is absolute. Dr. Wittschiebe is in charge here."

"This isn't the end of it," Lipscomb said. "You'll all be answering to me."

"Colonel," Bonnie said, "If this was your leg, what answer would you want?"

Lipscomb glared at her. "Don't try to confuse the issue. I will see this surgical team in Colonel Martin's office, the moment you're done here."

Which turned out to be two days later, when a fall-off in casualties from the battle for Seoul finally broke the cycle of cut/eat/cut again.

Bonnie, a stranger to her own cot for 72 hours, could feel the caffeine burning in her stomach, sizzling around her eyelids.

The angles of Colonel Martin's desk were too bright, the cross-stitch frame gleaming too brightly on the wall behind Colonel Lipscomb's head. Colonel Martin, evicted from his own desk chair by Lipscomb, leaned on his file cabinet like a man watching a ball game from behind the center field fence. Bonnie remembered the gist of his message to her in this same office a few days ago: *If you get caught, you're on our own.*

Lipscomb said, "I suppose with six apparently successful arterial grafts under your belts you folks are feeling pretty smug about your repeated violation of your military orders. That marine's leg was, in my opinion, damaged beyond repair. If he dies of gas gangrene, will that teach you the folly of what you've been doing?"

Going for the jugular. Bonnie forced herself to return Lipscomb's stare, even as her insides quivered with fear. If Private Barstow recovered, she'd be able to hold her head up even in the stockade but, checking him on the way over, she'd not found the improvement the team would hope for at two days postop. There was a pulse in his ankle, but it could have been stronger, and the skin had felt too cool.

"If you have to take the leg off now," Lipscomb went on, "in his weakened condition, he could die from the anesthesia."

Heat rushed to Bonnie's face. "You sound like you're hoping for that."

Lipscomb fixed her with an icy stare. "You're out of line, Nurse Brisbane. But that's hardly unusual for you, is it?"

Jeff said, "Lieutenants Brisbane and Reynolds are two of the finest nurses I've ever worked with."

"Thank you," Sally said in a faint voice. Beside her Hank Basham raised a finger as if to add his own praise, but no words came out.

Lipscomb shot Jeff a jaundiced look, then sorted through some papers. "Dr. Wittschiebe, I believe you were a third year resident when you were drafted. So, in fact, you haven't actually worked with that many nurses, have you?"

"Sorry for not being older, colonel. But I guess older docs have enough clout not to get drafted. And, for the record, I volunteered."

I knew it! Bonnie thought. Rumors that there was a volunteer among the young doctors had all but died away, but she'd continued to hope. Having volunteered, herself—and taken abuse for it from Laura and some of the others—at last she knew who her kindred spirit was.

Lipscomb peered at Jeff with clinical interest, as if he'd just confessed to wrapping his ankles in tin foil to keep the CIA from reading his thoughts. "Most of your colleagues were dragged here by the doctor draft, but you say you volunteered. How interesting. You thought in the army you could experiment on human subjects, is that it?"

"I resent that, colonel."

"What else would you call what you did two nights ago, and by your own confession, no less than six previous times?"

"I'd call it surgery. Sir, you seem to think 'experiment' is a dirty word, but surgeons do it all the time, deciding whether a drain will help or hinder healing of a particular wound, trying different opening incisions to find the best sites and angles for approaching hard-to-reach areas. Anything a surgeon does that he's not a hundred percent sure of is an experiment, so surgeons experiment every time they operate. I would guess that psychiatrists and medical administrators experiment as well, and when they do it there are, conveniently, no army regulations to prevent it."

"Ah, but there is an army regulation against arterial repair."

"Where is that written?"

Lipscomb sat back with a dismissive smile. "You were told. All medical personnel are informed in their initial indoctrinations and I'm confident Colonel Martin has reaffirmed that policy."

"Why isn't it written down, colonel? Every other Army regulation is."

Lipscomb flipped a hand as if shooing a fly. "That's a non-issue. As you know perfectly well, orders are orders, whether written or oral."

"Could it be because the Army doesn't want any written record of a policy that would deny U.S. soldiers their arms and legs?"

Lipscomb shook his head with a sad regret sold false by his cold smile. "It sounds like you plan to serve as your own defense counsel, captain. May I remind you of Abraham Lincoln's warning? 'He who represents himself has a fool for a client.'"

Jeff looked incredulous. "Come on, colonel. You aren't really going to court martial us."

"Oh, but I am."

Bonnie's skin went cold. She closed her eyes for a beat, then opened them again, but she was still here in the office with the little black and white magnet dogs on Colonel Martin's desk, the picture of his short, stout wife, the baseball glove in the out box. I came to Korea to help save lives, she thought, and now I'm going to jail?

"Are you sure you want the publicity?" Jeff's voice, confident until now, had lost some of its assurance.

"It will be done quietly. You are in the Army now, captain. In case you're thinking you can try this in the press like a civilian would, that's not the way it works with military courts."

"I wouldn't be so sure, colonel," Major Folsom cut in.

For a second, Lipscomb wouldn't look at her, his face reddening again. "Major, I'd advise you not to get mixed up in this."

"If I'm not mixed up in this then why am I here?"

"As a courtesy, since your nurses are involved. I have no evidence you were aware of these arterial repairs."

"She wasn't," Bonnie said.

"I can answer for myself, lieutenant," Folsom said tartly. "I did know about the repairs, colonel. Any charges you bring against my nurses, you'd better bring against me as well."

Bonnie wanted to hug Folsom. I was so wrong about you, she thought.

Lipscomb looked uncomfortable. "The decision of whom to charge will be up to me, not you, Major Folsom."

"What's wrong, colonel?" Folsom asked. "Don't want to try a senior officer who is regular Army? You just want to beat up on these young captains and lieutenants? If you think you can keep a trial like this, military or otherwise, out of the papers, you're quite mistaken, I'm sure."

Lipscomb glared at Folsom. "Very well, major, if you insist, I'll bring charges against you as well."

"No, you won't."

The room went absolutely still. With a heavy sigh, Colonel Martin took his elbow off the file. Bonnie's heart lifted. She hardly dared breathe.

Swiveling in Martin's chair, Lipscomb gave him a dumb-founded look. "Excuse me?"

"You will not bring charges against any of my doctors or nurses. Damn it, colonel, you're juggling grenades. Keep it up, and the pins will fall out."

"The regulation—"

"Is impossible, however well-intentioned or even well-founded. You know the issues as well as anyone in this room, and for every coldly logical argument you can make against the surgery, the most half-assed defense counsel can make a hotly emotional one for it—an argument even a jury of senior army officers will find hard to reject. We've got a young man in postop who might well be desperate to kill himself right now if these four people hadn't stuck their necks out to keep his body together. Might other soldiers die if this procedure catches on? Yes. But my money is on Private Barstow making it, because young Dr. Wittschiebe is very good at what he's doing. You want to make an example out of some poor army doctor whose only crime is trying to keep the entire bodies of wounded soldiers alive, at least have the sense to pick on someone who fails at it."

Lipscomb glared at Colonel Martin. "This is insubordina-tion, from the whole sorry lot of you. I must say, Chester, you of all people. . . well, I'm disappointed. I am the ranking officer here, and I will proceed how I—"

"For crying out loud," Martin said, "think. Inch'on is crawl-ing with journalists. They're bound to get ahold of this. Imagine Marguerite Higgins writing it up for the New York Herald Tribune. She'll want background on you. The entire medical staff was present at your lecture on the ship. What do you suppose she'd do with the information that you fainted dead away from the heat—the only one in the room to do so—after publicly suggesting that Lieutenant Brisbane was a weak female who'd pass out at the sight of blood? It wouldn't take much imagination for a woman like Higgins to slant her story that you had a vendetta against Brisbane, though all of us here know that couldn't possibly be the case."

Bonnie's heart swelled. This moment happening right in front of her was exactly what she'd hoped to find in her study of the male species. The most important man in her life had abandoned her and caused his wife and children great pain. At the same time, it seemed to be generally accepted that there were good men in the world. The history books had plenty of examples of men acting nobly, but in her actual daily life, men had disappointed her. Not just her father, but the dads of her girlfriends, who were present in their daughters' lives but seemed indifferent to them; her male high school teachers, droning on in class, escaping at the bell to the smoky sanctuary of the teacher's lounge. She'd grown up wondering if a good man ever came along in ordinary life, a man who cared, a man with even a smidgeon of the same stuff as a Lincoln, a Schweitzer, a Gandhi. Two days ago, Jeff had proven the answer was yes. And now Colonel Martin. Watch Chester Martin for a week or a month and you'd believe he wanted only to keep his head down, cover his ass, hide in his office from all the blood and death. But when it counted, he was risking the silver clusters on his shoulders for what he knew was right.

Why couldn't *he* have been my father? Bonnie thought.

"Are you blackmailing me?" Lipscomb huffed.

"I'm trying to save you," Martin said. "You start this ball rolling and it will get huge before it ends up rolling back to crush you and the whole Far East Command Surgeon's office. Think the Army will thank you for that? You'll embarrass yourself, hobble your own career, and for what? So you can send men home without their legs, wishing they were dead? Because, whether

235

that's the whole story or not, that's the story any court martial would tell."

Lipscomb glared at Martin, drummed his fingers on the desk. Bonnie could feel her heart thudding in her chest. Come on, she thought. Come on.

Lipscomb turned to Jeff, avoiding her now. "Doctor, will you promise to stop doing arterial repairs?"

"Sorry, sir. No can do."

Lipscomb slammed his hand down on Martin's desk, making the little dogs jump. The white one slid over, its face snapping to the rear end of the black one. Lipscomb stared at the dogs for a minute, then got up and left the office.

"I thought that went well," Hank Basham said.

South Mountain, 1330: Sam watched the South Korean sergeant light a Lucky and put it between the lips of the handcuffed captain captured in last night's skirmish with the North Korean People's Army. Sergeant Chun Mak Jimsuk—no press-ganged, poorly-trained KATUSA, this one, but a career non-com in the ROK Army. His hard eyes and shrapnel-scarred face belied the ingratiating grin he was displaying at the moment.

As for the prisoner, Captain Baek's expression as he accepted the cigarette was oddly relaxed, a glancing eye contact, a nod of thanks. He did not look afraid.

I sure would be scared of Chun, Sam thought. Hell, I *am* scared of him.

A raucous cry shattered the silence of the grove, a blue jay, scolding the odd little gathering from atop one of the surrounding pines. The trees screened off the clearing below, where other NKPA prisoners squatted in chains. Hard at the moment to remember that South Mountain was a city recreation area, like Central Park, or Rock Creek in Washington, D.C.—over 700 acres set aside for the people of Seoul to enjoy nature and get away from their city lives. The dirt trail that wound its way up here might well have been worn into the tall grass by lovers slipping away to kiss on the sheltered bench where the prisoner of war now sat.

Sam glanced at Kim, standing next to Major Anson, to see how he was taking the interrogation. Kim's mouth was tight, his shoulders stiff, resistance radiating from every line of his skinny body. But his gaze, fixed on the North Korean officer, betrayed a gleam of interest. What must he feel toward this arrogant captain from the army that had killed his family?

Sergeant Chun put another question to Baek, his voice soothing, deferential. He appeared to be trying to win Baek's trust. A tall order, it would seem, with the captain's hands cuffed behind his back and his ankles chained. By being solicitous, Chun was encouraging the prisoner to feel superior because, chains or no chains, he was a captain and Chun only a sergeant. Playing the dimwit so Baek might fail to watch his words.

Anson murmured something to Kim, who remained stony-faced. He won't look at me, Sam thought, not since we entered the clearing. Trying to make me feel guilty for going along with Anson—like I had any choice. Come on, kid, give it a chance. You might like it.

Chun asked another question and Baek nodded, smiling.

The sergeant's hand flashed out, knocking the cigarette from the captain's mouth. All of a sudden Chun was shouting, Baek staring at him, wide-eyed. Chun pushed Baek to the ground, the captain falling on his cuffed hands, his chained ankles flopping on the bench. The ROK sergeant pulled a pistol from his belt—a .38 revolver. Chun broke out the chamber, emptied the shells, then replaced one. Spinning the chamber, he pointed the pistol straight up and pulled the trigger.

The hammer clicked.

Baek, flat on the ground, had lost his blasé look, his face still impassive but going pale now. Chun seated himself on the NK captain's knees, pinning him, planting a booted foot on either side of Baek's face. He asked the question again, this time pointing the pistol at the NK's head.

Kim's expression shocked Sam from his paralysis. All of a sudden he looked pleased, an avid glitter in his eyes.

Sam started toward Chun.

"As you were, lieutenant," Anson murmured.

"Sir, we can't allow this."

Anson mouthed the word "blanks" then said in a loud voice, "He has to talk. We need to know the truth. If he won't tell us, he dies."

Sam hesitated, uncertain. If the gun held blanks, Baek was in no real danger. But was it all right to go that far terrorizing the man? He didn't know he was not about to be shot in the head.

"Major," Sam said, "the Geneva Convention—"

"Be damned. Better this scum should die than even a single one of our own men." Anson winked at him.

Sam felt a cold paralysis creeping over him. Could the Geneva Convention be stretched to allow such tactics if it would save American lives? He wasn't sure, he needed to think.

Chun repeated his question. Baek answered in a tremulous voice. Chun pulled the trigger, Baek flinched as the hammer clicked. Pressing the muzzle to Baek's forehead, Chun ground it in until it drew blood; asked the question once more. Baek's eyes crossed trying to see into the chamber of the revolver. He was trembling, now. He began talking, the words gushing from him with terrified urgency, his calm arrogance destroyed.

Kim leaned forward, involved now, urging Chun on with a savage grin. Sam smelled urine; saw the dark stain spreading in the North Korean officer's pants.

We're Americans, he thought, sickened. We don't do this.

Chun pulled the revolver from Baek's head and got off his ankles. Jerking the captain to his feet, he sat him on the bench again and turned to Anson. "He admits he lied when we questioned him before, major. There is no NK force moving in from the east. He hoped to freeze your battalion on this hill for a day or more, so you wouldn't go after his regiment, which is now retreating through the city."

"Very well. Thank you, sergeant. Would you be kind enough to return the captain to the prisoner compound."

Chun hauled Baek to his feet, supporting his arm as he shuffled from the grove, chains clanking, head lowered in shame. Kim looked at Anson for the first time. "Sir, how can you be sure he was lying at first? What if he's not?"

"It doesn't matter, private, because I'll recommend we get some mortars registered in on our flank and station a couple of platoons down there for early warning just in case. But I'd be very surprised if Sergeant Chun is wrong. He reads men under stress the way you and I read a postcard. And we have other intel, you see. The moment Captain Baek told us the regiment to be used in the surprise attack was from the NK 18th Division, I knew he might be trying to fool us. That's the enemy division that lost Yongdung-po to the marines. Two nights ago, air recon spotted a large column of NK abandoning the city, retreating north on the Uijongbu road, heading for Ch'orwon. Marine Corsairs from Kimpo and Navy Air from the carriers have been strafing and bombing them. Some wounded from the fleeing column ended up in our battalion aid stations, which is how we know it's the 18th Division."

Sam said, "If you knew all that, why put Captain Baek through psychological torture?"

"Because armies, like men, can never have too much intelligence," Anson replied in his mild, laconic voice, as if discussing the weather. "Lives are at stake. It's our job to collect a thousand notes that could play many different melodies and put them together into the right one instead of the dozens of possible wrong ones. Whenever a discordant note sounds, as it did here, we dare not discard it until we're sure it doesn't fit. Ignoring the discordant notes is what causes most intelligence failures."

"Like us deciding there were no enemy forces on the marine right flank outside Yongdung-po?"

As soon as the words had left his mouth, Sam wanted them back.

Anson held his gaze for a beat, then turned to Kim. "Private, would you excuse the lieutenant and me for a minute? Wait down the path, if you would, please."

Instead of moving off, Kim looked at his lieutenant.

"We'll catch up with you in a minute," Sam said.

Kim left the grove.

Anson settled on the bench and took a pipe from his shirt pocket. Scooping its bowl through a monogrammed pouch, he went to work with a silver tamp. "You continue to amaze me, lieutenant. What makes you think intelligence screwed up at Yongdung-po?"

"A sergeant from the 1st Marines. Ran into him when you sent me with those dispatches to Major Goss. Several of his friends were shot by enfilading fire which we were supposed to prevent. It was a problem all through their attack. The sergeant took a dim view of our regiment and Army in general."

A lighter of the same burnished silver as the tamp brought the pipe to life. Anson exhaled a stream of smoke that glittered in a stray shaft of sunlight; a leathery aroma replaced the pine scent of the grove. "Lieutenant, you have a knack for finding things out. I want both you and Private Kim to come work for me. I believe if I ask Colonel Faith to reassign you two, he'll do it. I'm confident you'd both be good at it."

Sam's indignation cooled—here it was, a bona fide offer.

He imagined the relief of having the duties of command lifted from his shoulders, never to have to order any of his men into battle again, never to fear who wasn't going to make it.

"No doubt you feel an obligation to your platoon," Anson said. "I respect you for it, but they'll adjust to a new lieutenant, and before you say 'no,' you need to think about the fact that your life might well be at stake."

A chill went up Sam's spine. "Why? You said yourself that the enemy is starting to flee north. Once we have Seoul, any forces left to the south are caught between us and Walker's 8th Army down in Pusan. All we have to do is take them prisoner and chase those we can't catch back to North Korea."

"Think MacArthur would leave it at that?"

"Why not? The North invades, we repel that invasion, declare victory, and go home."

Anson sighed. "That would be nice, lieutenant, and maybe even sensible, but no commanding general I know of, from Eisenhower to Bradley to MacArthur, could be content with simply restoring the prewar status quo if he felt he could do more. And for good reason. Leave a 'beaten' enemy intact and in control of his country, and you risk that he'll cause trouble in the future."

"Sometimes, sometimes not. We made no attempt to annihilate the British after we won our revolution. They did come back at us in 1812, but we let them go their way after that, too. Twice, we let them walk away, and they never fought us again. We're brothers now."

"We were brothers to begin with."

"Just as the North and South Koreans are. Would we still be brothers of the British if we'd tried to smash them when they were down?"

"There was an ocean between us and the British," Anson pointed out. "That had a lot to do with us not pursuing them. Here, the only physical barrier between democratic and communist Koreans is an invisible line of latitude. We are the best hope of democracy here; our armies are in place, more ready than they'll ever be again, and General MacArthur believes with all his heart that the world will be better off with communist North Korea erased from it."

"Even if he's right—"

"Hold on, lieutenant. If?"

"The South Koreans should not be forced into Communism—about that I have no doubt. But we've pretty much taken care of that. If the Koreans up north are fool enough to want to be commies, what gives us the right to say they can't?"

Anson watched the smoke of his pipe ascend through the pine needles. "What gives anyone the right to do anything? No, no, I'm serious, Sam. People believe in a lot of different things, and it's rare that fighting for one belief doesn't get in the way of others in the neighborhood. Your reasoning is fine, but the facts on the ground trump it. The man who gives us our orders, General Douglas MacArthur, will be determined to push into North Korea, throw out Kim Il Sung and end communist rule."

He's right, Sam realized. MacArthur's on top now, and he can smell their blood.

But once we've chased the enemy back onto their home turf, they'll have no place left to run. We'll be the invaders, and they'll fight like cornered rats. "When we cross the 38th parallel, what will our president tell the Chinese and Russians to keep them out of it?"

Anson shrugged. "I imagine our diplomats will be told to say we have no designs on China. They'll assure China we'll stop at the border—the Yalu River.

"If you were them, would you believe that?"

"Probably not. But that doesn't mean they'll find the nerve to intervene."

"The Chinese built the Great Wall for a reason," Sam said. "They're paranoid about invaders."

"True. But we just won a world war. They can't be eager to tangle with us. At most, they might sneak 'volunteers' from their army down to help their communist buddies across the border. That's why I need you, Sam. It would be our job, yours and mine, to help smoke out such a scheme. We'd put out patrols, do high altitude over-flights, then sift through the results, looking for any infiltration and assessing the numbers and significance. I think you'd enjoy that hunt, Lieutenant Foxworth. Join me, and you can help determine which one of us is right about the Chinese. If it's you, that only confirms my point that you have a gift for intel. If we do get into it with the Chinese, a lot of infantry lieutenants will die. I'm sure you're brave enough to face that, but it would be a foolish waste. You're no fighter. You're a thinker, like me. A young officer with your brains can do a lot more for the war effort in intelligence than you can leading a platoon."

Accept, Sam thought. What's wrong with you? "That day on the road, Major, you tried to make me think you didn't know of any North Koreans on the marine flank. But you're too good at what you do not to have known. You knew, and you told your superiors, and they did nothing about it."

Anson remained silent.

"Maybe it wasn't Colonel Faith's fault, maybe it was General Barr or someone above him. Whoever it was, I'm sure he thought he had good reasons—protecting his troops for another fight, or some other goal we're not privy to. But you told them, they ignored you, and there was nothing you could do about it. If they don't listen to you, how could I, a mere second lieutenant, hope to do a damn bit of good for the war effort?"

Anson tapped his pipe on the edge of the bench, knocking the ash out. "Sam, this isn't history, all prettied up for the textbooks. It's a war that is happening now, and this is how wars go. I started out as a 2nd lieutenant like you in the last one, and that war was no prettier, no nobler, and no neater than this one, whatever they end up writing in the history books. Mistakes are made, the ball is dropped, a certain number of our troops will be killed by friendly fire or failures of coordination like Yongdung-po. Galling as that is, it'll always be a small number compared to those who die in battle against the enemy because it's the job of our generals to buy enemy territory, hill by hill, town by town, with American blood. War is fucked, Sam. War is sending good men to get killed. It's ugly and messy, anathema for idealists like you and me who want to do what's best every time out. In a war, we can't. But we can do the best that's allowed us. If Army men had been killed or wounded by those NKs in the hills instead of marines, would that have been better?"

"I prefer not to be the one who has to answer such questions."

"Then you might be happier not asking them."

Anson stood. "I need your decision, lieutenant. Will you and Private Kim join me?"

"You could have Colonel Faith order us reassigned whether we want it or not."

243

"I won't do that—not to Kim or you."

Sam hesitated. *Damn* the man. All Anson had to do was make the decision for him and he could tell the platoon he'd had no choice. But he did have the choice, to stay or to leave them. Surely the men would be all right without him. In fact, their new lieutenant might well be more seasoned, someone better able to take care of the men. His own skin would be in less danger, not to mention Kim's. . . .

Sam remembered the ardent look on Kim's face as Sergeant Chun pressed the barrel of the gun into the prisoner's forehead. Private Kim might be safer, physically, with Major Anson, but what about emotionally? Shooting back at an enemy who had killed your family and was now trying to kill you was one thing. Being encouraged to terrorize helpless prisoners of that enemy, as Kim had just seen in the grove, was quite another—whether it could be justified or not. If Kim became an interrogator, how long before doing it turned him into another Sergeant Chun, with the scars on the inside?

If it's my decision whether to go with Anson, Sam thought, it's Kim's, too. He might look like a kid, but if he's old enough to fight in combat, he's old enough to make his own decision about this. If watching the sergeant work made him want in, I won't like it, but it's his decision.

"Major, I'm flattered to be asked, and I appreciate you giving me a choice in the matter. But I'll be staying with my platoon. I'll put the choice to Kim and let you know his answer."

Anson grunted. "He'll stay with you. He idolizes you, surely you know that."

"He doesn't even know me."

"Better than you think. Maybe even better than you know yourself. Sorry you won't be joining us. Good luck."

Sam shook the hand Anson offered. "Thank you, sir. Good luck hunting the Chinese."

On September 29, General Douglas MacArthur "returned Seoul to the South Korean people" in an impassioned service in the city's National Assembly Chamber. It would be the high point of the war for American and U.N. forces. The conflict was destined to drag on for years but at this moment the liberators were riding high. In just two weeks, the siege of Pusan had been broken, the North Korean Army routed and sent fleeing back above the 38th parallel, and South Korea liberated from the Communists. The People's Army lost an estimated 14,000 killed and 7000 prisoners of war. The triumphant X-Corps paid a sobering price for its victories: The 7th Infantry Division reported 106 killed, 409 wounded, and 57 missing in action. In the two weeks of combat the 1st Marine Division suffered the highest casualties—364 killed, 1,961 wounded, and 5 missing in action. Among the dead were 53 who succumbed to their wounds after receiving treatment in battalion aid stations and the 1st MASH.   (Ibid.)

16

29 September, Liberated Seoul, 1100: Harlan Hood sat near the back of the National Assembly Chamber, reliving the dream about high school. Not the one where he hadn't been going to math class, the other one, where he was sitting in Freshman English between Sharon Brightwood and Patricia O'Manian, the top two girls of his dreams, and he happened to look down and damn if his pants hadn't disappeared. Sitting there in his boxer shorts, filled with a dull horror, knowing if he so much as moved everyone would look and discover his pre"dick"ament.

Hood silently cursed Lieutenant Lui, sitting there beside him, so spiffy in his dress uniform. If Lui had given him even an hour's notice before collaring him, he might have been able to scrounge a clean shirt and a pair of decent service shoes to spit-shine. As it was, he'd barely had time to wire brush his boondockers. The six Brits beyond Lui must be curling their lips over how shabby the American noncom looked—the proper English Naval Officers, sitting there at attention, necks straight, turned out in pure white from their starched shirts to their. . .

Bermuda shorts and long stockings?

Forget the Brits.

Hood remembered scoping out Seoul from Hill 105, wondering if the National Assembly Building would survive the bombardment. Sitting inside it now gave him a weird feeling of time slippage. The protocol people had tried to spruce the place up

247

with some dark purple drapery but here in the auditorium the battle damage was too glaring to camouflage. Apparently the bombers and attack aircraft had been unable to steer entirely clear. Parts of the place had burned, and rockets and artillery shells had left gaping holes in the walls and ceiling. You could still smell the smoke, and through that, the singed-meat odor any combat veteran would recognize—

Everyone rose to their feet.

Startled, Hood pushed up with them in time to see Douglas MacArthur enter the chamber, arm in arm with Syngman Rhee, the American general dwarfing the Korean President. Together, the two strode to the lectern, regal as kings. Turning to Rhee, MacArthur said, "Mr. President, by the grace of a merciful Providence, our forces, fighting under the symbol of that greatest hope and inspiration of mankind, the United Nations, have liberated this ancient capital city of Korea. It has been freed from the despotism of communist rule, and its citizens once more have the opportunity for that immutable concept of life which holds invincibly to the primacy of individual liberty and personal dignity."

Couldn't have said it better myself, Hood thought.

A 155 millimeter howitzer boomed nearby, probably firing at a building hiding a holdout NK sniper. The vibration from the blast shook loose bits of glass to rain down from the auditorium's broken roof onto the platform and audience. All around, people flinched and covered up, but not MacArthur. Didn't even blink, just went right on with his speech. And then the speech was over and the audience started mumbling around Hood, and he realized the general was leading out in the Lord's Prayer.

Were those tears, running down MacArthur's cheeks?

Hood stared, embarrassed but also touched. General Douglas MacArthur might be an officer, and Army to boot, but there was something grand about him.

Looking at Syngman Rhee again, MacArthur said, "My officers and I will now resume our military duties and leave you and your government to the discharge of civil responsibility."

President Rhee grasped MacArthur's hand. "We admire you," he proclaimed. "We love you as the savior of our race."

Even Lui appeared impressed, eyes riveted on the front, his mask of blandness stowed for the ceremony.

The audience began filing out and Hood let the tide sweep him along until he stood outside in a throng of marines, ROK, and military police. Looking for a way clear, he spotted Corporal Bouden working through the crowd to him.

Jimmy threw Lui a salute, then turned to Hood. "Good news! I finally got through to the MASH. Not only is Barstow alive, they saved his leg."

"Great," Lui said.

Hood stared at Jimmy, afraid to believe, remembering the shredded meat of Barstow's leg, the spurting artery. It seemed impossible. "Who told you that?"

"A nurse. She says she knows you. Lieutenant Brisbane."

A sweet joy spread through Hood. If Bonnie Brisbane said Barstow's leg was saved, it was saved.

"She asked me how you're doing," Jimmy said. "I think she's sweet on you, sarge."

"Probably," Hood said. He felt like a million bucks. Barstow would live, he'd paid his price, that atonement he'd figured he owed because of the throats he'd cut. He could go home now to heal and, when the war was over, they'd all see him in a movie.

"We need to celebrate, corporal."

Jimmy glanced at the lieutenant.

"You two go ahead. I'm due at battalion."

After Lui had moved off, Jimmy said, "Define 'celebrate.'"

"How long since you've been laid?"

"That's what I was hoping you meant."

Hood surveyed the ruined apartments and shops of Seoul, nodding when Jimmy's constant patter seemed to require it. It felt good to be strolling along, loose and easy where only days ago the two of them had ducked, crawled, and sprinted with M-1s in their hands and their guts in a knot. The streets, while peaceful, had a grim, end-of- the-world feel. Fires had raged far and wide, leaving the smells of scorched furniture, the kerosene-like stink of melted tires, and the grim odor of roasted human meat.

Approaching an intersection, Hood was surprised to see no sign of the barrier that would have blocked it during the battle. The Koreans were already busy cleaning up their city, half a dozen firemen carrying body bags from a gutted apartment, its windows broken in by small arms fire or the blast percussion of a 500 pound bomb that might have fallen several blocks from here. The battle had left more glass work than could possibly get done before winter. The plywood slapped up in its place would make Seoul a city of sunless rooms—

Jimmy jabbed him with an elbow. "I said I heard the 7th Infantry is heading south to Pusan. That's your son's outfit, isn't it?"

"Yeah."

"That all you can say. The whole 7th Infantry is going south to Pusan while the North Koreans are running back where they came from. The war's almost over, sarge. Our next stop is Inch'on, bet you anything. We climb aboard the *Henrico* and head for the good old US of A. Home in time for Thanksgiving. Bertleson, he overhead a lieutenant in "B" Company say they're planning a ticker-tape parade for us in New York City—"

"I don't think we're going home, Jimmy."

"Sure we are. The war's over."

"I think we'll be chasing the enemy up north."

Jimmy blinked. "No, sarge. No way. Where do you get that?"

"Common sense. We got 'em on the run, now we're going to finish them."

"You're just saying that because it's what you want."

"I'm saying it because I know how brass thinks."

But Jimmy wasn't all that wrong. He wouldn't mind going north, see what was up there, kick some more enemy ass.

"My guess," Jimmy said, "MacArthur's going to have Walker's 8th Army take over from us. If the South Korean Army wants to keep chasing their northern cousins, maybe MacArthur will send some units from the 8th along so Army can have a reason to thump their chests. Either way, you and me'll be back home eating turkey. . . ."

Stopping in his tracks, Jimmy stared, then Hood stopped, too. A couple of Korean women had ventured onto the front stoop of an apartment building ahead and one was smiling at them. Jimmy waved, and the smiling woman waved back. The other, Hood realized, still had her eye on him, awaiting a cue from him, so he exchanged little waves with her, feeling silly even as his interest sharpened.

"Are these pretty ladies what I think they are?" Jimmy asked.

"Bouden, sometimes I worry about you."

"Don't give me a hard time, sarge. I been so long without a woman I'm startin' to see little yellow squiggles in front of my eyes. Are they or aren't they?"

"I think the one smiled at you is."

"You *think*? C'mon, man."

"If she isn't, what's the worst that can happen?"

"Their fathers come out with burp guns and let some air out of us. . ."

The woman crooked her finger at Jimmy.

". . .and that's a risk I'll just have to take," he finished, hurrying to her.

Hood followed to see where it might go with the other woman. The apartment building was dim and smelled of smoke like everything else, but it wasn't too bad, no evidence of fire in the hallway—the tattered floral carpet would have been first to burn. Jimmy, on the arm of the first girl, turned to wink at him.

"Make sure it's clear in there," Hood warned. "Any Korean men hanging around, you get them out first, and lock the door."

"Yes, Mother."

Hood looked a question at the other woman. She gazed back, not unfriendly, but still hard to read. She went into the next apartment, leaving the door open.

Inside smelled of lilac—not perfume but the coarser scent of bath beads. No cigarette smoke and no body odor. If she was a prostitute, he'd probably be her first man today, since it was early afternoon, but he still wasn't sure that's what she was. He pretended to admire the small apartment, looking through the living room, bedroom and tiny, neat kitchen with a professional eye, seeing no other men and nothing that might belong to one.

The woman put on a record; Dinah Shore began singing through a soft static that only made her weightless voice sexier.

"I've got some jazz," she said, "if you'd rather."

Her English, smooth and accentless, surprised him. She looked thirty, tall for a Korean, with glossy black hair down to her shoulders. Not much nose on her, but he'd gotten used to that in Japan, and she had those full lips he knew would be soft as velvet if she let him kiss her, which the Asian women usually did. She wore a dress of white satin, not tight but tight enough, with the mandarin collar and a slit up the side that revealed a smooth, brown thigh.

He realized his pants were starting to feel tight on their own, in front, like his .45 had slipped around to his zipper. If she wasn't selling it, she'd better tell him now.

She disappeared into the kitchen and returned with a bottle of tonic water and two jelly glasses. "Sorry, no gin," she said, setting the bottle and glasses on the sideboard of a napless blue divan that had been good quality once.

Pouring both glasses, he raised his to her. She tipped hers against his.

"To peace," he said.

It seemed to surprise her. With a nod, she drank hers off.

He sipped his more slowly, warm but not bad, the bubbles standing in for champagne. She's new at this, he thought. Maybe her friend is getting her started. He wondered if this was her place or if she'd been married to a policeman or soldier who'd been killed in battle when the North Koreans took the city. Surely a woman so lovely had a husband, or at least a boyfriend. Hood hoped that, if the man in her life had been killed, it had been long enough ago that she wouldn't start crying on him. She cried, he'd have to leave her be.

She did not look about to cry, seating herself on the divan, motioning him down, turning her perfect knees toward him. Tall as she was, maybe he'd be able to imagine Iris while they did it.

Something told him not to hurry her. "Where did you learn English?"

"In high school and at the Women's University here in Seoul. I went a year in the college before my. . .family needed me home."

"You speak it very well."

"Thank you."

Those dark eyes centered on him, none of the shyness you got with Japanese women. Most Koreans, it was hard to tell any difference physically between them and Japanese, though maybe that was just him not knowing which little details to look for. He'd bet the two races went back to one sometime long ago before they'd become such bitter enemies.

Time to be sure about this. "I only have scrip—no hwan."

Pain flitted in her eyes and he wondered if he'd been wrong after all.

"Scrip is fine," she said. "I'll spend it quick, before they print new. Would. . .ten dollars be all right?"

"Sure. What's your name?"

She looked startled. "You want my name?"

"Just your first name would be all right. Long as we're talking, I like to know what to call you."

She seemed amused. "Wait until Miju—my friend who is with your friend—hears about this. She says GIs never want to talk."

"I'm not a GI."

She focused on his uniform, then inclined her head. "I beg your pardon. The Chinese have a proverb: 'The beginning of wisdom is to call things by their right names.' So hello, Mr. Marine."

"My lieutenant is Chinese."

"How interesting. A Chinese Marine."

"Well, he's American, I mean. But his parents were born in China."

"My name is Jung-Sil—you can call me Sil. What's yours?"

"Harlan. But most people call me sarge."

Leaning forward she touched the stripes on his sleeve. "You are known by your profession."

He nodded, *profession,* pleased that she thought of it that way. An intelligent woman, knowing that a marine sergeant was not a draftee but a man who had chosen the career. In some odd way, though she was Korean, she *did* remind him of Iris. No physical similarity except for the graceful way she moved, but something inside her, that sense you got that you were amusing her in a way she needed to be amused.

Hood took the scrip from his wallet and put ten dollars worth on the end table. She slipped closer along the couch. Beyond her, a curtain of gauze fluttered in the breeze from her smashed-out window. A gentle rain pattered on the window sill, the breeze damp now, raising the scent of orange peel from her skin as he leaned his head into the crook of her throat.

He fumbled at the tong fastenings down the front of the dress.

Gently, she slipped her hands in, and he let her do it herself so he wouldn't tear what might be her only good dress. Underneath, she wore a threadbare slip and panties, which she let him take off.

He felt dizzy looking at her smooth, dusky skin. Sliding his lips across her belly, he tasted her dark down, then went lower to wet her, and found her already wet.

That drove him wild with desire.

Laying her back along the divan, he shucked his pants down and entered her as gently as he could. He came fast, locking a shout in his chest.

He stayed hard inside her for awhile, letting her hold his head to her, liking that she didn't want him off her now the way some of them did.

He lay there almost dozing, feeling her softness around him, too content to move. Dinah Shore was into the duet with Buddy Clark now, "Baby it's Cold Outside," throwing in those sexy sighs. How many times and places had he done this, and it never, not for a moment, helped him forget the woman he'd wanted as his one and only, to be loyal to her always, the way he would like himself to be.

Instead, he kept having other women, hundreds of them over the years, a bedroom or couch never his own, some whose names he hadn't even learned, and now Sil, whom he'd try not to forget. Need making him take the chances he got, even though each time it forced him to remember what he'd lost.

I really can't stay—
But baby it's cold outside
I got to go 'way—
But baby it's cold outside.

To have and to hold. He'd had Iris and couldn't hold her.

Sil gently pulled away and put her dress back on while he loaded and locked his pants and put another ten on the end table. "I hope things will get better for you," he said.

"And for you as well, sergeant."

She gazed at him as he backed to the door and slipped out.

Jimmy waited out in the hall. "What took you so long?"

"Gentlemen finish last." The joke felt hollow, even though Jimmy laughed. It was on him now, worse than usual—the feeling empty and let down and shabby for having to walk away from the woman.

"Yeah, well," Jimmy said, "I been waiting for you outside in the rain, and I was just about to knock."

"What's your hurry?"

"An MP jeep came along, spreading the word. Get this, sarge: 5th regiment is ordered to report back to the command post at once. They're going to truck us all to Inch'on, Sarge, just like

255

I was saying. We got a temporary billet in the Jinsin Electrical Works for while we load up the ships. We're going home!"

"They said that—home?"

"Well, not exactly, just that we're supposed to report back and get ready to load up. Jeez, sarge, when you gonna' believe it?"

"When I put my foot down in San Francisco."

"All right, be a skeptic, but right now we've got to haul ass."

"Yes, sir, corporal, sir."

Hood figured a fast walk was good enough, savoring the gentle rain on his face, trying to sort out how he felt about shipping out as they headed through the scarred streets for the command post. Going home would give him a chance to rest up, get himself back at a hundred percent for the next war.

If he could make it that far.

He was forty years old, and even if only another five years passed before the next dust-up he'd be long in the tooth for combat. He'd stay in The Corps as long as they'd have him, maybe become a drill instructor, teaching the new recruits how to be men. That wouldn't be too bad.

But face it, if Korea was really over he'd probably fought his last.

No more going up hills under fire or having that hollow feeling in your belly when you got in the LST and headed for shore. How had Sil just put it? You are known by your profession. How could he go home? Where he was now—walking the streets of a strange city he'd helped liberate with a buddy who'd fought at his side—this was home.

At the command post, they were issuing new equipment.

Hood trudged forward with Jimmy until they got to the supply sergeant.

"Here you go," the man said, stuffing a bedroll into his arms.

A cold weather sleeping bag!

Jimmy stared at it. The expression on his face brought to mind a marine Hood remembered on Iwo, who'd had his gut opened up by machine gun fire and was holding his entrails in his hands, staring at them with the same disbelief.

"Shit," Jimmy groaned.

"Yeah," Hood said in a sympathetic voice, hiding his relief.

Cold weather sleeping bags could only mean they'd be leaving Inch'on for some port up the northern coast, maybe in North Korea itself.

Not going home, gonna stay and fight some more.

A little scary how much he liked that idea.

The National Security Council advised President Truman not to pursue the North Korean People's Army above the 38th parallel, but General Omar Bradley and his Joint Chiefs of Staff disagreed. They won the argument. Truman ordered MacArthur to enter North Korea and destroy their military forces so long as Chinese and Soviet troops did not enter the conflict. On October 1, Zhou Enlai, premier of China's fledgling communist government, warned that China would not tolerate any invasion of North Korea. In the west, General Walker deployed his 8th Army just below the 38th parallel. Because Inch'on wasn't big enough to launch all of X-Corps at once, General Almond had to divide his forces. The 1st Marine Division sailed from Inch'on around the southern tip of Korea, then up the east coast to Wonson, North Korea. Army's 7th Division marched south to debark from Pusan. Not all NK forces at the Pusan perimeter had fled north after the US victory at Inch'on. If they could regroup, enough enemy remained in the southern mountains to attack the 7th Division on the road. . . .   (Ibid.)

17

9 October, Mun'gyong Pass, 0100:

Watching the convoy through his binoculars, Sam shifted his weight on the boulder. A headache gnawed behind his eyes—all that dust roiling in the headlights, making everything shimmer, forcing him to squint.

Lowering the glasses, he rolled his head around on stiff shoulders. From the corner of his eye he glimpsed the jagged peaks behind him, black under a sliver of moon. A chill ran up his spine. Was the enemy up there watching?

Probably just spooking himself, all alone on his little perch, looking down on the winding column of men and machines as an attacker would. G-2 had warned that thousands of North Korean troops could be hiding in these mountains—remnants of those who had fled north after their defeat at Pusan. If getting away was all the stragglers wanted, no problem. But if they could manage an attack, this pass would be a good place. With the road clinging to a steep mountainside, the division would be unable to mass its return fire, and there'd be no place to run.

Sam raised the binoculars. Quite a sight, twenty thousand infantry with their vehicles, weapons, food, and equipment battling 350 miles of roads so rough progress was coming in hours per mile, not miles per hour. Right now it was the vehicles that were slowing everyone down, drivers inching along fearing for their oil pans.

Be back by dawn, Sam—that's an order.

Anxiety welled in his chest. When was the 1st MASH going to show up?

A breeze stirred, drying his face, stinging his throat with exhaust fumes. He tracked a promising truck forward until a switchback hid it from view. . .

Here it came again. . . .

No. Just another water tanker, its shape rounding out in the haze as it got closer.

Sam swore out loud, unable to hear it over the din of engines and squealing gear shifts. Soon he'd have to hoof it back up the line empty-handed. With nothing but roadside bushes for toilets, everyone with a nose would learn the captain's secret.

Loomis would hate that, but he'd hate no Kaopectate *and* an A.W.O.L. lieutenant even more.

A horn blew, jagging along Sam's nerves. Below him a stalled Jeep was blocking the column. The driver got out and went for his jerry can of gas, flashing the bird at the impatient trucker behind him.

Sam slid down from his rock. "What outfit is this, sergeant?"

"Division Headquarters, sir."

"You wouldn't happen to know where the 1st MASH is?"

"Just beyond me."

"For real?" Sam's mood soared.

"Quarter of a mile, give or take. You can't miss 'em. Just make sure the drivers can see you, sir. The road is pretty narrow back there; you go off the edge, it's a long way down."

Grinning, Sam waved his thanks, already on his way. The stiffness in his legs melted as he headed back along the column, *Bonnie, here I come.*

There ahead, finally—a "box" ambulance, the shape he'd been searching for.

Next came a Jeep with a red cross on the door and a lieutenant colonel in the rear seat, probably the MASH CO.

Three more jeeps rolled past, two ambulances, and then a troop truck.

Pulling himself up by the tailgate, Sam peered into the dark cavern of canvas. Pale faces gazed back at him, four nurses and a bunch of guys, probably docs or medics.

No Bonnie.

Hopping down, he tried the next truck, and there she was, sitting at the tailgate.

"Lieutenant Brisbane."

Her eyes popped wide. "Uh, Lieutenant Foxworth?"

"Might I have a word with you," feeling silly at the formality.

"Um, of course."

Beyond Bonnie, nurses and medics were giving them knowing smiles.

Were they fooling anyone?

Who cares?

He gave Bonnie a hand down. No room on the shoulder to walk beside her, so he followed her back along the column until they came to another of the box ambulances rounding one of the hairpin turns. She climbed onto the running board for a quick conversation with the driver and then flashed Sam the "OK" sign. He scrambled after her through the rear doors, jerking them shut in time to evade headlights rounding the curve behind them.

As the inside of the ambulance lit, Sam saw that it was full of supplies—just enough room left in the rear to sit facing Bonnie, their legs alongside each other's, their backs against the walls. The crates rose high enough to block the ambulance driver's view into the back. And the windows in the rear doors were safely above their heads.

Sam felt his pulse pick up, total privacy!

"Please tell me you're not AWOL," Bonnie said.

He explained about the captain's dysentery.

"And he sent an officer chasing after Kaopectate?"

"Loomis wouldn't trust an enlisted man not to blab it to the whole company. When it comes to his bowels, the captain is a private man."

She smiled. "You seem to understand him pretty well. Why am I getting the feeling this little mission was your idea?"

"He'd have thought of it eventually. He's got enough to hold him until morning. And since I'm no longer falling behind, we can grab a little time for us."

"There's an 'Us?'"

"Don't be cruel. I've missed you. How's life been at the MASH?"

She settled back, gazing at him. "Not so bad, Sam, once the fighting stopped. I saw your fa—Sergeant Hood when we were packing up to truck out of Inch'on. He dropped by the MASH to visit one of his wounded."

She paused, as if expecting him to say something. When he didn't, she went on. "He told me his next stop was the new military cemetery in Inch'on. His lieutenant was KIA."

Despite himself, Sam felt a pang. Hood hadn't mentioned losing his lieutenant. Probably afraid talking about it would tarnish his tough-guy image.

She said, "Aren't you going to ask me how he's doing?"

"I saw him myself, not long ago." He told her about taking the dispatches to Major Goss and getting mixed up in the marine assault.

He heard a little intake of breath and then she touched his arm. "Thank God you both made it through alive. Did you have any chance to talk with him?"

"About what?"

"Come on, Sam. About what. You two fight the North Koreans together, then go right back to your own little war?"

"Cut me some slack, will you? You're not that close to your old man, either."

"What gives you that idea? Just because he and Mom—"

"You called him 'Uncle.' Your own father."

He could feel her sudden stillness in the dark. "That first night," he explained, "at Lulu's bar. You let it slip."

"I did?"

"Half way."

"I don't remember that. But you do. Wow."

The box ambulance lurched on groaning axles, dropped into a pothole and strained out the other side. Had he offended her?

She started it.

"'Uncle Daddy,'" she mused. "That's what we called him—my younger sister and I. I don't remember how it started. Maybe Mom's suggestion. She probably wasn't all that keen on him coming around, and who could blame her? She never told us we couldn't see him, but she didn't want us calling him 'Daddy' either. And she was right—he was a long way from being a proper father. That doesn't mean I'm going around angry at him. I mean, what good would it do?"

"Beats feeling sad."

"You feel what you feel."

"If you're a woman. Guys don't get that kind of pass."

"What do you mean?"

He gave a hard little laugh. "Didn't you notice that the boys in your fourth grade class never cried? Do that on the playground just once and you'd be mocked for the whole school year. Hell, most boys know not to do that by the time they're in second grade. . ." He shook his head. How did he get into this ridiculous conversation? A beautiful woman all to himself in a cozy, private place, and they were discussing playground rules? "Bonnie, can we talk about something else?"

"Like?"

"Our goodnight kiss back at Inch'on."

She laughed. "You're incorrigible."

"I can't get it out of my mind." Finding her hand, he drew it to his lips, then held the palm against his cheek.

"Sam." But she did not pull away.

"I'm crazy about you."

"You don't even know me."

"I know you're beautiful, smart, and interesting. Would it be so terrible just to hold each other? We might be dead in the next hour."

She groaned. "Oh, right, like I haven't heard that one before."

"Yeah, well, it happens to have become true, in case you haven't noticed. Bonnie, I want to kiss you. If the bullets start flying and I'm hit, I want the memory of your lips to be my last."

"Stop it."

"I'm serious."

"You seriously want to kiss me, but you aren't *serious*. I can hear you smiling."

He said, "You felt something when we kissed at the MASH. Don't tell me you didn't. Come on, what's with the wall? We're both adults and we do feel something for each other, you know we do."

She made a sound low in her throat. "I don't believe this. You, I. . . .this is exactly how my mother went wrong, Sam. Uncle Daddy was big and handsome, just like you, and he kept coming at her like you are at me, and she just couldn't resist. She should have. Instead, she got pregnant with my sister and me."

"You say that like it's a bad thing."

She groaned and then laughed. "Just shut up, will you?"

Rummaging in his pocket, he pulled out a condom and held it up in a passing band of light for her to see.

"Terrific. Like that's foolproof. What if we made love and then you found out I was carrying your child? Wouldn't you be in the same position as your father—having a child but not wanting to stay with its mother?"

He winced in the dark at the rhetorical thumb-poke in his eyes, at the same time feeling a grudging respect for her accuracy. "Who says I wouldn't want to stay with you?"

"You can't know that yet, and you don't. You want to have sex, sure, but you're scared to fall in love because, when you were a child, you loved your father but he went away. Sex is over in a few minutes until the next time, but love is supposed to last, and you think it can't with you. So you have to grab what you can in the moment, and forget about tomorrow."

He clapped slowly, controlling his frustration. *Let it pass; stay focused on the prize.*

But she was really starting to annoy him. "And what about you, Brisbane? It's the moment that scares you, am I right? You think sex is what got your mother in trouble, but it's not. What got your mother in trouble was Uncle Daddy being the wrong man."

Her silence told him he'd scored in return.

"I'm not afraid of intimacy, Sam."

"Sure you are."

The ambulance bounced, and in a flash of headlights from behind, he glimpsed her eyes, blue as a swimming pool. God, she was beautiful.

She leaned toward him, reaching.

Startled, he hesitated for a second and then slid to meet her, pulling her to him. Her lips, soft as plums, tasted salty sweet. The kiss went on and on, filling him with a delirious pleasure. He tried to empty his mind, just enjoy the feel of her, but instead he had a sudden, vivid image of her at a surgery table, working hour after hour to save the lives of wounded soldiers, getting their blood all over her but hanging in there, keeping at it. Images flared in his mind of living with her, coming home to her in the evening after teaching high school history all day. Taking her to a movie, or just sitting and talking.

Could he do that?

His stomach churned.

Later, he could think about it later. Now she could be his.

Stroking her hair, he slid his kiss to her cheek, her throat. Her breath came warm in his ear, sending a shiver up his spine. She slid closer, and he felt her breasts against his chest. He explored her back with his hands, the firm V that began with her shoulders and narrowed to a slender waist. Pulling her shirttail out, he circled her waist with his hands, rubbing his thumbs along her sides. Her hands slipped inside his shirt, molding to his ribs, pulling him hard against her.

He kissed her again, holding it until he had to breathe.

She worked herself onto his lap, straddling him in a way that made him groan with pleasure. He wanted to be inside her, right now, but another part of him longed for the touching and kissing to go on, to last as long as it could. Life was suddenly so sweet here in the middle of the night in a strange land, a caravan to nowhere, people dozing off all up and down the line, no one to intrude into their private world.

Sliding his hands under her rump, he lifted her to her knees, then worked to unzip his pants. She climbed off him, shucked her boots, and peeled down to her panties. He sprang loose from his own shorts and she straddled him again—

And gunfire sounded, the vicious rattle of a machine gun.

The ambulance braked, leaning them both against the crates. Voices outside shouted in pain and fear. Small arms began to pop, answering the long rips of the machine gun. Someone screamed for a medic.

"Sam!" Bonnie said in a horrified voice.

He pulled his pants on, the erection instantly gone.

Unbelievable. Only moments ago he'd said they should make love because they might be about to die, and now, suddenly, it wasn't a line.

Bonnie groped for her boots among the crates.

He grabbed his M-1. "Stay here," he said.

Throwing the door open, he jumped down.

She landed beside him.

"Bonnie—"

"Don't be foolish. I'm in this too. I'm needed."

The machine gun sounded much louder, more of them, above in the hills, answered by M-1 fire up and down the column. Bonnie grabbed his shirt, yanked him to her for a quick kiss, and then she was gone, dashing alongside the column.

Frantic that she might be shot, Sam circled around the ambulance and shot into the dark up the hillside, firing a clip off, blind.

Reloading, he took a deep breath.

He must calm down, look for the muzzle flashes.

Why weren't more people returning fire?

Because these were MASH and headquarters people. Had any of them ever seen combat?

They needed someone to get them organized.

Sprinting down the convoy, Sam corralled two men he saw huddling under a truck and a couple more who were crouching behind a jeep. One clutched an M-1, the others, carbines and side arms.

"We're going up the hill," Sam said.

"That's suicide," one replied.

"No. Sitting here is suicide. All their fire is focused on the roadway. They won't expect a counterattack this fast. And they sure as hell won't be able to home in on it in this dark. Just follow me."

"You're going first?" the same man said.

"Yes, damn it, are you with me?"

"Yes, sir."

The others nodded.

Sam led them between two trucks, then up hill. The slope was more gradual here, dotted with scrubby trees. He could see muzzle flashes forty yards up—a machine gun nest pouring tracers down on the column. The best approach would be to slant up from the side.

Glancing behind him, Sam realized with a shock that none of the soldiers had followed him. For a furious second, he thought of going back down to get them, then realized it was probably no use—and that machine gun needed silencing right now, or people would die.

Scrambling across the slope toward the gun, he felt a rock turn under his boot. He grabbed a bush to keep from falling. Pulling a grenade from his belt, he jerked the pin and lofted it underhand, swinging hard to give it some height. Too dark to follow its arc—

An explosion bloomed, and he saw a dark silhouette lurch away from the machinegun nest and fall. The gun remained silent.

Sam tried to back up, and his foot slipped again on loose shale, and then he was falling, grabbing at bushes, rolling over and over until a solid impact in the ribs stopped him. A deeper blackness closed in, then lifted as he sucked a lungful of air.

Damn, that hurt!

He saw that he was lying against the trunk of a small tree. Probing his ribs, he felt pain, but it was dull, not sharp—nothing broken.

He slid down to the road.

Bonnie—had she made it to the medical truck?

Running up the line, he passed a blazing troop truck, the canvas canopy set afire by a grenade or mortar. Ahead, he saw women bending over a fallen soldier. Another wounded man lay not far away, a dark-haired nurse holding up a bottle of blood as another set a needle in his arm.

Sam heard a weak cry for help—there, a man lying on his side between the grille of a jeep and the rear of a water truck. In the glow of the blazing truck the man made an inviting target. Slinging his M-1, Sam lifted the man over his shoulder and ran to the nurses. He saw with a rush of relief that Bonnie was there, bent over a wounded GI. She held a long cut open with her hands while a doctor inspected the wound with a flashlight.

Sam laid the wounded soldier behind Bonnie. A horrible gurgle told him the man had a sucking chest wound. Straddling him, Sam planted his hand over the wound. For a moment, the awful whistling sound of the man's breath stopped, and he felt the chest heave as it tried to pull air, and then the man went still.

Sam pounded the ground with a fist. Fucking North Koreans, this shouldn't be happening.

Bonnie's head swung around, her gaze focusing on him.

"Are you all right?" he asked.

She nodded. The doctor said something, and she turned back to the wounded man. I'm distracting them, Sam thought. They need me to fight, protect them.

Back on the road, he saw men firing up the hill from behind an overturned Jeep, trying to take out another machine gun that was pouring tracer-lit rounds into the column. One of the men pitched back from the hood of the jeep, yelling in pain, and Sam took his place. Bracing his M-1 on the hood, he fired at the machine gun's muzzle flash, his heart dense with rage. Dropping down to reload, he saw an abandoned half-track further up the column, no one manning any of its four .50 caliber machine guns.

Running to it, he jumped aboard and settled behind one of the guns. The handles pounded his palms as he fired a murderous stream at the tracers coming from the hillside. Almost at once, the tracers stopped, the gun silenced.

Gratified, he swiveled the mounted .50 back and forth until he saw more tracers, another machine gun nest. He fired a long burst at it, feeling the grips heat up.

Shells pinged off the armor of the half-track. A dim part of his mind realized he was taking return fire, but it didn't seem to matter.

A long, blank period, and then it was morning, and he was still firing, sitting behind the last of the four machine guns, burning through a final belt of ammo. Trucks and Jeeps burned on either side of him. He saw a sergeant up the line, spraying the hillside with a tripod-mounted .30 caliber machine-gun. Other knots of men had organized themselves and were fighting back.

Gradually, all firing from the hills died away.

Sam sat, exhausted, head down behind the emptied gun. God, so tired, and parched with thirst. Tipping his canteen back, he drained it. Water had never tasted so good. When he'd finished, he realized he was famished. Even the dry K-ration crackers would taste great right now. Probably some in one of the convoy trucks.

But first, Bonnie.

Climbing down, stiff-legged, from the M-19, he headed for where he'd last seen her. She was still there, on the road, directing orderlies as they moved a wounded man into an ambulance. His heart swelled at the sight of her, alive, unhurt. She nodded at him, and then the doctor from last night approached and started talking to her.

Sam stared at him with dread fascination. This was her doctor friend. In daylight, the scarring on his chin and neck were obvious. Handsome, in spite of it. Whatever he was saying, he had Bonnie's full attention. She hurried off with him without a backward glance.

Thinking he'd follow, Sam got two steps and then a knee gave out, nearly dumping him. Irritated, he stumbled to the base of the hillside, found a patch of moss and sank down. He'd rest here just for a minute, then find Bonnie when she wasn't tied up with that doctor, scare up some K-rations to share with her.

Leaning over, Sam felt the moss cushioning his side, soft as a mattress.

The world winked in and out, then faded to gray.

Chinese preparations to enter the Korean war began early, with great care taken to avoid alerting U.S. intelligence. After observing the course of the conflict through August of 1950, Zhou Enlai warned his People's Liberation Army it must prepare to go to war against the United States. Chinese intelligence had watched the build-up of American forces in Japan, including their preparations for an amphibious assault by the two divisions MacArthur had held back from the Pusan perimeter. China had, in fact, correctly guessed where the Americans would land and had warned Kim Il Sung to pull some troops from Pusan to help defeat an attack at Inch'on. The North Korean leader had chosen to ignore the warning, dashing all Chinese hopes for a quick victory. In the words of Zhou Enlai, China must "prepare for the worst and prepare quickly." Zhou emphasized that the military buildup for the coming conflict must be undertaken with the utmost secrecy, so that China could enter the war with a surprise attack and "give the enemy a sudden blow. . . ." (Ibid.)

18

22 November, Pukch'ong, North Korea, 1040:

With four shirts on, Bonnie couldn't be sure Jeff was flirting. Definitely snuggling his arm against hers, but maybe just to keep warm. Laura, sitting on her other side, shivered out of control, hair dotted with melting snow, her turned-up nose red. The little church was full of shivering people, the rows of folding chairs packed with doctors and nurses, their breath drifting up in ghostly plumes, as if their souls were leaving their bodies—

She shuddered—sheesh, morbid. Too many losses in surgery, lately.

The wind howled under the eaves, blowing down from Manchuria at thirty miles per hour. If this was only the start of winter, you could see why the people of Puk'chong had raided their former church for pews, altar, even the traditional wooden platform up front that had once supported choir and preacher. With religion outlawed by the communists, the church had provided the last full measure of its devotion in the form of fuel for people's stoves and fireplaces. Long since stripped bare of wood, the sanctuary was now giving up any remaining sacred identity to an influx of MASH equipment—a generator, the kerosene stove up front and the metal folding chairs, squeaking like crazed mice as people squirmed in their seats, knees pumping, bodies rocking in an effort to warm up.

273

Bonnie remembered her bit of bravado when Major Folsom had warned her of the North Korean winter. Better be ready if Folsom tried to tweak her about it. Act blasé, point out to the good major that there were only six inches of snow outside, and, gosh, the temp was five degrees above zero. Michigan got colder than this—it did. Look at all the sissies, shivering and griping about being forced outside for the five minutes it took to walk here from the MASH's main building. Up front, Hank Basham bent over to fuss with the stove, apparently unaware of how enormous his fanny looked. The man must be wearing at least three pair of pants.

He did have the right idea—layers. You never took off your long underwear, and if you had two sets, forget about saving one, put them both on. Next, three pairs of sox, which the nurses all needed anyway so their feet wouldn't swim inside the male-issue combat boots. Next, your summer fatigues, and then another set of your summer fatigues. If you went outside, you added jacket, mittens, and always your parka, with the hood cinched as snug as it would go around your face, no matter how silly it made you look.

Take sensible precautions, and the cold was no biggie.

Someone disparaged Hank's bottom, and he wiggled it suggestively, drawing applause and groans. The stove fire should have been started before the meeting, but the casualty load the past few days hadn't given anyone much time to think ahead.

Colonel Martin stomped in and continued stomping to the front, trying to get the snow off his boots. "Sorry for making you folks trudge through the evil weather tonight," he said, "but we're so full of wounded there's no place else we can all meet. Oh, to be back in Inch'on."

Amen, Bonnie thought.

Major Folsom *was* right about them missing Inch'on. Pukch'ong had supplied the MASH its own abandoned schoolhouse, but smaller than Inch'on's and not nearly as accommodating.

What was not smaller was the casualty load—mostly Korean soldiers from both sides.

As towns, the two locales couldn't begin to compare. Inch'on had been a bona fide city, with parks and theaters. Pukch'ong was a grubby village. About ten miles inland from the Sea of Japan, a scant eighty from North Korea's border with China, it offered not so much as a single ice skating rink or toboggan run. A real fun place.

"We need this meeting," Colonel Martin was saying, "to catch you up on new developments in the war, which will impact us. Please pass along the essentials of what I'm about to say to our colleagues who had to stay on duty in medical and postop tonight. As you know from the steady upswing of casualties this month, mopping up the North Koreans is not the walk in the park we hoped it might be. The good news is that, after four days of ground battle and three of supporting aerial attacks and bombing runs by our B-29s, the ROK 18th regiment up near Orangch'on is out of trouble and advancing again. So our casualty load from up north may decrease. Meanwhile, the 1st Marine Division is now concentrating about seventy miles west of here at the Chosin Reservoir."

Sergeant Hood! Bonnie thought. Her interest quickened.

"I must tell you," Colonel Martin said gravely, "that one of that division's regiments has encountered some stiff resistance from Chinese Communist forces."

The chairs stopped squeaking, leave only the throb of the generator and the howling eaves. Bonnie wondered which of the marine regiments had been attacked. Hopefully not the 5th, which was Harlan Hood's.

And what about Sam? The 7th Infantry was the other part of X Corps; wherever one went, the other wouldn't be far away.

"As the map enthusiasts among us will know," Martin said, "a bit north of Chosin and a little closer to us lies the Pujon Reservoir. Elements of the 7th Infantry Division are due south of that now, moving north and west toward Chosin to link up with the Marines. Like the Marines, the Army is running into some Chinese resistance, so we might also see some casualties from there."

Bonnie resisted an urge to interrupt. Elements of the 7th Infantry—couldn't he be more specific? Was it just the 31st Regiment, or was Sam's regiment there, too? She'd ask later. Damn Chinese, why can't they leave us alone? Our fight isn't with them. And didn't we just save them from the Japanese in World War II?

"Now, people," Colonel Martin went on in a soothing voice, "don't let any of this concern you overmuch. It's not clear these Chinese are anything more than a few raggedy-assed troops sent down here to show a token support for Kim Il Sung. At this point, the X Corps intelligence people don't think they'll be a major problem. They have asked us to assess any Chinese wounded we do get for possible referral to G-2."

"Not until after we treat them," Jeff said.

"No, of course not. And even then only if the wounded soldier is well enough to be questioned. If this is just a few volunteer units of the People's Liberation Army, we can still hope for an early end to this—not Thanksgiving, obviously, but maybe by Christmas. In the mean time, with the weather getting colder, we've seen some frostbite, and that's only going to get worse. For severe cases, where the damage appears deeper than epidermal, we'll start treatment with IV drips of procaine and heparin, but starting is all we're equipped for. We'll move all level-4 cases down to the 121st Evac at Hungnam as soon as they're fit to travel, since they'll need a thirty to forty day course of bed rest and IV treatment to save their toes, and we must keep room here for our acute postop caseload. So I want you doctors to keep moving the frostbites out ASAP.

Martin paused to check his notes.

"The cold weather is already sending our malaria rate way down, but we can look for flu instead. And this next is very important: The roads are so rough between here and Hungnam that the red cells in some of our whole blood shipments have broken up in transit. I don't need to tell you that ruins the blood, so I want close inspections of all whole blood before use, and let's have an aggressive reorder policy when we find blood with damaged RBCs.

"Finally, if casualties do go up, we may have to put in additional surgery teams drawing on some of you medical doctors. This will take you well beyond the shrapnel cleanups you've done on occasion. From here on, if you're not eating or sleeping, please grab every possible chance to observe our surgical teams."

"All right!" said several voices at once.

A smile flickered across Martin's lips. "Just don't start thinking you're really surgeons. Nurses, when it's your turn for triage, when all surgeons are working—and only then—start dishing the less critical cases to medical doctors. You've seen enough now to feel comfortable making those decisions. You medical doctors, don't get in over your heads. If you need help, yell to one of our surgeons. Any questions?"

Lars Hendricks, a neurology resident who still looked sixteen after two months in Korea, raised his hand. "Colonel, is the toe bone connected to the foot bone or the hand bone?"

"Very funny."

"He's serious," someone shouted.

"If there's nothing else, last one out shuts down the stove and generator."

Everyone got up and headed for the door.

As Bonnie started to rise, Jeff caught her arm. "Got a minute?"

She hesitated, her mind a sudden jumble. What was this? No, she knew what it was.

I'm not ready.

"I'll see to the stove and generator when we're through," Jeff added.

"Sure." She settled back in the chair.

"What do you think of Martin's little bombshell?"

"The Chinese?" she asked.

"No, letting medical doctors operate."

She shrugged. Was she wrong about why he'd collared her? He hadn't been much for small talk over the time they'd worked together. . .

And this wasn't exactly small talk either.

"As long as I don't have to assist Hendricks, it's all right with me."

Jeff smiled. Bonnie noticed he was keeping an eye on the others filing out of the church. Waiting for everyone to leave before he got down to what he really wanted to talk about?

"So, how are you doing?" he asked.

"What do you mean?"

"You've seemed a bit down since we got to Pukch'ong."

"Who wouldn't be? This place is a dump. I don't think the North Koreans are very fun-loving guys. Not that we've had much time to go out on the town anyway."

"Is that all?"

"I miss the orphans," she said.

He nodded. "I saw one of your puppet shows. You and Sally were terrific, and Laura, too. I'm sure the kids miss you, as well, but you can be glad they're not up here with us."

"True." She followed Jeff's glance to the door, everyone gone now, the two of them alone with the stove, thirty folding chairs, and the steady chug of the generator.

Jeff said, "I've been wondering about your friend the lieutenant."

Okay, here it was. "Which one? There's nothing but lieutenants all around me."

"The tall infantry guy."

"Sam?"

"I thought it was Stan—yes, him. I remember seeing him back in Inch'on a couple of times, and it was whispered around that you and he went out for a midnight stroll. And then, on the trip down to Pusan, he appeared out of nowhere, just before the column was attacked, and you two. . .well, word was you spent some time alone in the back of that ambulance we were using to ship equipment."

278

"What's your point, Jeff?"

He looked a little abashed. "I'm wondering if you and he are an item, or if he's just a friend. I don't mean to pry, it's just that I'm interested in you."

"In what way?"

"You're too smart to play dumb, Bonnie. You know I'm saying I'm romantically interested in you."

She felt her face growing warm. Jeff was a fine man, intelligent, dedicated to his patients, tremendous stamina and wonderful with his hands. Good looking, too. And she really admired his daring with the arterial transplants.

"You're not saying anything," he observed.

"I'm surprised—and flattered."

"But?"

"I'm also confused. We've worked together two months, sometimes twenty hours a day, and maybe I'm dense, but in all that time I haven't seen a single sign you thought of me as more than a co-worker."

"It wouldn't be proper in front of the others, and there's scant chance to be alone with you."

"What about on the ship? Coming up here, we were on the *Patrick* for almost two weeks, sitting in port at Pusan then dawdling while they cleared the mines at Wonsan, then changed our landing to Iwon. I nearly went crazy from boredom."

"I danced with you at those evening parties on the ship."

"So did every other doctor."

"I know," he said, sounding wounded.

"Jeff, surely you can't have expected me to save all the dances for you—not without some sign."

"If I'd given you signs, what then?"

"I don't know."

Truth was, she hadn't cared who she danced with, so long as she was dancing, using the contact to try and get Sam out of her system. What had she been thinking, letting him goad her, saying she was afraid of intimacy, so she decides right there on the spur of the moment to prove him wrong.

I don't have anything to prove, she thought, not to anyone. I've had sex, back in college. I did it with Andre because I was sure I *couldn't* love him. I liked his body and I wanted to, so I did. . . .

And then I felt like a slut.

Doing it with Sam would probably have been a huge mistake.

I really do like him, she thought, and maybe I could love him. If I'd had sex with him in the ambulance, afterward I'd have had to tell myself it was because I loved him. But how would I know if I really did or was just trying to not feel like a slut again?

I need to know more about men. . . .

But that wasn't entirely honest, either, was it? Men weren't the issue, Jeff was. She'd had plenty of time to get to know him, day and night for weeks. She *did* know him. He was the best kind of man, a healer who put his career on the line to keep men whole.

"How long have you felt this way?" she asked.

"Almost from the start."

She had to admit she'd gotten glimmers of it, but why only glimmers?

I'm trying to find things wrong with him, she realized.

Because I'd rather be with Sam.

Who may have a *lot* wrong with him.

"Maybe our working together is something of a disadvantage," Jeff said. "Standing on opposite sides of an operating table with blood up to your elbows for hours on end can't compete with being alone together in the back of an ambulance."

She laughed, and he looked perplexed, and she realized that was another difference between the two men. Sam knew how to make her laugh; Jeff had finally said something mordantly funny and didn't even realize it.

"And there's me outranking you, and a doctor besides. Those could both feel like barriers, especially to someone like you."

"What do you mean, someone like me?"

He gave her a surprised look, as if she were kidding. "You aren't exactly a shrinking violet, Bonnie, when it comes to how you respond to authority."

"Would you prefer I was?"

"No. You're smart and capable and you take initiative. I'm not in the least threatened by that."

And, thinking back, he didn't seem to be—another solid point in his favor.

If he could just say it without sounding like he was dictating a fitness report. "Jeff, for now, may we back up to 'I'm flattered?' I am. You're handsome, a terrific doctor, and I admire you very much. This is all pretty sudden and I need time to think about it. Maybe we can talk again in a day or two."

"That's fine."

He looked relieved. Had she overdone the encouragement?

Only if she'd already decided against Jeff.

She got up with him, feeling awkward, like she owed him a peck on the cheek or something, but he had already headed for the front to tend to the stove and generator.

As she stepped onto the concrete stoop of the church alone, the wind hit her, nearly tearing the hood of her parka back. She had to take her mittens off to find the string and cinch it close around her face. Pulling the mittens back on at once, she blew into them to warm her hands. She struck out for the MASH, following the footprints in the snow.

The sky was clear and black as coal, with a three-quarter moon. Stars beyond the moon's corona sparkled like fireflies rising from a black field. It made her think of home, ice skating on the Binder's Park pond during winter, or sledding with Mom and Diane on the big hill at the Kingman Arboretum.

Winter could be fun, it was all in your attitude.

She veered outside the beaten-down tracks so she could make the crisp, new snow crunch. A glistening blue-white, it sent a light of its own back up at the sky. Yellow squares marked the windows in town, flickering with the glow of kerosene lanterns or candles.

Cold, yes, and cold would get old after awhile, as winter always did in Michigan, but right now, she liked it.

Jeff, Jeff, Jeff.

Maybe once it sank in that he was attracted to her she'd feel it back at him. Sam, for all the risk he presented, made her feel warm inside. Jeff was a genuine hero who would one day be recognized among the pioneers of medicine. He'd done incalculable good for men who could still walk or hug their kids because of him.

But would she want to settle down with him?

With either of them?

This is *my* life, she thought. I didn't join the Army to find a man. I know the difference between sex and love. I don't want either one alone. When the right time comes, I want them both together.

She saw a tall figure walking toward her, dark in silhouette against the glow from the town. His parka rimmed his face, sinking it in shadow. Probably Colonel Martin coming back to make sure they were all right, or that the stove had been damped. Footsteps crunched behind her, and she turned, expecting Jeff, but it wasn't Jeff, it was a man in a strange uniform, hard to see in the low light, but it looked puffy, somehow, and now she could see diamond patterns of stitches—quilting!

The man brought up a weapon, nasty-looking, a Tommy gun. He barked something at her in a strange language.

Turning to run, she found herself facing the other man, now also pointing a machine gun at her. He repeated the first man's command, jerking the short barrel of his weapon up. Fear raced through her in an icy jolt. Raising her hands, she thought: *This can't be happening.*

The man motioned for her to follow him, and she felt the gun of the other prodding her back, and there was nothing to do but follow, through a break in a tall hedge, where a canopied truck was waiting. It looked like a U.S. Army truck, and after a second's confusion, she remembered all the American equipment Jiang Kai-shek had lost to the Communist Chinese in their civil war of just a year ago, and then she was climbing into the back of the truck, her heart pounding in panic.

Her two captors climbed in with her, and the engine started, and the truck bumped down the road, past the 1st MASH, through the grubby town of Pukch'ong and into the night, heading north, toward China.

By mid October MacArthur's Far East Command had numerous intelligence reports that China was preparing to enter the war. The CIA had led ROK irregulars in operations near the Yalu River bordering China. Their reports of Chinese troops moving into Korea were not communicated to MacArthur or Truman at that time. By November 3, the CIA "Weekly Summary" estimated that as many as 870,000 Chinese soldiers had entered Korea but also concluded these forces would not enter the war but were there to protect the Manchurian border and its hydroelectric plants. Apparently no one questioned that this was far more troops than would be needed for purely defensive purposes. On November 5, MacArthur told Bradley and the Joint Chiefs of Staff he did not believe the Chinese would enter the war in force—and if they did, he would annihilate them with air power. By November 15, the Far East Command had reports that twelve divisions of the People's Liberation Army had entered Korea. On November 24, "National Intelligence Estimate 2/1" held that China was capable of conducting massive offensive operations but that there was no indication that they would do so. . . .   (Ibid.)

19

23 November—Thanksgiving Day, Chosin Reservoir, 0930:
Near the summit, Hood ordered the squad to change their socks.

"Excuse me," Steinberg said, "I think something's happened to my ears."

"You heard fine," Jimmy snapped. "You and Bo clear the snow off that big table rock so we can all sit down."

Steinberg, continuing to whine, trudged with Bo to the rock, a nearly level slab the size of a barn door. The two began kicking the snow off, sheets of it whipping away in the wind that moaned across the summit. Joe Clemons helped without being asked, Hood noted with approval. Smart man—the best thing you could do for yourself in this cold was keep moving. Zero degrees, the air burning in his lungs as he sucked deep breaths, annoyed at his weakness. Five years ago, he'd have caught his wind by now even from a climb steep as this. Twice on the way up he had slipped, the second time puncturing his thigh on a sharp point, bleeding through his three layers of trousers before the fabric had frozen stiff, sealing the wound.

With his binoculars, he scanned the reservoir to the west, a vast field of snow-covered ice shaped like a lobster with its spine twisted sideways. From its upper body, two secondary lakes poked out to the north and west very much like lobster claws. With everything covered by snow, the reservoir's perfect flatness was the only way to distinguish it from the land around it—slopes and humps that started out low and rose away into high ridges.

Swinging the glasses south, Hood found Hill 1324, a peak east of the reservoir, about as high as here—a mile above sea level and 1200 feet above the road. Nosebleed altitude, if your blood didn't freeze before it could leak.

A shrieking blast of wind peppered Hood's face with snow crystals, stinging his numbed skin painfully awake.

"See anything?" Jimmy asked.

"Can't tell. The Chinese prisoners the 7th took had reversible uniforms. At the time they were caught, they were wearing the mustard side out. Now that we've got snow, they'll have switched to white. All I see over there is snow, but I can't be sure."

"I think everyone's ready for the sock drill."

Hood saw that the squad had settled on the rock. Bo was still panting from the climb, a big football player, couldn't be twenty yet. He looks as worn out as I feel, Hood thought, obscurely pleased. Clemons and Bertleson had their faces turned to the sun, and Steinberg was fiddling with the laces of his shoepacs.

"I hate these damn things," he said. "They're lousy in snow. I want my boondockers back."

"Stow your griping," Jimmy ordered.

"Shoepacs are okay," Hood said, "as long as you take care of them right. I assume all of you remembered to put yesterday's socks and the felt inserts under your armpits when you zipped into your sleeping bags last night, right?"

Clemons said he had, and the others, except the moping Steinberg, nodded.

"All right, take the shoepacs off, switch the inserts and change socks. After you've got the shoes back on, put the wet socks and inserts under your armpits so your body heat can start drying them."

"What body heat?" Bertleson, at least trying to be funny.

Sitting on the margin of the cleared rock, Hood worked on his own laces.

"Fucking nuisance." Steinberg again, the first time Hood could remember the kid all-out swearing.

Let it go—after all, he was right, shoepacs *weren't* okay, for the simple reason you couldn't take care of them right. The idea seemed good enough—if you knew nothing about combat. The shoes had lace-up leather uppers and thick rubber galoshes below. Into this you put a felt insert to help your socks absorb some of the sweat from your feet. Right now, because the rubber trapped body heat, every foot in the squad would be soaked with sweat from the climb. As they caught their breath and looked around, the heat would drain back from their feet, leaving their drenched socks and felt pads to freeze. At a time like now, with no enemy in sight, they could change the socks and do it right, but sooner or later, they'd be pinned down in a fire fight, their soaked feet slowly turning freezing cold, because they weren't moving around.

With bullets flying at you, the last thing you'd think about was changing out your socks.

Result: frostbite.

Platoons in the 7th regiment and a few in the 5th had already lost men to it, evac'd out because they could no longer walk or even stand, much less pull boots on their swollen feet. With Stempleford, Mendenhall and Hollywood gone and no replacements in sight, he couldn't afford to lose any more men. Taking his gloves off to lace back up, Hood hurried to finish before his fingers went numb. When he looked for his field glasses again, he saw that Jimmy had swiped them to take his own look at Hill 1324.

"Think we'll find any Chinks?" Jimmy asked.

"Better watch that talk or you'll slip up around the lieutenant."

"Damn, that's right. I forgot he's a Chinaman."

"I don't know if we'll find 'em," Hood said, "but we'll give it our best shot. We don't want them surprising us like they did Colonel Litzenberg's men. Forty-four marines dead at Sudong and a couple hundred wounded."

"But that was three weeks ago," Jimmy countered, "and the 7th ended up kicking their asses. What was left of them ran like rabbits."

"The thing to remember," Hood said, "is that Litzenberg had no warning. Forward ground patrols never picked the Chinese up. Hell, X Corps has been running daily air recon for months. They should have spotted them coming down from Manchuria, but they didn't. If the 7th regiment could be jumped with a surprise attack, so could we."

"Yeah, yeah."

Handing the glasses back, Jimmy pulled the string on his parka until his face looked out a narrow hole beneath his helmet. Snot had frozen on his upper lip, his face so numb he didn't know it.

The corporal turned away from a gust of wind, hugging his arms to him. "God, I hate this place. I ain't letting it show to the squad, but ever since we hit the Funchilin Pass, I've had a bad feeling, Sarge."

Hood agreed silently. Something spooky about the Taebek mountains, towering peaks that stuck up ever higher the further north you went, grim, gray, and unearthly cold. Until they hit the mountains, North Korea had seemed all right. It had been a big relief to get ashore after steaming back and forth off Wonsan for a week waiting for minesweepers to clear the harbor. "Operation Yo-yo," the comedians on board had called it. By the time the harbor was safe enough for an amphibious assault, the ROK had already taken the city from the land approaches and Bob Hope was there, cracking jokes about the marines out in the harbor.

So: An embarrassingly easy landing, then up the coast to the port of Hungnam, another normal-enough looking place.

Then General Almond had ordered the First Division up to the Chosin Reservoir.

Started out well enough, marching along a nice paved road, even had two lanes the forty three miles up to Chinhung-ni, walking along, taking their sweet time.

But then, above Chinhung-ni, he'd gotten the feeling they were crossing onto another planet, one he never could have imagined, even after being all over the world with The Corps. The road narrowed to one lane and started rising—2,500 feet in just the next seven or eight miles, twisting and turning ever upward through the Funchilin Pass to Koto-ri. Granite cliffs looming over you on one side of the road and plunging away at near vertical drops just beyond the outer edge. Colder every mile, the trees thinning out to scrubby pines.

Then it leveled off into a harsh, rocky plateau that stretched eleven more miles to Hagaru-ri, a bombed, burned-out relic of a town at the base of the Chosin Reservoir. First night there, the temperature had dropped to four below zero, freezing the hairs in your nose. Up all night, he'd had to make the rounds of foxholes, forcing the squad to crawl out and move to make sure they didn't freeze to death in their sleeping bags.

And now the reservoir itself—this strange-looking lake with its jagged lobster claw inlets poking out on both sides.

"I never thought I'd say this," Jimmy said, "but I miss Pusan. Remember how hot it got? You had to take salt pills or you'd collapse. Sun beating down like it was only seventy yards over your head? I swore if I could get out of Pusan I'd be happy forever, but this here where we're at now is something else, sarge."

Picking up the glasses, Hood stared across at Hill 1324 again.

There!

A piece of the white top of the hill had moved.

Hood tried to focus the field glasses, his gloved finger clumsy on the dial, the effort making him jitter off line and lose his place. He inched back across, found the place again, a furrow in the snow, and let his breath out.

Just a rock rolling down, or a small snow-slide.

"Listen," Jimmy said.

Hood pulled the parka away from his ears but heard only the whistle of the wind.

Jimmy crawled along the cleared slab to the edge, looking tense. Scooting over beside him, Hood hushed the squad with one hand. A snatch of sound came up to him from below—

A voice!

Jimmy grabbed his arm and he nodded to show he'd heard. Too garbled and distant in the wind to make out the language, but broken bits of speech floated up the slope opposite where they'd climbed up.

Marines?

Possible, if the division's recon company had sent their own patrol up here.

Another, longer burst of speech came on a gust of wind. Hood's gut clenched. Definitely not English. With no ROK forces near this area, it wouldn't be Korean, either.

He leaned close to Jimmy's ear. "I'm gonna ease down a ways, see if I can spot 'em."

"Why not wait here, ambush 'em when they come up?"

"They might not come up. They may just be skirting the peak, and I don't want them getting away. Lui sent us out for a prisoner, and that's what I aim to bring him. Disperse the squad and tell 'em to keep quiet. Then get where you can keep an eye on me. I raise my arm, you bring everyone down."

Jimmy nodded.

Easing off the rock, Hood unslung his M-1 and slipped off the condom Jimmy had given him to keep snow and dirt out of the muzzle. Twenty yards down from the rock slab, the slope steepened to nearly vertical, and he had to sling the rifle again and work his way lower, facing the cliff and grabbing for hand- and footholds until he got down to a narrow ledge. Lying flat on his belly, he removed his helmet and rubbed snow on his parka hood, then inched to the edge and looked over.

What he saw made him catch his breath. There, below, were seven, eight—no, ten men in white, quilted uniforms, trudging along a narrow shelf maybe twenty yards down, so close he didn't dare pull his head back for fear one of them would catch the movement.

Hood stared at the Chinese, chilled and fascinated. Instead of helmets, they all wore caps with earflaps, looked like those aviator caps, except fur-lined for winter. Their shoes appeared to be canvas, like a tennis shoe. How'd they keep their feet from freezing?

All of them wore grenade belts, he saw. The man in front had red piping on his pant-leg and one shoulder, must be an officer.

He and the man at the tail end of the column were toting burp guns strapped to their shoulders. Two men in the middle of the line carried a 120 mm mortar slung on a pole between them.

As they passed below him, Hood pulled his head back and rolled over, staring up slope for any sign of Jimmy. Couldn't see him, the vertical drop was too great, the curvature of the mountain screening him away from the flat boulder above.

Damn; he'd have to climb back up. It would take him half an hour. No way could he take ten Chinese prisoners by himself.

Rolling over for another look, he was shocked to see no sign of the patrol, even though the ledge they'd been on continued at least fifty yards before a jutting vertical column of rock ended it.

A *cave*, Hood thought.

At that moment, a head poked out below, peering both ways along the lower shelf—a lookout, in the cave entrance.

Turning back to the cliff above him, Hood saw a pair of shoepacs and a butt descending toward him, and then the same parts of two more men, he couldn't tell who. Relief flooded him, *take it easy up there, don't fall.* Jimmy, then Clemons, and then the rest of them slipped and slid down, landing on his ledge, Bertleson last, as always.

Pointing down, Hood mouthed "cave;" Jimmy passed it along the line. Taking a grenade from his belt, Hood mimed dropping it over, then pointed to Bo, Steinberg and Jimmy, motioning them to the right of the entrance. He signaled Clemons and Bertleson, and pointed to his own chest—follow me. He could feel his heart pounding. Combat—six against ten, and if the grenade doesn't do it, they'll shoot us off the ledge with those burp guns.

Pulling the pin, he waited a beat, then pitched it out just enough to clear the curvature.

Damn, too far, hitting the slope below the ridge and bouncing out. As it exploded harmlessly, he dropped the next, only a little push, and it blew before hitting the ridge, spraying shrapnel into the cave.

With a yell, Hood slung his legs off the ledge and started down, missing a handhold but grabbing another before he could slide out of control. Clemons snaked past him, and then he was down, running along the lower ledge toward the entrance—he could see it now, a black crescent.

A burp gun stuck out from the mouth of the cave and angled toward him, a stone outcropping stopping the barrel and forcing the burst wide.

Hood grabbed the Chinese's gun arm, jerking him from the cave and over the edge. The man plummeted away without a sound.

Hood saw Jimmy on the other side of the entrance pull a grenade, wait two, and chuck it into the hole. The blast blew stones out.

Hood charged inside, his .45 out front, seeing red-splotched bodies on the floor and two men coming from the back of the cave. He pulled the trigger, but it didn't move, *frozen, damn!* pulled harder, *Jesus, help me!* and then two Chinese stopped and put their hands in the air. Blood streamed from the face of one. The other looked unhurt. The red piping on his uniform marked him as an officer.

I did it!

"Hood, look out!"

From the corner of his eye, he saw one of the bodies roll over, then heard a shot. The body jerked and lay still and Jimmy ran up to him, the cuff of a condom encircling the smoking muzzle of his M-1.

Hood knew he should make a crack—something funny. Nothing came.

While the squad ate Thanksgiving dinner in an abandoned schoolhouse on the shore of the Chosin Reservoir, Hood stuck with Lieutenant Lui and the prisoner, Lieutenant Chang. He had to see this—an American lieutenant who was Chinese interrogating a lieutenant in the People's Liberation Army.

The jail in the village of Sinhung-ni was a big shack with a couple of cells in the back. Lieutenant Chang, tall and thin, with a small chin and disheveled, coal black hair, blinked as Lui ordered the MPs to unlock the cell he shared with the other Chinese. Chang said something in his own language, his voice high and urgent, as if he were amazed to find one of his own race in a U.S. Marine uniform.

Lui answered in a pleasant tone.

Hood kept his .45 out at his side, following the two Chinese as Lui walked Chang from the jail across the trampled snow to his own tent. A Coleman kerosene heater, going full blast, had dragged the temperature in the tent up to a balmy fifty degrees; Hood inhaled the warmer air gratefully.

Lui offered Chang a seat on a camp chair and a piece of pumpkin pie.

Chang ate the pie in big bites, nodding with obvious pleasure, while Hood waited, his stomach growling, not believing he'd decided to put off the best dinner the U.S. Marines served every year. Amazingly, the turkeys, which had been frozen solid when they arrived by truck from Koto-ri last night, had been thawed in time to cook, thanks to an ingenious plan by an officer from regimental headquarters. He'd had the cooks pile all the birds, hard as rocks, around two fired-up camp stoves, then covered the pile up with canvas, snow and brush. Somehow, enough oxygen had gotten in to keep the stoves burning, and by sometime this morning, the birds were thawed enough to cook. Watching Chang eat the pie, Hood thought of the promised menu—cranberry sauce, shrimp cocktail, turkey, dressing, fresh potatoes, fruitcake—

Stop thinking about it!

Chang gave Lui a little bow and put his plate down, the preliminaries over.

Lui started talking in a calm, conversational voice.

Chang answered in the same tone. They were like two casual acquaintances catching up on things. Hood began to feel strange gripping the .45, but he wasn't putting it away until Chang was back behind bars.

The talk went on for half an hour or so, and then Lui stood. Chang stood with him, gave a little bow.

"The lieutenant is ready to return to his cell, sergeant. I'll walk you both back."

Dark had fallen, and with it, the temperature, cold enough to sear Hood's face. He hoped the .45 had thawed out enough in the tent to fire if he had to. They crunched across the snow to the jail and turned Chang over to the MPs, both of whom were polishing off tin trays of turkey and stuffing.

Burning with curiosity, Hood said nothing until they were back in Lui's tent.

The lieutenant sat down on his cot and motioned Hood to his camp chair.

"How bad is it?" Hood asked.

"Bad enough. Lieutenant Chang is from the 377th Regiment of the 126th Division, which he says is waiting east of the reservoir, beyond where you were today. He says the 80th Division is also in the area, and that the 38th, 39th, 40th and 42nd armies have crossed into North Korea. He says the 20th, 26th, and 27th Armies are in our vicinity now. They marched at night, so our air recon wouldn't see them, and hid in train tunnels and other cover during the days."

"You got all that with just a piece of pie?"

Lui gave an impatient shake of his head. "You don't understand. Chang is my prisoner now. He feels no disgrace in telling me. Many men now in the People's Liberation Army fought against the PLA with Jiang Kai-shek's Nationalists right up until they were captured or surrendered. Then they were accepted straight into the communist army."

"You're kidding."

Lui said nothing.

"Any chance he's lying just to scare us?"

"Slim to none. Unfortunately, our own intelligence people are going to ask their interpreters that same question, and, like you, they will have a strong tendency to discount the answer."

"If I were captured by the Chinese," Hood said, "I'd tell them we had two hundred thousand men moving in on the reservoir."

"And they would know you are lying, just as I know Chang is telling the truth."

Hood looked at him, sitting there so calmly on his cot, a man of two different worlds. Did he really understand both?

"How many men in a Chinese 'Army?'"

"Thirty thousand," Lui said.

Hood did the math in his head and, for a moment, his mouth was too dry to speak. "Two hundred and ten thousand Chinese soldiers?"

"That Lieutenant Chang knows of."

Hood thought of the 7th Infantry Division. They were sure to be a part of this fight, probably on their way to join the marines right now, which would make a total of around 28,000 U.S. troops to fight off at least 90,000 Chinese who were in the immediate area right now, and 120,000 near enough to reinforce.

Hood's stomach shrank into a cold stone. He said, "Don't just leave Chang to our intelligence people. They're still painting a rosy picture, because that's what the top generals want to hear. You've got to go to Colonel Murray with this yourself, sir."

"I will."

"Not just see him, you've got to make him believe. Be so convincing he takes this to General Smith and General Smith takes it to General Almond and General Almond takes it to General MacArthur."

Lui gave a fatalistic shrug. "I'll do my best, sergeant. But I doubt any one man can stop what is coming."

Bonnie huddled in the darkness deep in the troop truck where a little heat leaked from the cab. Gusts of wind whipped the canvas canopy against her back; her teeth endured a spasm of chattering, as they did every few minutes.

At least they hadn't tied her hands or ankles. Why bother? She'd have to fight her way between them at the tailgate and then run away, a black silhouette on moon-white snow, while they riddled her with bullets.

ROK forces should have checkpoints up this way, she thought. Just be ready.

She tried to make sense out of what was happening. Why would the enemy take such risks to capture one nurse? Pukch'ong was the 7th Infantry's rear command post, and the MASH itself was protected by well-armed enlisted men who would have been more than a match for these three infiltrators. And yet they'd taken the chance, probably lurking around for some time, waiting for a stray they could grab.

Did they have wounded out in the mountains who needed tending? Or maybe a Chinese officer had been captured and they meant to trade her for him. These men were Chinese, not North Korean, she was quite sure. Both guards were taller than the average Korean—almost as tall as her—and she'd never seen a quilted uniform like these men wore on any of the NK wounded.

Peering out the back of the truck, Bonnie looked for a tree or outcropping of rock she might remember later. Nothing but road and hills, all covered in moonlit snow.

The truck slowed, and the two guards at the tailgate straightened. One leaned out around the opening to look ahead and then jerked back inside, saying something to the other guard in a low, sharp voice.

A checkpoint!

Bonnie's legs tensed. One of the guards pointed his machine gun at her, and hurried back, a finger over his lips. She battled to keep from shouting; as if sensing it, the guard pressed the muzzle of the gun into her parka just over her ear.

Stop us! Look in the back!

The truck slowed even further from its sudden leisurely pace, then began to pick up speed again. Beyond the guard, she could see black figures walking among larger blots that must be tents. She wanted to scream in frustration. They must have waved the truck through because it was U.S. Army issue, complete with the white star on the side.

The guard let his gun drop from her head. With a taunting grin at her, he returned to the tailgate. In her mind, she screamed with frustration.

No, calm down, think.

The road had forked three times now, the first after several hours, the second at around an hour, and the third after about as long as the first. At the forks, the truck had gone right, left, then right again. If she could escape, reversing that order would take her back to Pukch'ong—an extremely long walk in this cold, but one she would be glad to try.

It seemed incredible that, only hours ago, she'd griped to Jeff about Pukch'ong. What heaven it would be to be back there now, safe and warm in her cot near the kerosene stove in Pumpkin Patch II, hearing Sally mumble in her sleep. By now, the MASH probably had every available man and woman searching for her, but the truck was long gone, and no one would imagine until much later that she might have been taken prisoner.

The sky she could see out the back of the truck was starting to lighten now, more on the left than the right, which meant they were still heading north. With dawn near, it must be around 0730. She'd been abducted at midnight, give or take a few minutes, so they'd been on the road roughly seven hours. They'd probably averaged no more than ten or fifteen miles an hour because of the deep ruts and axle-threatening bumps. They could have come eighty miles by now, which was roughly the distance from Pukch'ong to Chinese territory. The Yalu River formed the border, and they had yet to cross any rivers, but it couldn't be far off.

Bonnie felt the weight of despair pressing her down. Face it, she wasn't going to escape. They had her and they were going to keep her.

Just survive, that's all.

Dozing, she woke with a start to see a wedge of light pouring in the back of the truck. The direction indicated they were now heading west. Had they crossed the Yalu while the sun rose and she slept?

The truck stopped, idled for a moment, then rolled forward again. The two guards sat straight on the bench in an attitude of expectation. Bonnie's heart sank as she saw a tall, chain link fence receding behind them, two men in quilted uniforms closing a gate.

They passed small mud huts with thatched roofs, then a row of larger cinderblock structures, windowless with roofs of corrugated tin.

The truck stopped again, and the cab door opened and slammed, and she heard voices in a rapid-fire exchange. One of the guards, peering back at her in the gloom, motioned sharply, beckoning her forward to the tailgate. Jumping down, she fell forward to her knees in the icy mud and dirt-stained snow that filled the ruts of the road. The other guard pulled her to her feet and turned her toward the front of the truck.

A tall Chinese with thick black hair parted from an immaculately straight line, gazed at her. His aristocratic posture, and the bent backs of the guards indicated he was an important officer. Instead of the quilted outfit, he wore a sharply-creased, dark green uniform, with the high collar she'd seen on pictures of Mao. A greatcoat hung from his shoulders back down to the tops of his polished boots. He was standing, she saw, on a wooden platform that held him above the muck.

The fine black eyebrows knitted together in a frown. He motioned her closer, and the guards marched her to him. He pointed to the hood of her parka. One of the guards jerked the bow knot open at her throat and yanked the parka back, freeing her hair to whip around her face in the wind.

The guards gasped.

The officer stared at her, shaking his head, then spat a torrent of harsh words. Both her guards stepped forward, heads hanging. He slapped each of them twice across the face with his palm, hard blows they took without moving.

He snapped an order; they grabbed her arms and marched her to a log building with a curving Asian roof and large windows. Inside, a wall of heat warmed her face; blinking, she made out a huge, ornate fireplace filled with blazing logs.

The two guards took off her coat and sat her in a wing-backed armchair, facing a massive desk of burnished mahogany, embellished with carved trim.

The officer handed his greatcoat to an aide, smoothed his uniform jacket, then seated himself in the leather swivel chair behind the desk. For a moment, he just stared at her, looking disgusted.

Then, composing himself, he gave her a pleasant nod. "I am Colonel Yuan Ching Tien. Welcome to my camp." A trace of Boston accent.

She told him her name, rank and serial number.

He sighed. "Lieutenant, I don't suppose there's any chance you're a doctor."

"Nurse."

He shook his head. "Of course. What else would you be? Only in America could there be so much talk about freedom and so little actual freedom, except for Caucasian males. I suppose if you'd tried to go to medical school they'd have told you it was not a proper job for a woman. In the People's Republic, you won't face such barriers. We value all of our comrades equally. When this war is over, you might like to go to medical school in Beijing."

Bonnie had trouble tracking his words. After the monotonous dark and chill of the truck, the room overwhelmed her senses. Behind Colonel Tien, a red tapestry woven in gold sparkled in the dancing light from the fireplace. Red draperies framed a large picture of Mao Tse Tung. A light fragrance soothed her raw sinuses and she noticed a pot of tea on the desk and two small cups. "Those imbeciles," Tien muttered.

"They thought the MASH had women doctors?"

"They thought you were a man."

Astonished, she glanced down at her bust and realized she couldn't see it—not under all the layers of clothing.

"Those boots," Tien said, "They are a man's are they not? A size ten or eleven, I would guess. You're tall for a woman and the hood of the parka hid your hair. Your shoulders are broad from all the shirts you must be wearing. Like most MASH doctors, you carried no rifle or sidearm—I'd told them to look especially for those who were unarmed. In the dark, they put it together, and concluded you were a MASH doctor." He looked at her a moment longer. "Your voice, on the other hand, is clearly a woman's, so I presume you did not speak."

She thought back over the capture. "I guess not."

"Curious."

"What would I have said? I don't speak Chinese." Frustration gnawed at her. She'd gone through hell the past eight hours when all she'd had to do was talk, say anything at all, and they would not have taken her.

But they couldn't have just released her either, knowing she'd raise the alarm. No, they'd have cut her throat, hid the body, and tried again, as fast as they could, to grab a doctor.

That she'd made no sound was the only reason she was alive.

Despite the warmth, she shuddered.

"Most women would have tried pleading with their captors," Colonel Tien groused, "whether they knew the language or not."

This from the man who'd said all comrades are equal? "I guess to Chinese, we westerners all look alike."

Tien gave the barest of smiles. "Pardon me. I'm being a poor host." He poured her a steaming cup of tea and handed it across the desk. She cradled it in her hands, savoring the warmth, then took a sip. The delicate taste brought tears to her eyes, and suddenly, she was crying. With an effort, she kept herself from sobbing, but nothing could stop the tears.

Tien's nostrils flared, and she saw a spark deep in the black eyes, and it occurred to her that he might be a connoisseur of tears. Not a pleasant thought.

She took a deep breath, clenched her teeth, and the tears stopped.

"Are you hungry?"

She wasn't, but who knew when she'd get another chance to eat? She nodded. Tien said something in Chinese, and the man who'd taken his coat stepped from the shadows and hurried off.

"Why do you want a doctor?" she asked.

"For the wounded and sick Americans who will soon be our guests here."

She swallowed more of the tea, her stomach contracting as she thought of the row of forbidding cinderblock buildings.

"By now, some of your countrymen are probably on the way here. In a few days, when those of you we do not kill surrender, there are sure to be more, many of them wounded. You're not a doctor, but you'll have to do. I assume I can expect your full cooperation?"

She felt muddled and slow, the warmth of the room dragging her down after the sleepless night. "In the MASH we treat North Koreans and ROK, along with our own soldiers. It's my duty to help the sick and wounded even if I weren't your prisoner."

"Excellent." Tien leaned forward. "This attitude, if you are sincere, is not that different from our communist ideal. There's hope for you, I think."

She kept her mouth shut. Survive, she told herself again. Do what you have to do, and watch for your moment to escape.

The colonel's batman brought a plate of steaming rice and two chopsticks. Fumbling with the sticks, she worked on getting rice into her mouth, using the time to think. Colonel Tien appeared to feel secure here, which meant they were in China—the truck must have crossed the Yalu when she dozed off.

She must learn what she could, in case escape became possible.

She said, "When may I see your hospital or clinic?"

Tien gazed at her.

Uneasiness pricked her. "You do have medical facilities, penicillin, bandages, disinfectants?"

Again, he did not answer.

All at once, she grasped the real use Colonel Tien would have for an American medical officer in his camp, and her stomach knotted with dread.

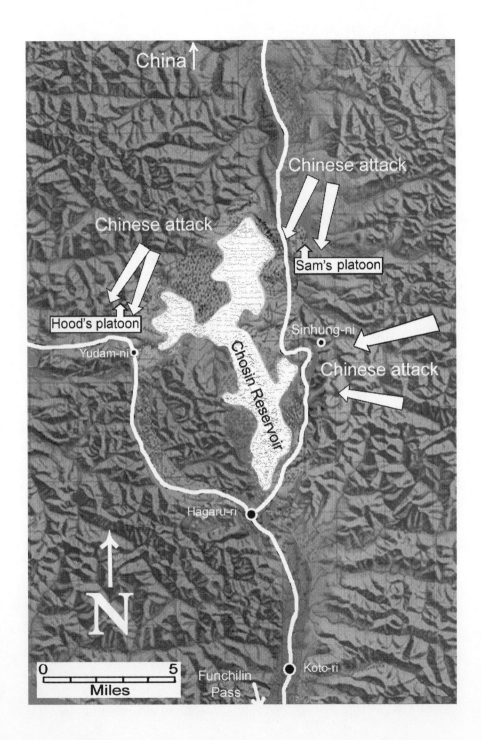

China↑

Chinese attack

Chinese attack

Sam's platoon

Hood's platoon

Chosin Reservoir

Yudam-ni

Sinhung-ni

Chinese attack

Hagaru-ri

N

0   5
Miles

Funchilin Pass

Koto-ri

As of November 24, General Walker's Eighth Army to the west in Korea, and General Almond's X Corps to the east had reported a total of 27,827 casualties in the war—21,529 in Eighth Army and 6,209 in X Corps. As the two forces prepared to launch a coordinated attack northward, the fronts for both were quiet. Recon patrols probing several miles forward encountered little or no enemy contact. It seemed the Chinese had withdrawn, leaving behind only rearguard forces. MacArthur decided the earlier clashes had been "spoiling attacks" to cover the retreat of North Korean forces into China and that only token PLA troops remained. On November 27, X Corps prepared to attack north, expecting only minor resistance. The 1st Marine Division had redeployed to the west shore of the Chosin Reservoir so that 7th Infantry's "Task Force Mac-Lean" could take over Marine positions on the east side. This army brigade included 3,200 troops, of which seven hundred were KATUSAs. Only the most leery in X Corps worried that they were about to be attacked, themselves, by the Chinese People's Liberation Army. . . .　　　　(Ibid.)

20

27 November, Chosin Reservoir, East side, 2130:
Staring out at the dark hills, Sam said a silent thank-you to the United States Marines. General Smith's leathernecks had occupied these hills on the east side just long enough to dig in before being ordered around to the west side of the reservoir.

Sam found himself smiling. How that must have pissed Hood off. The Marines bust their humps gouging out nice deep holes in the frozen ground, then General Almond orders these primo fortifications turned over to his "dogfaces"—bunkers so plentiful that even Second Lieutenant Sam Foxworth got one of his very own for his platoon command post. Far from the best one, to be sure, but better than anything his men could have put together in the half day they'd been here. Located on the forward slope just over the crest, it had a sturdy log roof covered with sandbags. From here, he had a clear view down to the road, as well as to the "A" Company positions on his left across the road and the rising ridge-line on his right defended by the rest of "C" Company.

Unfortunately a spur of that ridge-line rose to a separate peak; if any Chinese were hidden away up there, they could attack along that natural ramp from higher ground, a nasty advantage.

But that was "C" Company's problem.

His was any Chinese forces attacking from the north. The easiest route of attack would be the road that passed through a low saddle forward and to his left. Company "A" also had a platoon zeroed in on the road from the other side. Together, the two platoons could make life miserable for any enemy foot soldiers below.

Tanks were a different matter.

"S-s-sergeant Hartung."

"Sir?" The inky darkness of the bunker disembodied Hartung's voice. He did not sound cold, even though it was below zero and dropping.

Maybe I ought to take up smoking, Sam thought. At least my lungs would be warm. "Did we get that recoilless rifle from our heavy weapons company?"

"Yes, sir. Corporal Godfrey, one of Dog Company's finest. He and that gun are like Benny Goodman and his clarinet. He's up forward, there, with a real good angle down on the road."

"And the artillery is ranged in too?"

"Far as I know. You'd have to ask to be sure, but from what I saw before dark, the gun bunnies had it registered pretty good. Want me to ring up the CP and ask?"

"No, that's all right." Sam wasn't used to having a phone—another luxury of this bunker he'd inherited from the marines. Wire connected it to the battalion command post to the rear. Also to the rear, the big artillery had set up at the Pungnyuri Inlet—the widened delta of a stream that fed the reservoir. The inlet forced the road to curve away from the reservoir inland to where the stream narrowed enough to be crossed by a small bridge. The 57th Artillery Battalion had followed the 3rd Battalion of the 31st Infantry Regiment up to the reservoir from Hamhung, pumping up the total army forces on the east of the reservoir into a Regimental Combat Team. Starting in the afternoon, the big guns had lobbed shells forward until after dark. Nothing the past hour, which probably meant they were satisfied they had the range.

"Sir," Hartung said, "I think you need to relax. I know you enjoy expecting the worst, but the Chinks aren't out there. If they were, our recon patrols would have made contact. And even if there were Chinese out there, so what? We're dug in real well here."

"We don't have near enough men to fill the positions the marines left us."

"Doesn't matter. We've manned the best slots, and that'll be plenty good enough for anything we're likely to see tonight. Way I hear it, we're gonna be striking north in the morning. You can bet our artillery's homed in, and we've also got that heavy mortar company to give us supporting fire in case of trouble. My advice, enjoy this nice bunker, get some eyelid maintenance while you can before we have to hit the road."

"I'm worried about the men. It's damn cold."

"That, it is. They should have let us keep our warming fires. The big brass, excuse me saying so, are back in their nice farmhouse there at the command post, warm as toast, so they think everyone else is warm enough, too. Hell, if the Chinese are really out there, it don't take fires to tell 'em we're here. We were moving in all afternoon. All they had to do was look down from the hills."

Sam shook his head in the dark. The sergeant knew damn well that fires made a nice target for enemy mortars. Hartung just didn't believe any Chinese were out there. He had lots of company, including the top brass.

Please, God, let the optimists be right.

Feet crunched on the frozen ground outside. Sam jerked his .45 from the holster.

"It's the captain, sir," Hartung counseled in a whisper.

Loomis slid down through the observation slot into the bunker. Like everyone else, he looked bigger than normal because of all the clothes and the parka. "Everything all right here, lieutenant?"

"Everything's fine, sir."

"I was just going out to check the line," Hartung said.

"Carry on, sergeant." When he was gone, Loomis said, "We've got orders from Colonel Faith. At dawn we'll be leaving these positions to attack up the road toward Kalchon-ni."

"Yes, sir." No sense arguing. He was nothing but a second lieutenant and attacking north was the plan of a four star general, and if Chinese forces were waiting to turn it into a very bad plan, they'd all know sooner than they liked. "I'm just concerned about tonight, captain."

"That spur ridge?" Loomis asked, peering to his right.

"That, and we're too spread out. Either Colonel MacLean should bring his battalion up to fill the rest of the marine positions here, or he should have kept us back with him instead of letting Colonel Faith set us up nearly two miles to his north. If the Chinese do attack, our two battalions are too far apart to help each other much."

"I hope you're not scaring the men by mouthing that around to your noncoms."

"One of my noncoms mouthed it to me, sir, though I'd already had the thought."

"Hartung's always got some gripe."

"He's come around, sir. And he did learn a lot, fighting in the last war."

"Yes, well, I happen to agree with you and your sergeant in principle, but you've got to understand the politics, lieutenant. Colonel MacClean from the 31st got put in charge of the 32nd as well because someone has to command the RCT as a whole, and he outranks Lt. Colonel Faith. That doesn't mean Colonel Faith has no say. MacClean either didn't see a problem or figured the separation of forces wasn't enough of an issue to ruffle Faith's feathers by overruling him. You and Hartung just take turns checking up on your platoon, and let's try not to worry about the rest. That's what they pay the colonels and generals for."

"Yes, sir."

Loomis slapped him on the shoulder. This time he followed the side trench out, as he'd seen Hartung do.

A minute later Hartung returned and lit up a Lucky. "Those damn KATUSAs," he muttered. "All balled up in their sleeping bags, heads down like ostriches. Had to kick a few to get 'em to move a little."

Sam kept quiet. Nothing would make Hartung like having KATUSAs in the platoon, and as long as his beef was the language barrier and their lack of training, it wasn't something he wanted to argue about. Hartung was rough on everyone, and that was probably about how it should be, because the enemy was looking to be a lot rougher.

"At least your friend Kim has something on the ball," Hartung said grudgingly. "He was up and walking around, trying to keep his blood flowing, and he had that kid Choi he looks after sitting up with his carbine in his hands."

Picking up his M-1, Sam worked the bolt. It resisted, iced up, making the action sluggish. You had to work it on a regular basis or the oil would freeze. If there was a Chinese attack tonight, the damn thing might or might not give him automatic fire.

"I'll take the first watch," Hartung said.

"No. Let me go make my own rounds, then you can catch a few hours." Say this for fear, it kept you awake. Sam picked his way along the slanting rock of the summit. The moon had clouded over, making it hard to see. He found his way to Cinquemani's foxhole, nearest the road.

As he approached, Cinq said, "Mustard."

"Ketchup," Sam answered—the countersign. He walked on, checking the rest of the platoon, ending up with Choi and Kim. Kim was in his foxhole with Choi, talking to him. Choi had his back against the wall of the hole, like Hartung had said, just his head sticking up.

"Hi, boss."

"Everything all right there, private?"

Kim flashed him a thumbs up, and Choi smiled and copied Kim's gesture. A lot of the baby fat had gone from the kid, and he didn't seem as glum as when he'd got in trouble with Lee way back on the ship. Kim had been looking after him.

The young Koreans made him think of school kids bundled up to play in the snow. *Let me bring them through this, God. Let me bring all my men through. Let there be no Chinese. Let me get back with Bonnie, out of this war. Help me win her away from that doctor and stick with her. I'm afraid I won't. But right now, I'm more afraid of the Chinese. So get us all out of this if it's your will, and whatever happens, help me be a good lieutenant, God, because that's what these men need and deserve.*

Sam realized with surprise that he had just prayed. Hadn't been much for it before he'd hit Korea.

Back in the bunker, while Hartung slept, he gazed down at the road, blowing into his hands to warm them and thinking about Bonnie. All those doctors around her, especially that one on the road to Pusan. That had been the "Jeff" she'd mentioned—had to be. I'll get to her as soon as I can, he thought. I'll tell her I love her, and if she'll have me, I'll take her back to New York, show her the city. And then we'll settle down someplace warm.

And if I start feeling I have to leave her?

Gunfire popped across the road, the sporadic fire of carbines and M-1s.

"What the fuck," Hartung mumbled, coming awake. "Probably those damn KATUSAs firing at their own shadows."

Grabbing his field glasses, Sam tried to bring the road into focus, but there wasn't enough light. Wind blew into the bunker, stinging his eyes as he squinted at the road below and to the west. Maybe movement, maybe nothing.

The firing tailed off.

"That's better," Hartung mumbled; in a few seconds he was snoring again.

"Wake up, sergeant. I'm going out for a look. I need you on phone watch."

"Yes, sir," Hartung said in a resigned voice.

Sam worked his way down the slope toward Cinquemani's forward position. Squatting beside the foxhole, he peered down at the road. "See anything?"

"No, sir," Cinquemani said. "At least I don't think so."

Sam stared until his eyes watered. The sense of something moving grew on him. Firing started again across the road, and then some of his own men, the KATUSAs, were firing. All at once Sam realized what it might be. His scalp tingled.

"Cease fire," he shouted, and Cinquemani took up the call, but the firing continued.

"Stop," Sam yelled, running along behind the foxholes. The enemy was down there all right, and they were probing forward to draw fire so they could fix the U.S. positions for attack.

Finally, the firing along the American line died out.

Back in the bunker, Hartung had lit up another Lucky. Sam worked the bolt on his M-1, breaking the ice again, then took his .45 from the holster and slipped it inside his shirt. The frigid metal shocked his skin.

Time stretched, and he began to hope he'd been wrong, that no Chinese had ventured forward, that his men *had* been shooting at phantoms.

"I'm going out again—"

A bugle sounded up the road, an eerie sound piercing the night. Other horns started blowing and then whistles joined in, setting up a terrific racket.

Hartung looked startled, then scowled. "Fucking Chinks. Looks like you were right, sir." Rising, he unslung his rifle.

Sam shouldered his M-1. Gray shapes swarmed up the hill, lit by muzzle flashes from their submachine guns. He pulled the trigger again, again, until the magazine was empty, not sure if he'd hit anyone, fighting the bolt to reload. Flashes lit the charging Chinese and the bunker rattled with shells from their burp guns.

"Son of a bitch," Hartung yelled, and threw a grenade down at them. It bounced right into their midst and exploded, hurling the attackers to all sides.

Hurrying to the western exposure of the bunker, Hartung ran out his M-1. "Christ, sir, look at all those fucking Chinks." Chinese in white quilted uniforms raced up the hill on the other side of the road, running in behind "A" Company lines.

Squeezing beside Hartung, Sam fired the gun dry, reloaded, and kept firing, but fifty or more Chinese completed an end run around "A" Company's right flank.

Backing away to the phone, Sam tried to ring HQ. The line was dead—cut?

"We'd best watch each other's back, sergeant. They may be behind us, too."

"Fucking Chink slants."

More machine gun fire raked the roof of the bunker. Sam plucked a grenade from his belt, pulling the pin as he turned, Lord, twenty more of them, stumbling through the bodies of the last wave, coming straight at the bunker. Sam threw the grenade; an enemy soldier kicked it aside to sail harmlessly down the slope.

We're screwed, Sam thought, and then the attackers whirled and danced, toppling over dead. Sam laughed in relief, a harsh, barking sound he barely recognized as his own voice, as he watched the beautiful, wide muzzle flash of a heavy machine gun emplacement on "C" Company's line. The gun went on firing, mowing down more Chinese.

The bugles continued from the road, horns blaring, the din screeching along Sam's nerves above the furious rattle of machine gun and small arms fire. And then he heard the clank of treads below on the road, a Chinese tank—two. . .no the second was a self-propelled gun. The turret of the tank swiveled, firing a round that skipped on the slope and went high.

"Come on, Corporal Godfrey," Sam prayed aloud.

"Maybe they shot him already."

"I'm going over there—we've got to retrieve his gun."

"If they overran him, sir, they've got the gun by now."

Sam started out anyway and Hartung grabbed him and then the tank exploded in flames.

Hartung let go of him and cheered, and Sam yelled in triumph.

The long muzzle of the second gun swiveled toward Godfrey's position, and then the second vehicle exploded into flame, too, casting a brassy light over the slopes, and exposing a hundred Chinese who'd been hiding behind the two monsters. Charging up the hill toward Godfrey, they began toppling as the big gun mowed them down.

"I told you, sir," Hartung exulted. "Benny Goodman!"

On the ridge to his right, Sam saw one of the "C" Company machine gunners on his feet, cradling his 50 mm gun and tripod, hoisting it up to give him a better angle on the Chinese.

The road began to bloom with explosions—the heavy mortar company to the west of "A" Company, firing on the spots they'd registered. Movement caught Sam's eye; spinning toward Hartung, he saw the sergeant dry-clicking his M-1 as five Chinese sprang through the bodies of their comrades. Hartung went down under a fusillade from a Thompson sub-machine gun. Sam pulled his .45 from his shirt and fired until it was empty, four enemy at point blank range falling into the bunker on top of Hartung as the Chinese with the Thompson dashed past, up the hill behind.

Sam grabbed his M-1 and ran out the escape trench, firing into the back of the Chinese who'd shot Hartung. The soldier dropped. Racing back to the bunker, Sam pulled the bodies off his sergeant. In the glow from the burning tanks, Hartung seemed to be grinning. His eyes were open and Sam could find no pulse at his throat.

One of the Chinese he'd shot stirred; Sam rammed his bayonet into the man over and over, cursing. He backed out of the bunker, his vision blurred, trying to get his breath back.

He saw that "C" Company was being attacked from up the spur above, just as he'd feared. A machine gunner fell, and Sam ran to take his place, firing up the spur and then swiveling to fire down on Chinese still charging up from the road.

One of Cinq's stockade pals materialized beside him and fed a new ammo belt into the gun. Sam decimated a squad coming up from the road, but more followed, dear God, there must be thousands of them.

When the spur was clear except for Chinese bodies, Sam abandoned the machine gun and mounted the slope to the reverse side, rallying GIs who were crouched there.

"The Chinese are overrunning the middle of our line," he shouted. "We're going to take it back. You're all with me." Some rose to follow and some didn't, but he couldn't wait. He ran up the ridge line behind the heavy machine guns, feeling in his throat that he was screaming, but unable to hear the sound. He fired and kept firing, seeing Chinese drop and the remainder turn and run. He charged after them, bringing what had become a squad along with him, all of them yelling, but then men began to drop around him, as the Chinese counterattacked.

"Withdraw," he yelled, and the men retreated with him to the cover behind the reverse slope. He could hear firing behind the lines, too—nowhere was safe.

He found himself in Cinquemani's foxhole with Cinq and the dead body of Cinq's buddy, what was his name? Sam's jaws hurt. He felt himself grinning in horror, firing across the road at the Chinese still skirting "A" Company's flank, firing and reloading, grinning so hard it felt like his mouth was splitting.

Sunrise shredded the black heavens into bands of gray. Snow drifted down from a gunmetal sky, the flakes separating as they fell, spots of cool on the feverish hide of his face.

Where had the Chinese gone?

Piles of bodies covered the slopes, pile upon pile of dead Chinese, and too many Americans and Koreans Attached To the United States Army mixed in.

Sam listened intently to the silence. All firing had stopped. No more bugles or whistles, just the wind blowing snow in his face, and the moans of the wounded. Grief dragged his shoulders down, a weight in his chest hung hard on cables through his throat.

Cinquemani was saying "fuck" over and over in a soft voice, looking down at his dead buddy. Private Sherwood, that was it. Jim Sherwood, who had decided to stay in the reserves after

World War II so his three-year-old could go to Harvard some day.

"Let's take care of him," Sam said. "Get him back to battalion aide. I'll help you carry him. Then you help me with Sergeant Hartung."

Cinquemani turned raw red eyes on him. "Hartung, too?"

Sam nodded. I saved him from the white phosphorus. All that pain, and it bought him one more month, living scared in shacks or holes in the ground. It isn't fair. "Let's get him up."

They carried Sherwood to battalion aide, on the reverse slope. The bodies of other GIs were already there, frozen stiff on the ground. They laid Sherwood out, and Cinquemani covered his face with his helmet.

Hartung was heavier, a big man. They had to lay him on his side in the position he'd frozen. Sam found a poncho and spread it over Hartung. His eyes burned, the tears gelled by the wind, scalding him.

Leaving Cinq on his knees beside Sherwood, Sam trudged back to the line. He must find Kim. Kim would be alive, he would stand for nothing else.

Tremors in his legs made him stagger; he kept on. Nearing Kim's foxhole, he saw something at one end, a thing, and then it became a headless corpse, the remains of Choi.

Kim sat at the bottom of the foxhole, his shoulders shaking.

"What happened?" Sam asked before he could stop himself.

Kim's head came around slowly, an old man's face, wet with tears. "It was right at the start, when guh-guys in the other foxholes were shooting. I couldn't see anyone to shoot at, and Choi was scared, so I turned to calm him down, and suddenly his head flew off. A Chinese sneaked up and put a pole charge against him and it exploded. I shot him, but it was too late. I let him get Choi."

Kim bent his head down against his hands, shaking.

Settling beside him, Sam hugged him tight while Kim cried for both of them.

21

Yudam-ni, Chosin Reservoir, western shore, 2220:

A fat moon lit the trampled snow of Yudam-ni, throwing the thatched huts into dark relief. Trudging toward the lieutenant's shack, Hood shivered so hard his shoulders shook. Minus thirty-five on the rocks with a chaser of arctic wind—no chance this place would make his list of sites to revisit after the war. Didn't even have a decent view. High hills hid the reservoir to the east while higher ones rolled away west in frozen waves, stacking themselves against the towering Taebek mountains.

All the villagers had bugged out, leaving their huts to the marines.

Hood fought an urge to turn his back on the wind and re-trace his steps to the shack where he could content himself with dozing in the straw with Clemons and Bertleson while Steinberg wrote home in the glow of the lantern and Bo and Jimmy played gin for a penny a point. What could the lieutenant tell him that would change anything?

Like the other shacks, Lui's hootch looked dark behind blackout curtains, out of respect for any Chinese mortars that might be out there. Before Hood could knock, the door opened and a Chinese hand thrust a .45 in his face.

"Go ahead," Hood said, "put me out of my misery."

Lowering the weapon, Lui pulled him inside and shut the door against the howling wind. Hood took off his helmet, pushed back his parka hood and settled in a folding chair. The lieutenant had hung his poncho over the shack's one window to seal in the glow of a kerosene lantern. The only other furnishings, besides the sleeping bag on the floor, were more rusting metal chairs and a table supporting Lui's Coleman stove and his maps.

The stove cranked out a fair heat; Hood could feel his face prickling back to life.

"Smoke?" Lui shook out a crisp pack of Chesterfields.

Hood took one and lit up. The first drag roused the usual cough as it bathed his lungs with mellow heat. "Any change?" he asked.

"No. The 7th Regiment is still manning the first ridge line to our west. Our 2nd battalion is probing out beyond them."

"You know what I mean, sir."

Lui grunted. "Our orders are still to push northwest in the morning. At dawn, we and the rest of the 5th Regiment will move through the 7th's positions, join our 2nd battalion and lead the way west to Mupyong-ni."

On the table, Hood noticed a pamphlet covered with the slashing characters of Asian writing. "What's that?"

"You don't want to know."

"Okay. Except now I do."

Lui picked up the pamphlet. "It's nothing, really. Someone took it off a dead Chinese soldier. G2 thought it might be important, so they asked me to translate."

"Was it important, sir?"

Lui sighed and began to read: "Soon we will meet the American Marines in battle. We will destroy them. When they are defeated, the enemy will collapse and our country will be free from the threat of aggression. Kill these Marines as you would snakes in your homes."

"What have they got against snakes?"

Lui gave a harsh laugh. Rising, he paced to the door and back. "Want to hear *our* marching orders?" Before Hood could reply, he began to recite in a macho drawl, imitating someone from Command—a distinctly unflattering performance: "The 5th and the 7th Regiments will form half of a giant pincer. The other half of the pincer will be 8th Army. The two halves will drive north and snap shut at the Yalu River, crushing everything between them. These forces will then be relieved by an army of occupation and sent into reserve in the rear."

"Sounds good, but it needs something about killing the Chinese like rats."

Lui stared at him. "In China the rat is respected and considered a courageous, enterprising animal."

So tense, his shoulders hiked up, his normally half-lidded eyes wide. Was the lieutenant starting to lose it? "We'll be all right, sir. We'll attack like the plan says, and if the enemy tries any 'rear guard action' we'll kick their asses."

"We're talking sixty thousand Chinese, sergeant."

"Doesn't matter."

"Because they're Chinese?"

"Because they're not U.S. Marines, and we are."

"Good point." Lui sat down again and blew out a breath. "Heard anything about the other side of the reservoir?"

Sipping at his Chesterfield, Lui squinted through the smoke. "What do you care about a bunch of dogfaces?"

"Idle curiosity."

"You sure that's all it is?"

Hood realized with annoyance that one of his squad must have talked.

Lui relented with a wave of his cigarette. "I haven't heard a thing from or about Army. I've been monitoring the radio but we don't net on their channels. You check out north of the village?"

Hood pictured where he meant—the narrow space between hills where you could stand on the shore of the reservoir's western branch. From there, you could walk across the ice to Army positions on the eastern shore in half an hour. Trouble was, the lobster claw of frozen water curved too much. The high hills that lined it blocked any view of the other side just as they blocked all sound. One-fifty-five howitzers could be booming over there and you might not hear them on this side.

"Try not to worry, sergeant. I would guess Army's all right for the time being. Chinese are methodical in all things. In war, they like to coordinate their attacks. If they were hitting Army, they'd be on us, too."

Now the lieutenant was soothing him. Hood wished he hadn't brought it up.

"Don't be embarrassed, sergeant. If I had a son over there, I'd be worried."

Who had talked? Surely not Jimmy. Time for a lecture on keeping the private business of your brother Marines private. "It's his mother, lieutenant. If he gets himself killed only a few miles from me, she'll take a strip off me."

Lui reached beneath the desk and pulled out a bottle of Johnny Walker Red.

"Damn!" Hood said with approval. The lieutenant poured a shot into his tin mug and handed the bottle across. Hood filled the big cap of the bottle and raised it to his lieutenant, drinking with him, the scotch burning its way into his blood, thawing the chill.

"You have any kids, lieutenant?"

"A boy and two girls. The boy isn't quite old enough to fight, thank God."

Quite? Hood realized that Lui must be older than he looked if he had a son anywhere near combat age. Not surprising, come to think of it, given that Lui was a "mustang." He could have spent years as a non-com before his promotion to lieutenant.

"You're close with your kids?"

Lui nodded. "To the Chinese, family is very important. I was born in the U.S. but raised in the old ways by parents from mainland China. It's hard to describe, but I miss my kids very much. They're growing up without me."

"They rag you about not being there?"

"Sure." He knocked back a shot of whisky. "But they also understand about duty. They'll understand it even better as they get older."

Envy pierced Hood. They understand, he thought, because you're still a family. When you leave, they know you'll be back. I always went back, but then my son got another father, a real one, and my days as a weekend-pass-daddy were over. It wasn't how I wanted it, but he'll never believe that, never forgive me.

"You say something?" Lui asked.

He realized he'd made a sound deep in his throat. "Nope."

Lui eyed him. "Your son's a lieutenant, right?"

"Right."

"Well. His duty is to his men, as yours is to yours. It's only natural to worry about our sons, but when the shit hits the fan, I know you and I can count on each other."

A fast rattle sounded outside, like a stick dragged down a washboard. Lui yanked the poncho off the window. Green tracers flowed down from a ridge-line to the west.

"Chinese," he said. "Only they shoot the green."

Hood felt a push in his legs.

Rising, Lui went to the door, opened it a foot and leaned his head out into the wind. In a minute he pulled back inside, his face red with cold. "The 2nd must have advanced again and are taking fire."

Horns blared, mixing with the rattle of machine gun fire, and then whistles joined in, sounding like a tone-deaf marching band.

"What the hell is that?"

"A full scale attack," Lui said. "The Chinese like to make a lot of noise, try to spook the enemy. Our 2nd battalion can take care of themselves, and they've got the whole 7th regiment backing them up."

"All the same, I'd better get back to my men. Thanks for the drink."

A short time later, going on midnight, a company runner pounded on the door to Hood's shack. The 7th Regiment was in trouble on Hill 1282 and the 1st Battalion of the 5th was being called in to reinforce.

Excitement and fear beat in Hood's chest; he hurried the squad into their coats and parkas and out across the snow to where Company "A" was forming up. This was no rear guard delaying action to cover their retreat, the Chinks were attacking in force, driving the marines in the hills back toward the village.

Bo hurried over. "Come on, Jimmy. Heads up."

"In this cold? Forget it."

"Give it up, corporal," Hood advised.

Pretending to gripe, Jimmy took off his helmet and shucked his parka back, and Bo rubbed his bald head, the others falling in behind to give it a quick polish, and Hood rubbed it too, better safe than sorry, and then they were on the move with the rest of the platoon out of the valley heading north and west to the foot of Hill 1282. Its steep, snowy slope rose above them, glowing brassy orange under the parachute flares fired off by "E" Company. Breath streamed up from the skirmish line like the smoke from a musket volley.

Down the line, Sergeant Weiler waved forward, and Hood led his part of the line up the slope. Snow had accumulated, hip deep at the bottom. Churning through it, Hood sucked deep breaths and used the stock of his M-1 like a walking stick to help haul himself over jutting rocks. The snow dragged at him, making his lungs burn, and he felt his legs begin to quiver before they were halfway up.

"Damn, look at that," Jimmy said, pointing up the rise.

Hood's heart skipped a beat. The wavering drift of descending flares showed mounds of bodies, the remains of a Chinese charge down from the crest. The corpses seemed to writhe as their shadows shifted under them—must be several hundred dead Chinese up there, lying in tangles.

"They're moving, they're moving," cried Bo.

"It's just the shadows."

"No, Sarge, I saw one of them fucking move!" Bo raised his M-1 and fired off a full magazine at the pile of bodies.

"Knock it off," Steinberg yelped.

On the other side, Clemons tried to force the muzzle of Bo's rifle down before he could waste another magazine but Bo shoved him away.

Plowing through the snow, Hood threw an arm over Bo's shoulder. "Take it easy, big man, it's all right, you killed them, they're all dead," heaving breaths between each burst of words, remembering how he'd seen this same thing at Iwo, bodies seeming to move under flares.

"That's it," Clemons soothed. "You're all right now."

Bo blinked and heaved a couple of breaths, his eyes taking on focus. "Sorry, guys. I guess I got shook there for a minute."

Hood heard a new sound, the thump of 81 millimeter mortars zeroing in on the summit, where the Chinese waited. He cheered as dirt and rock exploded along the ridge line, raining down on the Chinks.

Taking point, he watched the mounds of bodies as they waded through, in case some of the Chinks *were* only wounded, still able to shoot.

The sky lit up—Roman candles, Vesuvius fountains, pinwheels, skyrockets, firecrackers going off, like the fourth of July, and he heard the bugles again, and cymbals crashing. A horde of white-uniformed Chinese ran down the slope at them. The skirmish line began firing, M-1s popping, then the chatter of machine guns as the heavy weapons squad scrambled to set their tripods. A Chink ran straight at Hood screaming, "Son of a bitch marine you die we kill you all—"

Hood fired, and the man dove headfirst into the snow, his cap with the earflaps flying off, but there was another man right behind him, and Bo shot him, and then the Chinese were among them, and Hood swung his rifle like a club, knocking men down around him until he could get a second to fix his bayonet.

"Look out," Jimmy yelled, and Hood lunged to the side as a Chinese bayonet caught in his parka. The soldier tried to pull it out. Hood punched him on the side of the head, and the Chink lost his footing and went down, rolling over and over down the slope. Someone was swearing—Bo—hacking at two Chinese with his K-bar. Steinberg waded in, slashing low at the tendons at the backs of their ankles with his knife and both attackers went down, screaming. Steinberg backed away as Bo finished them with his bayonet.

Suddenly, the Chinese were retreating up the slope.

No, don't let them.

"Go, GO!" Hood yelled, and fought his way up, slipping and sliding, forcing his legs through the knee-deep snow, not cold at all now, hot inside the shoepacs and all the clothes, eyes stinging with sweat before the wind whipped it away—damn, falling behind the retreating Chinese, but he couldn't go any faster. Glancing left and right, he saw the rest of the squad with him, all of them still alive and on their feet.

Higher now, he could see the long ridge of the summit. He passed a corpsman from the 7th regiment kneeling beside a fallen marine, the corpsman spitting something from his mouth—a Syrette of morphine, carried there to keep it from freezing—and then Hood was past and scrambling onto the summit, his lungs heaving. Fifty yards away along the ridge, he saw a Chinese bent over a dead marine, stripping off his parka. Beside him, another Chink rifled through the fallen soldier's C-rations. Hood tried to fire the M-1, but it spanged on empty. Fumbling another magazine in, he fired. The Chinese stripping the parka groped the middle of his back with both hands, arching and twisting, like a man with an itch, and then he fell backwards.

The other Chinese stared at him, his mouth full of C-ration crackers, and Hood shot him too, the crackers spraying with blood from the Chink's lung as he pitched forward.

The rest of the platoon, and the second platoon of A Company had gained the summit now, and Hood looked up and down the ridge-line for another Chinese to shoot, but there weren't any.

He sank to his knees in the snow, sweating and panting. *I'm too old for this.* The knowledge stabbed him through with a grief worse than pain.

No, damn it, not too old, still got it or he would never have made it to the top.

The ridge-line was bare of snow, blasted away by the mortars, the rock pulverized into pumice. One of the machine gun teams shouted a warning—Chinese had regrouped on the reverse slope and were charging the ridge. Hood fired down into the mass of men, damn, hundreds of them, screaming like madmen as they thrashed up the slope in wave after wave while the machine guns chattered on every side, mowing them down. A fool thing to do, charge with no cover into a hail of lead, coming as hard as they could, fatally bad tactics, but God were they brave.

Was this what Custer felt, his guts knotting as death swarmed at him, the last minute of his existence, and no one ever to know how it felt?

Hood threw his grenades until they were gone, others in the company raining explosions down on the Chinese until this wave, too, foundered and broke.

Signaling Clemons to follow, Hood led a run on Easy Company's ammo dump down the ridge-line, still intact, another tactical lapse by the Chinks, who'd let plundering the food of dead marines distract them when they'd held the summit. They must have been sent into battle on empty stomachs and many had died for it.

Hood grabbed a burlap sack of grenades and Clemons hoisted another, and they ran back to the squad, passing them out, hurling them down on the Chinese who were surging up again in another wave, shooting as they charged. Hood saw men falling all around him. A marine from Weiler's squad with a blood-soaked shoulder and shattered leg sat on his butt, legs splayed out in front, firing his M-1 one-armed, picking off target after target.

"Sarge, look." Jimmy, beside him, pointed at the sky to the east. It was turning a lighter gray. Dawn was coming, and with it the air cover would be back—Corsairs blazing away with their wing cannons and napalm.

The Chinese must have realized it too, because they were falling back, fading down the far slope, disappearing into the snow with their white uniforms.

"We made it, sarge," Jimmy grinning at him, and then Hood noticed a gash low on the corporal's forehead, a bad one that should have been pouring blood, but it was so cold the blood had frozen in the wound.

So hell freezing over is good for something, Hood thought.

He started laughing and couldn't stop, and Jimmy laughed too, the two of them doubling over on the summit, until Bo came along and cuffed them both on their helmets, as if he'd been the calm one all along.

A lieutenant from the 7th Regiment staggered up, his face crusted in blood. Hood's stomach took a queasy roll—the man's right eye was gummed shut, a black bullet hole puckering the flesh just under it. The battle high of a few seconds ago vanished and he felt sick. He took the lieutenant's sleeve.

"Go down the hill, sir. You've got to get yourself down to battalion aide. Able company's here, from the 5th, you are all right now. Go down, sir."

The lieutenant threw his hand off and spat out a mouthful of blood.

"Yancey!" Lieutenant Lui called with a stricken expression. "What happened, John?"

"Some son of a bitch shot me—popped my eye right out, hanging down my cheek. He was looking to shoot me again, but I got him first, with my .45, then I put my eyeball back in."

"You've got to get to battalion aide. You can't see."

"Tell that to the man I shot." He spat more blood.

A captain from the 7th walked up, took one look and said, "You—sergeant, take Lieutenant Yancey down the hill."

Lui turned to Jimmy. "Corporal, you've got the squad. Go, Hood."

The captain bent and picked up a stick from the snow. He put one end in Yancey's hand and the other in Hood's. "Just hang onto the stick, John. Sergeant, this man is the toughest

SOB in the U.S. Marines, and we can't afford to lose him. You make damn sure he gets to battalion aide."

"Yes, sir."

Hood started down the hill. Dawn had broken, but even full daylight wasn't much help to the one-eyed lieutenant. Keeping hold of his end of the stick, Hood threw back warnings over his shoulder about rocks and gullies, shouting to be heard above the wind. Yancey staggered along behind him. Other marines were helping the walking wounded down the hill, a steady stream on both sides, and Hood wondered how many they'd lost who'd never be walking again.

By the time he reached bottom his knees ached from the strain. Still holding the stick, Yancey followed him to the aid station. He was bleeding into his throat again, so one of the corpsmen tied him, sitting upright, to a tent post, to keep him from choking.

Hood wished him luck and headed out. Beyond the tent, he saw rows of marine bodies wrapped in their ponchos, men dragging and carrying more bodies in as he watched.

He started back up the hill, detouring around a soldier who sat in the snow, hugging his knees and shaking.

Hood realized it *was* a soldier—a GI, not a marine.

What the hell would an army private be doing this side of the reservoir?

Kneeling beside the man, he gripped his shoulder. A boy's face turned up to him, glittering with frozen tears, the eyes wide. "It's a massacre," he said in a thin, hoarse voice. "They just keep coming."

"Take it easy, son. What unit are you with?"

"Fuh, first battalion."

"Thirty-second regiment?"

The kid nodded.

Sam's outfit. "You're under attack?"

"They just keep coming. I was so scared, I ran away across the ice. It's a massacre."

Hood scanned the slope, feeling a desperate pressure in his chest—damn it, where was Lieutenant Lui?

Over there, heading toward the battalion command post!

Running to catch up, Hood grabbed Lui by the arm.

Lui looked down at his hand, and Hood let go.

"Sir, the Chinese have overrun Army positions on the east side of the reservoir."

"I'm sorry to hear that, sergeant. But we have our own problems, here."

"I thought we and Army were on the same side."

"They've got their orders and we have ours."

"You're asking me to choose between the Marine Corps and my son?"

"I'm asking you to do your duty."

"As a soldier or a father?"

"You know what your duty is, sergeant."

"Yes, sir, I surely do. Jimmy has the platoon. He should have been a sergeant long ago, but I've been in his way. He did great at Pusan. He'll do fine now. When I get back you can arrest me and promote him."

Lui took a step toward him. "Come on, sergeant. You're not even close to your son, you said so yourself."

"What has that got to do with anything?"

The lieutenant put a hand on his .45. "Sergeant Hood, I order you to stay with your squad."

"I'm going."

Lui pulled the .45, pointed it at him.

"If you mean to shoot me, do it." Hood waited a beat, then turned and headed toward the break in the hills, the ice that would carry him across the reservoir. Ten steps, twenty, waiting for the bullet to plow into his back, the pain, the darkness. If Lui was a good shot, maybe there would be no pain. They said you never heard the shot that killed you—

During the Korean war the Chinese, with some help from the Soviet Union, administered the majority of the prisoner of war camps in North Korea. Less well known is the fact that POW camps also existed in China. A U.S. military report in December of 1951 estimated that 2,500 American P.O.W.s were being held in camps in Manchuria and 1,500 in other areas of South China. The treatment in these camps was horrific. UN prisoners of war were starved, exposed to lethal cold, and were given foul water to drink. Chinese doctors experimented on some of the wounded with practices such as implanting bits of chicken liver beneath the skin. Pneumonia, rampant in the camps, was often treated only with cough drops. Surgeries were performed without anesthesia. Unquestionably the brutality of the treatment contributed to the fact that forty percent of prisoners held by the Chinese died in captivity.   (Ibid.)

22

28 November, Camp 2, China, near the Yalu River, 0900:
As the guards marched her toward Prison Row, Bonnie worked
on her fear. A lot like the hunger, actually, which wasn't so bad
after almost a week. Just a set of sensations, a hollow ache. Maybe
you couldn't escape it, hunger or fear, but you could look the
other way.

Bonnie focused on her feet crunching through the frozen muck, watching her Raggedy Anne shoes swing past each
other, concentrating on practicalities: The American prisoners
included some wounded, why else would Doody and Horseface
be herding her toward the miserable row of blockhouses? Six
GIs it had looked like, the spy hole in her mud hut too small to
be sure. Americans hanging onto each other, staggering while
the guards shouted and prodded them through the gate with
bayonets and kicks—

Lord, had she remembered to put out the fire?

Bonnie dredged up a memory of scattering the wood on the
baked mud hearth and smothering the bigger coals with her
blankets. Good. Being allowed to gather what few twigs and
branches she could find could end at any time, and in this place
you wasted nothing burnable or edible.

Shivering, she pulled her fatigue jacket tighter. She missed
her heavy coat, now the property of Doody—her name for the

guard with the bulgy cheeks, who made her think of the famous puppet. Doody had wasted no time stealing it. The ragged tennis shoes Horseface had "traded" for her boots had now finished rotting at the seams. He and Doody had probably placed side bets on how many more steps she could take before the soles fell away, leaving only socks to protect her from the ice and snow—

Horse grabbed her arm. Looking up, she saw they'd reached the first of the cinderblock barracks. Doody unlocked the padlock and wrenched the steel door open on a squeal of frozen hinges; he used his tommy gun to point her inside.

Ducking through the door, she took quick stock: the American soldiers she'd seen earlier lay on the dirt floor shivering. The rusted stove at the center of the barracks was empty and cold.

She turned to Doody. "Bring wood, please."

He stared at her.

She pointed to the stove. "Wood. We must make a fire now."

He understood—of course he did, but he didn't even bother to shake his head.

She pointed to his coat—her coat—then hugged her arms and pointed to the men. "They need heat."

"Pinch me," groaned a parched voice, "is that a woman I'm hearing?"

"And water." She mimed drinking from a glass.

Doody smirked.

"Water, or I will go to Colonel Tien. He brought me here to care for these men. Colonel Tien will be angry with you."

Horse, still outside, said something to Doody. Doody backed from the prison, slamming the door. She heard the padlock snick shut.

Turning back to the GIs, she did a quick assessment. Six men in tattered green uniforms sprawled in the dirt. One had a nasty cough that hadn't let up since she'd entered.

"I'm Lieutenant Brisbane," she said, "1st MASH. Who is the senior man here?"

"That would be me." One tried to struggle to his feet.

"Stay down. Conserve your strength."

He sank back. "I'm Lieutenant Charles DeForest, 7th Division, 31st Regiment, third battalion. My men and I were captured while on an advance recon patrol east of the Chosin Reservoir. . . ." Another fit of coughing took him, the rasping bark of bronchitis or maybe pneumonia.

She should have thought to bring her own canteen, still half full of today's ration. Next time she would—she could do that much.

The coughing eased enough for DeForest to suck a breath. "Chinks ambushed our patrol. That was two days ago. Been walking ever since. Some of my men can't feel their feet. The bastards stole our boots, first thing."

Tell me about it, Bonnie thought. "I'll keep after them for blankets, firewood and water. Did they give you anything to eat?"

"A ball of rice and sorghum this morning. First thing we need, one of my men, Dierdorf, here, is wounded. They shot him in the lower back, near the side. We had to carry him the last ten miles or so."

Bonnie knelt beside the man. He was shivering, his teeth chattering. His eyes looked through her, unfocused. She touched his forehead with the back of her hand, shocked by the heat. A serious fever, 102 or 103, at least.

"Lieutenant Brisbane," said DeForest, "what in God's name are you doing here?"

"They kidnapped me six days ago in Pukch'ong and brought me here to care for wounded POWs."

"You're a doctor?" The skepticism in his voice pricked her.

"A nurse. They thought I was doctor."

DeForest shook his head with disbelief. "And I thought the Chinese were smart."

"I was wearing a parka," Bonnie explained, "with the hood up and size ten combat boots. It was night and. . . ." *The hell with it.* "You had to be there."

"Dierdorf needs a hospital," DeForest said.

"I'm afraid this is it."

The lieutenant looked around. "There isn't even a cot in here. The ground is freezing. Why bother to bring a nurse or doctor up here under these conditions?"

"Strictly for show. They want to be able to say later that they provided medical care for their prisoners, as required by the Geneva Convention."

"But you'd just tell the truth."

Bonnie was aware, briefly, of the hollow in her stomach. Comprehension dawned in the lieutenant's face, and then she watched him try to hide it.

"It's all right, lieutenant," she said. "I've thought it all through long ago. I don't think they plan for me to survive this place. The day I arrived, they took a picture of me in the Chinese sick bay with one of their soldiers pretending to be American wounded. He was wearing a U.S. Army uniform shirt with sergeant stripes and his head was wrapped in bandages so he wouldn't be identifiable as Chinese. They can present that after the war, if they need to, and claim I was working as a camp nurse when I caught pneumonia or dysentery or some such and died."

"Bastards," Deforest rasped.

"Situations can change. We're alive now; let's focus on helping each other stay that way."

The lock rattled, and the door swung open. Doody stepped in, pointed the submachine gun at the prisoners, and motioned her to the door.

When she didn't move, Colonel's Tien's voice said, "Lieutenant Brisbane, would you step outside, please."

DeForest tried to struggle up again, but she held him down with a hand on his shoulder. "It's all right. This is good. Maybe I can get some blankets and wood for you now."

She stepped out into the cold.

The colonel, resplendent in his greatcoat and polished boots, looked her up and down. One groomed eyebrow arched. "Lieutenant, where are your boots?"

"Your guard stole them from me."

Tien glanced at Doody's feet, then Horse's. He said something to Horse, and the man replied softly, head down. "He says you traded him for his shoes."

"Does that sound reasonable to you, colonel?"

"Why not? After all, the boots were too big for you. And you have no need for them in your nice, warm villa. Surely you don't expect me to doubt my own man solely on the word of an enemy?"

"Your prisoners need water immediately," she said, "and food. And I must operate on one of them or he'll die."

"Operate?" Tien cocked an eyebrow.

"He was shot. The bullet is still inside him and infection has set in."

"No, no, I'm asking if you are capable of performing surgery."

"Why not? I've assisted in thousands of operations over the past two months. I've had my hands right in the wounds alongside the surgeon's, and I've stitched up afterward."

"Yes, but can you cut?"

"Certainly." *If I have to.* "Colonel, I'm sure you'd like to have a photo of me working on an actual wounded American whose face you won't need to hide. I will cooperate in that if you'll let me take Private Dierdorf to the clinic, remove the bullet, and treat him with penicillin."

"That clinic is for our brave Chinese soldiers, not murdering invaders."

"I'm a medical officer. I heal, I don't kill."

"And what do you think those men you send back into battle do with their restored health, lieutenant?"

"I'm responsible for healing, not controlling behavior. I have no say in what the people I help do after they're back on their feet."

"What a convenient rationalization."

She met his gaze, refusing to look down as his guards always did. What went on in that mind? Tien had obviously been highly educated, including schooling in the West, and yet he seemed to

335

see everything in a rigid, ideological way. We certainly haven't invaded his country, she thought. And a murderer is far different from a soldier who kills in battle.

"If you let me operate on Private Dierdorf, I'll operate on your soldiers, too."

"We have our own surgeons."

"Then I'll assist them."

"I could make you do that anyway."

"Could you?"

Tien shook his head with an indulgent sigh. "All right, lieutenant." Murmuring an order to Horse, he turned back to her. "Select two prisoners to carry the wounded man and follow Private Pao to our infirmary."

"Thank you. And will you please also give the prisoners food and water, right away, and fuel for the stove, so they won't freeze to death tonight?"

"Of course. That was to be done in any case."

The camp infirmary, kept exclusively for Chinese wounded, was warm and bright. It smelled of lotion and antiseptic, so clean and pleasant after her filthy mud hut and the frozen landscape of the camp that she stood a moment, overwhelmed, feeling faint. I had luxuries like these a week ago, she thought, and didn't even think about it.

Not trusting her voice, she pointed at an empty gurney; Lieutenant DeForest and his sergeant deposited Private Dierdorf on it. At once, Horse herded them out. As Bonnie started for the gurney, a man in white gown, mask and surgical cap, stepped in her way.

"No," he said. "You treat our wounded first."

She fought a furious impulse to push him aside and keep going. "He has a very high fever, doctor. We must get the bullet out at once, or he'll die of infection."

"You treat Chinese wounded first."

"Must I call Colonel Tien?"

336

"He say you treat Chinese first. You want me call him?"

"Can you at least give him penicillin while he's waiting, please?"

"Penicillin for Chinese."

"Aspirin, then—to get the fever down. If he dies, I'm finished here."

The doctor glared at her, then turned, gave a curt order to one of the nurses. She went to a medicine cabinet, got the aspirin and held up Dierdorf's head to a glass of water until he had drunk them down.

"You help us now," the doctor ordered.

"All right."

The operating room was small but well-equipped, two doctors and several nurses working around five tables under blazing lights. If only we had light like this, Bonnie thought as she plucked shrapnel from the leg of a Chinese soldier. The nurse across from her did nothing, watching over her mask. Bonnie had been working over an hour now, hurrying as fast as she could so she could get to Dierdorf, but as soon as she finished one procedure, they slid another Chinese onto her table. Stitching up scalp lacerations, removing shrapnel, irrigating and cleaning wounds that could have waited, conscious every second that Dierdorf's life was slipping away.

Hang on, private.

She plucked a last bit of shrapnel from her patient's leg, cleaned the wound and stepped back, gathering her will as orderlies wheeled the man off and brought another.

"No," she said. "I will take the bullet out of Private Dierdorf, now."

One of the orderlies called the doctor who'd first confronted her. He left his table, waving his bloody scalpel in her face. "Chinese first."

"How can you call yourself a doctor and ignore triage?"

"Triage for Chinese."

"In our hospitals triage is for humans. We take the most serious wounds first, whether they are North Korean or American. I'm sure Chinese soldiers are being treated right now in our battalion aid stations and the 1st MASH, in some cases, while American wounded wait. I will not treat another Chinese laceration or shrapnel case until I have removed the bullet from Private Dierdorf."

"You take this man." The doctor jerked his head toward the latest Chinese casualty, whose head was bloody from superficial scalp lacerations.

"Private Dierdorf," she said. "Now. If he dies, you won't get your picture."

The doctor stared at her. "You do him now, we take picture," he said, as if it were his own idea.

She hurried out, pulled Dierdorf's gurney into the OR, next to the table she'd been using. Another doctor was stepping in to that table's instrument tray. She pulled it away, over to the gurney, ignoring the doctor's angry protest.

Dierdorf lay on his side, unconscious, still in his bloody, ragged uniform. His breathing was shallow and labored, the skin of his face flushed an angry, feverish red despite the aspirin. Grabbing a pair of dorsal scissors, she worked the bent blade in and started to cut away the layers of shirt, then realized the guards would probably refuse to replace his clothes.

Instead, she cut out a small patch from the layers of shirt, exposing the wound, working fast, knowing someone might pull her away as soon as they'd got the photos they wanted. The skin around the bullet hole was dark and the wound oozed pus. Cold fear burrowed in her gut. *I can't do this.*

She looked around at the Chinese doctors. All had turned their backs on her.

Bonnie irrigated the wound with saline and then poured iodine all around it. As she picked up a scalpel to trim the ruined tissue away and enlarge her path to the bullet, her hand began to tremble. She heard a laugh behind her. She laid the scalpel on the wound and, as the blade touched flesh, her hand steadied and she cut with small, precise strokes, reducing the frayed edges of damaged skin. Blood welled up and she used her left hand to blot with gauze after each cut of her right. After more irrigation, she could see the flattened slug. Grabbing a curved Kelly forceps, she burrowed into the wound.

The bullet slipped away and she winced, terrified. Was she driving it deeper?

Forcing the forceps wide open, she found the edge of the slug and eased the jaws shut, finding a purchase at last. *Got it!*

She pulled the bullet out.

At that moment, a flashbulb popped in her face.

She hurried to clean the wound with more iodine. It was bleeding freely now, but not at a dangerous rate. A clot would form soon. From watching Jeff she knew not to close the wound, just irrigate and disinfect, then give it a chance to heal from the inside. If she closed with stitches, the wound would be more likely to suppurate from infection.

"You done now," said the Chinese doctor.

"After I bandage him."

"No bandage. Need for Chinese."

"Would you say that to me if I could see your face?"

The doctor stared at her. "You bandage him, then he goes. You stay here, treat more Chinese."

"Yes. Thank you. And you'll give him a shot of penicillin."

The doctor shook his head, then said, "one shot."

"Right now."

The doctor motioned and the same nurse as before drew a dose from a clear vial, the same sort used at the MASH. She injected it all into Dierdorf's shoulder.

"Thank you," Bonnie said. "Bring in your next patient. I'll help you all I can."

The Chinese surgeon gave her the slightest nod and swept an arm at his surgical table.

It was night when she got out of the clinic. Horse marched her toward her hut, no Doody this time. She ought to feel glad so

339

many Chinese had been wounded, because they were the enemy, and the more of them got taken out of action, the more American boys might live, but she could not feel glad.

So much suffering.

What she resented was that she had treated hundreds of enemy soldiers in her own hospital of her own free will, and would have here. She hated being ordered to do it.

She veered toward the prison.

Horse snapped an order.

"I must see my patient. You won't shoot me because you're too afraid of Colonel Tien."

He barked at her again; she kept walking.

He grabbed her from behind, spun her around, and she shoved him back.

He raised the tommygun; for a second she froze, an icy shock sweeping her scalp. Pushing the fear away, she resumed her march toward the prison. At the door, she pointed to the padlock.

He did not move, standing beside her like a statue. His face was backlit but she knew he was smiling.

She shouted, "Lieutenant DeForest!"

Horse said something in a low, cajoling tone.

"Lieutenant DeForest, I need to speak with you," yelling loud enough for the whole camp—including Colonel Tien—to hear.

Horse unlocked the door, shoved her inside, and locked her in.

The camp's security lights, up on poles, shed a faint glow between the panels of galvanized steel that made up the ceiling.

"Over here," said DeForest's voice.

She saw the men sitting against the wall, huddled together for warmth, covered in blankets, Dierdorf in the middle. The promise of firewood had not been kept; it must be below freezing in here, but maybe the blankets on top of their clothes would keep enough body heat in.

"How is Dierdorf?" she asked.

"We got him to drink and eat a little rice," said the sergeant. "His forehead doesn't feel as hot, and he even talked a little."

"Did he make sense?"

"As much as he ever does."

"Good, and they gave you food and water."

"Another rice ball apiece," Deforest said, "and a pan of water. I think it's frozen now, but we can break it up and suck the ice."

"You're from the 31st regiment, you said."

"Third battalion, yes."

"Do you by any chance know Lieutenant Foxworth? He's in the 1st of the 32nd."

"I'm sorry, no. They'd be deployed at the reservoir by now. He a friend of yours?"

"Yes." A friend of all women, Bonnie thought, and of no woman. She smiled in the dark.

"You saved Dierdorf."

"Let's hope." Meaning it with all her heart but if he did go on to recover, for what had she saved him? To die here of thirst or starvation or a beating?

No, she told herself. That is how Colonel Tien thinks. No matter what he says or does to me, I will never think like him.

By the 28th of November both Army and Marine forces at the Chosin Reservoir were in desperate trouble. Temperatures plunged far below zero at night. Three Chinese divisions surrounding the reservoir attacked repeatedly during the night when American air support was powerless to operate. Colonel MacLean was taken prisoner by the Chinese, leaving command of the Army Task Force to Colonel Faith. By November 29, General MacArthur had to face the fact that his plans for a quick, triumphant attack north by General Walker's 8th Army and General Almond's X Corps were not to be. He cut orders for X Corps to withdraw south to Hungnam, while the 8th Army, also weakened by Chinese attacks, was to try to hold onto P'yongyang. MacArthur's decision came fatally late. For the next two weeks, the 1st Marine Division and the far weaker Task Force Faith would find themselves in the fight of their lives, day and night, against overwhelming odds, to escape the Chinese trap. (Ibid.)

23

Chosin Reservoir, Hill 1475, 1030:

Sam forced himself to look at Captain Loomis's knee, ragged flaps of meat peeled back from the bone. The sight sent an adrenaline shock through him, better than coffee, clearing his head in the heat of the bunker. A medic poured benzalkonium chloride into the wound with the care of a gardener watering a prized flower. The antiseptic hit as Loomis started a question to his sergeant. Without looking, Loomis swung at the medic; the sergeant caught his arm, and Loomis finished his question as if nothing had happened.

Unaware of his narrow escape, the medic pulled a needle and suturing silk from his first aid kit.

Sam, drifting away again, felt a nudge on his chin, his head bouncing up from his chest. Falling asleep in the middle of a battle—too damn warm in here, the company command post simmering while the wind screamed outside. Mid morning, the mercury outside straining all the way up to -10, but here in the bunker the Yukon stove, fed by its jerry can of diesel, was as good as a general anesthetic, especially if you didn't care to be conscious. Josiah Hartung, gone; Choi, horribly gone, nothing left of his head; another KATUSA bayoneted in his sleeping bag during the first rush of the latest attack; a rifleman—a freckled kid whose name he could not remember, only that the kid had talked about missing his dog back in New Jersey; Cinquemani's buddy, Sherwood. Five sad letters—if he could survive to write them.

The Chinese were shelling the broken perimeter again. On the other side of the road, "A" Company was in trouble, their left flank overrun by Chinese creeping with the agility of goats around the steep, reservoir side of their hill.

Enemy in front and behind, no rear to the battle any more—you could take one in the back of the head while firing to the "front." The thump of mortars mixed with the incessant chatter of the heavy .30 caliber machine guns, still able to fire on automatic because of the antifreeze in their jackets. Most of the light machine guns could fire only single shots, the gunners having to jack the breech between each round.

A brace of Corsairs roared overhead, wing cannons thumping, angels of God.

"I'm gonna stitch you up now, captain. You want some morphine?"

Loomis gave the Syrette in the medic's hand a longing look and shook his head. "I gotta stay awake. Go ahead and sew."

The medic stuck his needle into one of the flaps and Loomis grimaced and turned back to his sergeant, reeling off more orders.

Afraid to close his eyes again, Sam squinted out the bright slit of the bunker toward the road. No Chinese visible down there now, not in broad daylight, but they were all over the hills on either side.

"Shit!" Loomis gasped.

"Sorry, sir. Almost done."

Sam thought of Bonnie back in Pukch'ong, all the men like Loomis she had treated, helping take bullets out or repairing torn organs. I should have told her I love her, he thought. Could have said it in the ambulance but I was afraid. Chicken, just like she said. God, how many times have I said it just to score, and when I could finally mean it, I choke.

"Okay, Foxworth." Sam turned back to Loomis. The medic was wrapping the knee in gauze now. The captain's face looked waxy, like a candle starting to melt, but his eyes were sharp from the pain. He said, "How many of your men are out of action?"

"Five dead, nine wounded too badly to fight."

Loomis closed his eyes a beat. "I want you to divide the rest into two assault teams. Hartung can take one and—"

"Hartung's dead."

Loomis coughed and swore. "All right, we won't split you up. The Chinks are still holding the high ground up that ridge. The Corsairs are pounding them, but they're dug in and they got Thompsons and heavy machine guns. If they come at us tonight, there is no way we can hold out against them. Right now, we've got Lieutenant Moore going at them with his platoon. You take your men and circle out, try coming at them up the North slope."

Sam battled an incongruous smile. Take my men, he thought. I don't even know where most of them are.

A private hurried in, brushing snow from his shoulders—one of Loomis's runners, all the com wires to the battalion command post long since cut by the Chinese.

The captain turned to him. "What about that artillery?"

"The 31st is under attack down there at the inlet, too, captain. They're getting the shit kicked out of them. All their artillery's tied up trying to hit the Chinese staging areas before they can send another wave."

"We need those 105s hitting that knob."

"I told them, sir. But it ain't gonna happen."

Loomis turned back and snarled, "You still here, Foxworth? Get going."

Outside the bunker the freezing air sucked the heat from his clothes in an instant, shocking him to a higher state of wakefulness that was still too close to sleep. He hunched into the wind, heading along what was left of the C Company line. More Corsairs, finishing the fifty mile run from their carriers off Hungnam, thundered overhead, firing at the high end of the ridge above C Company. Why didn't I become a pilot, Sam thought, instead of joining the reserves? I could be up there in a warm cockpit, pouring heavy ordnance on the enemy, then back to the carrier for a hot meal.

Of course, if you got shot down in a Corsair, you didn't have to worry about having your knee sewn up.

"Boss, I've got my men together."

Lifting his head, Sam saw Kim hurrying toward him, gripping his carbine as if offering it for inspection. Beyond Kim, the remaining five Koreans held their carbines the same way, stiffening to attention for him, looking scared but determined. Lee, the one who had tormented Choi on the ship, stepped forward and bowed, said something in a hard voice.

"Lee says they are going to kill some Chinese for Choi." Kim gave his carbine an angry shake. "I say that too."

"Good, Kim. Tell them that's just what we're going to do."

Kim spoke at length to his fellow Koreans, embellishing it into a fiery pep talk.

Taking his .45 from his belt, Sam made sure the safety was on and slipped it down inside the layers of coat and shirt. He unslung the M-1 from his shoulder and fired a shot into the air. The explosion of a mortar shell drowned out the report, but he felt the kick and knew it was working, enough heat left from the bunker that it hadn't yet iced up.

"Have you seen Corporal Cinquemani?"

"Forward slope, boss, keeping watch on the road."

"With Logan, Silverman and Hufnagel, I suppose."

"Most of the other men, too."

Sam had a fleeting sense of irony—the scrappers from the stockade, formerly avoided, were suddenly the friends to have.

A feeble confidence flickered in him. *Maybe we can do this.*

"Follow me," he said to Kim.

Trotting over the ridge line and down the forward slope, he saw the remainder of the platoon dug in near the top. The road, after a thorough shelling by the Corsairs, was clear of Chinese.

Slipping into the foxhole with Cinquemani, Sam told him the mission.

"Good," Cinq said. He looked scary-mad, his eyes sunken under dark eyebrows matted with snow and ice, a long cut down his right cheekbone, the blood frozen in the wound. Back in the States, he'd be heading for the emergency room. Here, he probably didn't even know he'd been cut.

"How we doing on ammo and grenades?" Sam asked.

"Silverman just got back from the dump. Ammo's running low, but he got what he could. Plenty of grenades."

"Pass them around, and then we go. I'll lead the way, and I want you and Silverman to take up the rear."

Cinq's eyes narrowed beneath the frozen brows. "With respect, sir, you want me and my guys up front, and you in the rear, to keep the KATUSAs from falling behind. They'll listen to you, and they'll just run from us. And if you were to die out on point, who would lead the platoon?"

"You would, so here's your chance."

"You can be right beside me, sir. We put Silverman and Hufnagel back there."

Sam realized Cinquemani was a force of nature right now, to be harnessed, not denied. "All right, but I want Silverman, Hufnagel, and Logan in the rear keeping the platoon moving forward and watching our backs."

"Fine. Did you send someone along the C Company line to tell them we'll be out there, so we don't get shot by our own men?"

Damn, Sam thought.

Seeing the answer in his face, Cinq said, "It's all right, sir, I'll send Logan right now, while we're passing out grenades, then he can head down from there and catch our tail." Cinq clambered from the foxhole and began giving the orders.

Pulling his .45 from inside his coat and shirts, Sam checked the action. He saw that his hand was shaking. Cinq had just saved him from what could have been a fatal mistake, exposing his men to friendly fire. From a hundred yards away the platoon could easily be mistaken for enemy. Hartung wouldn't have needed to point that out to him. He'd gotten in the habit of thinking each order through so the crusty bastard wouldn't second guess him. Josiah Hartung had kept him sharp, and now Hartung was gone and he'd have to keep himself sharp or his men would pay.

A shadow fell over Sam—Cinq, looking down into the foxhole. "All set, sir."

The quickest way to flank the Chinese on the high ground would be to lead the platoon along the front of C Company's patchwork line. But parts of that route would be visible from the heights he was trying to flank, and the Chinese would surely be watching it. The alternative was to descend to the road north and use it to round the base of the ridge. Only problem there was that a battalion or more of Chinese had come up that road last night, so there had to be a big staging area back there somewhere around the bend.

Sam pointed to the downhill route, and Cinq nodded.

Going down, Sam kept his eyes on the road and the steep rise on its other side. With luck, the enemy soldiers were all heading that way, pouring around the reservoir side of the hill as they continued to flank "A" Company. Good luck for us, Sam amended, bad for "A" Company.

He slipped and slid down the snow-covered rock this side of the road, hearing Cinquemani scrambling beside him. At the bottom of the hill the snow deepened and he slogged through it, his M-1 ready, praying the weapon hadn't frozen.

Rounding the bottom of the ridge, he made sure the road was clear and then began picking his way uphill to the east. A stinging wind raked his eyes, blurring his vision. The hill stretched away, pocked with holes and gullies, obstructed by boulders. The knob held by the Chinese was at least a mile's climb away. He heard his breath rasping, knew it must be streaming up behind him, the ragged remnant of a platoon sending up smoke signals saying, "Here we come."

God, let them be watching our lines instead of checking behind themselves. Just give me that and I'll never ask another favor of you.

Glancing behind, he saw the men strung out, following him, Kim right behind Cinq, Logan in the rear, looking back every few steps—

Sam blinked and squinted past Logan at the snow. It had seemed to move, and then he saw that it wasn't the snow but white uniforms, Chinese coming at them from the rear, at least fifty of them.

"Down!" he yelled, and at the same instant, the Chinese began firing, the stutter of Tommy guns, the pop of carbines. Sam hit the snow himself, on his belly, crawling to a rock outcropping. Cinq fired on the Chinese from above him.

"Kim!"

"Right here, boss." The kid slid in beside him.

Sam grabbed a grenade from his belt, pulled the pin and sailed it down the slope. A gout of snow blew up and he heard screams and groans. Popping his head up, he saw that he'd taken out three enemy soldiers, but closer in, his platoon was all down too, some firing, blood staining the snow around the rest.

Lee rose with a yell and hurled one grenade down, then another, before spinning around and falling to lie still.

Silverman and Hufnagel were still shooting and Sam squeezed the trigger of his M-1. The Chinese were almost to them now, firing as they charged, throwing their own grenades. He fired and saw an attacker go down, then heard Kim's carbine barking beside him. More Chinese fell, but there were too many, they kept coming, and now they had overrun the platoon and were bayoneting his men before they could rise, Silverman and Hufnagel, then others, as Sam watched in horror.

"Stop," he screamed, unable to fire for fear of hitting his own men. "Stay here," he yelled at Kim. "Keep down, cover yourself with snow."

Lunging up, he ran down the slope, firing his .45, missing everyone.

From the corner of his eye, he saw a Chinese aiming at him and knew it was too late, he'd be shot, and then the Chinese fell forward, shot from behind—

Behind?

Down the slope beyond the Chinese attackers, he saw a short, bull-shouldered man who looked like Hood running up the heels of the Chinese, spraying them with a submachine gun.

Two Chinese turned and fired back, and the man went down, flopping in the snow.

Sam emptied his .45 point blank, pushing between the two as they fell to the sides. He slipped and slid down the slope to the fallen soldier, knowing it couldn't be—

But it was!

Throwing himself down to stop his momentum, Sam rolled over in the snow, then dug hard back up-slope, Dear God, Hood, his eyes fluttering, the side of his helmet dented in.

Alive!

The snow puffed up around Hood, gunfire stitching a pattern past his left shoulder. Up-slope, Sam saw a dozen or more Chinese, running at them, firing, and he felt the .45 still in his hand—

No chance—they'll kill Hood.

Throwing the gun away, he raised his hands.

To keep his mind off dying, Sam tried to estimate how many miles he and Hood had marched. Dark now, snow-covered cliffs looming on either side of the road, only an occasional pine grove or bare outcropping to break the monotony. Heading north since noon, maybe four miles an hour for seven or eight hours—seven, fourteen, twenty-one, twenty-eight—his mind struggling with the simple math. Say thirty miles to the north, stopping only once, while the two guards ate and drank from their canteens. The Chinese border would be another forty-five miles or so.

"You all right?" Hood mumbled, the first time he'd spoken.

Sam's heart leapt. "Me? How about you?"

"Somebody split my head with an ax."

"You took a slug in the helmet. You've been marching, but I couldn't get a word out of you. A concussion, I'd guess." The moment flashed back: Seeing the Chinese lieutenant aim at Hood's head, throwing himself between, feeling the itch in his back as he waited for the bullets to hit. Then, when no bullets came, rubbing snow in Hood's face in a desperate attempt to rouse him out of his zombie-like state.

"Where are we?" Hood asked.

"Heading north. The border, I'd guess."

"What happened?"

Sam told him about flanking the hill, and the Chinese catching them at it. "What the hell were you doing there? Where did you come from?"

"Yudam-ni," Hood said.

For a second, Sam thought he said, "You damn me," and then it registered.

"Crossed the ice this morning," Hood said, "and found your captain. He told me where he'd sent you. The rest I can't remember. Concussion can do that."

"Why did you cross the reservoir?"

"To get to the other side."

A laugh exploded from Sam, blowing ice from his nose.

One of the guards snapped a command and he turned to see the man waving the Tommy gun menacingly. He held up his hands in apology. Apparently, prisoners weren't supposed to laugh. Must be getting giddy, faint from hunger and exhaustion, or he couldn't dream of laughing.

"Then you are AWOL," Sam said.

"I told my lieutenant I was going."

"And he agreed?"

"He didn't shoot me."

"You'll be court-martialed."

"Won't be the first time."

Sam swallowed. "You saved me. You shot that Chinese who had a bead on me. Another second, I'd have been dead."

Hood shrugged. "If you say so. I don't remember."

Sam only half heard him, thinking of the bodies of his men, staining the snow red. Kim—had he kept his head down or was he dead with the rest?

Pressing his eyes shut, Sam broke the forming ice of his tears. Too cold in North Korea to bleed, too cold even to cry. His lips had gone so numb he could barely form words. If he could rest awhile beside the road, but walking was the only thing keeping them alive. The layers of clothing would go on holding enough body heat in as long as exertion stayed high, but how much longer could they keep it up?

How much longer did he want to?

I've got the final say in this, he thought. I could stop right here, and they either shoot me or I freeze. If they decide not to waste a bullet, it takes fifteen minutes, half an hour at the most, and the pain is gone.

Then, if there's life after death, I look for Hartung.

"You all right?" Hood asked.

"I got my platoon killed." The bitter words escaped before he could stop them.

"Was it your idea," Hood said, "to take your men into enemy territory to assault a hill the whole damn battalion couldn't reduce, even with mortars and air attacks?"

"What difference? They were my men."

"You had to obey orders."

"Really. Like you did when you punched out that major?"

"I was wrong to do that."

"You disobeyed a stupid order and saved lives. You can't possibly regret it."

"I do, though." Hood made a harsh sound. "Oh, sure, I was a celebrity in the stockade. For years after, other noncoms came up and congratulated me. Every time one of them patted me on the back, I felt a little lower. I saved men right then at the time, true, but how many men have died because of sergeants who followed my example, disobeying orders that weren't as dumb as they seemed? No army can fight that way. Maybe your captain had no choice—if he didn't try it, you were all going to die anyway. Whether he was right or wrong, you were right to obey him. The platoon—you included—was his, and he's who lost it."

Sam took a deep breath, but the twisting in his chest persisted, sharp as glass. Sorrow for Cinq and the others, the Korean kids who were not kids at all, but men with small bodies and big hearts.

That gunfire up the slope as the Chinese had marched Hood and him away—had that been Kim, trying to save him?

"As long as I live, I'll feel I got them killed."

"You feel what you feel. I'd think less of you if you weren't sick about it. Just don't let your pain screw up your common sense. You were brave; you followed a desperate order that had no chance of success instead of waiting for the Chinks to kill you in your bunkers.

One of the guards snapped a command, motioning them to the side of the road.

Sam sat and Hood eased down beside him, scooping up handfuls of snow and eating it. One guard kept his Tommy gun aimed at them while the other took a rice ball from his pack and began gnawing at it. After a few minutes, he put the remains back in his pack and watched his prisoners while the other guard ate.

Sam patted his stomach, held a hand out to the one who was eating.

The guard grunted, shook his head.

"Eat some snow," Hood said. "You'll dehydrate."

Sam scooped up snow from around his legs and stuffed it into his mouth. Swallowing was painful, but the icy fluid soothed the rawness a little.

The guard who had eaten first took the remains of the rice ball he'd been chewing from his pack and handed it to Hood.

Sam's stomach growled. "I think he likes you."

Hood nodded at the guard, took a bite and handed the ball to Sam.

It was frozen solid. He managed to chew off a crumbling piece and handed it back. While Hood was chomping on it, it split, and Hood handed him half. Sam chewed the ice grains, swallowing eagerly, tasting a hint of sweetness like honey.

The guard barked an order, motioning them up. Sam offered Hood his hand, hauling him out of the snow, hiding his alarm at the strain on Hood's face. Stumbling back to the road, the old marine got it going again, plodding forward, head down.

He's tough, Sam told himself. Never any doubt about that.

"Did we pass any Chinese soldiers while I was out of it?"

"Not lately," Sam said. "A battalion early on and another just before dark. A few trucks going back the other way with Chinese wounded, I think. Why?"

"We've got to escape."

"That would be nice. How far can we get with a load of slugs in our backs?"

"We'll watch for our chance. Follow my lead."

"I'm in charge here. We'll try if and when I say."

With a grunt, Hood plodded on in silence.

"I'm serious, sergeant."

"Yessir." No sarcasm in his voice, probably too tired.

"Why are they keeping us alive?" Sam asked. "Why didn't they just shoot us back there?"

"They must have a use for us, sir."

"Knock off the 'sirs.' What use?"

"In the last war, the Japs used prisoners for labor, building bridges and clearing roads through the jungle."

"Slave labor."

Hood didn't answer.

Sam thought about it, crunching through the snow, leaning into the wind. Prison camp. Slave labor. It might be smarter to sit down in the middle of the road and let the guards shoot them both. But the urge had left him, its dark appeal gone.

"I'm glad you're with me," he said.

Hood laughed, and Sam realized how it must have sounded, like sending someone a "wish you were here" postcard from Hades. He laughed too, until the guard, with a perplexed look motioned for them both to shut up.

Educational TV, psychology texts, and novels like The Manchurian Candidate have linked the Korean War in the public mind with "brainwashing," a method of mental coercion used by the Chinese Communists to indoctrinate prisoners of war into abandoning their own beliefs and adopting those of their captors. In some cases the goal was simply to disrupt efforts of prisoners to organize and resist captivity. In others, it was to obtain from POWs formal confessions of crimes against humanity for use as propaganda. The victims were worn down by filthy housing, sleep deprivation and starvation. Fabricated confessions by other prisoners and physical torture were also used to increase the pressure. Whether or not the underlying principle was explicitly understood by the Chinese who used brainwashing, it is in essence an attempt to change someone's mind by first inducing or forcing him to change his behavior. This seemingly backwards sequence has since been validated by psychological experiments in "Cognitive Dissonance" by Festinger, Bandura, and others. Brainwashing can be traced back to the Inquisition. When successful, it leaves in its victims a guilt and depression deep enough to destroy their lives. . . .   (Ibid.)

24

29 November, Camp 2, China, 2130:
"What did you say?" Sam, jarred from his stupor, stared at the scarred face in the shadows.

"I don't know what we'd have done without her." Sergeant Lansing repeated.

"No, no—before that, her name, damn it!"

"Brisbane—Lieutenant Brisbane."

No! Sam thought. *Please, God.*

"She was here when they brought us in yesterday," Lansing went on. "She's looked in on us four or five times now, as often as they'll let her." The sergeant's big, homely face flickered orange as someone stoked the stove. "She flat out saved Dierdorf—he's under those blankets there with the other men. Took a bullet out of him, slick as any surgeon."

Hood, lying beyond the stove under a moth-eaten blanket, pushed himself up on an elbow. "What?" he rasped.

Before anyone could respond, he dropped back and resumed snoring.

Sam shook his head, stunned. Bonnie, here? But how?

His alarm, so sharp only seconds ago, was already fading. He could barely hold his head up. His butt ached against the dirt, his legs were still trembling, and his blistered feet throbbed, so swollen he couldn't get his shoepacs off. The prickle in his thaw-

357

ing face had deepened to a sting, needles of heat from the stove jabbing his cheeks and lips.

Despite the pain, the sheer physical relief of sitting was nearly overwhelming. To be in a room that was merely cold, finally at the end of the endless road, no more walking, the guards and their damn Tommy guns gone, nothing left but to bed down as near the stove as he could get.

But this—Bonnie, *Bonnie.*

Was there a way out of here? Staring around him, he struggled to hold onto the thought, his mind dull, as if he had taken Hood's concussion. Beyond Sergeant Lansing, four men slept together under a pile of blankets, their backs against the cinderblock wall. At the other end of the thirty by fifteen foot room hung a blanket. From the stink, it must hide a privy bucket.

A cold drip hit the back of Sam's hand. Looking up, he saw faint bands of sky between the corrugated roof panels, snowflakes dusting down. With Lansing boosting him, maybe he could force one of those creases wide enough to slip through.

If he could find the strength to get to his feet.

"She brought us some firewood for the stove today," Lansing mused, absorbed in the wonder of having his own Florence Nightingale to tend to him and his men. "We like to froze last night, but tonight is much better, thanks to her."

"Where are they keeping her?"

"One of those mud huts on the way in—that's what she told my lieutenant."

"There's another officer here?"

Lansing squinted at him. "Lieutenant DeForest. I told you that already. They took him out of here this morning. Fancy-ass Chink officer showed up and 'invited' the lieutenant over for a 'visit.' Colonel Tien, the camp commandant."

The air seemed thick with a deepening haze. "How did she look?"

"What?"

"Lieutenant Brisbane. Was she all right?"

"Seemed to be. Shadows under her eyes, and she looked a little pale, but who wouldn't in this place? She walked all right, nothing wrong with her feet. Half my men can barely stand." Lansing glanced at Hood. "That leatherneck over there give you any trouble on the march?"

Sam tried to think what he might mean.

Lansing leaned closer with a conspiratorial air. "In my experience, marines don't like taking orders from army. It's like they *blub the siffge. . . .*"

The words blurred; a blank moment passed and then Sam realized Lansing had him by the shoulders, holding him up.

"Sir, how long were you on the road?" talking through an invisible metal pipe, now.

"Day and a half," Sam mumbled.

Lansing's eyes widened. "You made it here from the reservoir, on foot, in a day and a half?"

"No stopping except to eat and piss."

"Jesus. I can see Chink guards pushing prisoners that hard, but themselves?"

"A Chinese horse patrol passed us about halfway. Their lieutenant let our guards switch off with two of his men."

Lansing grimaced. "Two fresh guards, upset at having to walk, so they took it out on you."

Sam nodded, chin tapping his chest.

"Sir, we can talk in the morning. You've got to rest."

Dragging his head back up, he forced his eyes open. "I'm all right. How did Brisbane look?"

"You just now asked me that. Don't worry, from what I've seen, she's as tough as she is pretty. She ain't goin' nowhere, and neither are we. Now just lie back there, that's it."

Sam tried to fight it but Lansing eased him back. He felt the floor melting into his shoulder blades, the rough rasp of a blanket at his chin, and then nothing.

Loud, metallic banging. . .not important. . .fading away.

More banging, swearing in a far-off place.

Then Bonnie bent over him, and he wanted to say hello, but his tongue wouldn't work. Why was she wearing that round Chinese cap? Serving him tea on a mat, telling him about a new ambulance she'd bought for Private Kim.

More banging, meaning nothing.

Rolling over, he went back to sleep.

Light slid across, burning through one lid, simmering his eyeball in a red stew. Men talked. For a minute he could make no sense of it, then one of the voices became Hood's, asking, "How long have I slept?"

Ten hours, someone told him.

Forcing his gummed eyelids open, Sam struggled to a sitting position, his joints stiff. The fire in the stove was still going, barely, a few tongues of flame licking at red embers. He pulled the blanket up around his shoulders.

Bonnie!

Galvanized, he tried to get up. His legs, flaming in protest, dumped him back on his butt.

Hood held out a tin mess kit cup to him. "Drink, lieutenant."

Sam was parched. The water tasted grand, waking his mummified tongue, and why was Hood being so formal?

"Drink it all, sir. There's enough," pointing to a tin pan on the floor, big enough to serve stew in a chow line, maybe a couple of gallons of murky water left in it, panes of ice floating on top.

Another man, someone he hadn't seen last night, sat with his back against the cinderblock, staring across at the opposite wall. A gold bar on one shoulder gleamed in a shaft of light. Sergeant Lansing was trying to get the officer to drink.

"Come on, now, Lieutenant DeForest, you need water."

"Need the nurse," DeForest croaked.

"We're trying. We asked the guard to get her when he brought you back, remember? And we been pounding on the door off and on ever since."

This time Sam was able to push himself up. His legs hurt like hell, the joints stiff from the cold ground.

"Drink up, sir," Lansing cajoled his lieutenant. "We'll call for her again, soon as you drink."

A fit of coughing shook the man, a harsh hacking from deep in his lungs. The sergeant held DeForest's head away from the floor and, finally, the spasm passed. Sam got his legs moving and limped over to introduce himself.

DeForest seemed not to hear. Up close, bruises showed on his cheekbone and along the backs of his hands. His lip was cut in two places.

"What did they do to you?" Sam said, horrified.

"Fucking Chinks," Sergeant Lansing muttered. "That colonel—Tien—is trying to make him confess to war crimes."

"Torture? That's. . . ."

Against the Geneva Convention, yeah, and so was marching prisoners for thirty straight hours on a few bites of frozen rice and all the snow they could eat.

"You'll be next," DeForest whispered, focusing on him at last.

"What does this colonel want us to say?"

"America's wrong, commies right." Another spasm of coughing took the lieutenant. When he straightened, blood flecked his lips. Sam felt a cold flush of alarm. Internal injuries? Or maybe advanced pneumonia. He needed medical attention right away or he'd die.

Stumbling to the door, Sam pounded on it. Lansing joined him, slamming his hands against the steel, yelling for the guards. After a minute, the door screeched open, revealing a black figure backlit against a blaze of sunlight.

"Sam!" Bonnie's voice.

His heart accelerated, though he still couldn't make out her features. And then she stepped through and the door slammed, and with the back-lighting gone, he could see her. She returned his gaze, a struggle waging itself on her beautiful face. That face looked thinner, but no bruises, thank God. Her field jacket hung on her, and she looked taller than he remembered—which meant she'd lost weight. His arms trembled with the urge to hug her, but a deeper instinct warned him not to.

She glanced past him and the distress on her face deepened. "Sergeant Hood, you too?"

"Lieutenant," Hood said. "I heard your name spoken last night and thought I was dreaming." His voice was heavy with the same regret Sam felt.

Looking from Hood to him and back, she shook her head, as if hoping they might yet turn out to be mirages. "I didn't see you come in. My hut is near the gate. I have a spy hole, but I didn't see you."

"It was after dark," Sam said.

She gave him a searching look he realized was a clinical once-over. "How are you? You look like hell."

"I'm all right but Sergeant Hood took a shell on the helmet, knocked him out."

"Over here, nurse!" Sergeant Lansing, his voice urgent.

She hurried to Lieutenant DeForest, kneeling to steady him as the coughs bent him nearly double. Taking the water from Lansing, she put a pill in DeForest's mouth and urged him to drink. Swallowing seemed hard for him, as if the muscles of his throat had been damaged.

Bonnie went to Hood next, asked him a few questions. Holding his head between her palms, she inspected his eyes, then motioned Sam to follow her to the curtain at the end of the room.

"I think your father's all right," she said in a low voice. "He suffered a concussion, for sure. If you notice any slurred speech not from the cold, or any sudden, extreme drowsiness, stay with him and walk him around, keep him awake. Right now, I'm more worried about Lieutenant DeForest's pneumonia."

"Are you all right?"

"Fine."

"You're thin. Are they giving you food?"

"Rice and sorghum. I needed to lose ten pounds anyway."

"Never."

She gave him a wan smile.

"How—?"

"I was walking outside the MASH," she said, "and they grabbed me up." Her voice was crisp, inviting no questions. Unable to resist any longer, he took her in his arms. She hesitated and then let her face rest against his, her soft cheek pressing against his bristles. She smelled of antiseptic, finer than any Paris perfume. He knew the others were watching—that, filled with their own needs, they wouldn't like what they were seeing, but damn it, he loved her.

He would give all he owned to have her back at the MASH under Dr. Jeff's watchful eye.

"I'll get you out," he said.

She stiffened against him. "Forget it, Sam. There's no escape. They've got guards patrolling all along the perimeter. I've been watching them for a week now, and they never stop. You must have noticed the fence as they brought you in. Chain link, it's too high, they would shoot you before you could get over."

"We're going as soon as I can figure how. You, Hood, me, and as many of these men as can walk."

Over her shoulder, he saw the others staring at them, some of them frowning. Sergeant Lansing looked like he was nerving himself to protest. Hood said something to his fellow non-com and Lansing gave a doubtful nod. Cold flushed through Sam's veins as he realized what an idiot he was being. It wasn't just what these men thought of him hugging Bonnie, it was the Chinese. That's why Hood was acting like a stranger. What if the colonel had one of these men tortured and found out what Hood and he were to Bonnie and what she meant to them?

What couldn't he make me do, Sam thought, by threatening her?

He eased back from Bonnie. "What do you know about Colonel Tien?"

She hesitated, as if marshaling her thoughts. "He's a strange one. Polite at times, rude at others. He speaks perfect English but he's a gung ho communist, as far as I can tell."

"He tortured Lieutenant DeForest."

She looked shocked. "Are you sure?"

"Didn't you see the bruises on his hands and cuts on his lip?"

"You've got bruises on your hands. Probably every man in the room does, from all the climbing and fighting. And the cuts could be from his own teeth—the spasms of coughing."

"No. I have it straight from DeForest. The colonel is trying to force him into denouncing America and praising communism. Stay clear of Tien."

"How can I? I need his cooperation to help these men."

The door banged open behind them and two Chinese with submachine guns entered. Sam watched as they scanned the room, settled on him. One of them motioned him over.

"If Tien calls you in," Sam said to Bonnie, "don't let on that you know Hood or me from before."

"I understand."

The guard stepped toward him, jerking the Tommy gun. Hood tried to walk out with him, but one of the guards shoved him back and waved Sam over.

"Mind what you say," Hood said in a low voice as he passed. "Every word."

A sudden heat flared in Sam's face. "I'm not an idiot. . . ."

Except I was, he thought bitterly, not two minutes ago.

Hood just looked at him, said nothing. *Will I ever see him again?* "Thank you, sergeant. I'll be all right." Catching Lansing's eye, Sam added, "Lieutenant Brisbane and I don't know each other."

"Don't worry about *us,*" Lansing said pointedly.

I deserved that.

One of the guards jerked him outside. The frigid air scalded his lungs. As the guards marched him ahead of them, he glanced around, trying not to be obvious about it. To the right, he counted five more cinderblock barracks, identical to the one he'd just left. No way to tell if they held prisoners yet, but clearly the Chinese expected this to be a major POW camp.

Near the gate were the mud huts Lansing had mentioned. A guard paced inside the high chain link fence, his breath streaming. The cold would make it harder to escape, keeping the guards wide awake and hustling up and down that fence to keep warm, if nothing else.

The guards turned him onto the road that came in from the gate. It had seen plenty of truck traffic, probably when the camp was built, leaving a maze of ruts in the muck, now frozen to brick-like hardness. Up ahead, he saw a jeep and two U.S. Army trucks parked alongside a log building. Its dark-stained timbers had been fitted together with skill and finished smooth. A massive stone chimney rose from the roof. Windows trimmed with empty flower boxes promised that spring came even to this frozen hell. If not for the horned pagoda-style roof, it might have been a resort lodge in Oregon.

Another nudge on his shoulder steered Sam off the road onto the flagstone walk that led to the building's only door, a solid-looking slab painted the blood red of the Chinese Communist Party.

The door opened, revealing an old man in a high-collared olive drab uniform, stiff and solemn as a butler. He led the way through a foyer into an office, warmed by a hearty blaze, crackling and popping in the stone fireplace. The heat felt wonderful, soothing Sam's face, warming his lungs. A Chinese officer in a uniform that might have been tailored on Saville Row sat at one of the grandest desks Sam had ever seen—burnished mahogany inlaid with gold and trimmed with exquisite carved moldings. On the desk sat a mechanical box with the lid up, maybe eight by fifteen inches. Two plastic reels were mounted in its center and a microphone was attached by electrical cord to the box.

A recorder.

Sam's mouth went dry. He was supposed to give Tien just his name, rank, serial number, and date of birth. But I have to talk to him, he thought, because, whatever he wants, I want something too—Bonnie, out of here.

Be careful. Let him bring her up first, if you can.

365

The colonel pointed across his desk to a plain, wooden chair with a crudely straight back. The guards on either side put their hands on his shoulders, forcing him down onto the hard seat and taking up position behind him. The colonel's cold gaze bored into him. His shining, jet-black hair was combed straight back. Looked young to be a full colonel—mid to late thirties. Not an ounce of fat. Hard to be sure, with him sitting, but he looked tall, maybe six feet.

"I am Colonel Yuan Ching Tien of the Chinese People's Volunteer Army."

"I thought it was the People's Liberation Army."

"Are you being smart with me? It's a bad way to start."

"I'm just asking a question, sir."

Tien eyed him. "Most of us are from the PLA, but that does not change the fact that we're all here as volunteers to help our Korean comrades and protect our homeland from your invasion."

"Colonel, with respect, didn't President Truman just promise the whole world that the United States will not set foot across your border?"

"Would you believe the same promise from us if we had invaded Canada and marched our army right up to your border?" Before he could answer, Tien spread his hands in a pacifying gesture. "But we're getting ahead of ourselves. You haven't yet introduced yourself."

"2nd Lieutenant Sam Foxworth, Company C, 1st Battalion, 32nd Regiment, 7th Army Division. Born December 13, 1938. Do you want my serial number?"

Tien gave a negligent wave. "Your birthday's coming soon, Mr. Foxworth."

Sam realized with a dull shock that it was true. In two weeks he would be 24 years old. Beyond that, it was hard to see much future for himself at the moment. "I hadn't thought about it, sir."

Tien nodded. "In war, you don't think about when you were born, you think about staying alive one more day. Such a shame."

"Sir?"

"You've let your government send you thousands of miles to interfere in a civil war that is not America's concern so the big corporations that run your country can get even richer making more tanks and guns and fighter planes."

Sam glanced at the box on the table. The plastic reels were not moving. "Excuse me, sir, but isn't China interfering in the same civil war?"

Tien sat back in his chair, fingering his chin. "You're polite, Mr. Foxworth. I appreciate that. The other lieutenant is rude, like most Americans."

"Because he's sick, sir. The prison is cold and he's forced to sleep on the ground. He needs to be in your hospital under regular medical supervision. I'm afraid he's dying. You don't want that on your conscience do you, sir?"

"You have your own medical officer, Lieutenant Brisbane. He is her responsibility, not mine."

Good. "If I may speak with you about that, sir, I understand from talking to the men and to Lieutenant Brisbane that she was captured alone just outside her medical facility. The Geneva Convention specifically states that medical personnel are not to be targets of combatants. Given that the MASH hospital was close at hand, and that she was unarmed, her captors had to know she was a non-combatant medical officer. Which means you purposely targeted her even though China signed the Geneva—"

"Not my China, Mr. Foxworth. In case you weren't paying attention, a year ago the corrupt government that signed this paper you cite was overthrown by the Chinese people."

"Surely, sir, you don't mean to tell me that the communists are renouncing the treaty. That would look barbaric to the world."

For the first time Tien seemed uncomfortable. "That is not something to be hashed out at our level, Mr. Foxworth."

Why won't he call me lieutenant?

"No, sir, but after this war is over, the world community will be looking into how China behaved toward her prisoners, and at this camp *you* are China, are you not?"

"I'm touched you care so much about my reputation."

"I'm just saying would you want it to get out that you captured a woman so you could force her to care for your wounded?"

"We haven't forced Lieutenant Brisbane to treat our wounded. She's doing it on her own. We have Chinese doctors and nurses to treat our wounded."

"And a well equipped, warm clinic, I'm told. So why continue to hold Lieutenant Brisbane when her capture was illegal? Your own medical people should be treating the prisoners. The Convention clearly states that *captors* shall provide the best treatment possible to all wounded, prioritized solely on the severity of the patient's medical condition regardless of which side he's on. What will the world think, sir, if they find that your Chinese doctors wouldn't treat prisoners, forcing you to kidnap a woman—"

Tien slapped a hand on the desk. "Oh, come now, Foxworth—*chivalry?* What a sham. In the name of cherishing and protecting your women, you Americans deny them full and equal citizenship."

"That's not true, sir."

He shot up from his chair. "Isn't it? Where are your women soldiers? Not nurses and clerks, I'm talking about fighters?"

"Keeping women out of harm's way is not a sham of protection, it is protection."

Tien's lip curled. "How considerate. Your men can fight and die for your country, but you won't let any of your women, no matter how strong and capable, do the same. We all die, Foxworth, and life is full of wounds. How noble can your nation's causes be if you deny one half of your population the right to suffer or die for them? Your society doesn't do half enough to keep its women from being raped and murdered by strangers, or beaten and killed by their husbands but it absolutely *forbids* them to risk taking a blow for their country."

Does he expect an answer? Sam wondered.

"You seem informed," Tien said, "about things like the Geneva Convention. Dare I hope you know any Chinese history, 1934, for example—our Long March?"

"I've read about it."

"Ah. I was twenty-three, Mr. Foxworth, about your age now. We communists were, at that time, only a small band of patriots, hunted by the huge armies of a corrupt government and its warlord allies. They had us bottled up in Hunan. I was there with Mao Se Dong and Zhou Enlai and other heroes of our revolution. Mao wasn't our leader then, though the march would make him one. We broke out of the encirclement of the huge nationalist army, which then pursued us over high mountain passes in the freezing cold, across a score of rivers. You think your little stroll up from Chosin was rough? Six thousand miles they drove us, from south China all the way to Yenan in the northwest. More than a dozen times we fought them off our flanks, taking many casualties. Often we had no food or water. During that year, I had nothing to eat for days at a time, not once, but many times. When we broke out in October of 1934, there were a hundred thousand of us. When we reached Yenan, only 8,000 of us remained alive—less than one in ten who had started out. Did you know that several thousand of our soldiers were women? Yes. Some of the bravest human beings I have ever been fortunate enough to know."

Turning away toward the fire, Tien gazed into it. "One of those women, whom I knew well, was captured. She was later returned to us, her feet strapped to a Manchurian pony. Her head they kept." His voice was sharp as broken glass.

Sam felt an involuntary pang of sympathy. *Your wife?*

Your wife or your lover, yes.

You won't say it, though. You dread the sympathy of an enemy.

Beyond Tien, Sam noticed a sword and scimitar cross-mounted above the grand stone fireplace. The hairs at the nape of his neck bristled. The scimitar would be an excellent weapon for loping off heads.

Returning to the desk, the colonel leaned on it and rolled his shoulders as if to shrug away tension. "Women in your hollow democracy are second class citizens. And you want to deny Lieutenant Brisbane the right to distinguish herself."

369

A cold foreboding swept Sam. What did "distinguish" mean to Tien? Would Bonnie's head on a platter seem like a distinguished end to him?

Or justice, perhaps, for the woman he'd lost?

"Colonel Tien, I'm simply asking, with all respect, that you observe the Geneva Convention, on simple humanitarian grounds, if no other. Maybe our forces are holding one of your officers and you could trade Lieutenant Brisbane for him."

Tien cocked his head. "You are here only a few hours and already Lieutenant Brisbane seems to have caught your eye. Curious. Is that what this is about? You're attracted to her and you want to be her knight in shining armor?"

"If that were so, would I be trying to get you to return her to her MASH unit where I'll probably never see her again?"

"It depends on how unselfish you are, Mr. Foxworth."

"Sir, I am not Mr. Foxworth, I am Lieutenant Foxworth, and I'm just as selfish as the next guy but, as one of the ranking officers among your POWs, I have a duty to speak up for the Americans in this camp."

Tien gazed at him. "If you really want to help Lieutenant Brisbane, there's a way."

"How?"

"By admitting a simple truth: that none of you have any business here so far from home, interfering in the affairs of another nation."

"Admit it to you, sir, or to that machine on your desk? A Magnetophon, right? The Nazis developed amazing tape recorders, I've heard. They were the first to achieve high enough fidelity to match a recorded voice to a specific individual."

Tien shook his head, smiling. "You think I'm doing this just for 'propaganda,' as you Americans like to call any words but your own. As if the United States were not the capital of lies, with it's mandarins of Madison Avenue making whatever outrageous claim they please to sell their products. You capitalists buy and sell everything and let the buyer beware. Well, here's your chance to buy preferential treatment for any prisoner you choose. Just admit what you already know to be true—that you have no business here. Have the courage and honesty to tell the truth, even though it embarrasses you. Set an example for the other young men your robber barons want to send here to their deaths just so they can make more money."

Sam found himself considering it. His weakness sickened him, but surely it would do no harm just to think about it. What did preferential treatment mean? If I offer to denounce America, he thought, in return for Bonnie's release or exchange, how would I know that Tien would keep his end of the deal?

What could I do if he didn't?

Not a damn thing. He can do whatever he wants once he's got my treason on tape. And I'd have turned Bonnie into a weapon he can use against me or Hood whenever he wants. In the end, it could even get her killed.

"Mr. Foxworth?"

"Colonel, the Geneva Convention expressly forbids any form of duress. Denying proper medical treatment to force treasonous statements from a prisoner for propaganda purposes is clearly—"

"Stop!" Tien pinched the bridge of his nose between a thumb and forefinger as if to ward off a headache. "What duress? You don't understand. I'm not trying to force you, I'm trying to educate you, and if motivation will help, I'll provide that. You don't realize how indoctrinated you already are. Let me help you and other young men who might listen to you. Forget about the tape recorder. It's off, and you'll know if I turn it on. Just think about what I'm asking. Why have you done it—come all this way to fight in Korea? What's wrong with you Americans that you can't stay out of other people's fights but instead you go around trying to force the world into your mold, threatening everyone who sees things differently? What gives you the right?"

Sam sensed he was hearing not a rhetorical question but a real one from Tien's heart. He remembered asking Major Anson almost the same question—and the major's answer, which had seemed so specious: *What gives anyone the right to do anything?*

"Colonel Tien, I don't know what gives us the right, any more than you know what gives you Chinese the right to interfere in the same war. If you believe you have the right because you *are* right, that's the same thing Hitler and Hirohito believed in the last war. How many of your comrades did Hirohito's men kill for the 'right' as they perceived it? Everyone in this war believes they're right, so this can't be about that. It's about how our two countries see the world and each other."

"Really. And how, pray tell, is that?"

"China has always feared outsiders," Sam said, ignoring the sarcasm. "That's why you built the great wall. We Americans are the ultimate outsiders. Except for the Indians of America, our parents and grandparents are all from somewhere else, a nation of foreigners—foreign as in different; different as in individuals. That's where we get our strength. It's why we get riled when the North Koreans try to make everyone in the south be the same as them. You Chinese are the ultimate insiders. You believe in co-operation and unity and uniformity. That's where you get your strength, and that's why you're backing your Korean "comrades" in their effort to make all of their country communist. That, and you fear us outsiders coming too close to your gates."

Tien looked unimpressed. "That's all theory, Mr. Foxworth. It has no practical use. The fact is, Korea is on our border, and it's thousands of miles from yours. It's simple logic that what happens in Korea is far more our affair than yours. China's revolution liberating the people is a great force that will sweep all of Asia. A Communist Korea is inevitable. You won't be able to stop it. So why die trying? Are you willing to do that, Mr. Foxworth, to die for your theories?"

Sam thought of Hartung and Choi, Cinquemani and the others, and felt the soreness around his heart that had dogged him since their deaths.

"With respect, colonel, that's the wrong question—am I willing to die. You and I aren't here to die, we're here to kill. The North Koreans started it, and now America and China and other countries are all in it. We're ready to kill and kill, end thousands of lives, maybe hundreds of thousands on all sides. When it's over, we'll shake our heads and say how tragic and regrettable it all was. The mothers and fathers and sweethearts and kids who loved the dead will have holes in their hearts, and the rest of the world will get over it, without ever knowing what was lost. Most of the dead will be young men, barely more than kids. Multiply them two or three times over, and you'll have the children they would have fathered, several million of them who will never be born because of the war. That might just be the biggest loss of all. Humanity won't even comprehend how staggering is that absence of human beings who should have been born."

Tien made a dismissive gesture. "Now you're being sentimental."

"I'm being pragmatic, sir. Sure, most of the missing kids probably wouldn't have made much difference. They'd have grown up and lived their lives, some good, some bad, then died. But one of them might have been our next Confucius or Einstein. We're both educated men, colonel—you more than me, or I'd be speaking Chinese right now. You appreciate civilization, I can see it in this office. Because of what you and I and the North Koreans are doing, a human being of great ability the world really needs—perhaps several—will never exist. The human race will go without the cure for cancer one unborn person might have discovered, or the disease-resistant wheat another might have developed, or the next step up from the light bulb. Instead of asking me if I'm ready to die, we should all—everyone in this goddamn war, starting with Kim Il Sung—be asking ourselves why we are so ready to kill."

Tien shook his head. "You're showing why America will lose this war. You are weak."

"Because I hate killing?"

"Because you're an idealist. You see man as you wish he was instead of as he is. You won't answer my question but it, and it alone, will decide this war. Are you willing to die for what you believe?"

"I'm here, aren't I?"

"That's not an answer."

"What would be a better one? Words?"

Tien glanced at the tape recorder on his desk, then rubbed his forehead. A steady, measured click emerged from the background crackle of the fire, and Sam realized there must be a grandfather clock in the room behind him, a part of the beauty this communist colonel clearly loved.

Turning away from him toward the fire, Tien flipped a hand. The guards pulled Sam up from the chair.

"We'll talk again. . . .lieutenant."

C: If the captor permits medical personnel and chaplains to perform their professional functions for the welfare of the POW community, special latitude is authorized these personnel under the Code of Conduct as it applies to escape.

D: Medical personnel and chaplains do not, as individuals, have a duty to escape or to actively aid others in escaping as long as they are treated as "retained personnel" by the enemy.

The Geneva Conventions, Code of Conduct: Special Allowances for Medical Personnel and Chaplains
(Article III, C & D)

25

5 December, Camp 2, China, 0100:
"I can't go with you," Bonnie whispered.

Sam stared at her, stunned, groping for words.

Before he could say anything, a cough cut through the wind outside the hut. Beside him, Hood pulled his homemade knife from his belt. Bonnie motioned them both to the wall beside the door. Grabbing her field jacket, she flung it down over the hole Hood had dug through the base of the wall, then rolled onto her cot, pulling the blankets up and closing her eyes.

Sam pressed his back into the mud wall, Hood crowding up tight beside him.

The guard's key rattled around the padlock, his hand no doubt shaking in the cold. Had he seen the hole at the back of the hut? Once they'd crawled through, Hood had shoved hunks of the hardened mud back into the hole, and the night was overcast, but a flashlight beam would pick the hole out in two seconds.

Not going?—she has to go!

The key slid home. In the same instant, Bonnie's coat settled, revealing the top of the hole in the flickering light of the fire. Sam gave a soft hiss; Bonnie's eyes popped open, and he motioned toward the coat. Staying on the cot, she reached over and plucked the coat up to cover the hole again.

The padlock snicked and the door creaked inward.

Through a narrow crack, Sam could see the guard—the one Bonnie called Doody—staring in at her. Hood raised his blade, a triangular edge from a corrugated roofing panel of the prison barracks, bent back and forth a thousand times until the weakened fold of metal had snapped along its length. Hood had spent a day sharpening one edge on a stone, then wrapped the handle in a felt insert from his shoepac, sticking it to the metal with sorghum from his daily rice ball.

One makeshift knife against a Thompson submachine gun.

Even if they came out on top, a single burst from the guard's gun and the escape would be scuttled.

Doody took another step, bringing him to the edge of the door.

On the cot, Bonnie shivered and opened her eyes, then sat bolt upright, as if surprised, holding the blanket up to her chin. "What are you doing? Get out of here or I'll scream."

Doody paused in mid-step.

"I mean it! Colonel Tien will punish you."

Sam felt his teeth clenching. Did the bastard mean to rape her?

Doody murmured a few words in Chinese and bent over, his hand extending past the door as he laid a package wrapped in cloth on the dirt floor. Sam smelled fish. Beyond Bonnie, he saw her jacket starting to settle again.

"Oh, a present," she said, peering over her blanket at the package. "Thank you—*shay-shay.*"

The top of Doody's cap bowed in past the edge of the door. Bonnie's field jacket settled another inch, revealing the top curvature of the hole. It might look like a shadow to the guard, but not if the jacket sank any lower.

Get out, Sam thought, go!

"*Zye jee ahng,*" Bonnie said.

With another bow, Doody backed out. The door closed, the padlock clicked shut, and the sound of feet swishing through snow faded in the wind.

"Damn," Hood breathed.

Bonnie unwrapped the cloth. Inside, swaddled in butcher paper, were a dozen pickled fish, the briny smell flooding the room.

"It seems I have an admirer," she whispered with a grim smile.

"That same guard would shoot you in a second," Sam told her, "if Colonel Tien gave the order."

Bonnie gave him a disbelieving frown. "Why would Tien do that?"

"You must come with us."

She wrapped the fish again, set it at the foot of her cot. Against his will, Sam felt the juices flowing in his mouth; his stomach growled. At the fireplace, Bonnie poked the log with a stick, sending up showers of sparks. The chill receded as the fire flamed. Wind howled in gusts outside, making her field jacket flutter over the hole.

"Sam, there are thirty prisoners now, and we have to assume more on the way, along with plenty of Chinese wounded. Lieutenant DeForest is doing better, but I have four additional cases of pneumonia, fifteen of frostbite, and eight bullet wounds just starting on penicillin that will worsen again if it's cut off—which it surely will be if I anger them by escaping. As it stands, Doctor Huan will not treat our prisoners himself. If I were to escape, he would cut off all meds, everything. I'm the link. As long as I go on helping the Chinese wounded, I'll be allowed to treat our own as well. Who knows, maybe I can even start getting the worst cases moved to the clinic."

"That'll never happen."

"Whether it does or does not, if I bug out, men will die. I'm all they've got."

You're all I've got, Sam wanted to say, but the selfishness of it stopped him. How could he say, "It's me or them," when it wasn't—he would love her no matter what, and if she stayed, he'd love her even more, God help him.

But she mustn't stay. There was a very good chance she'd die in here, especially if the Chinese army suffered reverses.

Images flashed in his mind—a headless woman strapped to a horse, the scimitar mounted over Colonel Tien's fireplace. He said, "It's our duty to escape."

"Your duty," Bonnie corrected. "Under the Geneva Convention, non-combatant medical personnel needed for the treatment of prisoners are considered 'retained personnel.' So long as they are allowed to treat POW wounded, they are exempted from the duty to escape."

"Who told you that?"

She did not answer.

"Tien?"

"It doesn't matter."

"That self-serving bastard. He despises Americans and wouldn't shed one tear if you or any of the rest of us died. It's too late for you to back out now. We've dug this damn hole into your hut. What will they do when they find it?"

"They'll know you tried to get me to escape with you, and that I stayed here instead, to help their wounded and my own. I'll tell them that, and they'll believe it because it's the truth, and because no other explanation would make any sense. If anything, it will make Tien treat me better."

Sam shook his head in an agony of frustration. "Hood, help me out here."

"Let it go."

Sam turned to him shocked. "What do you mean, let it go? If she stays, she could die."

"She might die out there, too. It might take more than we've got to make it back to our lines, wherever they are by now."

"At last!" Bonnie said. "Common sense. You need to listen, Sam. Sergeant Hood is in no shape for another eighty mile hike—"

"I never said that, lieutenant. I'm fine—"

"You're not fine, either of you. If it made sense to try an escape now, in this cold and snow, Lieutenant DeForest would be letting his men make the attempt with you instead of ordering them to wait for better weather."

"Bonnie," Sam said, "Colonel Tien has hauled me in twice, trying to get me to sell out. He's apparently mistaken my tendency to look at all sides of an issue for a weak mind or a lack of patriotism or both. He can do whatever he wants to me and I won't put word one on his tape recorder—unless he threatens you. He already suspects you are more to me than a fellow officer in the U.S. Army. The longer we're together here, the more likely he'll know how I feel about you. If he then brings you into one of our sessions and threatens to hurt you, Tien can give me the music and I'll sing like Kate Smith."

"Sam," she said with dismay. "No, you mustn't."

"What I mustn't is be put in that position. We have to get out of here, all of us."

She gazed at him, then down at the floor, as if calculating. "You do have to go, then." Her voice was barely audible now, all animation gone from her. "But I can't. I won't."

"Bonnie—"

"It's just until the war's over."

"I can't let you stay." Saying it, Sam felt the lack of weight in the words. He had no authority to back them up. Bonnie and he were both second lieutenants, and even if he was a general, her chain of command was in the 1st MASH.

Hood said, "Sam, this is Lieutenant Brisbane's decision. It doesn't matter what you and I think, but for what it's worth, I think she's right, and you do too, if you'll let yourself see it. What if we could bully her into leaving the wounded and sick behind, and we make it out, and then she hates herself for the rest of her life for leaving her patients. You want that between you?"

Sam wanted to shout at Hood to shut up. This was insane. Surely, Bonnie could never hate him for taking her out of this hell hole.

It wouldn't have to be hate. Resentment would be enough, always there in the back of her mind, the feeling she'd failed in her duty because she'd done what he wanted. Carrying that for the rest of her life because he'd forced it on her.

Jesus, how the hell had Hood, who couldn't keep his own marriage together, seen that?

All right, he'd call off the escape. He'd stay, too.

As soon as he thought it, he knew it was wrong. He could not stay. His duty was to escape. He must get back to his division, to Captain Loomis, find Kim if he was still alive, and any other remnants of his platoon. If there were no survivors, he'd be duty-bound to assume command of a platoon that had lost its lieutenant.

"Son, don't risk what put you two in love in the first place."

He turned on Hood. "Goddamn it, when did you become a goddamn authority on love?" a lifetime of anger burning through him—a low blow, he knew, but the words were out.

"Begging the lieutenant's pardon," Hood said evenly, "but if we learn from our mistakes, I'm just about the world's leading authority on love. If you're as smart as I think, you don't have to put yourself through what I did to know what I know."

Sam barely heard him, like he was speaking a foreign language. He gazed at Bonnie, a vision, right here close enough to grab and hold. "How can I leave you?"

Hood eased his knife back into his belt, eyes averted, and went to uncover the hole. Bonnie held out her hands to Sam. Taking them, he pulled her close, kissed her, held her to him.

After a moment, she pulled back. Her eyes glistened, but she did not cry. "It is what it is, Sam. I have to stay, and you have to go. We can't always hold onto what we love, only the love itself. Can you do that, Sam?"

He gave a single mute nod.

She touched his cheek, tears in her eyes. "Then I will see you after. We'll have our chance, I promise you—I *promise* you."

Sam let her turn him toward the hole. Feeling trapped in a nightmare, he bent to follow Hood out.

"Wait!" she said. "Take the fish."

A laugh caught in his throat. "Those are your final words— 'take the fish?'" Accepting the packet from her, he stuffed it down inside his parka and shirts, so it wouldn't freeze.

"I love you, too," she said.

He cradled her head, held her face to his, determined to remember how her lips felt, to remember this kiss forever.

Then followed Hood into the cold.

In December of 1950, severe cold mounted a constant, deadly assault on every aspect of military operations in North Korea, and, indeed, on survival itself. No meteorological data were kept in North Korea in the 1950s, but during the same period in 1970, the average daily high in the Chosin region was minus five degrees Fahrenheit and the average low, minus 18. Survivors of Chosin reported temperatures as low as minus thirty-five to minus fifty in some accounts. Prolonged exposure rendered men incoherent. Rations froze and canteens became blocks of ice. Frostbite numbed the fingers and toes, turning the skin white and hard, ending in amputation for those fortunate enough to survive. . . .

"The Korean War" chapter in: U.S. History, St. Clair Press, New York, 1972, 1991, 2009.

26

Watching the floodlit fence from a copse of pines, Sam whispered, "Remember, we mustn't kill him. They'll take it out on Bonnie."

Hood nodded.

The wind shrieked, spraying a sheet of snow onto the deep drift building against the base of the fence. In the glare of the floodlights, the snow sparkled like mica. Sam scanned the low pine scrub stretching out to either side. It would screen them from the camp as long as they kept low. But if they went clambering up the fence, they'd be visible all the way back to Tien's lodge.

Which was why they must go under the chain link, if they could.

"Maybe we can make it before the guard doubles back," Sam said.

"We need his gun."

Sam took a deep breath. His legs were itching to move, go, but Hood was right—stick to the plan. The sergeant's homemade knife wouldn't be much protection on the long trek back. Even if Tien didn't chase them, they'd likely be dodging and weaving through Chinese forces between here and the reservoir, especially if they couldn't hack the hills and had to stick to the road. With a gun, they might stave off recapture.

Would Tien chase them?

Hood had said that some of the Japanese POW camps during World War II were so remote they didn't even have walls. The prisoners were assured if they escaped they'd surely die in the jungle. This frozen ass-end of the earth was more inhospitable than any jungle. An escape would stick in Tien's craw, but maybe he'd console himself with mental images of them freezing to death.

Hood's teeth chattered, and Sam felt his confidence plummet. Did the old man have a chance in hell of making it? Forty years old, still recovering from the forced march to the prison, how much of his toughness was used up? Had to be twenty below, the wind lashing them even here in the shelter of the trees.

"This is nuts," Sam said. "Let's go back to the barracks."

Hood looked at him. The wind had blown snow into his eyebrows and beard, making him look like Father Winter. He said, "On the diet they're giving us, we'll never be stronger. We're going."

"You can't make it."

"We're going."

The guard tramped into view again down the fence, keeping his pace brisk, the flaps of his quilted hat flopping with each step. The wind obliterated his tracks with drifting snow almost as soon as he'd made them. That same wind would steal their body heat on the long trek and eat away at their stamina, but at least it would make them a lot harder to trail.

Sam held his breath to keep the approaching guard from seeing the vapor. The Chinese tramped past, his body now leaning back into the following wind. When he was fifty yards down the fence, Hood said, "You ready?"

"I can go anywhere a jarhead can go."

Without giving himself time to think, Sam bolted from the bushes to the edge of the fence, hearing Hood right behind him, hoping the guard wasn't hearing it, too.

Now the hard part.

Hood lay down on his back, and Sam scooped snow over him, covering even his face, except a small hole to allow him to breathe.

Lying down beside him as close as he could get for the warmth, he did the same to himself, scooping the snow up around his body and, finally, his face. The snow was so cold it burned.

What if we can't hear him coming back?

Then Bonnie will have a couple more wounded to treat.

Or we'll be dead.

At least we wouldn't be cold any more.

Sam grimaced. Great as not being cold would be, he did not want to die. He wanted to survive, make it through the war and be there when the Chinese repatriated their POWs, waiting at the exchange point to throw his arms around Bonnie and take her home and make love to her in the warmth of a summer evening, with kids playing in the spray from a fire hydrant and cabs honking their horns and pigeons cooing in the eaves. . . .

Sam felt the grainy thump of the guard's boots through the snow, minute vibrations against his back that grew stronger, *thud, thud, thud,* and then stopped right beside him, and a gloved hand brushed snow off his face, and he saw the guard's eyes widen beneath the quilted hat, and for a second his arm would not move, and then he drove his fist into the man's jaw, snapping the head back.

The soldier pitched over in the snow.

Hood rose, sputtering, from his white grave and scrambled to the base of the fence, hacking at the ground beneath with his homemade knife. Sam knelt over the guard. His eyelids fluttered, his jaw hanging open. Pulling the strips of blanket from his coat pocket, Sam tied the man's hands behind him and knotted his ankles together.

The guard's eyes opened.

Sam raised his fist.

"Qing—qing!" the guard gasped.

Scrambling over, Hood put the blade against the man's throat.

"No!" Sam said.

"Just giving him more to owe us." Hood took the blade away. "He came to awfully fast."

"I suppose if you'd punched him, he'd be out for a week."

"You said that, I didn't."

The guard heaved a shuddering sigh, obviously savoring the air flowing in and out of his still-intact throat.

"Can we trust you?" Sam asked.

Sensing a question, the guard nodded vigorously.

"No," Sam said, "of course we can't. But what can you do tied up? And if I knock you out again you might freeze to death in the snow. You're gonna need to squirm to survive."

Tearing off a trailing piece of blanket, he used it to gag the guard. He'd be free to keep his blood flowing wiggling and trying to craw in the snow, but the wind should drown out any cries he made. He'd crawl his way to help or his relief would find him, and either way should take an hour or two.

"I can't cut through the crust," Hood said. "The frozen ground is too hard."

"So it's Plan B. Let's go."

Hood stuffed the guard's ammo pack into his coat and strapped the Tommy gun onto his shoulder. Sam cradled Hood's boot in both hands and heaved as Hood clawed his way up the chain link. For an agonizing time it seemed that anyone in the camp could see him in the floodlights, and then Hood made it over the top and dropped into the drifts on the other side. Sam scrambled up behind, climbing with desperate speed, then dropping the ten feet into the snow.

He listened for shouts or gunshots.

Nothing but the howl of the wind.

Free!

Yeah, free to freeze or be shot by anyone in the four Chinese armies between here and the Chosin Reservoir.

"We should have taken one of the trucks," Sam said.

"They'd have sh-shot us at the gate," Hood said. "And if they didn't, they'd have come after us with the other trucks and jeeps. Colonel Tien couldn't afford to have transport stolen, not to mention the 'face' he'd lose from it. This way, he can just let us die out here."

Sam scooped up a handful of snow, scanning the road below as he ate it for the water. Nothing in sight and no sounds either, except the screaming wind. Dawn couldn't be far off, and if the clouds had broken maybe the sun could warm them up to, say, zero degrees.

And make them visible to any truck or horse patrol coming down the road.

"Can you feel your feet?" Sam asked.

"Stop mothering me. I'm the sergeant here. I'm responsible for foot hygiene."

"Can you feel them or not?"

"Is there any more of that fish?"

Sam drew the pack from his chest and slipped a herring to Hood. He ate it with obvious relish. Sam was glad to see he had an appetite, but it worried him, too. He'd have thought it best to ration their food—the four rice balls DeForest's men had insisted on pitching in before they crawled out the hole in the roof, and the unexpected bonus of fish. But Hood had prevailed, arguing they should stoke up so they could go as fast as they could, because if they were out here more than two days it would be because they were lost or pinned down, in which case they'd freeze to death anyway.

"We have to risk staying on the road," Sam said. "We can make four miles an hour down there, and probably four hours a mile stumbling along up here."

"You're right."

"Eighty miles to the reservoir. The rate we're chewing through our food, we don't have much choice. We'll watch and listen, get off the road if we see anyone coming."

Hood nodded as if it were as good as done, but he had to know they were taking a huge gamble. Only luck would show them the enemy before the enemy saw them.

They scrambled down the rocky hillside to the road, stepping out through the drifts. The sky was turning from black to gray. The road had four inches of fresh snow, but beneath, it was packed hard and smooth, the way it would be if thousands of feet had tramped every inch of it.

Not a pleasant thought.

Sam set an easy pace, mindful of the long march ahead. "It's been nine days since we were captured. Do you think the marines and army are still at the reservoir?"

"We'd better hope they are," Hood said.

"You don't sound hopeful."

"From what I saw coming through your forward positions, there isn't a chance in hell the Army could have held out this long east of the reservoir. They're cleaned out by now, and the best we can hope is that they managed to fight their way back down to Hagaru-ri. Even in a rout, some of your men could walk the ice the few miles south, but either way, it's finished on that side of the reservoir."

"Hate to say it," Sam muttered, "but I agree."

"The marines, I don't know. Their first stop would also be Hagaru-ri at the south end of the reservoir. They're further from it than army because the road south loops out around a little mountain that borders the reservoir on their side. A ten mile trek, maybe, from where I left them at the little village—what was it?—Yudam-ni. The Chinese would have set up roadblocks where they could attack from the hills. General Smith wouldn't leave Hagaru-ri until his 5th and 7th regiments had fought their way back and he had his division intact. If we can get there before he pulls out, we're set. If not, we'll just have to keep pushing on, try and catch them further south. Right now, the main thing is to get back to where we were captured, hope we can find some C-rations the Chinese missed and then get our asses on down to Hagaru-ri as fast as we can."

"And avoid the Chinese while doing all that."

"Well, sure."

Demoralized, Sam looked back the way they had come, a dark wilderness of rock and blowing snow. An image of Bonnie came to him: sleeping on her cot in the hut, the warm glow of the fire caressing her face. He suppressed a bitter laugh that Camp 2, a hell hole, could now seem like paradise.

What if Tien decided to punish her?

Sam's throat ached. I'd take a bullet for her, he thought. If I was there, maybe I could protect her, but I'm not there, I left her, and if she dies, or they—

"Sam."

He realized Hood had been saying his name, repeating it. "What?"

"You did the right thing. If you'd stayed, you couldn't do a damn thing for her."

"Every step I take away from her. . . ."

"I know. It's the hardest thing you'll ever do."

Sam tried to harden his will. Hood was right, if he were back at Camp 2, he'd have no power to help her. Tien or the guards could do anything they wanted to her and he wouldn't know until it was too late. Right or wrong, he had done what he'd done, and now he must stop thinking about her and concentrate on keeping himself and Hood alive.

He said, "I wish we had those white quilted uniforms. It would make us a lot harder to spot."

"While you're wishing, why not wish we were back in Georgia?"

"Manhattan, you mean. Tavern on the Green, steak and eggs for breakfast."

"Ruby's Diner," Hood countered, "out in Bucks Head. We could go fishing on the Chattahoochee, like that time I took you. . . ." He let it hang.

Yeah, Sam thought. We had fun.

And the fun only made it harder. If you had never visited, maybe I could have forgotten about you. But no, you came every chance you got. You made me love you, you did it over and over, and every time, you went away again. You left my mother and you left me.

And now I've left Bonnie.

Hood said, "Would you really sell out your country to save her?"

"Bet your ass."

"What about honor?"

"Honor matters. But not more than Bonnie. Letting them hurt her when I had any hope of stopping it, just so I could preserve my honor—that would be caring more about myself than her. I'd rather be called a traitor the rest of my life."

Hood nodded.

Sam felt a dim surprise. Could it be the answer he was looking for? Surely not—not a gung ho, hard-ass jarhead. Duty, honor, country were the ideals that made marines so full of themselves. Hood had probably never had an unpatriotic thought in his life.

A gust shrieked into their faces, stirring up a whirl of snow, and for a second Sam could see nothing but white ahead. His eyes stung. "Mom still loves you."

"What?"

"I said, how could you leave her?"

Hood walked faster, kicking up clouds of dry snow.

Sam lengthened his stride to keep up. "I asked you a question."

"It was the only way to keep her."

"Visiting on the few weekends when you had leave, you call that keeping?"

"It was the only keeping possible for us. You think a few days with you two every couple of months would have been enough for me if I could have had more? I left because, to stay together, one of us would have had to lose their soul."

"Bullshit. You couldn't give up your beloved Corps."

"Yeah, right. After you were born, I had two months left in my hitch. I told Iris I wouldn't re-enlist."

Sam wondered if he'd heard right. "What?"

"She hit the ceiling. Said a Marine was what I was supposed to be, and she couldn't bear to have wrecking that on her conscience. Told me deep down inside I'd blame her the rest of our lives together."

"And you let that stop you?"

Hood said nothing.

"*Would* you have blamed her?"

"Hell, Sam. I want to believe I wouldn't have. But she wasn't often wrong about me. And what she said about holding it against her—she didn't intend to be talking about herself too, but I saw that if she was right about me, the same reasoning would have to apply to her. In her heart, she really was determined to stay with me. But I saw that if she did, I'd be destroying the woman I fell in love with."

"How convenient for you," Sam said bitterly. "You had to leave her for her sake."

"Can you see her as an enlisted man's wife?"

Sam set his mind to imagine it, tried to put her in that frame.

"She needs beauty," Hood said. "Art and music and plays; friends who can talk intelligently about those things and appreciate them with her. She wasn't meant to live my life—dusty military bases, being scared all the time that I'd be hurt or killed."

"You make her sound so shallow—"

"No. Your mother is anything but shallow. She was ready to give up everything she loved for me. She tried her best to make my life hers, to become a good military wife and make us both believe it was what she wanted, but I could see her dying inside. It's like Bonnie. If she'd come with us because you wouldn't take 'no' for an answer, it might have destroyed the very things you love about her. Love is two things—what you feel and what you do. The first doesn't mean much without the second. I mean, what you feel for Bonnie is great—for you. What you just *did* for her, even though it's breaking your heart, now *that* is love."

Sam felt a welling pain, as if something was tearing loose inside him. Everything Hood had said had the ring of truth. But how *could* it be true? He thought, If that's really how it was between him and Mom, what right do I have to be angry? To blame Hood for what I've suffered?

No. He's just trying to wiggle off the hook.

"You deserting Mom and me is nothing like what just happened with Bonnie."

"If you say so." Plodding forward, Hood pulled his parka tighter against the wind.

"Don't do that. You started this. Talk to me—you've got some more explaining to do."

"Let me know when you're ready to listen."

"Screw you, Hood."

They walked in silence, one foot following the other, the wind driving into their eyes.

"I could no more live your mother's life," Hood said, "than she could mine. It was either let her go or destroy her. The tragedy is what it did to you. You have every right to hate me."

Damn straight. Sam opened his mouth to say it, then closed it. *Listen. This is Hood admitting he was wrong. This is what you've wanted.*

"I knew I could never make up for it," Hood said, "but I had to try. That's why I kept coming around. I loved you, Sam. I'd have kept you with me if I could, but then it would have been your mother you lost, your mother you ended up hating, and it would have destroyed her, the woman I loved." His head gave a slow, drunken roll, like a man trying to shake off a blow. "Your Ma and I made you somewhere in the first acts of love between us. I'm sure the experts on marriage would be against us having a child so fast, before we understood that love wasn't enough, that too much else stood against us. But I will never call you a mistake. For all my sins, helping put you on this planet is the best thing I've ever done. You've grown into a good man, a strong man. I know it wasn't my doing, and that's what hurts the most. It's a pain I deserve. You don't. For what it's worth, I'll be sorry until I die."

Sam glanced over at him, a blurry image of a weary old leatherneck, plodding along wrapped in the parka and helmet, looking fat with all the clothes, the same man who'd used to walk through Mom's door, smelling of shaving soap, lean and grinning, hugging him against that snappy, creased uniform.

Sam's throat tightened. I could never stop loving you, he thought. That's what really pissed me off.

Say it. Tell him.

Let Hood off the hook?

No. He wasn't ready.

Tomorrow, maybe. They had time together now. If what he was feeling he still felt tomorrow, he'd say it then.

During the first week of December the fate of Army's Task Force Faith on the east side of the Chosin Reservoir, and of the 1st Marine Division on the west side, hung in the balance. Colonel Faith led his task force in a desperate attempt to evacuate with their wounded. The retreat was doomed by the overwhelming numbers of encircling Chinese forces, which riddled the unarmored trucks with machine gun and small arms fire. The task force was beaten down by repeated attacks as the senior officers at every level were killed or wounded so badly they were taken out of action. Men died from the tail end of the column to the head, a sharp turn several miles south where the road was blocked. By December 4, only 181 men of the original 1053 in the 1st Battalion, 32nd Infantry, had survived. The marines, with superior equipment, training, and numbers, fared far better, fighting their way south from the reservoir and shredding the four Chinese armies that attacked from all sides. General Smith's insistence on keeping his forces together despite General Almond's earlier pressure to string them out paid off. The skill and sheer grit of this veteran Marine division was the other key factor enabling them to avoid Army's terrible fate. What happened at the Chosin Reservoir, while tragic, was also one of the finest hours of the United States Marines.

"The Korean War" chapter in: *U.S. History,* St. Clair Press, New York, 1972, 1991, 2009.

27

7 December, Chosin Reservoir, 2010:
"Dear God Almighty," Sam said.

A ghostly line of Army trucks, their snow-capped canopies phosphorescent in the moonlight, stretched as far as he could see up the road flanking the Chosin Reservoir. Gutted Sherman tanks blocked the head of the column, their cannons skewed up at the black sky.

Here in this back alley of a frozen-over hell, the 7th Division's regimental combat team had made its last stand. Ice sculptures of Chinese, South Korean, and American soldiers sat and lay in the snow all along the column.

A white, quilted uniform would be easy to come by now.

Sam stared at the ghastly tableau, sick with horror. Until this moment, he'd actually felt lucky. Only two patrols between the prison camp and here; one had failed to see them scrambling from the roadway, and the other clearly had seen them but had been in too much of a hurry to bother trying to chase down two shadowy figures in the distance who might be nothing more than North Korean refugees. Lucky with that, lucky after their food had run out to find C-rations in an outlying foxhole above the Pungnyuri-gang inlet where Sam's battalion had fought on the day he'd been captured.

Only two more miles to the south end of the reservoir and they would know if whatever was left of the Army and Marines were still at Hagaru-ri.

Now he must accept his luck at being spared the death of so many brothers.

And, if that "luck" held, find a way to live with it.

"We should move on," Hood said.

Sam followed him, sticking close to the trucks, glancing into the cabs and backs in case someone had somehow survived.

No chance.

Many of the trucks had been burned. In others, men lay in stacks of stretchers collapsed onto each other by the gunfire that had shredded the sides of the canopies. Frozen together, perfectly preserved in the cold, frost gilding their faces. Moonlight gleamed off the teeth of a Chinese by the road, his stomach torn into meat by a machine gun. Men sat slumped in the cabs, chins on their chests, as if sleeping, except that no fog of breath rose from them.

Horror. Horror.

"How long do you think they've been here?"

"No way to tell," Hood said. "Could be a week, could be a couple of days. In this icebox, they'd look exactly like this two years from now." He shuddered. His bristles had grown to a beard coated in ice, crackling in the crease of his parka. His voice had the rusty quaver of an ancient. "Awful, to leave them like this."

Criticizing Army again.

Exhausted, Sam could muster only a thin irritation. So superior, the Marines, stressing how they always brought out their dead. But surely sometimes you couldn't because if you tried you'd be dead yourself, and your first duty was to the not-yet-dead who would die if you weren't giving everything you had to them.

"The roadblock stopped the column," Sam said. "The trucks had no way around the tanks because of how these damn hills close in. The road is basically a narrow pass, here, and the

Chinese used that to block and swarm the column. Our boys still had some ammo, but not enough." He sucked a breath. Should be saving his energy, but you couldn't see this and say nothing. Take off your helmet and throw back your parka and your ears would freeze, but you could at least say a few words to honor their desperate courage. "You can see the black scars where the Corsairs dropped napalm, but that didn't stop it either. All the Chinese had to do was hide in the rocks and blast the convoy with machine guns. Canvas canopies, the wounded had no chance. The only hope for those who could still use their legs was to desert the trucks and try to run away across the ice."

Hood stared at the smashed convoy, his expression stark in the moonlight. "Lot of brave men here died at the wheels when they could have run to the reservoir—and probably should have. No marine could have done better."

The praise, so unexpected and generous, brought a dry heave of grief to Sam's throat.

A thought drifted through his mind that they should be keeping an eye on the hills in case Chinese stragglers were still up there.

Trying to hold the idea, he could not.

He wondered what he'd just been thinking.

The trucks slid past, telling him he was still walking—he could hear his feet crunching in the snow but couldn't feel them, like walking on someone else's feet. He hoped they were just numb, not frozen. Tired, so damn tired, no sleep in two days, nothing but walking, putting one foot in front of the other.

Reaching the cab of the next to last truck, he put the foot-like thing at the end of his leg onto the running board and hoisted himself up. He almost didn't recognize the face of the driver because a major wouldn't usually be at the wheel of a troop truck; Anson should have been in a jeep, or, if wounded, in an ambulance, not here, trying to drive enlisted men to safety.

Sam's eyes prickled. "Damn. God damn."

"Someone you know?"

"He taught me things. He liked to act like a cynic but he was an optimist to the end. He never believed the Chinese would fight us in strength."

"The Marine brass had all the signs too," Hood said, "and went right ahead."

A sudden, desperate urge to be away from this place seized Sam. "The ice will be quickest. Let's go." He led the way down through the frozen marsh and onto the snow-covered ice. More bodies lay all around, on their backs or curled up on their sides, frozen to the ice. The Chinese had seen them running, had hurried to the shore and mowed a lot of them down, the ones that were still close enough to shoot, not a speck of cover to hide behind.

Look at this poor devil, his legs shredded by a submachine gun. Maybe he didn't die right away, the cold freezing the blood to seal the wounds so he wouldn't bleed out. So he'd frozen to death, cold, so terribly cold, and then warmer, feeling like he was falling asleep, maybe trying to hold onto a last image of his mother or sweetheart.

And now, gone where nothing else could ever happen to him.

Sam's heart clung to one small hope: He hadn't seen Kim. Maybe he had survived. *Please, God. Let Kim be alive.*

He kept his feet moving, plodding and slipping ahead through the snow. The ice was too cold to be slick, a small mercy. "Shouldn't we be seeing lights ahead?"

"Yeah," Hood's voice was low, stricken, the single syllable an effort.

Sam's heart sank. *We're too late.*

They tramped into Hagaru-ri, where the 1st Marine Division had headquartered, the tents, trucks, and artillery gone, most of the town burned down, nothing left but a few shacks that had somehow escaped the fires set by the departing Marines to deny the Chinese any use of the place. Where the ammo dump must have been, a huge, black hole yawned in the ground—the leathernecks blowing up what they couldn't carry. Parachutes littering the hills around the town told of airdrops to supply the breakout. No generators hummed, a burned and sacked town, no lights, no Marine Corps, no Army.

No American bodies, either, though there were plenty of Chinese.

Sam said, "Looks like they were able to take along what they didn't burn, bury, or blow up."

Hood made no response.

Fear for him lit a desperate spark of energy in Sam. After two days of non-stop exertion, Sergeant Harlan Hood was at the end of his rope. He'd been hanging on, pushing forward in the hope that the marines would be massed in Hagaru-ri, but it was empty, even the airstrip the marine bulldozers had scraped from the frozen ground outside the shantytown.

Now, with his hope dashed, Hood couldn't whip his body any further.

"I have to rest," Sam said.

"No."

"There's a couple of shacks right there that didn't burn. We'll get in out of the cold, thaw out some C-rations, eat, sleep. Just for a few hours."

Hood stopped, teetering on his feet, his head down. "Every hour we sit," he mumbled, "they get further away."

"I can't go on."

Hood raised his head, eyed him from under a shaggy, frozen brow. "All right, you big pussy."

Sam put an arm around his shoulders, guiding him into one of the shacks that had escaped the fire. Short pieces of phone wire tangled on the pine board floor along with a broken handset and some scattered, blank sheets from a log book. No sleeping bags but in one corner, under the shack's only window, a bed lay waiting, an actual bed, the mattress too big to take along. As was the wood stove, the beautiful, blessed wood stove.

"You stretch out," Hood mumbled. "I'll get us a blaze going."

Sam walked him to the bed, eased him down. He was out in seconds.

Sam broke up two of the chairs and used matches from the C-rations, and some of the log book pages to start a fire in the stove. Within minutes, heat welled, beating back the frigid cold of the room. On the bed, Hood snored. Sam tossed a couple of frozen tins of beans and franks onto the fire and sat on the remaining chair. He was afraid to take his shoepacs off. How could his feet be so cold? They'd been moving constantly for two days, never resting long enough to freeze up. But the body, pushed far enough, began to run down mile by mile, the blood finally retreating back up the legs toward the vital organs, the capillaries in the feet too far a reach for the laboring heart.

Hell with it. Only one thing mattered: Rest and then push on. Just a few hours, and then they'd have the strength to catch up.

Sam used Hood's homemade knife to fish the cans out of the fire, letting them cool a bit, then puncturing them and ripping them open with the knife. Raising Hood to a sitting position, he spooned the beans and meat into his mouth, then eased him down again. He ate his own can, then checked the Tommy gun, which was starting to thaw out. Another half hour and it would probably be able to fire on automatic.

I'll stand the first watch, he thought.

The mattress rose up behind him, enfolding his back.

He did not dream.

Shivering woke him, the fire down to embers, and he stumbled outside to the flattened remains of another shack, only half awake, a gust of cold wind knocking him down on the way back with the boards. He got up, not sure it had happened, and continued to the shack. Hood didn't wake up as he fed the boards onto the embers. Gazing into the fire, he imagined Bonnie back at the prison camp in her mud hut, her own fire burning. *God, please keep her safe. I'll never ask another thing. If she dies in that place after I left her there, it'll be the end of me, too.*

He awoke in the chair, stayed conscious long enough to get himself to the bed.

Shivering woke him a second time. Now it was light outside—

And a Chinese soldier was staring in the window.

Sam groped for the Tommy gun, his mind throwing off sleep as he saw the Chinese raise his burp gun to fire. The glass broke, showering down on Hood, who leapt into motion, grabbing the barrel of the intruding burp gun and shoving it to the side as the gun chattered, perforating the stove in a spray of sparks.

Snatching up the Tommy gun, Sam hosed the window at point blank range. Hood tore the burp gun from dead hands of the Chinese soldier.

Shouts outside.

Sam dived to the floor and scuttled away with Hood as a barrage of shells showered the rest of the window's glass down on the bed.

The fusillade broke off, leaving Sam's ears ringing.

"Guess we overslept," Hood said. "I make it three of them."

"What do we do, sergeant?"

Hood looked up to the rafters. "Boost me up there and then I'll pull you up."

Keeping away from the window, Sam cradled his hands for Hood's shoepac and lunged up with all his strength. Hood caught the beam and clambered up with stiff awkwardness, then reached his hand down. The beam, nothing more than a two by four, creaked ominously, and Sam could see it shimmying. Shaking his head, he handed the burp gun up to Hood, then hid behind the overturned stove, clenching the Tommy gun to his chest.

For a long moment, there was nothing but the rasp of their breath, and then the door burst open, two Chinese racing in. Hood cut loose from above with the burp gun and they both went down. From the corner of his eye, Sam saw movement at the window and swung the Tommy gun around, killing the Chinese as he drew a bead on Hood.

Three more dead, Sam thought, but he felt nothing but a vast relief.

Hood took the machine gun from his hands, slung it on his shoulder. "You did good, Son."

"I should have been dead back there," Sam said. He'd fallen behind, letting Hood lead on the road to the Funchilin Pass. Cradling the burp gun so he could shoot at any second, he searched the ridge lines.

Hood did not answer.

"When you grabbed the barrel," Sam prompted, "and pushed it to the side. He had me. That's the second time you saved my life."

"I'm sure you'll put it to good use." More energy in Hood's voice now after the food and night's sleep. But he was limping all the same. And this bump in their energy wouldn't last.

"Other fathers just take their sons on camping trips."

Hood snorted. "It wasn't my idea, you being here."

"Mine either."

"Then why did you join?"

Sam hesitated. How many times had he asked himself that, and always a toss-off answer was all he could come up with. Time for a stab at the truth. "I liked the idea of it," he said. "The way it might feel to commit myself. Hell, I don't know."

He remembered telling Bonnie he'd put on the uniform to get dates. More likely he'd done it because a part of him, against all logic, had yearned to look as Hood looked in his memories, coming home for the weekend.

"You're sure they'll blow the bridge?"

"At the Funchilin pass?" Hood said. "No question about it. The second they get the last man, tank, and artillery piece across it, that baby goes." He didn't add what he must be thinking: that it was probably gone already.

Sam pulled out his recollections of the bridge, a huge structure at the Changjin power station, spanning North Korea's scaled-down version of the Grand Canyon.

Of course the Marines would blow it, and that would end any Chinese pursuit.

And our hopes of catching up, too.

It might be possible to climb down through that gorge and back up the other side, if you were reasonably rested, strong and blessed with steady nerves. For two men near the end of their ropes, flat impossible.

And even if they could make it, the time it would cost would leave them so far behind the division they'd have no hope of running it down. They'd probably freeze to death in the pass.

So we'll just have to get there before they blow it.

"Are you afraid?" Sam asked.

"Of dying?"

"No, of having your skin chapped by all this wind."

Hood's shoulders humped in a gruff chuckle. He tramped along for a moment, and Sam thought he wasn't going to answer, and then he said, "I've seen a lot of men die, and from what I've seen, it usually hurts less than shutting your finger in a door. What scares you is knowing that when dying gets close you won't want your life to end but it will anyway. If being scared could change that, I'd be for it. But making yourself miserable over what you can't change is a waste of time you could use trying to be happy. Happy is what life's about, right?"

Sam looked at him, impressed. Harlan Hood, philosopher—without all the big words. "So you're not afraid."

"Sometimes I slip up."

They rounded a bend. Ahead, a marine troop truck sat by the side of the road. For a second, Sam's heart swelled with irrational hope that it had men in it, a nice warm ride waiting for Hood and him, going to take them over the Funchilin pass, down to the well-defended port of Hamhung and safety.

But the truck was abandoned, of course.

The hood was up. Maybe the driver had stopped to let men relieve themselves, and the carburetor had frozen, or it had simply run out of gas.

The key was still in the ignition. Hood tried it. Nothing, the battery sucked too dry by the cold for even a whisper.

But the truck was at least an omen, along with tire tracks not completely drifted over yet. The column might be only a few miles ahead. And if that was true, there would be Chinese regiments even closer, in pursuit on the road and hills on either side. Live Chinese, not the dead they were beginning to see, draped over rock outcroppings, or lying in the snow where they'd tumbled from the cliffs.

If we get close enough, Sam thought, how will we get through the Chinese line to link up? We could strip the white uniforms off a couple of the corpses, but our faces would give us away to Chinese on the road. We'll have to go up in the hills, and with the marine column rolling ahead on the road, we'll never catch up that way. Chinese forces will be spread along the ridges, too.

Maybe the old man has a plan.

Rounding another curve, Sam saw a convoy of trucks off the side of the road, this time facing north. As he got closer, he saw that the trucks had been shot up, their drivers dead at the wheels, like the convoy by the reservoir, bodies scattered all around, along with a mail bag, torn open, letters fluttering in the snow. "What uniforms are those?"

"Royal Marines," Hood said. "The Limeys are getting into it with us, helping us like we did them in the last war. This would be the 41st Independent Commandos—a recon unit. They were attached to our division in November. They must have been coming up to reinforce Hagaru-ri before the evacuation order."

Hood took his helmet off and rolled his parka back, baring his head, the black hair giving Sam a small shock—longer than he'd ever seen it, plastered down to Hood's skull with sweat that would freeze in seconds if he didn't cover up. . . .

Sam bared his own head in respect and quickly covered up again. "I've heard others are here or on the way, Turks, Canadians, Australians, lots of others, coming to help the South Koreans."

"God bless them all," Hood whispered.

"It'll be good not to be alone in this," Sam agreed. "Should we look for rations? Maybe some warmer clothes?"

"If we don't get to the pass in time, we won't need any of it. We keep going, fast as we can."

Hood covered his head again and turned back to the road. Sam tugged one of the envelopes from the snow, reading the name, a Private Smythe, addressed in a child's scrawl. Dropping the letter back in the snow, he followed Hood.

The sky was growing dark, though it was only late morning, heavy, lead-colored clouds dimming the frozen white landscape to a pewter glow.

Within a mile, they came upon stacks of Chinese bodies beside the road and another U.S. Vehicle, this time a jeep, off on the shoulder, all four tires shot out, the radiator holed. Frozen blood on the seat, but no dead, the marines taking them along.

Sam touched the hood. Stone cold, but in this freezing air it would turn that way minutes after the engine quit. A Chinese soldier, frozen solid, had been set at the edge of the road on a mound of snow. In one out-thrust hand was a pack of Luckies.

With a harsh laugh, Hood plucked a frozen cigarette from the pack. "Thanks, don't mind if I do." He tried to light it, but the match sputtered out.

Sam shuddered. If only there was a way to tell whether the marines were days ahead, or only hours. His teeth chattered, though the wind was in his back, whipping his parka forward. "What are you going to do after the war?"

"Good ways to go in this one."

"But it'll end at some point."

"There'll be another."

"But if there isn't?"

Hood gave him a blank look, and Sam realized he couldn't answer, didn't know what he'd do when he could no longer fight. Even now, when it must be clear to him that he was too old for this sort of thing, he had not thought past it.

Time for him to do so. Hood was smart, determined and experienced. He could be a. . . .a. . . .

Sam kept drawing blanks, rejecting each possibility almost as soon as he thought of it. Banker? Carpenter? Milk truck driver? He couldn't imagine Harlan Hood as anything but a soldier.

"I suppose you'll teach history," Hood said.

"That's the plan."

407

"You're sure as hell living history. This will be in all the books, like the World War II battles."

Sam thought about the folks back home still trying to piece their lives back together from the World War, dismayed and resentful that the nation must fight another so soon after—one where the rationale and goals were murkier. Colonel Tien had been right about one thing. Korea was a long way to come to fight for someone else's freedom. A people whose culture and history were a mystery to most Americans.

Hood said, "I fought at Iwo Jima and that was no picnic but the Chosin Reservoir? Fighting at midnight in minus 35 degrees, winter trying to kill you before the Chinese can, climbing these mountains, freezing your feet, having your gun not work half the time. No one ever fought such a battle before in the history of the world, not us, not the Chinese, no one. It'll go down with D-Day, Iwo Jima, the charge of the light brigade."

"A retreat."

Hood stopped on the road, turned to him. "Son, what we're seeing here is not a retreat. A retreat is where you have a rear to go back to. We were surrounded up at that reservoir, the main supply route cut, Chinese attacking from all directions, which means there was no possibility of retreating. This is an attack you're seeing here. An attack by the U. S. Marines, and a successful one, a breakout, like the Germans did in the Battle of the Bulge. This is Custer fighting his way clear at Little Big Horn and taking his men and horses and guns out with him to fight another day. We may not, at the moment, be going in the direction General MacArthur had hoped, but this war is a long way from over, and the 1st Division of the U.S. Marines is on the attack. If you need more proof than these piles upon piles of Chinese bodies, just remember that dead Chinaman with the Luckies back there. That little display wasn't left by a whipped dog. It was left by a pack of wolves, pissing to show their territory."

Before Sam could think of an answer, Hood took off walking again, pumping those short legs, scanning the hills, left and right, under a sky the color of slate. For a moment, all Sam could do was watch him, eyes prickling. So sure the folks back home would remember and appreciate him, so steadfast in his commitment to defending his country, a warrior without equal.

Magnificent.

A heavy sadness filled Sam as he thought of what really awaited Sergeant Harlan Hood. If they did manage to catch up with the 1st Division, the marines might well court martial him for desertion. He could lose the way of life he loved, and it wouldn't matter that he'd gone to be with his son.

This time he chose me.

Ahead of him, Hood stumbled and went down. Stepping forward to help him up, Sam noticed a patch of red in the snow under Hood's cheek, the look of surprise in the one eye he could see.

The breath froze in Sam's lungs. Falling to one knee, he looked ahead and saw them, white against the road, five of them in their quilted uniforms. One still had his rifle up, and the muzzle flashed, and Sam's helmet rang, twisting on his head. No sound of a shot, the wind blowing toward the Chinese, ripping it away.

"Get down," Hood barked.

Sam flattened himself beside his father, unlimbering the Thompson, no good at this range, but the patrol was closing on the run.

"Get behind me," Hood gasped.

"Hell, no!"

"I'm bleeding out, won't last a minute. God damn it, get behind me, or they'll get you too."

Sam saw with horror that the circle of blood had spread out to both sides of Hood, pouring out of him and freezing on the ground. His face had gone white as the snow.

Sam's shoulder took a whack and went numb, and he realized he'd been shot. Stunned, he clung to consciousness. He could feel his father crawling in front of him, Hood's body shaking with another impact, the closest Chinese about fifty yards away now.

"I always loved you," Sam said.

"Even when you hated me?"

"Yes." Sam felt his heart breaking.

Hood grinned. "Son, tell your mother I love her."

"I will."

Hood's eye held his a second longer, then rolled back.

Rage gripped Sam. He tipped Hood up on his side like a sandbag, feeling the body jar with another impact, as the Chinese kept firing—

Come on, just a little closer, you killed us, we're both dead, so come on—

Close enough; he rolled the Thompson over Hood's body and pulled the trigger. Nothing happened, the damn gun frozen. Hood's burp gun lay a yard away, the Chinese still coming. Sam grabbed it with his good arm and fired off the magazine, spraying the gun back and forth, watching the Chinese spin and slam down on their knees, falling into each other, screaming.

All of them down now, but two trying to crawl away.

He grabbed another magazine from inside Hood's coat, jammed it home and walked up to the Chinese, feeling very light, one arm numb and hanging, but the other plenty good as he sprayed them, the bullets pocking up tufts of their quilted uniforms, their blood pouring out red against the white.

Returning to kneel over Hood, he felt for the pulse he knew was gone.

"I'll tell her," he said again. Rising, he stared down at his father, and as he stared, Hood's blood faded to white, and Sam realized it was snowing.

He took off the Marine helmet and put it on his own head, throwing his away. Dropping the gun, he hooked the fingers of the arm that still had feeling into the hood of his father's parka and began walking down the road, dragging the body along the icy surface behind him. The cliffs on either side of the road faded out, a full scale blizzard, a white out. He could see only a foot or two in front of his face.

He did not think, because there was really nothing he wanted to think about.

He kept walking, dragging Hood along behind him through the fresh snow.

After awhile, he made his way between the pale snow ghosts of soldiers speaking to each other in a foreign language—Chinese flickering in and out of the snow on either side of him, trudging with fatigue, drifting back as he pushed himself forward, more of them ahead but none in a hurry, and they fell behind, too. He knew he should be afraid, but he wasn't. In the blizzard, he was just another Chinese, dragging God knew what, a bag of grenades maybe, everyone around him too bone weary for curiosity.

After awhile there were no more ghostly figures, and he was alone on the road, the world vanished around him. In the void, he started to care again and at once fear welled up, a deeper cold inside him. This was useless, the marines were long gone, the bridge blown, he should let go of his father, he could make better time.

Hood would *want* him to let go.

His arm hurt from the strain, more pain than he could ever have imagined.

Keep on.

And then he was walking among men again, more Chinese? No, he could hear someone cracking a joke, about a rabbi, a priest, and an atheist going into a bar.

"Will someone help me?" he said, and shadows emerged from the white around him, these men not too weary to care.

Some time later, he couldn't be sure how long, he lay in the back of an ambulance, feeling better than he wanted to with the morphine from a Navy Corpsman's kit soothing him, one arm around Hood. The body was cold, but no colder than everything else. Sam dozed off, maybe a couple of times, and then a familiar face was bending over him, not quite looking at him, but definitely talking to him.

"How far did you bring him?" the face said.

"What?"

"Hood. They say you were dragging him. How far?" Bald headed, tears frozen on his face.

411

Recognition dawned—Corporal Bouden, Hood's corporal, here in the ambulance with him and Hood.

"I don't know," Sam said.

Bouden was fussing with Hood's frozen uniform, tidying it up here and there.

"The bridge," Sam said. "I thought you'd be long gone."

"We woulda' been, and you'd have been royally screwed, but the Chinks blew the bridge up before we got there, and that slowed us down. Sons of bitches meant to keep us from crossing so they could wipe us out. Instead, we kicked their asses on the road and in the hills all the while our planes airlifted sections for a new span in. We kept killing Chinese while the engineers put the new bridge together, then we went across. When everyone was on the other side, we blew the bridge we'd just got done building and stranded whatever Chinks were left on the other side. We're going downhill now, closing in on Hungnam. The 1st MASH has moved there. They'll take that bullet out of your shoulder, then we'll get you on a hospital ship. You'll be in Tokyo, soon." Bouden patted Hood's chest.

"I'm sorry," Sam said.

Bouden looked at him at last. "Your old man was the best."

"Yes."

"And you're a piece of him, or you'd never have brought him out. When you get well, I want to know how the hell you managed that."

Sam could find no words—the morphine, or maybe his heart would break if he tried to talk about it.

"Rest, now" Bouden said. "I'll look after you both until we reach the 1st MASH. They have a lot of pretty nurses. Your old man told me about one of them that took care of him in Tokyo, said she was really special. You'll be meeting her soon."

Before Sam could explain that Bonnie was a prisoner in China, he passed out.

One million, seven hundred eighty-nine thousand American soldiers, sailors, airmen, and marines served their country in Korea during the war. Several hundred thousand are still living down the street from us or across town. Chances are, we don't know their stories, but the living memories of these senior Americans preserve and honor the 33,665 killed in action, the 92,134 wounded in action, and the 8,176 still missing in action. For the survivors of the Korean War, who risked all they had and were to restore freedom to strangers in a strange land, the armistice signed on July 27, 1953, is not a quaint curiosity from a forgotten era. It is a cease-fire that can be broken at any time. They, and the American troops who have taken their place, watch the Korea above the 38th parallel tout its nuclear missiles. They worry that America, like last time, is too preoccupied with other things.

"The Korean War," Sam Foxworth's chapter in: *U.S. History,* St. Clair Press, New York, 1972, 1991, 2009.

EPILOGUE

27 July, 2009, Centralhatchee, Georgia, 8 A.M.:
Looking for Sam, Bonnie found him at the bay window in the dining room, gazing out at the little branch of the Centralhatchee Creek that bordered the back yard. There, on the table, lay his cell phone. She made a mental note of it for later, when he was sure to ask her where she'd put it.

"Who was the call from?" she asked.

Turning from the window, Sam threw her a smile, and her heart did a couple of dance steps. Still handsome at eighty-one, his thick hair, once black as a raven's wing, now a blazing white. Maybe it was partly memory superimposing itself but his shoulders looked as broad to her as when she'd first seen him glide with that uncanny, silent grace onto her ward in Tokyo.

"It was Dr. Kim," he said.

She nodded. Kim always called on Armistice Day. Could it really be fifty-six years today since the Korean War had settled into its endless pause? She and Sam preferred to celebrate on August 5, when "Operation Big Switch" had begun—the exchange of prisoners with the Chinese. They'd go to dinner at The Palm and she would call up her memories of how he'd looked waiting with the other families, craning his neck to spot her. How she'd started crying, this huge grin pasted to her face, knowing life would be good after all.

"How's Kim doing?" she asked.

"He's been appointed to the Advisory Council on Democratic and Peaceful Reunification. He'll report directly to the president of South Korea."

"Wow!"

"He's sure reunification is just around the corner. I asked him if that would be before or after North Korea hits Hawaii with a missile and he gave me his tolerant laugh. I can't get over him. When he was in my platoon he *hated* the North."

"Nobody believed the two Germanies would get back together."

"That's what he said. I told him I'd believe it when Nicole Kidman gets back with Tom Cruise." Leaning a bit too far forward, he stabilized himself with a nonchalant hand on the dining room archway. She suspected he still felt the missing toes sometimes—the seven dwarfs as he called them, amputated fifty-nine years ago in the 1st MASH at Hungnam. Sometimes, in the middle of the night, she'd hear him in the bathroom, the furtive rattle of the aspirin bottle, and know he'd been wakened by the burning sensation frostbite victims suffer off and on for the rest of their lives. She'd pretend to be asleep when he crept back into bed, so he wouldn't have to act macho—a tactic that had rubbed off on him during his brief time with his father.

Bonnie thought of Sergeant Harlan Hood, killed on the road to the Funchilin Pass, a place that, unlike the Alamo and Little Big Horn and Pearl Harbor, few remembered because too few had heard of it to begin with. America had spent blood and treasure in the Korean War to restore South Korea's freedom. Nearly sixty years after the North Korean invasion had been repelled, the south was a flourishing democracy. World War II had ended with a Germany as divided as Korea, but that hadn't stopped America from thanking its veterans with a tickertape parade.

Somehow, for the Korean War vets, there had been no such parades.

Out the window, Bonnie saw Harlan walking along the stream with young Ethan. Actually, she needed to stop calling him that—he was nineteen. Following her gaze, Sam watched their son and grandson approach the house. "Gonna miss 'em," he said.

"They'll be back at Christmas."

With the original Harlan fresh in her mind, Bonnie marveled once again at how much her son resembled him. Writing Sergeant Hood into her notebook at Tokyo General, she'd never dreamed his genes would find their way into her son. Her Harlan had a softer gut than his grandfather, but then, emergency medicine physicians tended to work out less than United States Marines. He certainly had his grandfather's square jaw and cleft chin, the big shoulders and piano legs. He even had his height—at five-eight, he was a lot closer to Sergeant Hood than to Lieutenant Foxworth. She imagined Hood peering out from Harlan's eyes, the primordial warrior marveling at his reincarnation as a healer.

Ethan veered to the south end of the house, leading his dad toward the guest bedroom window.

"I'd say his mom is about to get her wake up call," Sam observed.

"I tried brewing coffee. Even the smell didn't do it. Linda hates mornings."

When Harlan and Ethan were out of sight, Sam picked something up from the table. She saw it was one of her notebooks.

"I've been reading through these," he said. "You ought to turn them into a book."

"Fiction or non-fiction?" she joked.

"A novel, actually. I think fiction would do the best job of putting readers inside what happened. My chapter in the history book was an overview of the war from the perspective of the generals and politicians. I'd a lot rather it could have been about what the war was like to the privates and sergeants and lieutenants who did the fighting. Your notebooks are full of that—the feelings, the view from the ground, not just the combatants, but the nurses and doctors." Thumbing through a few pages, he began reading: "Surgery for six hours today. We did arterial transplants on two NKs and one U.S. Marine. Strong pulse in all three limbs. Jeff should get a medal for this, but if we get caught, they'll probably court-martial us all."

He lowered the notebook. "That's an incredible story right there, Bonnie, and not many people know it."

"Shall I put in the parts where I compare you and Jeff?"

"Why not? I beat him out."

"It was touch and go there, for awhile."

"Yeah, right," he scoffed.

Clearly, he'd forgotten what a shaky prospect he'd been at the start. Korea had changed Sam from an uncertain playboy into a man who had proven young just how much he was capable of. The rest of the journey they'd made together, a good one.

"There's a lot about the war I'd just as soon forget," she said.

"I understand. But there's so much in here. People would be fascinated."

She thought about the trip she and Sam took every December, on the date of his father's death, to the vast military cemetery in Pusan. The long rows of American graves amounted to only a fraction of the total UN casualties of 120,000 from twenty-two countries. A hundred thousand Korean War veterans had carried scars out of the war like the ones in Sam's shoulder and on his feet. Two hundred thousand South Koreans dead, three hundred thousand North Koreans and as many as a million and a half Chinese—numbers sobering enough to end war for all time.

Of course, war hadn't ended and probably never would.

Her war had been Korea. She'd gone into it hoping to learn about men, and she had. At the same time, the one thing about men she would never understand was war. So horrific, so costly in every way.

And for all that, if Sam and Harlan Hood and all the others had not done what they'd done, all of Korea might be the starving and browbeaten nation the North was now. The blood of the fallen UN allies had bought hundreds of millions of people a future far brighter than they could possibly have lived under the dictator. The people who had given up their lives for the freedom of strangers might be the closest thing on Earth to angels. The survivors of that war were fewer every year. When they were gone, who would know what had happened there?

So much would be lost.

Maybe I'll do it, she thought.

She started thinking about how to describe Sam that first time she'd seen him on the ward in Tokyo.

"How about it?" Sam said. "If you don't want all the attention a novel might bring, you could always use a pseudonym. I'll help you—I'll be your editor."

You'll be a lot more than that, she thought.

Today, North Korea announced the unilateral end of its truce with South Korea. After 56 years of stalemate, it may attack the South at any time.

May 27, 2009, reported in newspapers across America and around the world

Made in the USA
Charleston, SC
03 March 2010